ALSO BY CHRISTOPHER REICH

RULES OF BETRAYAL

Christopher Reich

Century · London

Published by Century 2010

2 4 6 8 10 9 7 5 3 1

Copyright © Christopher Reich

Christopher Reich has asserted his right under the Copyright, Designs
and Patents Act 1988 to be identified as the author of this work

First published in Great Britain in 2010 by
Century
Random House, 20 Vauxhall Bridge Road,
London SW1V 2SA

www.randomhouse.co.uk

Addresses for companies within The Random House Group Limited can be found at:
www.randomhouse.co.uk

The Random House Group Limited Reg. No. 954009

A CIP catalogue record for this book
is available from the British Library

ISBN 9781846058714

The Random House Group Limited supports The Forest Stewardship
Council (FSC), the leading international forest certification organisation. All our
titles that are printed on Greenpeace approved FSC certified paper carry the
FSC logo. Our paper procurement policy can be found at:
www.rbooks.co.uk/environment

For my father, Willy Wolfgang Reich,
In Memory.

RULES
OF BETRAYAL

PROLOGUE

Above Camp 4
Tirich Mir
Northwestern Pakistan
May 30, 1984

"Did you hear that?"

The climber dug his ice ax into the snow and cocked his head, listening.

"What?" asked his partner, perched a few feet below on the near-vertical face.

"A scream." The climber squinted, trying to locate the shrill sound hiding inside the untiring wind. His name was Claude Brunner. He was twenty-two years old and considered France's finest alpinist. Suddenly he caught the high-pitched wail again. It seemed to come from far away, and for a moment he was certain that it was approaching. "There!"

"A scream?" asked Castillo, a Spaniard ten years his senior. "You mean like a person shouting?"

"Yes," said Brunner. "But not a man. Something else. Something bigger."

"Bigger? Up here?" Castillo shook his head, and chunks of snow fell from his beard. "I don't hear anything. You're tired and imagining things."

The wind calmed and Brunner listened intently. This time he heard nothing but the pounding of his heart. Still, the sound stayed with him, and he felt a stab of fear between his shoulder blades.

"How many hours' sleep did you get last night?" asked Castillo.

"None."

"It's your mind playing tricks on you. The only thing you can hear this high is the jet stream. It makes you crazy."

Brunner hammered a screw into the snow and affixed his rope. Castillo was right. He was tired. Bone tired. They'd left Camp 4 at 24,000 feet at two in the morning. It had taken eight hours of steady climbing to make it past the shoulder. Not bad, but not as fast as he would have liked. Not as fast as the American, who'd left their side two hours earlier to break trail.

Brunner looked down the precipitous incline. A string of six climbers approached from the ridge. In their brightly colored parkas, they resembled a Nepalese prayer flag. Red was Bertucci from Italy. Blue was Evans from England. Yellow was Hamada from Japan. And the others were from Germany, Austria, and Denmark.

The expedition was a UN-sponsored "Climb for World Peace," though the idea had been the brainchild of the Reagan White House and seconded by Margaret Thatcher. Over the next mountain range, barely 160 kilometers away, a force of some 100,000 Russian troops had overthrown the government of Afghanistan and installed their own puppet, a wily dictator named Babrak Karmal.

Brunner gazed up. High above, emerging from the shadows of the great ice serac, was the final member of their team. The American.

"He's moving too fast," said Castillo with concern. "The snow up there is bad. We lost two men on my last attempt."

"I think he's trying to set some kind of record," said Brunner.

"The only record that counts is getting to the top and back down alive."

Overhead, an untrammeled blue canopy stretched to all points of the horizon. The peaks of the Hindu Kush rose in a saw-toothed crescent. The wind, though blowing at a constant fifty kilometers an hour, was calmer than at any time in the two weeks they'd camped on the mountain. It was as fine a day as a climber could ask for to summit.

Brunner cut another step out of the hard ice, stopping as a cry cut the air. It wasn't the shrill sound he'd heard before. It was something else entirely. Something he knew all too well.

Looking toward the crest, he spotted the American's dark form, shrouded by snow, hurtling pell-mell down the incline and making a beeline for them.

"Put in another screw," said Brunner. "Hook me in. I've got to stop him."

"It's suicide," said Castillo. "If the impact doesn't kill you, he'll take both of us with him."

Brunner motioned toward the climbers below. "If I don't try, he could kill all of the others. They won't see him coming until it's too late. Just make sure the screw holds."

Castillo hammered a screw into the snow while Brunner two-pointed across the face in an effort to position himself in the American's path. "Is it in?"

"Another second!"

The American bounded closer, desperately clawing at the mountainside. Brunner could see that his eyes were open and hear him grunting with every rock he hit. Amazingly, he was conscious. Brunner moved a few feet to his left and dug in his crampons. The American struck an outcropping and lifted off the ice entirely, spinning until his head was below his feet.

Brunner shouted his name. "Michael!"

The American stretched out an arm. Brunner threw himself at the hurtling figure. The impact knocked him off the mountainside, and he plummeted headfirst down the face. But even as he fell, he was able to wrap his arms around the American's waist.

The rope caught, halting Brunner's descent. The American slipped from his grasp, his body beginning to slide across the ice. Brunner flung an arm at his leg, mitten curling around a boot, the force wrenching his shoulder clear of its socket. Brunner screamed, but maintained his grip.

The two men hung that way, suspended head below heels, until Castillo down-climbed to their position and fashioned a bivouac. A gash on the American's forehead was bleeding heavily, and one of his pupils was dilated.

"Can you hear me?" asked Brunner.

The American grunted and forced an ugly smile. "Thanks, bro. You really hung it out there for me."

Brunner said nothing.

"Why did you take yourself off the rope?" demanded Castillo.

"Had to," said the American.

"Why?" asked Brunner.

"Had to get everything set up."

"What do you mean, get everything set up?" asked Castillo angrily.

The American mumbled a few unintelligible words.

"Tell us," said Castillo. "What were you setting up?"

"Orders, man. Orders." The American's eyes rolled up in their sockets, and he lost consciousness.

"Orders? What does he mean by that?" Castillo grabbed the American's pack and freed the straps that held it closed. "What the hell?"

"Find something?" asked Brunner.

Castillo pulled out a large cardboard box. On its side were the words "Property of United States Department of Defense." He shared a look with Brunner, then said, "It must weigh twenty kilos. And still he beat us up the mountain. You know anything about this?"

Brunner shook his head. He was no longer looking at the box or the American. His gaze shot up to the serac hanging above them, and past it to the sky. This time he didn't need to ask if Castillo heard the sound. It was no longer faint or shrill. It was the full-throated, ear-splitting roar of a jet engine in the throes of mechanical failure.

A shadow passed in front of the sun, and then he saw it, and his breath left him.

Claude Brunner knew that they were all going to die very soon.

The aircraft passed directly overhead, its wing coming so close to the mountain that it appeared to slice a sliver of ice from the crest and launch a million snowflakes into the air. One of its engines was on fire, and as he stood rooted, watching, it exploded, causing the aircraft to tilt wildly to the left and assume a downward trajectory. He recognized it as a B-52 Stratofortress, and the large white star painted on the underside of the wing identified it as American.

For a moment the pilot righted the aircraft. Its nose lifted, and the engines no longer whined so angrily. And then the right wing snapped from the fuselage. It separated so cleanly, and so rapidly, that the action appeared to be a normal occurrence, and for another moment the plane continued to carve a perfect trajectory, framed by the brilliant blue sky. Abruptly, the bomber lost all airworthiness. The nose dropped and the jet began to spin, heading directly at the far mountainside. Debris tumbled from the aircraft. Several large cylindrical objects hurtled through space. The jet's engines howled like a dying beast.

Five interminable seconds passed before the jet struck the face of the neighboring peak, three kilometers distant. Brunner saw the fireball before he heard the explosion. The sound came seconds later, buffeting him like a gale-force wind.

Brunner looked over his shoulder at the giant lip of snow and ice hanging above him. *The serac.* The mountain shuddered. The overhang began to tremble.

The serac broke free. Two million tons of snow separated from the mountain and fell.

The last thing the Frenchman saw was a wall of infinite white plummeting toward him.

In the morning sun, the snow sparkled like diamonds.

1

Zabul Province, Afghanistan
Present day

They formed on the plain at dawn.

Man and beast and machine spread across the hard brown dirt in a line one hundred meters across. There were horses and jeeps and pickup trucks with heavy machine guns mounted on the flatbeds. They numbered only fifty men, and the villagers counted one hundred times that, but they were committed men. Warriors united under the banner of heaven. Sons of Tamerlane.

The commander stood in the rear of his Hilux pickup, binoculars to his eyes, surveying his target. He was tall and formidable, and he wore his black wool turban piled high on his head, the trailing folds wrapped tightly around his face to guard against the bitter cold. His name was Sultan Haq. He was thirty years old. He had been imprisoned for six years, twenty-three hours a day, in a small, clean cage in a hot place far, far away. In deference to his name, and to his habit of growing his fingernails long and keeping them as sharp as a bird of prey's talons, his jailers had called him "the Hawk."

The Hawk studied the cluster of low-slung mud buildings situated among the foothills two kilometers away. Through the mist, he could make out the town bazaar. Already shopkeepers were at work setting out their wares. Vendors cooked meat over brazier fires. Children and dogs ran up and down alleyways.

He lowered his binoculars and looked at his men. Arrayed on either side of him were six vehicles identical to his own, battered Toyota four-by-fours with mounted .30 caliber machine guns. His men crouched at the base of the armament, Kalashnikovs clutched and ready, spare clips tucked into the leather bandoliers strung across their chests. Several among them carried old Soviet-era RPGs. In between the trucks, twenty or more horses moved anxiously, steam issuing from their nostrils, hooves pawing the ground. Their riders held their mounts at bay, waiting for the signal.

The men wore no common uniform. Their clothes were ragged and dirty. But they were an army all the same. They had trained and drilled together. They had fought and been blooded. They were without mercy.

Sultan Haq raised a hand into the air. As one, the gunners cocked the machine guns. The sound of metal striking metal reverberated across the barren landscape. The horses whinnied madly. He closed his fist, and his men rose to their feet and let out a fierce cry. Throwing back his head, Haq joined them, feeling the spirit of his ancestors rise within him. Closing his eyes, he envisioned the rampaging horde. He saw thundering hooves and flashing swords and smelled acrid smoke filling the air. He heard the screams of the vanquished and tasted death on his tongue.

He opened his eyes and returned to the present. Once more he was at home on the flatlands of eastern Afghanistan. He pounded his fist on the roof of the cab, and the pickup roared to life and accelerated across the fallow fields. In a few short months, these same fields would come to life as the poppy awoke, grew, and bloomed. Last year these fields had yielded three thousand kilos of raw opium, earning its farmers millions of U.S. dollars—more than enough to purchase stores and weapons to equip a thousand of his men.

The village must be brought under the Taliban's white flag. It was a question of economics, not religion.

A bullet cut the air above Haq's head, and a split second later the crack of the gunshot reached his ear. Dispassionately, he watched as the villagers armed themselves and formed a hasty skirmish line. Still he held back from giving the order to fire.

Seconds passed, and the air was alive with gunfire, lead whizzing past like a swarm of angry bees. A shot splintered the windshield of the pickup next to him. He glimpsed a spray of blood, and the vehicle peeled off.

"Commence firing," he said into his two-way radio.

The first mortar landed in the center of the village bazaar. A geyser of dirt shot into the air. A second mortar exploded, followed by a third. Confused, and unsure of where to direct their fire, the skirmish line broke.

The Hawk looked on with satisfaction. He had positioned two squads on the higher ground south of the village to deliver fire from the rear while he attacked from the front. It was a classic hammer-and-anvil maneuver as taught by the United States Army *Handbook of Infantry Tactics*. Remarkably, he had found the handbook in the prison library. He had committed every page and illustration to memory.

The truck climbed a rise and the village came into full view. It was a scene of chaos, with men, women, and children scrambling in every direction, seeking cover where none was to be had. Turning, he tapped the gunner on the shoulder. The machine gun roared to life, spraying the square in disciplined bursts as gunners from the other pickups opened fire. Bodies dropped to the ground. Entire walls of shops and offices disintegrated and collapsed. A house caught fire.

In his free hand, Sultan Haq clutched a Remington long-barrel sniper rifle pried from the fingers of the enemy. It was a fine and accurate weapon with a polished maple stock and the words "Barnes" and "USMC" carved into the butt. It fired only a single round, but a single round was enough. As a boy, he'd hunted bighorn sheep in the rugged mountains of Kunar Province in the north. He knew how to shoot.

He signaled for his truck to slow and, raising the rifle to his eye, found a target, a young man running up the hillside clutching a woman's hand. He closed his finger around the trigger. The rifle kicked pleasurably. The young man fell to the ground. Pleased, Haq shouted for the driver to accelerate. The truck mounted a final hillock and barreled into the village.

An elderly mullah ran in front of the truck, waving his arms furiously. "Stop!" he shouted.

Haq halted alongside the man and jumped to the ground. "This village is now under my control," he said. "You will follow the dictates of Abdul Haq and the Haq clan."

The elder nodded abjectly, tears rolling down his wrinkled cheeks. "I surrender."

Haq raised an arm. "Cease fire!"

He waited as his soldiers shepherded the townsfolk toward a water fountain at the center of the bazaar. When they arrived, he ordered the elder to his knees. The old man complied. Haq put the barrel of his rifle to his head and shot him.

Stepping away from the body, he removed a list of names from his pocket. "Where is Abdullah Masri?" he called.

There was no answer. He aimed his rifle at a weak man with an insufficient growth of facial hair and shot him dead. Then he repeated the question. A stout man emerged from a store that had been selling DVDs of Western movies and Japanese television sets.

"You are Masri?" asked Haq.

The man nodded.

Haq took his time slipping a bullet into the rifle, then shot the man in the head.

"Where is Muhammad Fawzi?"

One by one, Sultan Haq called out the names of the village's leaders. He executed the schoolteacher and the grocer. He executed a homosexual and a woman suspected of adultery. For months he had been spying on the town, readying for this moment.

There was one last thing to do.

Climbing into the cab of his pickup, he pointed to a large whitewashed building that housed the village school. Like most of the buildings in the region, it was built with stone and mud. The driver positioned the truck's tail at the front of the school. A second truck came alongside. Moving backward, then forward, then backward again, the trucks battered the wall until it collapsed. Then they moved to the next wall and did the same, until the school was no more.

Afterward, his men walked among the rubble, gathering books, maps, and any learning materials they could find and dumping them into a pile. When they finished, he hauled a jerrican from his truck and doused the pile with gasoline.

As he was about to light it, a boy ran forward. "Stop," he pleaded. "We have nowhere else to learn."

Haq eyed the brave child. He was interested not in the boy's words but in the fiberglass cast on his left arm. To the best of Haq's knowledge, there was only a rudimentary clinic in the village. In his country, broken limbs were set in plaster, not fiberglass. He had seen this advanced medical treatment only once before. "Where did you get this?" he asked, touching the cast.

"The healer," said the boy.

Haq's ears perked up. He hadn't heard about a healer in these parts. "Who is this healer?"

The boy looked away.

Haq grabbed the child's jaw in his immense hand, the sharpened nails raising welts on his cheek. "Who?"

"A crusader," someone shouted.

Haq spun. "A crusader? Here? Alone?"

"He's traveling with an assistant. A Hazara who carries medicine for him in a bag."

"Is the healer American?" asked Haq.

"A Westerner," came an answer. "He speaks English and some Pashto. We didn't ask if he was American. He cured many people. He fixed the khan's stomach and repaired my cousin's knee."

Haq released the boy, shoving him backward. His heart was racing, but he hid his anticipation beneath a veil of anger. "Where did he go?"

An elder pointed toward the mountains. "There."

Haq looked at the foothills that rose and eventually formed the massive mountain range known as the Hindu Kush. Tossing the lighter onto the pile of books, he walked back to his truck, paying scant attention as the flames climbed into the sky.

"Go," he said to the driver. "To the mountains."

2

Jonathan Ransom woke and knew that something was wrong.

Bolting upright, he pulled his sleeping bag to his waist and listened. Across the room, Hamid, his assistant, slept on the ground, snoring. Beyond the shuttered windows, a camel brayed. Outside, a pushcart rolled past, its arthritic axles in need of oil, followed by a trio of voices raised in conversation. The cart, he had learned during his week in the village of Khos-al-Fari, belonged to the butcher, who was presently transporting his daily supply of freshly slaughtered goats to the town bazaar to be displayed hanging from tenterhooks in the front of his stall.

The cart continued down the hill. The voices died away. All was silent but for the ghostly roar of the Gar River churning through the nearby gorge.

Jonathan remained stock-still, the frigid air stinging his cheeks. It was only mid-November, yet in the steep, inhospitable foothills of eastern Afghanistan, winter had arrived with a vengeance.

A minute passed. Still he heard nothing.

And then the crack of a rifle. A single shot—high-caliber, judging by its report. He waited, expecting more gunfire, but none came, and he wondered if a hunter had taken one of the big-horned Marco Polo sheep that roamed the mountainside.

It was almost five a.m. Time to begin the day. With a grunt, he unzipped the sleeping bag to his feet and stood on the dirt floor. Shivering, he lit the kerosene lamp, then hurried to pull on a second pair of woolen socks and a beat-up pair of flannel-lined cargo pants.

A camp table in one corner held a washbasin, a jug of water, a cup with his toothbrush and toothpaste, and a washcloth. Jonathan poured water into the basin. The water had partially frozen overnight, and islands of ice floated on the surface. He washed his hands and face, then ran the washcloth over his body, scrubbing vigorously to stop his teeth from chattering. Finished, he dried himself, brushed his teeth, and put on his shirt and jacket. His hair was too long and tangled to tame with a brush, so he combed it with his fingers for a few moments before giving up on it.

"Hamid," he said. "Wake up."

To combat the cold, Hamid had disappeared inside his sleeping bag. Jonathan crossed the room and kicked him. "Move it."

A head of unruly black hair popped out of the sleeping bag. Hamid peered angrily around the room. In the dim light, the circles under his eyes gained depth and he looked older than his nineteen years. "That hurt."

"Get your butt out of the sack. We've got a lot to do today."

"Just a sec—"

"Now."

Hamid sat up slowly, pulling his cell phone out of the bag and checking it for messages.

Jonathan observed him, wondering for the hundredth time how a village could not have electricity but manage to have cellular phone service. "Your mom call?"

Hamid didn't look up from the phone. "Not funny."

"Yeah, well, put that thing away and get moving. I'll see you at the clinic."

Jonathan picked up the duffel that held his equipment and swung it over his shoulder. Pulling on his pakol hat, he opened the door and sniffed the air. Wood smoke, damp foliage, and peat: the smells of the world away from civilization. It was a scent he knew well.

For eight years he had traveled the world as a physician with Doctors Without Borders. He had worked from the top of Africa to the bottom. He had spent time in Kosovo, Beirut, and Iraq, too. Wherever he was located, his mission was to bring medical care to those who needed it most. Politics was not a factor. There were no good guys or bad guys. There were only patients.

He'd arrived in Afghanistan two months before, but he no longer worked for Doctors Without Borders. Events in the recent past prevented him from working in an official capacity as a physician or surgeon for them or anyone else. The man at the American embassy had told him he was crazy to venture into the Red Zone—the Red Zone being anywhere outside Kabul. When Jonathan said he was traveling alone, without bodyguards or weapons or any personal security whatsoever, so that he might offer medical care to people in the remotest villages, the man called him "suicidal." Jonathan didn't think so. He had calculated the risks, weighed them against his responsibilities, and found the balance equal, more or less.

Now, standing outside his one-room shelter in the predawn darkness, his boots sinking into the icy muck, he listened again. It wasn't noise that unsettled him, but the lack of it.

"One hour," he said to Hamid, then shut the door.

A soft rain fell as he walked along the path zigzagging down the hillside. Below, shrouded in clouds on a spit of flat terrain tucked between steeply descending mountains, lay the village. All the structures looked the same: low-slung, rectangular slurries of rock, timber, and mud that seemed to have grown out of the earth itself. A thousand people lived in Khos-al-Fari. Many times that number visited from the surrounding valley to trade at the bazaar, sell crops and timber, and conduct a rudimentary social life.

Hands thrust into his pockets, Jonathan made his way through town. He was tall and broad-shouldered, and he walked purposefully, leaning forward as if to combat a rising wind. To look at him, one would think he was a native. He wore the baggy trousers and untucked shirt known as a shalwar kameez. To protect against the cold, he wore a herder's sheep-fleece vest. His beard was coarse and long, black cut through with gray. But a closer look revealed his European ancestry. His nose was prominent and well shaped. His teeth were straight and white and, most tellingly, in complete order. His skin was smooth, and except for the crow's feet at his eyes, youthful for a man of thirty-eight. His eyes were the color of tar and, even at this time of day, lit with resolve. Nowhere in his face was there a hint of Mongol blood, or of the tireless suspicion born of millennia spent repelling invaders. There was only competence, tenacity, and hope.

Jonathan Ransom was an American.

The patients were lined up outside the clinic when Jonathan arrived. He counted fifteen in all, including several children in the company of their fathers. Some had visible infirmities: badly healed burns, gliomas, cleft palates. Several were amputees, the victims of the land mines and bomblets left behind by the Russians. Others simply looked wan and tired, and were most likely suffering from the flu. Jonathan greeted them with respect, taking care to shake every man's hand while ushering them inside and explaining that they must wait an hour until he could see them.

One father stood apart from the others. His daughter leaned against him, a scarf covering the lower half of her face. Seeing the tall foreign doctor, she turned away. Jonathan knelt in front of her. "I'm happy to see you," he said softly. "We're going to make you better. You won't have to wear this scarf anymore. You'll be able to play with the other children again."

"You are really going to do this?" the girl's father asked in halting English. "Today?"

Jonathan stood. "Yes."

He entered the building, lowering his head so that he didn't strike the lintel. He had divided the clinic into five rooms: a waiting room, two consultation rooms, an office, and an operating theater. The conditions were dismal, even by local standards. Hard-packed dirt floors. Low ceilings. No electricity. No running water.

Upon arriving, he had discovered a battered wooden desk inside with the words "Médecins Sans Frontières: où les autres ne vont pas" carved into it. Roughly translated, it said, "Doctors Without Borders: Where Others Dare Not Venture." And below it, also in French, "The Doctor Is Always Right," and the year "1988." His colleagues had preceded him to this remote village more than twenty years earlier. To Jonathan, it was confirmation that he had made the right decision in coming.

He walked into his office and dropped the duffel onto the ground. Inside was everything he needed. Scalpel, forceps, and Metzenbaum scissors for surgery. Cipro and Ancef for antibiotics, Pepcid for ulcers, iron supplements for the women, and multivitamins for the children. Lidocaine in 30cc bottles for use as a local anesthetic and Ketamine for putting a patient under. There was prednisone, Zyrtec, norepinephrine, and a host of pharmaceuticals to treat a gamut of ailments beyond most doctors' imagination. And sutures, syringes, Band-Aids, ace bandages, and lots and lots of alcohol swabs.

Jonathan spent an hour equipping the clinic for the coming day. He started a fire, boiled water, and sterilized his instruments. He swept the floor of the operating room and laid a clean plastic sheet over it. He arranged his supplies and inventoried his medicines.

At seven a.m. he saw his first patient, a boy of ten missing the lower half of his right leg and walking with the help of an ungainly wooden prosthesis. Three years earlier he'd stepped on a Russian mine while playing in the fields. The amputation had been badly done. Over time the flesh had withered because of a lack of circulation and become infected. The skin needed to be debrided and cleansed and the boy put on a course of antibiotics.

"You'll just feel a little pinch," said Jonathan, preparing a syringe of lidocaine. "It won't hurt at—"

Hamid burst into the room. "We have to go," he said, gasping for breath.

Jonathan regarded him impassively. "You're late."

"Did you hear me?" Hamid was short and skinny, twenty pounds underweight, with narrow shoulders and an eager, bobbing head. Jonathan had found him outside the offices of a medical aid organization in Kabul shortly after his arrival. Or rather, Hamid had found Jonathan. A second-year medical student, he'd offered his services as a translator, guide, and doctor's assistant for $50 U.S. a week. Jonathan offered him $40 if Hamid would find him a decent four-by-four and accompany him into the Red Zone. Hamid agreed, and a deal was struck.

"Yeah, I heard you," said Jonathan.

"They're coming."

"They" meant the Taliban, the orthodox Islamic fighters locked in a struggle with the American and Afghan forces to retake control of the government and the country and reassert Islamic law over its population.

"It's Sultan Haq. He took a town sixty-five kilometers from here yesterday and massacred the village elders."

Jonathan considered this. He'd heard of Haq, a particularly vicious Taliban drug lord who captained his own militia in Lashkar to the south, but he was confused by his presence. Khos-al-Fari was a poor village far from the poppy belt, with no apparent strategic value. "What does he want?"

"I don't know," answered Hamid wildly. "Does it matter?"

The father took his son by the shoulder and hurried him out of the room.

"Tell the others to come back tomorrow," said Jonathan. "All except Amina. She can't wait. Set out a standard tray in the operating room. Make sure I have some extra anesthetic."

Hamid eyed Jonathan as if he were mad. "You're going to operate on her?"

"It's her turn."

"That's a four-hour procedure."

"Longer. You never know with reconstruction."

"Just give her medicine for the infection. You can come back and take care of her another time."

"She's waited long enough."

The blast of a distant explosion caused the room to tremble.

"Mortars," said Hamid, rushing to the window. "Sultan Haq's men killed eighteen people yesterday. He executed ten of them himself. An American will be at the top of his list."

"What about Pashtunwali?" asked Jonathan. "The villagers will watch out for us."

"Pashtunwali" referred to the Afghans' code of honor and hospitality, which demanded that they protect a visitor taken into their home or village.

"It doesn't stand up very long in the face of superior firepower. We have to get out of here."

"Set up the tray, Hamid."

Hamid retreated from the window and came closer to Jonathan. "Leave, or you will die."

"I'll take my chances."

"And me?"

"You said you wanted to learn. I respected that. Now's your chance. You've never seen me perform this procedure. Think of it as an opportunity."

There was another explosion, closer this time. An exchange of automatic-weapons fire, then silence.

"They'll kill me, too," said Hamid. "I helped you. Besides, I'm Hazara."

Jonathan dug in his pockets for the keys to the truck and tossed them to Hamid. "Go. I understand. You've been a great help. I owe you."

"But you won't be able to operate on Amina without me."

"It'll be harder, but not impossible."

Hamid studied the keys in his palm, then put his head against the wall and moaned. "Damn you," he said after a minute.

"Set up the tray," said Jonathan.

3

It was snowing in the resort of Les Grandes Alpes. Large, fluffy flakes tumbled from a curiously clear sky onto the mountainside. Translated, the resort's name meant "the Big Alps," but the slope was nowhere near Switzerland, nor any other mountain range in Europe, and its runs were anything but grand. The entire skiing area consisted of a single well-groomed piste that descended in three sections, like flights of a staircase, steep, then flat, and finally a gentle decline to the bottom.

The woman named Lara Antonova attacked the hill expertly, skis pressed together, hands at her waist. It was just past three and the slope was crowded with skiers. Most were novices. The snowplow was the rule, and the majority had difficulty mastering even that. Dressed in white stretch pants and a turquoise down parka, her auburn hair pulled into a ponytail that hung past her shoulder, she carved a sleek line among the other skiers, her eyes casting about for a familiar face.

Lara Antonova had not come to Les Grandes Alpes for the skiing. Born in Siberia and raised a ward of the state, she was a highly ranked operative assigned to Directorate S of the FSB, the Russian Federal Security Service. Directorate S was responsible for foreign clandestine operations: intelligence-gathering, blackmail, extortion, and in the rare case assassination. Lara Antonova had come to Les Grandes Alpes on assignment to meet the most powerful arms dealer in southwestern Asia.

Reaching the halfway point, she came to a crisp parallel stop. She removed her goggles and surveyed the slope. Despite their lack of skill, most of the skiers were dressed as if they were habitués of the finest alpine resorts. A survey of equipment turned up nothing but the latest Kastle skis, Rossignol boots, and Bogner ensembles. Still, even among the raft of colorful attire, she had no difficulty spotting her mark. He stood fifty meters down the hill, a trim, diminutive man clad in a conservative navy ski suit, skiing slowly and with great caution down the center of the slope. Surrounding him, arrayed like a battle fleet protecting the prized carrier at its center, were six very large men in black-and-gray parkas. It was a retinue worthy of a head of state. Then again, her mark was royalty. Lord Balfour, by name if not lineage.

"I've got him," said Lara as she bent to check her bindings. "He's got six crushers with him."

"Six?" Her controller's gravelly voice spoke to her from the miniature receiver planted deep in her ear canal. "That's up two from the last time. He must be in trouble."

The person in question was named Ashok Balfour Armitraj, a.k.a. Lord Balfour. Hair: black (dyed); height: 5'5"; weight: 160 lbs.; age: 52. Bastard son of a Muslim mother and a British father, brought up in Dharavi, Mumbai's worst slum. A childhood on the streets. An early bent toward criminality, or, his word, "entrepreneurship." Member of a gang at age eight. A chieftain at fifteen. Then, at twenty, the big move to start his own crew.

Balfour dabbled in everything, black and white. On the legitimate side, there were real estate and raw materials and even online brokerage. Less legitimately, there were drugs, white slavery, and counterfeit merchandise. But in the end it always came back to arms. Guns, artillery, helicopters, even jets. If there was mention of it in Jane's Defence Archive, Lord Balfour could get it for you.

Down the hill, Balfour had come to a halt. His men gathered around him, forming a two-layer defensive perimeter. Judging by the heft of his jacket and the way he kept his zipper undone to his breastbone, the bodyguard closest to Lara was carrying an Uzi. And if there was one machine gun, there would be others. Balfour wasn't one for half-measures.

"Where's the merchandise?" Lara asked her controller.

"On the ground at Tehran International. Three-hour transit time inbound to you."

"All there?"

"Down to the last bullet."

She had negotiated the transaction herself and knew the packing list by heart. Fifteen hundred Kalashnikov assault rifles, 1,000 grenades, 200 antipersonnel mines, 2 million rounds of ammunition, 100 Advanced Night Vision goggles, 500 kilos of Semtex plastic explosive. There was big stuff, too. Twenty shoulder-held ground-to-air missiles, 10 fifty-caliber machine guns, 100 antitank weapons, and an ample supply of munitions. A grand total of $10 million worth of arms and matériel. Enough to supply a reinforced infantry battalion of Taliban insurgents.

"Sounds good," she said. "We're a go."

"Just get us our money."

Lara slid her phone from her pocket and hit speed-dial. A cultured British voice answered. "Hello, darling."

"I'm just up the hill." She raised a pole and the man below glanced at her.

"Aren't we dashing?" said Lord Balfour.

"Tell your boys to let me through." Lara pushed off and skied down the hill, cutting past the phalanx of bodyguards without a glance and coming to a dramatic halt next to Balfour.

"You don't ski like a Russian," he said with admiration.

Lara considered this. "Unfortunately, *you* ski like a Maratha."

Balfour threw his head back and laughed richly.

Everything he does, he does in spades, Lara remembered. He laughs too much, talks too loudly, and kills too freely. Looking at the small Indian, his hair slicked back with pomade, his Mississippi gambler's mustache just so, his eyes warm and friendly, she forced herself to remember that he was a volatile and dangerous man.

"But really, where did you learn to ski like that?" Balfour's smile was stretched to breaking.

"Switzerland, mostly."

"Gstaad?" He pronounced it perfectly. *Sshttaad.*

"Why, yes." In fact she'd never set foot in the Swiss resort, but she knew better than to embarrass him twice. "How did you know?"

"I have a friend who lives there. A doctor. He says the Russians have positively overrun it. Is that where you went while on your sabbatical?"

Lara sensed something amiss. "Excuse me?"

"I mean when you left the FSB. I understand you stopped working for Moscow for a number of years. Isn't that correct?"

"You tell me."

"Rumor is that the FSB dumped you when they ran out of money back in the nineties. You jumped to the other side of the Atlantic and went to work for American intelligence as some kind of freelancer. They chucked you out a few months ago and you went running back to Daddy."

Lara smiled casually, but inside, her alarm bells were sounding. This wasn't a rumor. It was a full-fledged leak. "I wouldn't believe everything you hear."

But Balfour wasn't so easily put off. "I couldn't care less," he explained with exaggerated earnestness. "I built my first house with money from the CIA. Even today the director has me on his speed-dial. 'Balfour,' he says, 'Congress won't allow us to arm the Waziris. You do it for us. Here's a check for twenty million from the black fund. You can double your commission if you buy American.' Frankly, I consider myself an honorary agent. No, it's not me who's concerned about whether or not you worked for the Americans."

"Then who is it?"

"My client. I don't need to tell you that there is no love lost between the prince and Uncle Sam. In fact, he's convinced they're trying to kill him."

The prince was Crown Prince Rashid al-Zayed, youngest member of the Zayed clan, rulers of the United Arab Emirates, and secret financier of all causes Islamic.

"The papers reported that his private jet lost an engine," said Lara. "That's common enough."

"Granted. But last week a Predator drone missed him by five minutes when he was visiting friends in the tribal areas near Peshawar. Killed ten of his closest friends. Nothing accidental about that."

"He may be right, then," said Lara. "He's arming their enemies, after all. Taliban, Hezbollah, FARC."

"And how do you know that?"

"Rumors," said Lara. "My boss, General Ivanov, is well informed, too. Last I checked, he wasn't too keen on the Americans either. I am correct in assuming that it was you who initiated contact with our organization on the prince's behalf?"

Balfour stared into Lara's eyes for several seconds. The smile was gone, as was any indication of warmth. He was a hardened criminal sizing up a contact and deciding whether or not she was to be trusted. "And so?" he said finally, with his usual vigor. "Is the shipment complete? The prince is adamant that he receive everything."

"One hundred percent fulfillment. All sitting on the tarmac in Tehran waiting for the prince's go-ahead."

Balfour raised an eyebrow, impressed. Turning his head, he placed a call and spoke in rapid Arabic. "The prince asks if midnight would be all right," he said after hanging up.

Both of them knew it was not a request.

"Midnight will be fine." Lara gazed casually up the slope. Her eyes landed on two men dressed in decidedly inferior gray ski suits. "Tell me, Ash, is everything all right between you and your client?"

"Never better," replied Ashok Balfour Armitraj. "We are as close as brothers."

"Then why does your brother have two of his hoods watching you?"

Balfour followed Lara's eyes to the two men. "Them?" he chuckled, his humor firmly back in place. "They're not His Highness's men. They're ISI. Pakistani intelligence. I consider them my backup protection."

"Really?"

"They see to it that the boys from Indian intelligence don't get their hands on me. Delhi is convinced that I had a hand in the Mumbai attacks. They say I armed the bad guys. They're out for blood."

Hence the Uzis. "Did you?" she asked.

"Of course," said Balfour. "But that's beside the point. I was just the broker. I sold them their toys. They could've bought them from anyone. In point of fact, the weapons were yours."

"Mine? I didn't even know you then."

"I mean Russian. The lot. AKs, grenades, fuses, even the phones. It was a Russian package from stem to stern."

Lara looked at her watch. They had been standing together conspicuously on the slope for ten minutes, which was nine minutes too long. As a contact, Balfour was a nightmare. Somewhere along the line, he had gotten it into his head that he was not a criminal wanted by the law enforcement agencies of a dozen Western nations but a legitimate businessman. In Germany or Britain, his brand of flagrant behavior would have gotten him either killed or jailed for life. In Pakistan, where he made his home, it made him a king.

"And so?" she said. "Midnight. At your hangar at Sharjah Free Trade Zone."

"I'll have one of my aircraft ready to transship the merchandise."

"Where's it going?"

"Tsk, tsk," said Balfour. "That's the prince's business."

"We like to know where our weapons end up."

"There's only one war going on in the region that I know of at the moment. Use your imagination."

Business concluded, Lara waited as Balfour and his men skied to the bottom of the hill. On cue, the pair of Pakistani intelligence officers followed them down the slope.

She spent another hour at Les Grandes Alpes, taking the chairlift to the top of the hill several more times and skiing down. Certain she wasn't being trailed, she made a final descent, took off her skis, and returned them at the rental desk, along with her boots and poles.

Leaving the rental desk, she proceeded into a changing room, where she removed her ski attire and packed it neatly in a shoulder bag.

She emerged five minutes later, wearing denim shorts, a tight black tank, and low heels. She'd exchanged her oversized Uvex goggles for Ray-Ban aviators and freed her hair from the ponytail, letting it take its usual ungoverned course, falling around her face and shoulders.

Walking past the base of the ski slope, she glanced up to the sky, where giant snow machines hidden in the rafters continued to shower perfectly formed snowflakes onto the mountain. Not bad, she thought to herself, for a desert kingdom thousands of miles from Europe. What did the Quran say? If Muhammad won't go to the mountain, bring the mountain to Muhammad.

A moment later she pushed through a pair of tall double doors and stepped into the harsh sunlight and ninety-degree temperature of a late fall day in the sprawling metropolis of Dubai City, on the shores of the Persian Gulf.

As soon as she reached her car, she placed a call. Not to Moscow, but to Washington, D.C.

"It's Emma," she said. "It's a go. Midnight at the duty-free zone in Sharjah. The prince himself is coming."

4

Her name was Amina. She was a nine-year-old wisp of a girl with fine black hair and doe eyes that bore a hole into Jonathan's conscience the first time he saw her. He knew nothing more about her, whether she was in school or knew how to read, if she enjoyed embroidering or was a tomboy who played soccer. Amina couldn't talk, and Afghan parents didn't discuss their children with strangers. None of this mattered. As a surgeon, all Jonathan needed to know was evident the first time he examined her. He'd taken one look at her wounds and sworn that he would help her.

Amina lay sedated on the operating table. There was no respirator to ensure a steady flow of oxygen, no blood gas machine to monitor the anesthesia in her system, and no readily available blood should she hemorrhage. He didn't even have scrubs or surgical masks. He had only his skill, generic pharmaceuticals, and what the Afghans called "God's will."

"Where do we start?" asked Hamid.

"With the face. It's the most difficult and will take the most time. We do it while we're fresh." The temperature inside the clinic hovered at a damp fifty degrees. Jonathan massaged his fingers in an attempt to rub away the chill. "Okay, then, it's eight-fifteen by my watch. Let's do it. Scalpel."

He rolled the instrument between his thumb and forefinger, examining the child's features, plotting his steps. There was a hole the circumference of his pinkie beneath her jaw, where the bullet had entered, and a much larger wound where the bullet had exited, destroying most of the girl's upper palate and nose. Amina was not a victim of war, at least not in the usual sense. She was a victim of carelessness, and a culture where automatic weapons were as common in homes as brushes and brooms.

A month earlier, while playing with her older brother, she had picked up her father's AK-47 and used it as a crutch or support, placing both hands over the barrel and resting her chin on her hands. No one knew what happened next, whether her brother pushed her or inadvertently kicked the rifle. All that mattered was that there was a bullet in the chamber, the safety had become dislodged, and somehow the trigger had been pulled, firing a 7.62 mm copper-jacketed bullet through Amina's hands, through the soft flesh beneath her jaw, and into her mouth, where it passed through the palate and into her sinus cavity, striking bone (thus saving her life) and altering its trajectory ninety degrees, after which it left her skull, tearing away most of her nasal cartilage and flesh.

The tragedy didn't end there.

Still traveling at near its initial velocity, the bullet continued on its new azimuth and struck Amina's brother in the temple, entering his brain and killing him instantly.

The procedure would represent a test of Jonathan's skills. He had no illusions about the result. He could never restore Amina's beauty. The best he could hope for was a face that would not provoke gasps and might one day help her find a husband.

An hour passed. Outside, the sounds of battle rose and fell, long periods of silence interrupted by staccato bursts of machine-gun fire and the thud of mortars and grenades. Each progressive clash brought the fighting closer.

"Clean up some of that blood," said Jonathan.

Hamid dabbed the wound with gauze, looking up from the girl every few seconds to gaze out the window. "Haq's reached the village."

"If he comes, he comes. There's nothing we can do about it. I need you here. Not just your hands but your mind."

Jonathan concentrated on cutting cartilage from Amina's ear and using his scalpel to pare it into a slim strip that would define her nose.

A shell landed one hundred meters away. The building rocked, loosing a veil of dust. Amina's father clasped his arms to his chest but said nothing. Jonathan leaned closer to the girl, driving the noise and distraction from his consciousness. Somewhere beyond his world, a woman wailed, but he did not hear her. All that mattered was this little girl.

A bullet tore through the wall, spraying dust and wood splinters.

"Shit," muttered Hamid, ducking.

Jonathan stepped back from the table. Despite the cold, he was sweating and his shirt clung to his back. "What do you think?"

Hamid stared down at the girl. "You're a magician."

"Hardly, but it just might do." Jonathan pulled back skin and straightened the cartilage. "I don't know if it's an Afghan nose, but in Beverly Hills it might be the next rage."

Just then a volley of automatic-weapons fire rang out close by. It was loud enough to make Jonathan wince and Hamid cry out. Amina's father held his daughter's limp hand, eyes to the ground, saying nothing.

Hamid hurried to the window, pulling his phone out of his pocket and clutching it as if it might save his life. "Why do they keep firing? No one's trying to stop them."

"Get back here," said Jonathan. "There's no one to call."

Hamid swallowed and slipped the phone back into his pocket. Lowering his head, he returned to the operating table.

"Let's close up this palate so this girl can eat some solid foods again," said Jonathan. "Get me a syringe with five cc's of lidocaine."

Hamid didn't answer. His eyes were fixed on a funnel of smoke rising from the far end of the village. "That's near our house."

Jonathan looked at the smoke, but only for a moment. "Lidocaine, Hamid. Five cc's."

A camel was braying continuously. A gunshot rang out and the animal went silent. Several vehicles approached, engines whining as they battled the terrible road.

"Hamid."

"Yes, Dr. Jonathan."

"Lidocaine."

Hamid handed him the syringe.

"Did I ever tell you why I came to your country?" Jonathan said.

Hamid met his eyes. "To do this. I mean, to help."

Jonathan went back to his work. "That's part of it. I had other reasons. I came to make up for some of the things I've done."

"You, Dr. Jonathan? You've done bad things?"

"Not just me. My wife, too."

"You told me you were never married."

"I lied. I was married for eight years. Officially I still am, but after what she did, I'm going to call that game rained out. For the entire time, I was married to a government operative and I didn't know it. She married me because my job with Doctors Without Borders provided her with cover and got her into politically sensitive spots in Africa, the Middle East, and Europe so she could carry out her missions."

"Missions? I don't understand."

"Bombings, extortion, assassination."

"She killed people?"

"She did. She worked for a secret organization called Division . . . She was their star." Jonathan paused, and his tone dropped a notch. "I killed, too. I had to. There was no other way. Even so, I'm still not good with it. There's more to it than that, but that's why I'm here. To make up for her sins as well as my own. I figure if I was dumb enough not to know that the woman I shared my bed with was a spy, then at least I ought to own up to part of what she did. The funny thing is that I didn't even know her real name until three months ago. It's Lara. She's Russian. Not even American. Crazy, huh?"

Outside the window, a pair of pickups with machine-gun mounts pulled up to the clinic. Taliban fighters jumped from the rear and entered the clinic. The door to the operating room opened. A tall, powerful-looking man entered the room, carrying a hunting rifle with a scope. A shorter man followed close behind, grabbed Hamid in an armlock, and forced him to his knees. A half-dozen agitated fighters entered the room and pointed their weapons at Jonathan.

Jonathan stepped away from the table. "I'm operating," he said, mustering his calm. "Let go of my assistant and please leave."

The tall fighter ignored his instructions and held his ground. "You are the healer everyone is talking about," he said in unaccented English.

Jonathan studied the fighter more closely. It was the first time he'd heard American English in weeks. "I'm a doctor."

"I must ask you to come with me."

"We can talk when I'm finished."

"You will come now."

Another fighter approached, pulled a pistol from his belt, and pressed it against Amina's head. His eyes went to the leader for approval.

The taller Afghan pushed the man's hand away, then looked at Jonathan. "How long might that be?"

"Three hours. I asked you once already to leave. Now I'm telling you. Get out of my operating room and take your men with you."

"A bold response for someone in your position, Dr. . . . . ?"

"Ransom. And you are?" asked Jonathan, though he already knew the answer. He noticed the fighter's long, curling fingernails and followed his hand past a chunky Casio G-Force wristwatch to the rifle, where the name "W. Barnes USMC" was carved into the stock. "I take it you're not Barnes."

"My name is Sultan Haq." Haq ordered Hamid to be freed, then handed the rifle to one of his men. "Who is she?"

"Her name is Amina. She had an accident." Jonathan explained what had happened and how he was repairing her face. Haq listened as intently as a resident accompanying an attending physician on rounds.

"You are gifted," said the Hawk. "I see this. You may fix her face. But her hands can wait another day."

"She's waited long enough," said Jonathan.

One of Haq's men burst into the operating room. "Drone," he shouted, rushing to the window and pointing to the sky.

The assembled fighters began talking all at once. Several ran from the building and continued on foot into the village. Others raised their fists at Jonathan and hurled threats his way. Only Sultan Haq did not move. He eyed Jonathan from a greater distance than the meter separating them. "You are CIA?" he said at length, in the same imperturbable voice.

"No."

"MI6? Mossad, perhaps? You have come to kill me."

"No."

"Then why are you here so far from where anyone can help you?"

Jonathan looked at the sleeping girl's form. "For her."

"Then you really *are* a crusader," said Haq, with respect.

A dirt-streaked face pressed against the window. "All clear," the man shouted, using the English terminology. "No drone. A fighter. It is gone to the north."

Haq put a hand on Jonathan's shoulder. "This is your lucky day, but not his." Turning, he drew a pistol from his belt and put it to Hamid's forehead. "Dr. Ransom, you have fifteen minutes to finish or I will shoot him. And if you're not done fifteen minutes after that, I will shoot the girl. You're my prisoner, and you'll do as I say. "

5

Emma Ransom, a.k.a. Lara Antonova, sped down the eight-lane superhighway, a lone courier in the night. The windows were down, and warm air filled the BMW M5 with the scent of saltwater and scorched earth. The digital clock's numerals glowed 11:47. Ahead, like the first rays of a rising sun, a scythe of light cut the horizon in two. She passed a sign saying "Sharjah Free Trade Zone—5 km."

"This is a final systems check," she announced to the empty cockpit.

"We have you loud and clear," came a gruff American voice from deep inside her head.

"How's the picture?" A microdigital camera embedded in the top button of her blouse delivered the pictures to her cell phone, which transmitted the images to a suite of offices at Fort Belvoir, Virginia, across the Potomac from Washington, D.C.

"If you're driving two hundred kilometers per hour like the speedometer says, the camera's working fine. Now slow down."

"Just tell me if it's in focus and aimed straight ahead."

"Yes and yes. Now remember, all I want you to do is hand over the shipment, get General Ivanov his money, and get the hell out. Are we clear?"

"Yes, Frank, we're clear."

"Whatever you do, don't wait around for him to try that gun."

"That gun" was a VSSK Vychlop 12.7 mm sniper's rifle, the most powerful weapon of its kind in the world.

"How did you rig it?"

"You don't need to know."

"I don't go in blind."

"We engraved three bullets with his name and the royal family's coat of arms and included them in the case. Two of them are good. We put fifty grams of C4 in the third. When the firing pin hits it, *bang* goes the breech. And I mean *bang*, as in a serious shrapnel burst. You don't want to be nearby when it goes off."

"Thanks for letting me know," she said. "I'm glad you're looking after me."

"*Me* look after *you?* Since when?"

The comment provoked a laugh. Maybe because it was so patently true, or maybe because she wished it weren't. "Talk to you on the other side."

Emma pressed her foot against the accelerator, locking her arms against the wheel as the car gained speed—200 . . . 220 . . . 240 kilometers per hour—and the wind buffeted her.

"Slow down," said Connor.

Frank Connor was the head of Division and Emma's boss. She ignored him.

The free trade zone came into view. It was a city of warehouses, hangars, cranes, and fences built on a gargantuan scale. The highway narrowed from eight lanes to four. A sign advised her to slow to 80 kilometers per hour. Her response was to press the pedal harder and watch the speedometer jump to 260. She stared at the unbroken white stripe leading her on, enjoying the hum of the automobile's five-liter V10 engine, the world beyond her reduced to a blur.

"Emma . . . I said, slow the hell down!"

She kept her foot on the accelerator: 280 . . . 290 . . . 300.

And then she braked. The car decelerated rapidly, the g's forcing her forward against the seatbelt, making her aware of her anxious stomach and her rapidly beating heart. She drew a breath and calmed herself. The butterflies vanished and her heart rate fell to its normal fifty beats per minute. She was no longer Lara or Emma. She was an operative. Names didn't matter. It was her work that defined her identity, her mission that formed the core of her soul.

Leaving the highway, she turned in to the east entry and stopped at the security checkpoint. A tall fence topped with rings of barbed wire blocked her path. A uniformed guard looked her up and down but didn't ask for her name or her identification. She was expected. "Continue straight ahead for two kilometers," he said. "You'll be met at Warehouse 7."

The fence clattered on its track, and Emma advanced into the complex. She passed a succession of warehouses, each five stories tall and as large as two city blocks. Even at this hour the area was alive with traffic: trucks loading and offloading goods, forklifts zipping back and forth, cranes lifting containers from trains to flatbeds.

Finally she reached Warehouse 7. A second checkpoint blocked the road. As she approached, the gate slid back. A police car was parked a few meters ahead. Its flashers lit up and began to strobe. A hand emerged from the driver's window and motioned for her to follow.

She tailed the police car across a wide asphalt expanse to a smaller hangar two kilometers away that was situated at the farthest corner of the free trade zone. Its giant barn doors stood open, and bright lights burned overhead. Her eyes scanned the building. For a moment she caught a shadow perched on the rooftop, the glint of a rifle, but when she looked closer it was gone.

Balfour had already arrived and stood alone beside his Bentley Mulsanne Turbo. His retinue of bodyguards had dwindled to one, a six-foot, six-inch Sikh she knew as Mr. Singh.

There were, however, a dozen uniformed policemen to see to his well-being. This was the prince's territory, and the prince would guarantee Balfour's safety.

Emma killed the engine and stepped out of the car. A policeman frisked her, then nodded for her to go ahead.

"Ah, Miss Antonova," said Balfour, who greeted everyone as if he'd just run into them at a cocktail party. "I see that you've found us."

"Where's the prince?" asked Emma.

"Due any minute. Where's the plane?"

"On schedule."

"So we wait," said Balfour.

"So we wait," said Emma. "I've never seen you without your pack of wolves. Don't you feel naked?"

"I have Mr. Singh. Besides, the prince and I have a relationship of long standing."

Emma raised a brow. She was skeptical of such relationships.

"And," said Balfour, "I have something the prince wants."

"I thought I was providing the merchandise."

"Not that," said Balfour. "Those are just guns. Playthings. I have something else. Something far more interesting."

"I'm sure you do," she said. But instead of probing further, which was an intelligence officer's first instinct, she walked out of the hangar and stared into the black sky. The air buzzed with aircraft taking off, one after another.

"They're mine," said Balfour. "Cargo planes. They're on their way to Iraq. For eight years the Americans pumped that country full of everything you can imagine. Now they want to take it all home in eighteen months. I'm more than happy to help."

To the east, Emma made out a set of red landing lights. She checked her watch. The time was 11:58. It was the Tupolev, inbound from Tehran.

"Is that our plane?" asked Balfour.

"The prince said midnight. The Swiss aren't the only ones who are punctual."

"So you can be relied upon?" The promise of conspiracy lay heavy in his voice.

"Have I ever failed you?"

Balfour smiled his fox's grin. "No. But that doesn't mean I can trust you." He stepped closer and lit a cigarette. "Just how high do your contacts reach in Moscow?"

"As high as necessary."

"The director? General Ivanov?"

Emma met Balfour's eye. She said nothing. She knew that she had something he wanted.

Balfour glanced over his shoulder at the cadre of policemen

standing near their vehicles. Taking her arm, he led her toward a grass berm bordering the runway. "I've found something," he said. "Something in the mountains. A device of some sort. I need help to extract it and bring it down."

Still Emma refused to exhibit the least interest. "That's not what we do," she said. "I'm sorry."

"It is an explosive," Balfour continued. "American."

"Really? What kind?"

"I don't know. I only have a photograph. It's much too far away for me to venture. I suffer from asthma, and it's at high altitude. All I can tell you is that it is large and appears to be very heavy."

"I'm an intelligence agent, not a mountain guide. What kind of help do you think I could provide?"

"Equipment. Experts. A whole team, I should think."

Beneath her veil of nonchalance, Emma was keen to learn more. The words "large American explosive device" had coalesced into a tempting image. "Do you have the photograph with you?"

Balfour glanced over his shoulder once again. "Quick. Before he gets here." A hand delved into the inner pocket of his cream-colored sports jacket. "Take a look. Tell me what you think."

Emma studied the photograph. It showed a length of silver metallic skin buried in snow. Stenciled in black paint were the letters "USAF." A few feet away, a square fin protruded. She brought the photograph closer. The problem was scale. There was nothing to indicate the object's size. It could be one meter or ten. "Looks like a bomb or a missile."

"Yes, but what kind?"

"Don't you have one with a little less snow on it?"

Balfour hesitated. "Unfortunately not."

Emma kept her eyes on the picture, fully aware that Balfour was lying to her and that he knew more than he was letting on. "Where exactly did you say you found this?" she asked.

"I didn't." There was noise of motors approaching. Balfour snapped the photo out of her fingers and slid it into his pocket. "Our secret."

"Of course."

Emma turned to see a convoy of seven black Mercedes SUVs speeding across the tarmac. Small UAE flags flew from the antennas. Balfour returned to the hangar. Emma followed at a distance. As she walked, she glanced up at the roof of the hangar. The shadow she'd seen earlier was there again, and this time he wasn't hiding. Nor were the three other snipers positioned on the rooftop. Either the prince was exceedingly conscious of his safety or something was wrong.

"Are you getting that, Frank?" she said under her breath. "They've got shooters on the roof. Something's up. He's never done that before."

Emma waited for the voice to answer, but no one responded.

"Frank?" she whispered.

A faint, high-pitched whistle filled her ear. The whistle indicated the presence of a jamming device designed to seek out and defeat all wireless transmissions in the immediate area. She could no longer hear Connor; she could only hope he was able to receive her voice and her pictures.

Effectively isolated, Emma quickened her pace, watching as the fleet of Mercedes pulled to a halt. The driver's door opened and a man wearing the tan uniform and green shoulder boards of a general in the national police got out.

The prince had arrived.

6

His full name was Prince Rashid Albayar al-Zayed, and he was the twelfth son of Crown Prince Ali al-Zayed, the sitting president of the United Arab Emirates. Thirty-two years of age, Prince Rashid stood a strapping six feet tall, with broad shoulders, a matinee idol's smile, and flashing brown eyes that captivated all with their sincerity. Rashid was not one of the lazy royals who lived off his family's name and squandered money as if it were an Olympic discipline. He was the opposite thing. A graduate of Phillips Exeter Academy, Cambridge University, and INSEAD, all with honors, he had returned home to commence a career in his government's service. In six years he had moved from commissioner of customs and excise to deputy minister of foreign affairs, and now he headed the country's national police.

In his off hours, Prince Rashid chaired a pan-Arab summit on climate change and served as the royal family's representative for the Emirates Hunger Challenge, a charity that had raised over $200 million for starving children in sub-Saharan Africa. His wife was a Lebanese beauty, and Christian. His four lovely children attended a French *lycée* in Dubai City. To all eyes, the prince was the model of a modern secular Muslim and a postage-stamp representative of the UAE.

But the file on him painted a darker portrait. It suggested that his public activities were for show and nothing more than a workaholic's laboriously constructed facade to camouflage his true calling: the funneling of arms and matériel to fundamentalist Islamic terrorist organizations.

As he walked across the hangar floor, arms outstretched, Prince Rashid turned up the wattage on his smile and made bold use of his flashing eyes. In the Middle East, a greeting says everything about a relationship.

"Ashok, my dear friend," he said, taking Balfour into his arms and hugging him. "I'm so very glad to see you. I can't thank you enough for helping me . . . *and my friends.*"

"The pleasure is mine," said Lord Balfour. "May I introduce Miss Lara Antonova of the Russian FSB?"

"I thought Siberians were blond," said Prince Rashid, bowing slightly.

"Not all of us," said Emma. He was shaking her hand, and for a moment she thought he was not going to let go. His hands were large and surprisingly callused. Another snippet came back to her. The prince was a devotee of martial arts. Rumor was that he enjoyed sending his sparring partners to the hospital.

"If I didn't know General Ivanov better, I'd say you were British," the prince went on.

"Moscow prefers that we speak the queen's English."

Rashid laughed, and they were joined a moment later by his cadre of police officers. Just then his phone rang. He spoke briefly. "Miss Antonova, your plane has requested permission to land. It will be on the ground in two minutes."

The prince rubbed his hands together and strode onto the tarmac. Balfour and Emma accompanied him, careful to stay the requisite step behind. The twenty-odd police officers, all dressed in the same crisp short-sleeved khaki uniform as their commander, followed.

The Tupolev landed and taxied to the near end of the runway. The cargo hatch dropped. The plane's crew began to unload pallet after pallet stacked high with wooden crates painted an olive drab and stenciled with Cyrillic words.

The next hour passed quickly. Prince Rashid strode among the cargo, pointing out random crates to open and inspecting the contents against his packing list. Lord Balfour walked at the prince's side, saying, "It's all here" again and again. "One hundred percent fulfillment, as requested."

Emma stood off to one side, arms crossed, her eyes shifting

between the prince and the snipers positioned on the rooftop. It was while she was checking over her shoulder that she noticed the man for the first time. He was small and lithe, bearded, like nearly every male present except the prince, but very different in manner. He stood next to the prince's Mercedes, and she suspected he must have ridden in the passenger seat, which made him a VIP. His skin was dark, and even standing, one hand clutching the SUV's open door, he appeared hunted, as if afraid of being spotted. He was dressed in traditional Arab garb but not a rich man's robe, just a simple white dishdasha and headdress with a coiled black rope. His clothes marked him as a common man, but no common man rode shotgun with Prince Rashid.

Emma looked at him long enough for her camera to get a nice shot for Frank Connor and the boys back at Division.

The man was the end user: Prince Rashid's terrorist of the month. Emma had no proof, but she knew it all the same. Experience.

"One hundred percent fulfillment." This time it was the prince speaking, and she turned to see him approach. "I'm impressed. I look forward to doing more business with General Ivanov in the future." He signaled to an aide-de-camp, and a minute later Emma was in possession of two stainless steel briefcases, each containing $5 million.

"The pleasure is ours," said Emma. "In fact, the general has asked me to present you with a gift on his behalf."

"Really?"

She stared at the prince, wondering if his surprise was genuine or if his sincerity was always so transparent. She signaled to the airmen, and a few moments later they descended from the Tupolev carrying a lacquered black rifle case between them. "Put it there," she said, gesturing to a nearby crate.

With ceremony she opened the box, revealing the Vychlop sniper's rifle embedded in maroon velvet. Directly beneath the rifle, each in its own compartment, were three five-inch-long bullets with the circumference of a Cohiba cigar. Each bore the prince's name and family crest engraved on its brass jacket. More important, each was capable of penetrating an armored Humvee at a thousand yards.

Prince Rashid put the rifle to his shoulder. It weighed twenty-two pounds, but he clasped it as if it were a Daisy Repeater.

"I hope it meets your satisfaction," said Emma.

"What kind of question is that?" asked the prince, lowering the rifle and passing a well-manicured hand along its barrel. "It is a thing of beauty. An instrument of death rendered elegant."

"I'm glad you like it." She checked her watch. "Excuse me, but I have a three a.m. flight to Zurich. I'm sorry to leave so soon—"

"Nonsense," said Prince Rashid. "I'll call the airport and see that it's delayed. You must stay and try General Ivanov's gift with me."

Emma sensed an insistence that had not been there before. A false, predatory insistence. "Really," she continued, a voice within her ordering her to run. "It's late and I must be going. General Ivanov is expecting me."

Prince Rashid flashed his movie star's smile. "But I spoke with Igor Ivanovich earlier. He's more than happy for you to stay. He called you his country's finest ambassador. Now that we've met, I see that he spoke the truth."

Emma's eyes went to the roof of the hangar. The snipers had taken up position. Each was curled over his weapon. She had little doubt that her head was centered in the crosshairs of their scopes. She decided that Rashid had been expecting the rifle and that it was not a surprise. She looked at Balfour, who knew nothing about the gift. It was Connor's play and Connor's play alone.

"Surely you can stay," added Balfour, his eyes sterner than his voice.

"But of course," Emma consented, if only to buy time.

The prince rattled off a command, and a patch of scrub adjacent to the hangar was suddenly illuminated as bright as midday. At the far end was a wing-back chair. On it sat a mannequin dressed in the uniform of a United States Marine. Emma had her proof. Rashid had been expecting the weapon.

The prince handed her the rifle. "Please. I would be honored if you took the first shot." He selected a bullet from the case. "I insist."

Emma cleared the breech and slipped the shell into the chamber, slamming home the bolt with authority. Her odds were one in three. She'd faced worse, she told herself as anger replaced apprehension. She'd been betrayed. She knew too much, and knowledge was a double-edged sword. It was that simple. Whatever the case, she would proceed in style.

"Come," she said, motioning to the prince to come closer. "Let me show you how to shoot it. The rifle is heavy in the barrel. It's necessary to put weight on your back foot. To aim, you have to lay your cheek flat against the stock. Step closer. You can't see from there."

"I can see perfectly," said Prince Rashid.

"As you wish." Emma sighted the rifle on the mannequin's chest, positioning the butt against her shoulder. "The trigger is surprisingly light. Squeeze gently and get ready for the biggest goddamn kick of your life."

One in three.

She pressed her cheek to the stock, drew a breath, and tightened her finger.

The explosion was deafening.

The prince cowered, raising an arm to protect his head. Downrange, the mannequin sat in his chair just as before, but his head and half of his left shoulder were gone.

"A little high." Emma shrugged, not entirely dissatisfied, and handed the prince his rifle. "I'm sure you'll do better."

Weapon in hand, the prince walked to the lacquered case, selected a bullet, and slid it into the chamber. Without a word, he returned to the firing line, drove home the bolt, raised the rifle to his shoulder, aimed, and fired.

The shot was wide and low, loosing a cloud of dust.

"A devil of a kick," said Prince Rashid, rubbing his shoulder. "My wife will wish to know how I received such a bruise."

One bullet remained in its velvet cradle. Rashid thrust the rifle toward Balfour. "What about you, Ashok? Game?"

Balfour raised his hands. "I just sell the bloody things. Look at it. The damned thing is nearly as big as I am."

"That's two excuses," said Prince Rashid. With a glance at Emma, he plucked the final bullet from its case and slid it into the carriage. "Perhaps you can help me this time," he said to her. "How should I sight it?"

Emma stepped behind the prince and placed an arm around his shoulder, guiding his head so that his cheek lay in the proper position against the rifle stock. With her left hand, she helped raise the weapon so that it was aimed at the mannequin. "Don't touch the trigger until you have the bead centered on the target. I suggest aiming a half-meter low to compensate for the kick. Press your front foot into the ground. Harder. Now tense your stomach."

Emma stood just to the side of the prince, watching his finger caress the trigger. "Softly," she said. "Take a breath and squeeze."

The prince looked at her from the corner of his eye. "Softly," he said.

"That's right."

Suddenly the prince stood tall, lowering the rifle. "Dammit," he said, striding away.

"What's wrong?" asked Balfour, rushing to his side.

"I just can't do it to my shoulder," said Prince Rashid. "It will ruin my golf game for a month."

The gathering went silent; then a few of his underlings laughed and the laugh became contagious. Prince Rashid handed the rifle to a short, corpulent man in a captain's uniform. "Let's see if Captain Hussein can hit the target. As I recall, he used to be a shooting instructor at the academy."

Hussein walked to the firing line. With care, he raised the weapon and sighted it on the mannequin. He would not disappoint his ruler.

"Softly," said the prince, staring at Emma.

An instant later, the rifle backfired as the bullet exploded inside the barrel, blowing apart the bolt and chamber.

The police captain lay writhing on the ground, his face ripped clean off his skull, eyeballs, cartilage, and teeth mashed together to resemble nothing more than a crushed pomegranate. The police officers ran to the horrifically wounded man. Balfour shouted for an ambulance. "On the double!"

But Prince Rashid remained where he was.

"You," he said to Emma, grasping her by the arm. "You will come with me."

7

The trek led upward, hugging the contours of the mountain. The truck surged and slowed, rocking like a lifeboat on a stormy sea. The foothills had disappeared hours ago, replaced first by sparse pine forest, then the featureless, ever-steepening slopes of scree. Now even that was gone, cloaked by gray cloud. It was just a patch of hardscrabble in front, a precipitous drop to the side, and the incessant grinding of the motor struggling at altitude.

"I would do anything for my father," said Haq. "Wouldn't you do the same?"

Jonathan sat between Haq and his driver, too uncomfortable to be scared. "My father's dead."

"This is fate," said Haq with conviction. "When I was a boy, I was struck by shrapnel from a Russian grenade. My father carried me on his back for three days to reach an aid station. He had pneumonia at the time. It was winter. He nearly died to save me. I promised myself that one day I would repay him."

Jonathan looked at Haq. "You destroyed a village to help your father?"

Haq considered this, his eyes indicating that he was not unaware of the moral complexity. "The village was of strategic value," he said finally.

Jonathan looked straight ahead.

"What brought you here?" asked Haq. "You're not a missionary?"

"No," said Jonathan.

"But on a crusade nonetheless."

"What about you?" asked Jonathan. "Where did you learn your English?"

"I was a guest of your country for several years."

"You were in the States?"

"Not exactly. Camp X-Ray at Guantánamo Bay. I was captured in November of 2001. I surrendered, I'll admit it. It was the bombs. Every day the planes would come. They flew high, so you could not hear them. The bombs would arrive without warning. We were dug in, but a mound of earth is no protection against a five-hundred-pound bomb, let alone hundreds of them. The fury. You have no idea." Haq looked away, his eyes staring in horror at a point far beyond the windshield. And then he snapped back. "I'm glad you find my English acceptable. We learned from the movies."

"You had movies there?" Jonathan's surprise was evident.

"Not at first. No, at first there were no movies. At first we lived in dog cages outdoors. At first we had interrogation, not movies, but after a while, when the CIA decided we had told them as much as we knew, we were allowed books, and a few months after that, movies. By the time I left, the library had over seven thousand volumes and four hundred films."

"What did you watch?"

"War movies mostly. *Apocalypse Now. Platoon. Patton.* These are very fine films. But my favorite was a musical."

"A musical?"

"You find that amusing?"

"No."

"*On the Town*, with Gene Kelly. You know it? 'The Bronx is up and the Battery down.'" Haq hummed a few bars. "For me, that is America. Three sailors happily singing and dancing while their country oppresses the rest of the world. Mindless tyranny. I tell myself, if I ever go to America, I must see this city. Have you been?"

"Yes. It's impressive."

"Six years I was in prison. One day they decided I could go free."

"Why?" asked Jonathan.

"I lied to them," said Haq, fixing him with kohl-smeared eyes. "The secret is to believe your lies no matter what they do to you."

The Toyota rounded a curve, the trail flattened, and the truck accelerated drunkenly. They were no longer climbing the mountain; they were in it, hemmed in by vertical slabs that climbed all the way to heaven.

"Tell me about your father," said Jonathan. "How old is he?"

"I would guess seventy. It is his stomach. It gives him much pain. He has not eaten in a week."

"When did the pain begin?"

"Several months ago," said Haq, "but it has worsened in the last week."

"Has he suffered any blows or injuries?"

"We are warriors. Nothing more than the usual."

"Does he speak English?" asked Jonathan.

"He thinks I'm a traitor for saying hello," said Haq, laughing suddenly.

The driver laughed too, and Haq was quiet.

Jonathan asked a few more questions, but Haq had lost interest. The fighter fired off a series of commands to his driver, then without warning leaned across Jonathan and cuffed the man on the head. Jonathan said nothing. It was not the first time he had witnessed a violent and unprovoked exchange. He guessed that Haq had warned his driver against discussing any of what he had witnessed.

The steep cliffs fell away and the road fed into a narrow clearing. One hundred meters ahead, Jonathan spotted a number of vehicles parked beneath a camouflaged canopy. A group of men ran toward them, crying *"Allahu akhbar."* *God is great.* It was the Afghans' all-purpose expression, used to signify victory and defeat, happiness and heartbreak.

The truck halted. Haq climbed out and Jonathan followed, asking, "Where's Hamid?"

Haq scratched his cheek with a long nail, as if reconsidering his promise, then walked to the last truck in line and hauled Hamid out of the flatbed. "Here's your assistant," he said, shoving Hamid to the ground. "A Hazara. Weak."

Jonathan helped him to his feet. "You okay?"

Hamid brushed the dirt off his pants. "Thanks for looking out for me."

"Yeah, well," said Jonathan, "I got you into this."

Haq walked away, and Hamid fished in his pocket for his phone.

"Put that thing away," said Jonathan. "He'll kill you if he sees that."

"No reception," said Hamid, thumbing a few keys angrily. "Crap."

"What did you expect? Now put it away."

Hamid stuffed the phone into his pants and looked at the sky, shaking his head.

A dozen men crowded the area beneath the canopy. Several wandered close to peer at Jonathan, one or two rushing forward to touch his sleeve as if he were some kind of talisman.

"Where are these guys coming from?" Jonathan asked.

"Over there. " Hamid pointed to a hole cut into the mountainside. A crude door fashioned from worn floorboards hung open. "We're in Tora Bora. There are caves all over the place."

Tilting his head, Jonathan gazed up through the netting. A narrow band of sky was visible between the towering granite aeries. From high above, the clearing was just one more inaccessible ravine among thousands. He swallowed. It would be impossible to find them.

Sultan Haq cut a swath through the men. "My father," he said, gesturing for Jonathan and Hamid to follow. "If you please."

The warlord pressed toward the cave, ducking his head as he passed through the door, and disappeared into a murky twilight. Jonathan walked close behind him, his shoulder bag of medical equipment feeling heavier than its weight. Inside the cave he slowed to allow his eyes to get accustomed to the dark. The dark, however, was only temporary, an anteroom walled with heavy curtains. Haq parted the curtains and stepped into a large, dimly lit chamber the size of a school auditorium. "This way."

Jonathan noticed at once that a great deal of work had been done to make the cave habitable. The walls had been smoothed and the ceiling raised to a height of five meters. Somewhere there was a generator, because a track of lightbulbs had been drilled into the rock overhead. The air was bitterly cold. Supplies were stacked neatly against the walls, food in one corner, ammunition in another. Here and there men slept on the floor, wrapped in woolen blankets.

Haq walked across the chamber and advanced down a short passage. The ceiling was lower here, the walls uneven, rock jutting out at sharp angles. Every few meters a room opened up to their right or left. The first held sacks of rice marked with a NATO stencil. In the second, several men were sleeping on the dirt floor. Something caught Jonathan's eye. He was looking at a pair of muddy combat boots sticking out of a pair of desert fatigues. Squinting, he made out not one but three soldiers, lying side by side. He couldn't miss the American flag stitched on the shoulders of their uniforms. A guard sat in the corner, an AK-47 propped against his knee.

Haq peered over his shoulder. "Prisoners," he said. "None of your concern."

Hamid shoved Jonathan from behind, and Jonathan turned to see if he was all right. "Move," said Hamid, in an unfamiliar and threatening voice.

Jonathan hurried to catch up to Haq.

The Afghan's father lay on a bed of colorful blankets in the next room. Haq had said he was seventy, but his beard was black throughout and his eyes were alive and vital. Only the papery texture of his pale skin testified to his years. Sultan Haq dropped to his knees, and it was apparent that he was pleading with the old man to allow the American doctor to examine him.

"It's Abdul Haq," whispered Hamid to Jonathan. "Once he was minister of defense with the Taliban government. During the war he captured a brigade of his own soldiers crossing the lines to fight for the Northern Alliance. Eight hundred men. To set an example, he beheaded them all. Today he's commander of all Taliban forces in the north and chief of their intelligence network."

"How do you know all this?" asked Jonathan.

"Everyone knows," answered Hamid, dark eyes flashing.

"Dr. Ransom, you will come," said Sultan Haq, waving him close. "My father agrees to let you treat him. I will be watching."

Jonathan looked at the armed guards to his left and right. He set his medical bag on the ground and kneeled to the right of Abdul Haq.

"You have pain in your stomach?" asked Jonathan. "Show me where, please."

Sultan Haq translated and his father pointed to a spot a few inches below the rib cage. Jonathan unbuttoned the man's shirt. The abdomen was visibly distended, the flesh a purplish pink. He ran two fingers over the discolored area. The old man tensed. His eyes widened, but he uttered not a sound.

"It's all right to tell me if it hurts," said Jonathan.

"A man does not howl," said Sultan Haq.

"It will help me localize the problem."

"Surely you can discover the problem yourself."

Jonathan took the old man's blood pressure, temperature, and pulse. All readings were well above normal.

"What is the matter with my father?" asked Sultan Haq.

"Without an X-ray, it's impossible to be sure. My guess is that he's suffering from an acute abdomen caused by a peritoneal abscess. That means there's a tear in his colon or stomach that has allowed bacteria to escape into the abdominal cavity. Normally, if it goes untreated this long, it kills you. Since he isn't dead, it means that his system has walled off the infection."

"He is a strong man."

"Yes, he is. But he has a big pocket of pus in there that needs to get out. And I mean now." Jonathan looked at Abdul Haq and did his best to offer a comforting smile. The old warrior scowled in return, his eyes wishing Jonathan a long and painful death.

"What can you do?" asked Haq.

"We need to take him to a hospital in Kabul. The sooner, the better."

"That's not a possibility," responded Haq. "I ask you again, what can you do?"

Jonathan sat back on his haunches, running a hand over his mouth. "I don't have the equipment to perform that kind of surgery. Look around you. These aren't exactly sanitary conditions."

"I didn't bring you up the mountain to do nothing."

"Take him to a hospital and he'll be better in two days."

"You will heal him here, *now*."

"I will not harm your father," said Jonathan. "He needs proper medical care."

"Then I will have to kill you and your friend." Haq barked a command, and one of the guards grabbed Hamid and put a knife to his throat, drawing blood.

"Stop!" shouted Jonathan, jumping to his feet. "All right. I'll do it. Let Hamid go."

Haq waved away the guard and Hamid slumped to the ground, gingerly exploring the wound on his neck.

"But the best I can do is open him up and drain the pus," Jonathan continued. "That will relieve the pain, but it won't solve the underlying problem. Even if I find a perforation, I doubt I can close it. I don't have the tools."

Haq held Jonathan's eyes. "You will cure my father or you will not walk out of this cave."

Jonathan gazed down at the old man lying on the bed of colorful blankets. As he did, he observed a large black centipede scurrying beneath the pillows. He looked around the room for a table or some firm surface he could lay the man down on. There was nothing.

"I'm going to need water," said Jonathan. "Lots of it, boiled and sterile. Hamid, put a bandage on your throat, then get me two syringes of lidocaine. I'll need gauze, scalpel, forceps—that should do it."

He turned to Haq. "Your father won't feel anything, but you and your men"—he pointed at the guards standing nearby—"you're not going to like it. I suggest you wait outside."

"They're used to blood," said Haq.

"I'm not talking about blood."

"We will stay," said Sultan Haq.

Jonathan injected three cc's of lidocaine into the area around the infection. He waited several minutes, then made a five-centimeter incision and with his fingers separated the fascia. "Mosquito."

Hamid inserted the mosquito, a small rake-shaped clamp, to hold the incision open. Jonathan injected another cc of lidocaine directly into the fascia. Already he could feel the pressure from the abscess throbbing against the muscle.

"You guys might want to back off," he said, eyeing the guards, who stood with the barrels of their AK-47s aimed at his back.

The guards looked at Haq. Haq shook his head sternly.

"Don't say I didn't warn you." Jonathan cut through the last layer of fascia. A jet of pus erupted, shooting vertically out of the abdomen and striking one of the men squarely in the face. The man cried out, frantically wiping away the warm liquid.

"Be still," commanded Haq.

Jonathan widened the incision and glimpsed a large mass of yellow pus. Officially the pus was termed a "fibrous, proteinaceous exudate." As a resident in general surgery, he'd preferred to call it what it actually was: "gross nastiness."

Inserting his fingers, he pulled out a wad of pus and wiped it on the gauze. It was then that the odor wafted from the wound, and the first guard bent double and retched. A second guard turned his head, his eyes watering.

Nothing on earth smelled as awful as a long-festering anaerobic infection. The smell was worse than a Lagos latrine on a 100-degree day. Worse than a three-day dead rat plumped with maggots. Worse than anything Jonathan had ever experienced.

"Like that, eh? There's more. Don't worry." Reaching back into the abdominal cavity, he retrieved a second, larger wad, this one the size of a Coke can. The guards covered their mouths and rushed out of the room. Even Haq jumped to his feet and charged the door. Only Hamid remained rock-steady, unflinching.

"What do you think got to them?" asked Jonathan.

"No idea," said Hamid. "Guess the sight of blood makes them squeamish."

"Guess so," said Jonathan. "Now, let's clean this out."

For the next few minutes he pumped syringe after syringe of sterile boiled water into the cavity. Leaving behind even a trace of bacteria would result in a second infection. Abdul Haq might be Public Enemy No. 1, but for the moment he was a patient in grave danger, and Jonathan did his best to save him.

Satisfied that the infection had been cleaned, he tacked the muscle together. To allow any residual pus to escape, he fashioned a Penrose drain from a short length of rubber tourniquet and inserted it like a candle wick into the cavity. Ten stitches closed the incision.

Jonathan looked at the doorway, where Haq remained, his face a curious shade of yellow. "We're done."

"Will he live?" asked Haq.

"That's up to you. He needs to recover in a clean environment. If the infection comes back, I wouldn't count on him making it through a second time. He's tough, but not that tough."

Abdul Haq probed the stitches gingerly. "I am all right?" he asked in Pashto.

"Yes," said Jonathan. "You're going to be fine."

Suddenly the old man was beaming. Free of the crippling pain that had plagued him for weeks, he grabbed Jonathan's hand and held it to his chest. "God sent you. Blessings upon your house. You are a great man."

Sultan Haq touched Jonathan's shoulder. "I thank you for saving my father's life."

"You're welcome," said Jonathan. "But if you really want to thank me, let those soldiers go."

"They're my enemies," said Haq. "They have killed many of my men. They know where we live."

"So do we." Hamid kneeled beside Abdul Haq to apply a sterile bandage to his abdomen.

"Did I speak to you?" thundered Haq, looking down at the slight assistant.

"Well?" asked Jonathan.

"You are welcome to stay," said Haq with forced kindness. "You say you came to my country to help its people. You may help us."

"Is that an invitation or an order?" Hamid stood, and Jonathan thought he appeared taller, no longer so timid.

Drawn by the sound of the raised voices, one of the guards poked his head back into the room.

"Hold it, Hamid," said Jonathan. "Finish putting on the bandage. Okay?"

"Your work is done, Jonathan," continued Hamid. "Now it's my turn."

Jonathan looked hard at Hamid. It was the first time the assistant had ever called him by his Christian name. He could feel the tension ratcheting up, everyone looking at everyone else too expectantly.

A second guard returned to the room, holding his machine gun at the ready.

"I will decide when the healer's work is done," said Haq, incensed by the challenge to his authority.

"You don't understand," said Hamid. "The healer works for me."

"You? A Hazara?" Haq spat the words with disbelief.

"No. Me, the United States government."

In a blur, Hamid dropped to a knee and ripped a scalpel across Abdul Haq's throat. A fountain of blood sprayed into the air. The old man arched his back, his hands reaching for the gaping wound. His mouth formed a perfect O, but no sound came out. His eyes rolled back into his head and he fell back on the bed.

Abdul Haq was dead.

8

The first kick hit Emma in the side, and she heard a rib crack. The next glanced off her shoulder, and then he was on her, driving a knee into her stomach and grasping her clothing with his powerful callused hands, striking her chest with curled knuckles, just as they'd taught her at Yasenevo so many years ago.

"Who do you work for? The CIA? The Pentagon? You will tell me, do you hear? A confession is what I'm after. When I talk to General Ivanov, I will give him the truth!"

The prince was screaming, his handsome features made unrecognizable with rage. Between slaps to the face and yanks of her hair, Emma decided that he had no idea how to conduct an interrogation. Fear made a person talk. Violence made them shut up. And then she realized that this was no interrogation. The prince already knew the answers to his questions. This was sport.

They had driven for an hour into the desert, Emma in the front seat alongside Prince Rashid, her wrists cuffed in front of her. At one point he stopped the car and climbed out to bleed air from the tires. From there the journey proceeded off-road, sand dunes alternating with expanses of sun-hardened earth. They stopped, and she saw that there were two cars accompanying them. A dozen of the prince's police poured from the vehicles, forming a semicircle on the hard-pack. Balfour was not among them. She recognized only one face: the hooded eyes and intense stare of the prince's client.

"Who?" railed the prince. "Tell me and I will stop. You will die quickly."

Emma didn't respond, and her silence goaded him more than any lie.

"If you will not talk, then you will at least eat." The prince scooped up a handful of sand and stuffed it into her mouth.

She thrashed violently, spitting it out. A new pair of hands held her as the prince forced her mouth open and filled it with fistfuls of sand. She spat them out, gagging, but he continued, undeterred.

"Some fine Arabian sand for my would-be executioner. I hope you enjoy the taste."

Emma could not breathe. She could not swallow. She struggled and spat.

And then the powerful hands released her. Emma rolled away. She knew that at least one rib was broken. Something else was wrong. Something worse. A pain deep inside.

"Look at her," said Prince Rashid, arms spread wide, turning to face his men. "Do you know what she is? She is a cow. A fat, lazy cow. And do you know what cows need? They need to move."

"No," she said. "It's enough."

A white-hot pain seared Emma's back and a barbed current traveled up her spine, causing her body to shudder.

Prince Rashid withdrew the cattle prod. "There," he said, looking at the man with hooded eyes. "That made her jump. Shall we try again?"

The prod touched her buttocks, and the odor of burned flesh filled the air.

"Move, American whore! Your friends in Washington can't help you now. They sent you on a fool's errand to kill me. Your errand is finished. You failed. It's not so easy to kill a prince."

Rashid struck her repeatedly with the prod. On her belly, her thighs, her breasts. She opened her mouth to scream, but no sound emerged. The electricity coursing through her body had locked her vocal cords.

"Who's your controller? It is a housekeeping matter, actually. I need to know where to send your body." He stood laughing, and all his men joined him. All except the man with the hooded eyes. He stood apart, saying nothing, his unblinking black eyes never leaving her.

"Has this cow had enough exercise?" Prince Rashid turned a circle, imploring his men to answer. No one said a word. "I don't think so either," he said finally. "She still looks rather lazy to me. I think she needs a tour of our lovely desert. Strip her."

Emma could offer only perfunctory resistance. When she was naked, someone yanked her hands above her head and passed a chain around her cuffs. She squinted, watching one of the policemen attach the other end of the chain to the rear bumper of the prince's Mercedes.

"No," she said, hearing a desperate voice cry out inside her. "Please. I'm—" She rose to one knee, but the car was already accelerating. The chain grew taut and yanked her to the ground.

The prince drove slowly across the desert floor. He dragged her over rocks and thistles and sage and sand gritty enough to peel paint. When the pain was too much, she lost consciousness. Against her will, the waking world found her. She didn't know how many times she passed out or how long they drove, only that at some point she was no longer moving and someone had removed the handcuffs.

A hand slapped her cheek and she opened her eyes. Stars glistened like tears in the sky above.

The prince glared down at her. "If your friends know so much about me, surely they'll figure out where I took you. The question is, my darling, will they find you before the sun dries you out?"

Emma watched Rashid climb into his car and drive away. The sound of the motor faded. In a minute the desert was silent.

She was alone.

And then pain began in earnest.

Emma put her hands to her stomach and cried.

9

For an instant, shocked silence ruled the cave chamber.

"What the hell did you do?" gasped Jonathan. "You killed him! Jesus Christ!"

Hamid paid no attention to his words. The scalpel was no longer in his hand. In its place was his cell phone. Oddly, he was pointing it at the nearest guard. There was a bang and a flurry of blood and the guard dropped to the floor. The phone was a concealed handgun. Before Jonathan could react, Hamid fired at the second guard, another head shot delivered with devastating accuracy. The guard fell backward, colliding with Sultan Haq, who was scrambling for his rifle.

"Who are you?" asked Jonathan.

"Watch it!" Hamid shoved Jonathan to the ground, turning as he did so to fire at Sultan Haq. There was a welter of gunshots, one on top of the other, the explosions painfully loud in the confined space. Bullets ricocheted off rock. Someone cried out. Jonathan covered his head. As quickly as it had begun, the gunshots died. The air quieted and he looked up. Haq was gone, as were the two remaining guards.

"Get a rifle." Hamid picked up one of the slain guards' AK-47s, checking the magazine and making sure that a round was chambered. "We've got to move before they can regroup."

Jonathan rushed across the room and pried the machine gun from the dead warrior's fingers. He had too many questions to ask, so he didn't ask any.

"You know how to fire it?" Hamid asked.

"I've plinked at some cans."

"Great, they told me you'd done this before." Hamid snatched the weapon from his grasp, released the banana clip, rapped it against his thigh, then shoved it back into the stock, finally flipping the rifle onto its side and chambering a round. He was no longer the shy, whining doctor in training. This was another Hamid altogether. He was bold, decisive, and thoroughly professional.

"You've got a full mag," he said, slamming the rifle against Jonathan's chest. "Fire low and in short bursts. Now come on. We've got to get our guys before Haq takes care of them."

Jonathan stared at the elder Haq's corpse, then at the rifle in Hamid's arms. The scope of the operation came to him in its entirety. Hamid worked for Division, and Division had used Jonathan as cover to put their operative in place to kill Abdul Haq.

A volley of automatic-weapons fire rattled through the cave. Hamid poked his head into the dim passage. "Stay on my tail. When I move, you move. Ready?"

Jonathan nodded. He was shaking badly.

Hamid slid the barrel of the machine gun around the corner. With crisp, practiced movements, he leaned into the cave and fired at the ceiling. The lightbulbs shattered. Darkness was immediate. There was a breath of wind where Hamid had been standing and a voice called from down the passage, "Come on!"

"Shit." Jonathan ducked into the tunnel. Gunfire lit the cave. Bullets struck the wall above his head and a shard of rock stung his cheek. Bent double, he ran as fast as he could, his shoulder scudding the wall. Staccato flashes of machine-gun fire illuminated their progress like frames from a stuttering projector. He saw Hamid a few steps ahead, raising his weapon. A rifle responded, the noise deafening, and for a second Jonathan glimpsed the tall, turbaned figure of Sultan Haq, the Kentucky hunting rifle pressed to his shoulder. Jonathan threw himself to the ground as rock burst from the wall above his head.

"In here," shouted a voice to his left.

Jonathan commando-crawled the last few meters into the opening and rolled onto his back.

Hamid popped a glow-bright bracelet. "You okay?"

Jonathan tried to speak, but his throat was too tight and he had no idea where his voice had gone. He moved his jaw and finally formed a word. "Yeah."

The captured American soldiers stood in a semicircle facing him. The lifeless body of a Taliban fighter lay at their feet, his head twisted at a grotesque angle. "I don't know who the hell you are, but I'm glad to see you," said one of the soldiers, who had a captain's twin bars sewn to his collar. There was a Ranger tab on one shoulder and jump wings on his chest. "When we heard the commotion and saw old Muhammad here freak out, we figured it was our only chance. I take it you came for Abdul Haq. You get him?"

"Dispatched with prejudice," said Hamid. "You boys are gravy. Consider this your lucky day."

"A-fuckin'-men," said the captain.

"How you guys holding out?"

"We're good to go."

"Outstanding." Hamid handed a roll of medical gauze to each man.

Jonathan got to his feet, confused. "Is someone hurt?"

Hamid peeled away the bandage to reveal an olive-green metallic canister. "Sorry, doc. Had to use your equipment to smuggle in what we needed." He turned to the soldiers: "Four grenades is all we have. Two antipersonnel. Two Willy Petes. You guys got any extra clips?"

"Just the one," said the captain. "You?"

"One spare, and the doc's AK has a full mag."

"You mind?" One of the soldiers, a sergeant, reached for Jonathan's rifle.

"Be my guest." Jonathan handed over the Kalashnikov.

"I take it you got a plan to get out of here," said the captain.

"There's a SEAL extraction team waiting in Kunduz," said Hamid. "I got off a signal that I was going in, but I didn't get confirmation that they were inbound. With all these mountains, it's doubtful they got a good read on my GPS. Otherwise, they'd have been here by now."

Jonathan felt his stomach sink. "What does that mean?"

"It means there's a fifty-fifty chance no one's going to be waiting for us when we get out of here."

"How many Tabbies are out there?" asked the captain, "Tabby" meaning Taliban.

"I counted fifteen armed," said Hamid. "You can add on a couple of camp followers. And then there are the thirty-caliber machine guns on the jeeps. That's what worries me. Any of you got a good arm?"

"That'd be me," said the sergeant.

"What do you think, cap?" asked Hamid.

The captain extended an arm into the passage. There was no fire. "They're waiting for us to show our faces. Doesn't look like they have night vision, so we've got that in our favor. We'll cover and roll, make 'em keep their heads down until we can chuck a grenade their way. We need to force them outside the cave and into the open where the chopper can hit them."

"If the chopper's even here." Suddenly Jonathan wanted a machine gun very badly.

"Have faith, doc," said Hamid. "When you get out, keep your head down and your legs moving."

"Let's do this." The captain tapped his sergeant on the shoulder. The sergeant nodded, then ducked into the passage and opened fire. The Rangers ran out first, then Hamid, and last Jonathan. He'd made it five steps when there was an explosion in the main entry chamber. He glimpsed a body launched into the air and heard a scream. A grenade. Keeping a hand on Hamid's back, he kept moving. The corridor grew light. The Rangers kneeled at the mouth of the passage, firing. Jonathan heard a smack, and one of the soldiers collapsed.

"Man down!" shouted the captain.

A second grenade exploded near the doorway and the Taliban fighters escaped outside. Jonathan rushed to the wounded Ranger. He could see blood spreading from a chest wound. He felt for a pulse. Nothing. Then, a faint tremor.

"How is he?" asked the captain.

"Unconscious. He needs attention fast."

"Can you carry him?" asked the captain.

Jonathan nodded. Bending double, he hoisted the soldier onto his shoulders in a fireman's carry. "Let's get out of here."

The officer ran toward the doorway, followed by Hamid and the sergeant. Jonathan took a breath and staggered into the large chamber. Exhaustion, adrenaline, and the din of combat blurred events. He saw the captain firing in disciplined bursts. He saw Hamid cross the chamber, throw open the exterior door, and lob a grenade. He saw the sergeant bolt upright, with half his head shorn away, then stumble backward and fall to the ground.

And then Jonathan was at the door leading to the clearing, the captain and Hamid next to him. From high in the sky came the dull, rhythmic chop of a helicopter. A moment later, an earsplitting roar louder than anything Jonathan had ever heard filled the air. The ground shook. Men screamed.

"Gatling gun," said the captain. "Let's move!"

"What about the sergeant?" asked Jonathan.

The soldier lay a méter away, his brains spilled on the ground beside him.

"He's gone."

Hamid opened the door and tossed the last grenade. There was a flash of light, and a stream of white smoke curled into the air. The captain ran ahead, turning every few feet and spraying the area with machine-gun fire. Hamid pushed Jonathan out the door.

"Run to the far side of the plateau. Don't stop for anything."

"You don't have to tell me that twice." Jonathan jogged unevenly behind him, head down, his only thought that he must deliver the wounded Ranger to safety. He sensed rather than saw the helicopter hovering overhead. Geysers of dirt and crushed stone erupted from the Gatling gun's rounds, spraying his face. Dead Taliban lay everywhere. To his right, the pickup trucks burned magnificently. Afghan fighters dashed across the clearing, seeking shelter from the withering cannon fire.

The helicopter touched down at the far end of the clearing. SEALs jumped to the ground and ran toward them. Jonathan transferred the wounded Ranger to their care, then pulled himself into the open compartment. The captain hauled himself in next to him. "You did good, doc," he shouted, barely audible above the rifle fire and rotor wash. "We could use you on our team anytime."

Jonathan looked at the Ranger, seeing him clearly for the first time. The captain had shorn blond hair and wide, knowing blue eyes that were too hardened for a young man. The name Brewster was stenciled on his uniform.

"No thanks," said Jonathan. "Never again."

Gunfire raked the helicopter. Jonathan saw an Afghan fighter nearly enveloped in flames manning the .30 caliber machine gun. Another burst of fire struck the helicopter. Something hit close to Jonathan. Captain Brewster was flung onto his back. A string of bullet wounds laced his chest, and Jonathan knew immediately that he was dead.

A moment later, an explosion rocked the pickup truck and the machine gunner vanished.

"We're outta here," called the pilot over his shoulder. "Strap in."

The aircraft lifted off.

Jonathan spotted Hamid trapped behind a rock outcropping twenty meters away. "Don't go. We've got a man pinned down back there," he shouted. "Put down."

"No can do," said the pilot. "It's too late."

Jonathan waved his arms, motioning for his assistant to join them. "Come on! Run!"

Hamid broke from the rocks and sprinted toward the chopper.

Jonathan grabbed the captain's rifle and began shooting at the figures scurrying across the clearing. A man went down. Then another. "Hurry!" he shouted.

With a leap, Hamid grasped the skid. The chopper climbed higher. Jonathan threw aside the rifle and reached out for Hamid's hand. "I've got you."

"Don't let go!"

A flurry of bullets struck the engine mount. The helicopter lurched to the side. Jonathan slid halfway out of the open bay, manag-

ing to grasp a safety strap at the last moment. Another bullet ricocheted near his head.

"Get your feet onto the skid," he yelled.

"I'm trying!" Hamid flailed as the helicopter gained height, working time and again to kick his legs over the landing skid.

"Hold tight," said Jonathan.

At last Hamid managed to hook a foot around the skid. With
Jonathan's help, he pulled himself up and placed the other foot on the
metal rail. "Thanks, man. I didn't think we were—" Suddenly Hamid's
eyes rolled back in his head. The report of a high-powered rifle
cracked the air like a bullwhip and his grip weakened. His feet fell off
the skid and he slipped from Jonathan's grasp, plummeting to the
ground. It was over in a second.

Jonathan fell back against the bulkhead wall. As clouds closed
around the helicopter, his eyes remained glued to the clearing below,
where Sultan Haq stood with a dead Marine's hunting rifle at his
shoulder. Haq was looking at Jonathan and Jonathan was looking right
back. The warrior raised his arm and pointed a finger and its long curling nail at him. Then he put his head back and cried out for revenge.

White enveloped the chopper and Jonathan could see no more.
But the warrior's eyes stayed with him.

One day, he swore to himself. *One day* . . .

10

Frank Connor was still in shock.

"What the hell happened?" he demanded, spreading his arms wide.

Barely two hours earlier, he had watched his best operative being taken away to be murdered. The satellite link to Emma's com unit had faded in and out, because of either a technical glitch or, more probably, a jamming unit at the airport. The last image he'd received of Emma showed her handcuffed and being forced into Rashid's car.

Connor, director of Division, turned from the dark video screen and stared out the window. Seven thousand miles from the desert emirate of Sharjah, in Falls Church, Virginia, the afternoon was gray, damp, and bleak. The forested countryside had surrendered its last leaves a week ago. A vista of barren, spindly trees beckoned in every direction. Winter lurked at the door.

"Let's go over this again," said Peter Erskine, his deputy and the sole other occupant of the office. "All we can assume is that she's in Rashid's custody."

"Really? I think we can assume quite a bit more than that." Connor shook his head, dizzy with frustration. He knew full well that they could assume that Emma Ransom, in the guise of Lara Antonova, major in the Russian FSB, had been defrocked as a double agent in the pay of the United States of America, and his meticulously planned operation to assassinate Prince Rashid had quite literally blown up in his, or rather Emma's, face.

"He knew, Peter. Someone tipped him off about our little gift."

"We can't be certain. He did take a shot with the rifle."

"He had no other choice. He had to save face in front of his men."

"How many people knew about the rifle?" said Erskine. "You, me, Emma, a couple of our transport guys, and the gunsmiths at Quantico. Rashid is rightfully paranoid. That's all. Who wouldn't be, after the close calls he's had?"

Connor eyed Erskine skeptically. "You telling me it wasn't you who gave him the heads-up?"

Erskine took the jibe in stride. "He's on my speed-dial, didn't you know?"

Connor thought about what he was suggesting. "I hope you're right and it's just that Rashid's got a case of nerves." He rubbed a meaty hand over his face. "Contact the CIA station chief in Dubai. See if he has any men in place that know the area. I want my girl back."

"Sir, if I may be so bold," said Erskine, "any action we take to find Emma will constitute an acknowledgment on our behalf that she's one of ours. We might as well call up Rashid and tell him that the United States government tried to assassinate him."

Erskine was tall, urbane, and handsome in the way that only third-generation Grotonians could be. He wore his father's tortoise-shell eyeglasses and his grandfather's navy blazer and spoke with his great-grandfather's Beacon Hill lilt. At thirty-five, he was a young fogey in the prime of his life.

"I think the prince knows that by now," said Connor.

"Even so, there's a difference between knowing and *knowing*. Our two governments still have to do business. Then, of course, there's the Russian angle. I don't think Igor Ivanov will be pleased."

"Screw Ivanov," said Connor, referring to the chief of the Russian security service. "It's my job to turn his agents and his job to do the same to mine. Five will get you ten that Rashid is on the phone to Ivanov right now, giving him the news. All I care about is finding Emma."

"Rashid wouldn't kill an American agent," said Erskine. "He doesn't have the guts."

"Doesn't he? He's a ruthless bastard. I'll give him that. Besides, technically Emma isn't an *American* agent. She's Russian born and bred, and an honor graduate of the FSB academy at Yasenevo. She might be married to an American, but otherwise she doesn't have a single official tie to our country."

Erskine nodded, pushing up his eyeglasses on his patrician nose. "And her years at Division?"

"I don't think her time with us is on the record books, do you?"

Erskine offered a look of sheepish resignation. "That puts her rather on her own."

Connor looked away, despising his assistant's easy cynicism. The fact was, he owed Emma. He'd handpicked her from the open market in the days when Russia was in the tank and a bankrupt FSB had been forced to let nearly all of its agents go. Division was in its infancy then, a brand-spanking-new outfit set up in the deepest corridors of the Pentagon to do the things the White House wanted done but didn't have the intestinal fortitude to carry out.

The first jobs were in-and-out affairs: assassinations, kidnappings, thefts of classified information. Muscle jobs that emphasized brawn over brain. Operatives were drawn from Delta Force, the Green Berets, and the SEALs as well as the CIA's Special Operations Group. But as the successes mounted, Division grew more ambitious. "Proactive" was the watchword. More complex plans were drawn up. Even the most heavily protected targets were deemed game. Operatives were called on to assume false identities and spend long periods in foreign locales. To bolster language capabilities, Division began looking for talent outside the fold. Freelance personnel from Britain, France, and Italy were recruited. And from Russia.

Division was the president's secret weapon and operated at his sole command. Covert foreign policy conducted at the barrel of a gun, with no congressional oversight allowed.

But times changed. The outrage that followed 9/11 faded. There had been no further attacks on American soil, though Connor knew firsthand that plenty had been thwarted. If Americans had a short memory, he liked it that way. It meant that his country was safe.

Connor looked at Erskine and made a decision.

"You're right," he said. "I was being hasty. We can't go out there running around like a chicken with its head cut off."

"I'm pleased you see it that way," said Erskine. "The last thing this agency needs is to get into hot water again. As far as everyone outside this office is concerned, Emma Ransom is Lara Antonova, a card-carrying FSB spook."

"You're right, Pete. This is no time to get emotional."

Erskine evinced a grimace, as if to say he shared Connor's concern for her welfare. "Look at it this way. If anyone can take care of herself, it's Emma Ransom. She's one tough cookie."

"That she is."

"We have to tie this operation off at the source. There's no other way. Don't take it hard, Frank. The woman knew what she was getting herself into."

"Did she, Pete? You really think so?" Connor shook his head ruefully. "And did your wife? Did she know she was going to be an intel widow, or did you wait till after the marriage to tell her?"

Erskine was a newlywed, six months in, and married to a gal who worked reasonable hours as an attorney over at the Justice Department. He was at the part where he had to call his wife every evening to explain why he wouldn't be home at seven.

"Sometimes, kid," Connor went on, "I wonder if any of us really know what we're getting into."

At fifty-nine years of age, standing five feet nine inches tall and weighing 260 pounds, Frank Connor was the poster boy for heart disease, diabetes, stroke, and all the perils to personal health that accumulated after a life spent eating, drinking, and working to excess. His chin drooped over his collar. His thatch of ginger hair had thinned to a wisp, and his cheeks were decorated with enough broken capillaries to map the United States interstate system. His blue eyes, though, were still vital and stood ready for a challenge.

During his thirty years in Washington, he'd worked at Treasury, in the Pentagon, and for the past ten years at Division. Everyone knew that Frank Connor was going to die with his boots on. Connor knew it, too, and he wouldn't have it any other way.

"All right, then," he said. "What's that they say about lemons and lemonade? Let's see what we can make out of this fiasco."

"Do let's," said Erskine, with exaggerated brio.

"Take a look at Rashid's pal. Recognize him?"

Connor sat at his government-issue desk staring at the image of Prince Rashid's associate filling his computer screen.

"Never seen him," said Erskine. "What do you think? Distant cousin? A warlord over from Afghanistan?"

"Too spiffed up. This one's got some class."

"One of his Wahabi pals from Riyadh?"

"Why would he need Rashid to do his shopping for him? Plenty of fundamentalist nut jobs can do the job right there. Besides, if he were a Saudi, our assets would've pinpointed him by now. With all the eyes and ears we have on payroll in the royal palace, we'd know his name, blood type, and favorite scotch."

"A friend of Balfour's?" suggested Erskine.

Connor dismissed the suggestion with a snort. "He's with Rashid all the way. Did you see the way the prince kowtowed to the guy? He respected him. Whoever our new friend is, he's a mover and a shaker. He's either done something to impress Rashid, in which case we should have a trace of him on our books, or he's going to, in which case we may be in deep shit. Get a still blown up and send it over to tech services for cleaning up. When it's finished, pass it over to Langley, MI6, and our friends in Jerusalem. Maybe they can put a name to a face."

"Right away." Erskine jotted the notes on a digital assistant, then slipped the device into his jacket. He walked to the door, but instead of leaving, he checked that it was properly closed, then crossed the office and perched himself on the corner of Connor's desk. "You know what really concerns me, Frank?"

Connor leaned back in his chair. "What's that?"

"The weapon Balfour mentioned finding."

"That? Probably a five-hundred-pounder we were sending to the mujahideen way back when."

Erskine narrowed his eyes and shook his head, having none of it. "I don't think he'd ask Emma if she had a direct line to Igor Ivanov if it were a conventional munition. Mind taking another look at the feed?"

Connor restarted the digital recording, watching closely as Balfour handed Emma the picture of the bomb. The images were so crisp that Connor wanted to reach out and kiss her for framing the photograph so perfectly. Erskine rose from his chair and approached the fifty-inch screen. "What if it isn't just a five-hundred-pounder?"

Connor put his elbows on the desk and leaned forward. "What are you trying to say?"

"What if it's something bigger?"

"Like what? A bunker buster?"

"I don't mean bigger in size," said Erskine menacingly.

Connor leaned back in his chair, hands behind his head. "You're out of your mind," he said. "We'd have known."

Erskine crossed his arms and looked at Connor over the top of his tortoiseshell glasses. "Would we?"

11

It was past midnight when Frank Connor returned to his town house on Prospect Street in Georgetown. Mounting the stairs, he paused at the front door long enough to punch in the alarm code and watch the pinlight turn from red to green. Despite the alarm and the two-man security team parked somewhere up the street to keep watch on him, he had few illusions about his safety. He'd been in the business long enough to forget more enemies than he could remember. If someone wanted him dead, he would die without seeing his assailant.

Safety was one thing. Security another.

Instead of unlocking the door and stepping inside, he put his fingers to the brick just below the alarm and slid it to the right, revealing a second numeric touch pad. This was his own alarm, a motion detection system set to register any activity inside the home and notify him privately. He was pleased to see that the light burned amber. All clear. It wasn't his life he was worried about so much as the information inside his home.

He tapped in his six-digit code—his mother's birthday—and then thumbed the brick back into position. With a muted click, the door opened automatically. Connor stepped inside and set down his briefcase in the vestibule. A single lamp burned in the living room, casting light on a chintz couch and an antique Quaker chair. The house was decorated in traditional bachelor style, which meant there was really no style at all. Still, he was careful to follow the dictates required of a ranking official who'd maxed out on the Special Executive Service pay scale long ago. He had an oak dining set and fine Meissen china. He had a mahogany secretary and prints of old U.S. sailing ships. There were no photos of friends or family anywhere in the house. He had none that he cared about. The only piece of furniture he gave a hoot about was his old leather recliner, dating from his days as a law student at the University of Michigan.

Connor was a man of habit. As always, he walked to the kitchen and poured himself a glass of milk, turning the lights on and off to mark his progress through the house. Next he went to his second-floor den, sat down in his recliner, and made himself watch one of the late-night television hosts' monologue. Ten excruciating minutes passed before he rose and walked up the last flight of stairs to his bedroom. He drew the curtains, changed into his pajamas, then lay on his bed, leafing through an issue of *Foreign Affairs*, not seeing a single word.

In his mind, a single phrase played over and over. *Someone is watching.*

At twelve-forty he turned off the lights. Frank Connor's official day was over.

Five minutes later, he threw off the covers, lumbered out of bed, and walked through the bathroom and into a musty back closet reserved for discarded clothing. Pushing aside a few moth-eaten blazers, he set his shoulder against the wall and pushed. The wall spun on a gimbal to reveal a comfortable study beyond, outfitted with green carpeting, a sturdy desk, and a large captain's chair. The room had come with the house, courtesy of its original owners, abolitionists who had helped slaves escape on the Underground Railroad. (There was a secret stairwell, too, leading to a garden shed on an adjacent property. He was not the first occupant interested in escaping from prying eyes.) The air inside was cool and smelled of lemon. He pushed the wall back into place and pressed a button that secured the door with a sixteen-inch titanium rod. Safe in his private office, Connor sighed. He could finally go to work.

He sat down and logged onto Intelnet, his agency's secure server. His first order of business was to access his mailbox. He was pleased to note that the Strategic Air Command had finished cleaning up the picture of the American munition that Lord Balfour had shown to Emma. Computer processing had sharpened the focus tenfold, and as he gazed at the weapon he could make out the rivets on its steel skin.

"Jesus, Mary, and Joseph," he whispered.

Peter Erskine was right: it was no five-hundred-pound conventional bomb. Not by a long shot. An attached simulation showed what the weapon would look like when freed from the snow. Anyone with even a rudimentary knowledge of military technology would recognize it as a cruise missile. SAC had labeled the weapon an AGM-86.

Connor had more than a rudimentary knowledge of military technology. Before joining Division, he'd worked as a procurement officer for the Defense Department and spent much of his time with companies like General Dynamics, Raytheon, and Lockheed. He knew all about a cruise missile's specs. He knew that it could fly close to the speed of sound with a range of over a thousand miles. He knew it could be launched from a ship or dropped from a plane, and that either way it could hit a target the size of a Volkswagen Beetle with 98 percent accuracy. He knew that it could carry a conventional warhead containing high explosives or a nuclear warhead with a yield of up to 150 kilotons, ten times the size of the bomb that fell on Hiroshima.

One hundred fifty kilotons.

Connor sat up in his chair. He felt short of breath. A sharp pain speared his chest and he stiffened. Desperately he opened his mouth to breathe, to relieve the profound discomfort, but an immense, unyielding pressure had clamped down on his chest. His throat and lungs were paralyzed.

And then it was gone. The pressure lifted. The pain vanished. Connor sucked down a draft of air, feeling his entire body come back to him. The episode had lasted fifteen seconds.

Stress, he told himself as he stood and poured himself four fingers of Mr. Justerini and Brooks. Anyone would feel the same if he'd just gotten a glimpse of Armageddon.

One hundred fifty kilotons.

He lifted his glass and toasted a world gone to hell.

He was aware that the air force had lost nuclear weapons on a few occasions, but to the best of his knowledge it had recovered them without incident. He also knew that as a safety precaution, the air force had halted all bomber flights with armed nuclear weapons in 1968. The cruise missile in question wasn't manufactured until the 1970s. Logic therefore dictated that whatever Balfour had found, and wanted Emma to help retrieve, was not an armed nuclear weapon.

But where was logic in explaining how that kind of weapon, either conventional or nuclear, had ended up high in the mountains of Pakistan or India in the first place?

There were two things that Frank Connor had learned during thirty years of government service: people lie, and anything is possible. He took these as the fundamental truths of his profession, and it was his ruthless exploitation of both that had fueled his climb to the directorship of Division.

Which brought him back to the present.

Somewhere there was a bomb, *possibly nuclear,* and somehow he had to get it.

He glanced at his wristwatch. The time was 1:23. It was an appropriate time for a mission to begin.

Connor logged off Intelnet. For a while he sat in the dark, contemplating the events of the day. Unlike Erskine, he was more concerned about Emma Ransom than about the discovery of the cruise missile tucked away high in a distant mountain range. For the moment the missile was contained. It was a threat. It posed near unimaginable danger if in fact it carried a nuclear payload, armed or otherwise. But any imminent danger was a way off.

On the other hand, Emma Ransom was either dead or faced torture and imprisonment. Either prospect pained him greatly.

Emma was special. Emma had sacrificed. Emma had given of herself, as he had given of himself.

Connor rose and crossed to the far corner of the room. With difficulty, he kneeled and pulled back a section of carpet, revealing a safe with a biometric lock. He opened it and retrieved a sturdy leatherbound volume. He needed a breath to regain his feet, and several more to make it back to his desk. Seated, he cracked the volume and turned the pages slowly, staring at the photographs affixed to each page.

Against every rule of practice, Frank Connor had assembled an album of every man and woman who had worked as an operative at Division. There were only photographs. No names. No dates. Just faces. Still, it was a fundamental breach and he knew it. He had no excuses. His heart needed none. They were his family.

He stopped at a page halfway through and looked down at the young woman with twisted auburn hair and spectral green eyes. She looked so young. Not innocent. Emma had never been innocent. But young and eager, and, by God, so willing. He had never known anyone so capable and so driven.

He closed the book and raised his eyes toward the ceiling. Something stirred inside him. Not sorrow. Certainly not guilt. He had forsaken his conscience years ago. Something stronger. A call to duty. He owed her.

Connor picked up his phone and placed a call to the Middle East. A male voice answered.

"Don't you ever sleep?"

"I've got an assignment for you," said Connor. "Strictly off the record."

"Isn't it always?"

12

It was one o'clock in the afternoon in the United Arab Emirates when the man pulled onto the shoulder of the highway from Dubai to Sharjah. He put the Land Rover into park and stared out the window. A sea of undulating dunes spread to all four corners of the horizon with nothing to differentiate one patch of earth from the next. For a final time he checked the coordinates of his handheld GPS against those he'd received two hours earlier from Frank Connor. The map indicated his position as twenty-six kilometers southwest of the Sharjah Free Trade Zone. He was in the right place.

Climbing down from the cab, the man made a circuit of the vehicle. He stopped at each tire, inserting a pen into the air valve until he'd bled fifteen pounds of pressure. Finished, he ran a sleeve across his forehead while looking in either direction for approaching vehicles. No cars were visible. Even so, he wouldn't have been overly concerned. Tours of the desert were popular among visitors. The logo of Dubai Desert Adventures adorned the vehicle's doors. To all passing eyes he was just one more guide. If anyone wished to look closer, the glove compartment held a valid guide's license, his operating permit, and a log of customers dating back two years. As cover it would withstand a cursory inspection, but little beyond that. It was the best he could do on short notice.

The man slid behind the wheel and shoved the gearshift into first. The Land Rover lurched forward, the underinflated tires gripping the sand nicely. Sky filled the windscreen as the vehicle climbed a dune. The next moment the nose fell, and blue was replaced by brown as the car slid down the back side. His destination was an anonymous point in the desert thirty kilometers due west, where Emma Ransom had last been seen. Satellite imagery taken after her video feed was cut showed the heat signature of six vehicles departing from the airfield and traveling deep into the desert. Enhancement of the images identified five of the vehicles as belonging to the national police. The sixth was a Mercedes SUV and belonged to Prince Rashid.

"One of my operators is missing," Connor had said when he'd called hours earlier. "This one is a priority. To be found at all costs."

The man drove for an hour, his neck growing tense from the vehicle's continual rising and falling. One kilometer from the destination, he crested a rise and braked before the Land Rover could plummet down the other side. Cautiously, he stepped out. The dune sea ended just ahead, giving way to a moonlike expanse of hard sand, rock, and scrub. With his binoculars, he scanned the landscape. Almost immediately his eye caught a patch of color where none should be. There, precisely where the satellite had last mapped Prince Rashid's position, was a black garment impaled on a thorn bush.

Lowering his binoculars, he listened. The desert was a vacuum and sound traveled far. He heard nothing. Senses on alert, the man guided the vehicle down the last dune. Leaving the motor running, he walked to the bush and removed the garment. It was a cotton T-shirt, and he noticed at once that all of its labels had been cut out. It was a spy's garment, and as such, verification that Rashid had brought Emma Ransom to this place. One corner of the shirt was dry and crusted, and when he ran a thumb over it, it came away the color of rust.

A few meters away, tire tracks raked the dirt. The man approached and observed a storm of footprints in a semicircle around a smoothed patch of sand. Cigarette butts littered the area. Kneeling, he ran his fingers through the sand. He came away with various rocks and pebbles and sticks. There was something else, too. A tooth. A human molar with a silver filling.

The man returned to his car and drove over to a dune that looked down on the spot where Emma Ransom had been tortured, and more than likely executed. Using his binoculars, he studied the area. After a moment he spotted a set of tire tracks leading farther into the desert and, centered behind the tracks, a rough furrow. He knew the rumors about the prince. It was not the first time Rashid al-Zayed had dragged someone behind his car.

The man followed the tracks until they ended abruptly one kilometer farther on. He stepped down from the car and surveyed the area, but he found only a single set of men's footprints. One impression was exceptionally clear and showed a partial name of the shoe brand. He snapped a few photos with his telephone and sent them to Connor with the hope that some of his technical whizzes might be able to deduce something or other. He kicked around the sand, feeling miserable.

And then he saw it—a chunk of plastic no bigger than a thumbnail. He brought it closer. It was a cellular telephone's SIM card, the all-important chip containing the telephone's user information: numbers, addresses, photographs, and records of calls made to and from that apparatus. Near the SIM card, blood had dried into a hardened pool, as black as obsidian.

Rising, he made a final walk around. With a heavy heart, he placed a call to Connor.

"You were right. Rashid took her out into the desert with all his buddies and had some fun with her."

"Any sign of her?"

"I found her shirt, a tooth, and a SIM card. There's a lot of blood, too."

"Jesus."

"I wouldn't hold out much—" The man stopped mid-sentence. "Holy shit."

"What is it?" demanded Frank Connor.

The man bent at the waist and peered at something in the sand. "She's alive."

"How do you know?"

"Because I'm looking at her footprint. She walked out of here."

13

The MV-22 Osprey flew high over the blue waters of the Persian Gulf, maintaining a speed of 180 knots on its course south-by-southwest from Bagram Air Base in Afghanistan. Seated in the passenger compartment, Jonathan Ransom glanced out the window as a pair of F-18 fighters whizzed past a mile to port. The helicopter passed directly above a guided missile cruiser, the Stars and Stripes flying boldly from the fantail. For the last ten minutes they'd been overflying the naval vessels of Carrier Task Force 50. He'd left one war zone only to enter another.

"Touchdown in six minutes," said the pilot.

Jonathan checked his shoulder harness, making sure that the belt fit tightly across his chest and waist. The Osprey dipped its nose and began a rapid descent. He had the sensation of being sucked into a vortex against his will.

Since climbing onto the chopper at Tora Bora one week earlier, he'd been constantly on the move. From Tora Bora to Bagram. Bagram to Camp Rhino. Camp Rhino to the embassy in Kabul. Back to Bagram. At every stop he'd endured another debriefing. He'd related the events as best he could. He'd asked to go home. Always he received the same answer: "In due time." And he waited to be moved again.

The aircraft touched down. Two MPs led the way to a hatch in "the Island," the imposing tower rising from the flight deck. Jonathan followed, climbing a set of stairs to reach the flag bridge. His destination was an anonymous wardroom with a table and chair and an American flag stuck in one corner like an afterthought.

The hatch opened and a stocky middle-aged man dressed in a rumpled gray suit entered. He was carrying two china mugs and held a leather folder beneath an arm. "You drink tea, right?" he said, thrusting one of the mugs toward Jonathan. "I got you Darjeeling. Two bags and plenty of sugar. Figured you needed something to keep you going. Me, I'm a coffee guy. Don't care what kind as long as it's black."

Jonathan took the mug and looked on as the man struggled to set his coffee and dossier on the table, spilling quite a bit in the process. "Want to join me?" he asked as he pulled out a chair and sat down. "No? Suit yourself. Me, I have to sit. I swear these long flights give me thrombosis in my legs. Hurts like the dickens."

"You should make sure you walk around during the flight," said Jonathan. "Helps the circulation."

"Yeah, that's what they say."

The man unzipped his leather folder and took out a legal pad and some papers and arranged them neatly, as if he were a clerk setting up for business. Jonathan knew better than to be fooled. Whoever this man was, he was anything but a clerk.

"Some shit-storm you went through," said the man. "You all right?"

"I'm fine. The other guys weren't so lucky."

"You want to tell me what happened?"

"You want to tell me your name?"

"What's the point? I'd probably be lying to you."

"You're Connor."

The man pulled his jaw into his neck, either surprised or bewildered. "Emma told you?"

"She might have let something slip when we were in London. She said you were a prick. I just put a face to a name."

Connor found this amusing. "Did she tell you anything else?"

"That you tried to have her killed when she was in Rome."

"I understand you're upset. No one likes to be manipulated without their knowledge."

"I'm still working on your sending a man to put a knife in my wife's back."

Connor lost his friendly tone. "We'll get to that later," he said, and for the first time Jonathan was aware that he was in the presence of a formidable individual. "Sit down, Dr. Ransom. I didn't fly seven thousand miles to give you a handshake, a hug, and a kiss on the cheek for serving your country. We have some important issues to get through."

Jonathan sat down. "Eight years wasn't enough? I thought I'd served my time."

"Believe me, we're grateful for all you've done. Especially for your actions in Switzerland. No one more than me. If it's worth anything, I'm sorry that we had to drag you back into this. I know you went to Afghanistan to get away from it all."

"I went to Afghanistan to get back to doing what I do best."

"From the little I heard about how you acted under fire, you might want to reconsider what that is."

"I did what anyone would do."

"Not everyone would carry a wounded soldier through a hail of gunfire at considerable risk to himself. They give medals for that kind of thing."

"I don't want a medal."

"I know you don't. I couldn't give you one anyway. But so you know, Dr. Ransom, the man you led us to, Abdul Haq, was a first-class sonofabitch. We'd been trying to get at him for months without any luck. Drones. Informants. Rewards. Nothing worked. Then we got word he was sick and we saw our way in. You happened to be in that neck of the woods. You didn't leave us much choice."

"So that's how it goes? I don't get a say in the matter."

"No, Dr. Ransom. Sometimes you don't. Ain't life a pile of shit?"

"And Hamid?"

"Hamid signed up. He grew up in Kabul, then emigrated to San Francisco. He joined the army to do some good for his country."

"And that's when you stepped in?"

"He possessed a unique skill set that was very much in demand. Hamid wanted us as badly as we wanted him. Afghanistan is a safer place without Mr. Abdul Haq."

Jonathan put the mug to his lips and drank down the warm, sweet tea. He thought of Hamid dropping from his grasp. It might as easily have been him. "You know, I've been wondering about something. How was it that you guys found me all that time ago?"

"Even if I knew, I couldn't tell you."

"Of course you know," said Jonathan. "A guy like you knows everything."

"Don't count on it."

Jonathan stifled a nasty rebuke. "And Emma? How'd you get your hooks into her?"

"I can't tell you that either. 'Need to know,' Dr. Ransom. It's the first rule of the game."

"Do you know where she is?"

"Like I said, I can't discuss your wife's past or present." Connor paused and set down his coffee. "At least, *not yet.*"

Jonathan felt something shift in the room, a change in the dynamic between them. If he weren't mistaken, an offer had been made. "What does that mean?"

"It means I came to talk to you about helping us."

"You mean Division?"

Connor nodded.

"You're serious? You want me to work for you?"

"We think you have certain skills that can—"

"No," said Jonathan.

"Just hear me out."

"Absolutely not. I'm finished. Done. Over."

"I've come an awfully long way—"

"Well, that's awfully tough shit." Jonathan shoved himself away from the table, knocking his chair over as he stood. "Now you can get in your plane and fly an awfully long way back. Goodbye."

"Please, Dr. Ransom, I understand you're upset. Just give me a—"

"I said I'm finished."

Connor stared at Jonathan. "Fair enough," he said. "It goes without saying that none of what happened in Tora Bora can ever be repeated.

The intel boys aboard ship will give you some papers to sign. When you're done, tell them where you want to go. They'll make it happen. Ticket, passport, whatever you need. I've been authorized to pay you for your work. I've got a check for fourteen thousand dollars made out in your name. That's two months' hazardous duty pay at major's rank."

"Keep it," said Jonathan.

"It's yours. You earned it. If you want to give it to charity, that's your business."

Connor set an envelope on the table, then gathered up his papers and replaced them in his briefcase. Jonathan noticed that he hadn't written a word. It was a show, just like the lousy suit, the scuffed-up shoes, and the Joe Sixpack delivery. He was the voice of America.

Connor stumbled as he rose to his feet and extended an uncertain hand for balance. Jonathan rushed around the table. "You okay?" he asked, grasping his arm for support.

"It's the leg." Connor waved him off. "I told you already. Lousy circulation."

Jonathan took a better look at Connor, seeing him as a doctor would a patient. He took in the burst capillaries in his cheeks, the bags under the eyes, the air of dissipation. Up close, he could hear Connor's breath, rapid and shallow. "Do you know where Emma is? Please. I just want to know if she's all right."

Connor lifted his satchel onto the desk. "What if I were to tell you that everything you currently know about your wife is false?"

Jonathan hesitated before answering, wondering if this was just another ploy to lure him in. "Like what? That she didn't try to kill me in France?"

"Among other things."

"I wouldn't believe you," said Jonathan, but his response was a reflex. There was something about Connor's manner that bespoke honesty and earnestness. Or maybe it was something inside Jonathan. Maybe he just wanted to believe.

"And if I told you that Emma was in danger—possibly grave danger—and that you were the only person who could help her?"

Jonathan looked hard at Connor, trying to see past the artifice. He saw only a man who was fifty pounds overweight, with a bum leg and a heart condition, telling him the truth. "Sit down."

14

"All right," said Jonathan. "I'm listening."

"The first thing you need to know is that Emma never stopped working for us. By us, I mean Division, and by Division, I mean the United States of America. There was a time after the events in Switzerland when she struck out on her own. Days—weeks, even. She was frightened that we'd seek retribution. I won't lie. There were some in the organization who wanted their pound of flesh. On the surface, Emma had betrayed us, and they wanted her punished. I was not of that opinion. I knew that Emma had done us an immeasurable service, and after things cooled down, everyone else began to see it my way. In fact, I realized that not only had her actions prevented a catastrophe of unimaginable proportions, but they'd presented us with a unique opportunity. Emma and I communicated, and I convinced her that she could be of more use to us staying out in the cold."

"But you tried to have her killed," said Jonathan. "I saw the scar on her back. I read the hospital report in Rome. She almost died from loss of blood."

"No, Dr. Ransom, she didn't. A very fine surgeon like yourself cut her and sewed her back up. The rest was smoke and mirrors. It's what we do."

Jonathan resisted speaking. His mind had come alive with the events of the past July, when Emma had visited him in London and he'd witnessed her detonating a car bomb that had left several people dead and numerous more wounded. He knew he should be sifting through the steps he'd taken afterward to track her down, but he couldn't get past the night they'd spent together at the Dorchester Hotel. The night before all hell had broken loose.

He had a vision of them making love on the floor of the hotel room. Emma was an active and passionate lover, but never before had she given herself to him so completely. Their hours together affirmed his love for his wife, and even deepened it. She'd risked all to be with him.

The memory was wonderful, but all too short-lived. Her subsequent unveiling as an operative in the employ of the Russian Federal Security Service had revealed her true reasons for coming to London. Visiting her husband for a romantic tryst figured far down the list. What he'd taken to be an expression of love was artifice or, worse, simple convenience. The realization had wrecked him.

"But why?" asked Jonathan, even as the pieces began to fall into place.

"Once we decided to run Emma as a double—to reintegrate her into the FSB—it was imperative that all doubts about where her loyalty lay be erased from the Russians' minds. The Russians are paranoid to a fault, and no one more than Sergei Shvets, at the time director of the FSB, the man who was Emma's first controller as well as her first lover. Emma had worked for us a long time by then."

"Eight years," said Jonathan.

"Longer," said Connor. "There was no way Shvets was going to take her back unless we gave him a reason. If we wanted her dead, he could only assume it was because she had betrayed us. Nothing less would have convinced him."

"And the rest? I mean, the explosives in the nuclear plant in Normandy? The car bomb in London? What about that?"

"That is none of your business." Connor raised a hand before Jonathan could protest. "You already know much too much about what happened last summer. I only told you this much because you're her husband and I figure we owe it to you."

"So you weren't aware that she was going to visit me in London?"

Connor laughed gruffly. "Do you think that's the kind of thing she'd clear with me?"

Jonathan looked away. "And so . . ."

"If she saw you, it was because she wanted to. You do the math. I will say this, however: it was a stupid, rash decision in contravention of every last tenet of her training. She risked her life and the mission by doing so, and you'd better believe I chewed her ass out about it when I found out."

Jonathan grabbed his mug of tea and drank it down. A steady hum reverberated through the carrier's hull. There was a loud *whoosh* from above their heads, and the boat shuddered as if it had taken a body blow.

"Flight ops," said Connor. "That's the catapult launching a plane off the deck."

The boat stilled, and Jonathan noted the pervasive scent of diesel fuel that hung in the air. "You said that Emma was in danger. How can I help her?"

"By finishing what she started."

"I think you have the wrong person. I'm a doctor, not an operative."

"Precisely. As it so happens, that's exactly what I'm in the market for." Connor laid his meaty fists on the table. "First off, I need you to tell me how you're feeling. No bullshit. What you went through in those mountains is enough to derail a strong man. I've seen soldiers with twenty years' experience lose it after something like that."

"I'm okay," said Jonathan.

"Nightmares? Sweats?"

Jonathan shook his head.

"Hold out your arm."

"Excuse me?"

"Come on. Stick it out straight in front of you. Hold your hand flat, fingers as straight as you can keep 'em."

Jonathan extended his right arm. His hand shook visibly. He balled his fingers into a fist, and when he released them, the fingers were steadier. Connor eyed him, unsure.

"When I was younger, I lost a few friends climbing," said Jonathan. "We were up high in dangerous spots, where things can happen quickly. Someone is there and then they're not. It's too fast to register what happened and what it means to you. I feel the same now. I'm freaked. Maybe I'm even in some kind of delayed shock. Part of me wants to give in to that, but there's too much going on. I have to take care of the now, now, or else I'm not going to get down alive. Does that make sense to you?"

Connor considered this. "Yes, Dr. Ransom. It does."

"Do me a favor. Would you stop calling me Dr. Ransom? My name is Jonathan."

"All right, Jonathan." One of the meaty hands rose from the table for a shake. "Frank Connor."

"And that's your real name?" asked Jonathan as he tried to match Connor's grip.

"As far as my mother told me." Connor laughed and loosened the knot of his tie. "Okay then, *Jonathan*, this is where we start. Everything I'm going to tell you from this moment on is classified, or a helluva lot higher than that. I don't have any papers for you to sign. That can wait. But make no mistake, from here on out, you work for me, and by that I mean the United States government. Are we clear?"

"Yeah, but you can leave that military bullshit at the door. *Are we clear?*"

Connor's eyes narrowed and a hint of red flushed his cheeks. "There's something else I should tell you. The job I'm asking you to take is extremely dangerous. You will be going into the belly of the beast, and there is not going to be anybody there to hold your hand. You will be alone behind enemy lines, and I mean that in the real sense of the word. There is every chance in the world that you will be caught. And if you are, I can't do a damn thing about it. The good news is that you won't have to rot for fifty years in a Pakistani cell. The bad news is that you'll be summarily executed."

"Hey, Frank, don't sugarcoat it. Tell how it's really going to be."

Connor didn't appreciate the joke. "I will steer you where you need to go. I will tell you everything you have to do. Follow my instructions and you'll make out just fine. The most important thing is to keep your wits about you. Are we cl—" Connor caught himself. "Do you understand?"

"Yes," said Jonathan. "I get it. It's dangerous. Go ahead. If it's something to help Emma, I'll do it."

"All right, then let me read you in on your wife's activities. For the past two months—since September—Emma's been stationed at the FSB's residence in Damascus, doing penance for her role in the attempt to assassinate Igor Ivanov. They have her doing menial tasks—running Arab diplomats, low-level sneak-'n'-peeks, the occasional theft of corporate secrets. These days industrial espionage is a state activity, especially if you're as far behind the eight ball as Russia. One of her jobs is handling Ashok Armitraj, a big-time gunrunner working out of South Asia. Armitraj is half Indian, half British and calls himself Lord Balfour. Ever heard of him?"

Jonathan said he hadn't.

"Soon you're going to know every goddamn thing there is to know about him. He's going to be your bestest and closest friend. Anyway, a month back Balfour contacted Emma with a shopping list he wanted for a client. Usually no one cares who the end user is. Balfour gives us a country and we put that on the export documentation."

"Us? America sells to this guy, too?"

Connor nodded. "We have a lot of fine companies to keep in business. Anyhow, the Russians don't mind who the end user is. They're shipping this stuff out the back door as it is."

"What do you mean, the back door?"

"Think of them like the Mob. The stuff Balfour buys from the Russians has all fallen off the back of a truck. In this case, the truck is a government arms factory controlled by the FSB. There's legit production and there's the back door. Legit sales go on the books. The back door goes into the generals' pockets."

"So who was Balfour's client—the end user?"

"We don't know. What we do know, and what opened our eyes, was Prince Rashid's involvement in the deal. According to Balfour, Rashid was brokering the sale and guaranteeing payment on his client's behalf."

"Prince Rashid from the Gulf? He's a benefactor of Doctors Without Borders. He's a good guy."

"Oh?" Connor's eyes darted away and he shook his head, as if somewhere there had been a gross misunderstanding. "Maybe we're talking about two different people. The Prince Rashid I know is one of the world's notorious terrorist financiers. He funnels money to Al-Qaeda, the Taliban, Laskar-e-Taiba, and any other Islamic organization bent on destroying the West, to the tune of two hundred million dollars a year."

Jonathan sat back, chastised. "I hadn't heard."

"Of course you hadn't. You're too busy being wowed by his good works and his blond wife and his beautiful blue-eyed children. Rashid wouldn't have it any other way."

"If you know all this, why haven't you made it public?"

"Think of what you're saying. The prince's family is the United States' staunchest ally in the Gulf. The accusation alone would sour relations for years. This isn't the kind of thing you air in public." Connor leaned forward, as if sharing a secret. "This is the kind of thing we take care of privately."

"So you used Emma to get at Rashid through Balfour?"

"No comment." Connor pursed his lips, as if struggling to decide what he might or might not say. His expression made it all too evident that something had gone terribly wrong. "All we know is that she disappeared while overseeing the transfer of weapons from Balfour to Rashid."

Jonathan envisioned the scenario without difficulty: Emma acting as a Russian agent to get close to Rashid and kill him. She'd pulled off similar feats in Lebanon and Bosnia and too many other places to name, let alone remember. It was not an occupation without risk. "Is she dead?"

"We have good reason to believe that she's not."

To Jonathan's ear, "good reason" sounded like spy-speak for a fifty-fifty chance at best. "So Rashid was onto her?"

"We don't know. But before I tell you what we do know, I want you to get a grip on yourself. A temper isn't going to help anyone, especially Emma."

Jonathan drew a breath, tamping down his nerves. "I understand," he said.

"Prince Rashid has a thing he does to people he thinks screwed him. Business, politics, whatever. He likes to take them into the desert and put the hurt on them. I'm not going to go into detail. It's nasty stuff."

"Like what?"

"You don't want to know."

"Like what, Frank?"

Connor set his forearms on the table and sighed, as if he were going against his better instincts. "Chains," he said. "Cattle prods. Cigarettes. Sometimes he drags them behind his car."

"And he did this to Emma?"

Connor nodded.

Jonathan looked away, an ungovernable rage building inside him. The thought came to him that he would stop at nothing to punish the animal who had inflicted such punishment on his wife.

A steady ringing filled his ears, but he wasn't sure whether it came from inside him or from the carrier. "You just said you had good reason to believe that she isn't dead."

"We have evidence that indicates she survived the beating."

"Did someone see her?"

"No."

"Then what? This is my wife you're talking about. 'Good reason' doesn't cut it."

"We found what we believe to be her footprints walking away from the spot where she was left. It appears she was driven from the scene. At this point, that's all we know."

"Cattle prods? He dragged her behind his car across the desert?"

Connor frowned. "He's a bad one. I'm sorry."

Jonathan felt something cold and hard and merciless settle inside him. He had never been one to harbor grudges, to catalogue wrongs done to him, slights received, indignities and insults, in the vain, misguided hope of one day paying them back. In his younger days, he had had his own method of dealing with assholes, and that method invariably involved a bottle of Jack Daniel's Tennessee Sour Mash Whiskey and his fists. He found his method to be cheap, expedient, and effective at resolving matters between individuals. Unfortunately, it was also illegal, and landed him overnight stays in jail in ten cities across six counties. As he grew older, and (eventually) matured, he'd learned that violence was not a means to an end. It was just a means to feed the devil inside you. Instead of hitting people, he ignored them. He traded mayhem for a medical degree, fists for a scalpel and forceps. He needed his hands in good condition for surgery.

But all the while, the devil inside him waited, biding his time, doing pushups in the deepest corner of his soul, gathering strength for the moment of his return. Jonathan knew this, and, ever vigilant, had kept him at bay these many years.

Chains . . . cattle prods . . . cigarettes . . . sometimes he drags them behind his car.

Connor's words penetrated to that deepest corner, and now, seated at the table as the carrier shuddered with the launch of another jet, Jonathan felt the demon stir inside him, the hounds bay for revenge.

Payback.

"So this is about getting to Rashid?" asked Jonathan, with a new and improved outlook on the matter.

Connor shook his head. "Not just yet. The situation is fluid. Rashid doesn't matter at the moment. We're more interested in finding out the identity of the man for whom he purchased the weapons. If he's a new player, we want a name. If he's an established entity, we want to know that, too."

"But Rashid hurt Emma. You can't just let him—"

"Rashid is an SOB, and one day he'll pay. You've got my word. But right now there's no way we can get close to him. He knows we're watching. He'll have his defenses buttoned up tight. The only way in is through Balfour. You see, Balfour doesn't just supply weapons, he flies them to wherever his clients need them. If we can find out where Balfour delivered those guns, we'll know who Rashid's mystery friend is. As I said, we need to get close to Balfour, and you're the only one who can do it."

"I already told you that I don't know anything about him."

"That doesn't matter. It's what you can do for him that counts."

Connor spent several minutes explaining Balfour's history, his rise to power as an arms trafficker, and his subsequent fall from grace as a fugitive on Interpol's Red List. When it was done, Connor paused and leaned back in his chair, his shrewd eyes fixed on Jonathan. "Still interested?" he asked.

"Keep talking," said Jonathan.

"Balfour is in trouble and he knows it. The Indian government is closing in on him. The Pakistanis may pull the welcome mat from beneath his feet at any time. He needs a way out and he needs it now. The problem is, there's nowhere for him to hide. So . . . Balfour needs someone to alter his appearance so that he can start a new life incognito. He's in the market for a plastic surgeon, and he wants him to perform the procedure at his compound in Pakistan. We would like you, Dr. Ransom, to be that surgeon."

"You want me to change his looks? To turn him into someone else entirely?"

"Hopefully, you'll never have to perform the operation," said Connor. "Balfour conducts all his affairs from offices inside a palatial compound outside Islamabad. We want you to use your status as Balfour's guest to locate information telling us the identity of Rashid's client. There'll never be a better opportunity to get inside his business. Rashid's client is just the tip of the iceberg. If things go well, we'll get enough information to turn the arms market inside out."

"How long will I have?"

"You tell me. How long does that sort of procedure take?"

"Start to finish? A lot depends on just how radically he wants to alter his appearance. Nose, chin, implants. We'll have to see. In any event, I'll have to do a full workup on him, a physical, blood panels, that kind of thing. We're talking two days minimum if we can get results back quickly. What kind of equipment does he have?"

"Knowing Balfour, he'll have the best."

"In that case, the surgery itself will only take a half-day. But he'll need to rest for a few days afterward. There's no way he can get on a plane for at least a week."

A klaxon sounded on the ship's internal speaker system. A man announced that chow was being served in the enlisted mess and that the movie for that night was *Batman Returns*. Jonathan spent a moment running over all that Connor had told him. "You said Balfour's in the market for a surgeon. Has he chosen someone?"

Connor said yes.

An uneasy feeling took hold of Jonathan. "What's going to happen to him?"

"He'll be taken out of the picture," said Connor matter-of-factly.

"Taken out of the picture?"

Connor nodded. "Obviously, we need to get him out of the way."

"You guys just don't get it. I can't trade Emma's life for his."

Connor stared with obvious disappointment across the table. "Is that how you see us? A bunch of amoral killers willing to do anything to accomplish our objectives? You, of all people, should know how seriously we value human life."

Jonathan didn't miss the unspoken message. He, a civilian, had been privy to several of Division's operations. He knew far more than any civilian should. If Division made it a policy to eliminate any and all individuals they considered a risk, he would've been dead a long time ago. "Yeah, maybe," he admitted. "It's just that I'm not too good at figuring out who has to live and who has to die."

"You leave that part to me. Right now, you just need to do as I tell you. You good with that?"

Jonathan said that he was, but already a voice was sounding inside him, saying that Connor was holding something back. "So what happens now? How much time do we have?"

Connor checked his watch. "Jesus, where did the time get to? You'd better haul your butt upstairs to the flight deck. Your carriage is waiting."

"Now?"

"This minute." Frank Connor guided him out of the wardroom and down several flights of stairs, stopping at the pilots' ready room. He barked a few orders, and an officer emerged with a flight suit and a helmet.

"Put 'em on," said Connor. "Now."

"Where am I going?" asked Jonathan.

"To see some friends of mine. You've got a lot to learn before I can send you into Balfour's den."

Jonathan looked at the flight suit and helmet. "Hold it a second," he said, keeping his hands at his sides. "What about Emma? You told me she might be in danger. Isn't this about her?"

"It certainly is. The best way you can help your wife is to finish what she started," said Connor. "Lord Balfour was one of the last people to see Emma before Rashid tortured her. If anyone knows what happened to her, it'll be him."

15

Frank Connor stood on the flight deck, watching from the safety line as Jonathan climbed into the rear seat of the F-18/A. An airman leaned into the cockpit and tightened Jonathan's harness and acquainted him with the plane's features. At one point the airman pointed to something at Jonathan's feet and then crossed his hands over each other dramatically while shaking his head, and Connor knew that Jonathan had just been advised not to pull the ejection handle except in an absolute emergency.

The airman closed the canopy and leaped down from the ladder. Farther up the deck, a flight controller waved a green flag. The pilot gave a salute. The sound of the aircraft powering up was like an industrial turbine red-lining. Connor saw Jonathan glance his way. Feeling that something was expected of him, he forced an arm up and gave a thumbs-up. It was an awkward gesture. He'd never been good at the rah-rah stuff. It wasn't that he didn't have much practice at it. Rather, it was that he felt it disingenuous in a business that made its home in the gray regions of the human condition, where success was measured by acts of greater or lesser evil and death was ever-present. Still, he was the director now, and it was his duty to offer encouragement. He smiled, and Jonathan nodded.

The flight controller dropped his flag. The lights on the meatball went from red to green. The F-18 shuddered, then burst from its chocks and thundered down the flight deck, shooting like an arrow into the sky. The engine glowed orange, then red. Connor watched the fighter bank hard right and assume its direction to the north. An amateur, he thought darkly. He had sent a rank amateur without a day's training to do a professional's work. He thought of Balfour and the men that protected him, hardened criminals all. One in particular stood out, a six-and-a-half-foot-tall Sikh named Mr. Singh who did Balfour's dirty work. Ransom was entering a nest of vipers, and he didn't even know it. Connor stood rooted to the spot until the plane was nothing but a gray speck. Finally it disappeared altogether, swallowed by the sky.

Connor turned and began to walk back to the Island. He had his own flight home to arrange, and he was in no condition to sit like a goddamned daredevil in the back of one of those jets. A helicopter to the nearest major airport would be fine. He walked to the hatch and stopped a step shy, a force beyond him compelling him to take a last look into the sky.

"Godspeed," he whispered.

16

Midday traffic in Islamabad was no more horrendous than usual. Cars, vans, light trucks, and juggernauts, motorcycles, bicycles, tuk-tuks, and auto rickshaws clogged the broad, well-manicured boulevards of the government district, everyone vying with everyone else for the right to advance another ten meters. Horns blaring, the convoy of white Range Rovers peeled away from the curb in front of the Colonial Building and fought its way onto Kitchener Road.

"Where's our escort?" asked Lord Balfour, checking over his shoulder for a sign of the ISI agents who had been their constant companions for the past two months.

"They haven't been on us all day." The driver caught Balfour's eye in the rearview mirror and grinned. "We're safe now, boss. No one's coming after us."

Balfour said nothing. The truth was the opposite. He was as safe as a wounded fish in a shark tank.

"What did the solicitor say?" asked the driver, a young man he'd brought in from the streets and trained himself. "All good, I'm sure?"

"Everything's fine," said Balfour, forcing a pleasant tone. "Just get us home, will you? There's a good chap."

"Yes, sir." The driver smiled broadly and leaned on the horn to show he meant business.

Balfour sat back, the polite smile vanishing as he replayed the meeting from start to finish.

"The Indian police have furnished the Pakistani police with proof of your involvement in the raid," the solicitor had begun nervously, as soon as Balfour sat down. "The serial numbers from two of the machine guns used by the terrorists in Mumbai match those on a shipping manifest that passed through your warehouses a month before the attack."

"How the hell do they know that?"

"They possess a copy of the shipping manifest."

"Impossible," said Balfour, restraining himself from saying that he alone had a copy of the manifest. "But those guns could have gone anywhere in between. A month is a long time."

"Not likely," said the solicitor. "Your reputation precedes you."

Balfour didn't bother protesting. His dislike of his native government was well known. It had been a private pleasure to arm the band of fighters and point them in the direction of his homeland. The surprise came in learning how successful their attack had been. One hundred eighty killed, dozens more wounded. Mumbai, or Bombay, as he and anyone who had ever lived there still called it, held hostage for three days. A metropolis of millions paralyzed by the actions of twenty brave men. A pleasure indeed.

The solicitor, however, was not so sanguine. "Your meddling has become a political football. Delhi is willing to forgive several border incursions in Srinagar if you are promptly turned over to the government."

"And Islamabad?" asked Balfour, meaning the Pakistani government.

"I've placed a call to General Gul. Unfortunately, I haven't heard back."

"He'll call back. He enjoys his fifty thousand U.S. a month."

"It may be beyond even him."

"Nonsense," said Balfour. "This is Pakistan. Everyone's for sale. Call the PM."

"I have," said the solicitor. "He refused the call."

Balfour had nodded and put up a good front. "I hope to hell you got a copy of the evidence."

The solicitor said that he did, and produced a copy of the shipping manifest. "I'm afraid there's very little we can do except wait. I trust you've taken precautionary measures. The Indians will know immediately that you've lost your official protection. I wouldn't put it past them to come after you. Do be careful."

Balfour had not answered.

That had been thirty minutes ago.

Now, in the safety of his automobile, Balfour unfolded the manifest and studied it closely. It was genuine—no doubt of it. Aware of the sensitive nature of the order, Balfour had chosen to oversee the shipment himself. Only one person besides him had access to the paperwork. He placed a call to his personal aide.

"Yes, Mr. Medina, I'm just on my way back from the city. Tell the grooms to tack up Copenhagen. No, it's not a special occasion. My solicitor gave me some good news, that's all. This whole thing about Mumbai looks to be blowing over nicely. An afternoon ride is just the ticket."

Balfour placed a second call. The respondent was his Sikh chief of security, Mr. Singh. "We have a problem. Mr. Medina has been talking out of school. I'll be meeting him at the stables in an hour. Make sure our guest has an unobstructed view of the punishment. It's important to send a clear message about the rules of betrayal. Have the thoroughbreds ready. Thank you, Mr. Singh."

The Range Rover slammed to a halt as a string of porters carrying bales of saffron-colored cloth on their heads crossed the road in front of them. Balfour looked out the window at a boy crouched beside a brazier, selling chicken kidneys at ten rupees a skewer. Beside him a woman with crippled legs sat in the dirt.

Balfour rolled down the window. "Two skewers," he said.

The boy chose his two finest and thrust them into the car. Balfour handed him a five-hundred-rupee note. "Give the rest to your mother," he said.

The boy took a closer look at the banknote and cried out in delight, jumping up and down.

Traffic picked up. Balfour waited a few seconds, then rolled down the opposite window and chucked the kidneys out. A passing cement mixer blasted a cloud of exhaust into the car. Balfour sank back into his seat, coughing. He couldn't get out of this damned country fast enough, he thought to himself.

But where to go?

To calm himself, he ran a hand over the buttery leather upholstery. It was Alcantara leather special-ordered from Spain at a cost of $51,000. The Range Rovers were armored by Alpha Armouring Panzerung of Munich and equipped with supercharged V-12 engines, at a cost of $225,000 apiece. There was little chance he'd be allowed to export them.

Balfour caught sight of his reflection in the window. He had dressed for his meeting in a Brioni suit, Egyptian cotton shirt from Ascot Chang, and Hermès tie. His shoes were handmade, from John Lobb of London. Even his underwear was tailor-made: monogrammed silk boxers from Hanro of Switzerland.

His obsession with luxury was hard-earned. His work demanded a steady state of paranoia and forbade him friends. He had only associates and colleagues, and too many underlings to count. He enjoyed the company of women, but distrusted them on principle. Material possessions offered lasting tactile satisfaction while providing an ever-visible reminder of his success. He had sold chicken livers on the street once, too.

The convoy left the highway and followed a razor-straight two-lane road toward the rolling Margalla Hills. After a few kilometers, they approached an armed checkpoint. Guards clad in black utilities and Kevlar vests, with Heckler & Koch MP-5 submachine guns at their sides, ran to lift the barrier. The cars passed without slowing. A sign nearby read, "Private Property—No Trespassing" in Urdu, Hindi, and English. The skull and bones below needed no translation. The road continued dead straight for exactly two kilometers. Apple orchards gave way to oranges and then almond trees. Balfour rolled down his window to smell the sweetly scented air. His desire to leave Pakistan faded.

Ahead, he made out the stately gateposts that signaled the official entry to his property. A guard box painted with black-and-white diagonal stripes no different from those at Buckingham Palace stood to one side. No Queen's Guard in a bearskin cap; just another member of his private army, clad in black head to toe, his machine gun at the ready. The ornate wrought-iron gate rolled back. Balfour waved to the guard, and the guard threw his best parade-ground salute in return.

The Range Rover drove for another two minutes before Balfour caught sight of the man-made lake. The cars crossed a plank bridge and swept into a gravel courtyard, continuing past the front entry and around the back to the stables.

Balfour had named his home Blenheim, in reference to the Duke of Marlborough's grand palace in England. And Blenheim was a two-thousand-square-meter Palladian palace built to rival its namesake.

Mr. Medina was waiting beside the cross ties as a black stallion was being saddled. Medina was a thin, meticulous man with pince-nez glasses and hair swept off his forehead in a pompadour. Balfour had originally hired him as an accountant, only to be impressed by his near-photographic recall and his willingness to work all hours.

Balfour walked directly to Mr. Medina and handed him the copy of the shipping manifest. "Did you supply this to the Indian police?"

Medina examined the paper and his hand began to tremble. He glanced over his shoulder. Mr. Singh stood a few feet away, clad in immaculate white attire, except for his turban, which was maroon. Medina nodded.

"Why?" asked Balfour.

"A man from Delhi contacted me. A policeman. He paid me to get the information. I'm Hindu. When you fight against my countrymen, you fight against me."

Balfour took back the manifest. "I will care for your family."

Medina thanked him. With care, he took off his glasses and handed them to Balfour.

Mr. Singh bound Medina's hands and feet. Two horses were brought from the stables, thoroughbreds rescued from the racetrack in Abu Dhabi. One cable was passed through the ropes binding the hands and another through the ropes binding Medina's feet. Medina began to cry. Sensing death, the horses grew agitated, neighing and tugging at their bits. Each cable was attached to a saddle. Riders mounted the thoroughbreds and turned them in opposite directions. Balfour raised his hand, and the riders whipped their horses.

Medina was flung into the air. He remained horizontal for less than two seconds before falling back to the ground. The horses dragged his arms and legs for a half-mile. They were very spirited.

Medina lay on the ground, very much alive. Mr. Singh beheaded him with a kukri, the curved machete favored by Nepalese Gurkhas. Balfour regarded the head, then said to Singh, "Find the family. Kill them, too. I don't want to spend the rest of my life looking over my shoulder."

Mr. Singh strode away, the traitor's head dangling by its hair. The head would be placed on a spear and displayed at the entrance to Balfour's property. Fair warning to those who thought of following a similar course.

Satisfied that justice had been done, Balfour turned and looked behind him. Gazing down from a second-floor window stood a European woman with unruly auburn hair. He noted that her bruises had faded and the bandages were no longer on her cheeks. She would be ready to leave for the mountains any day.

The sooner, the better.

17

Jonathan had exchanged the blue of the Persian Gulf for the brown of the Negev Desert. The F-18/A landed at exactly twelve noon at Tel Nof Air Force Base south of Rehovot, Israel. The aircraft taxied past the control tower, past a squadron of F-16 Falcons, and past a dozen hangars, continuing to the farthest tip of the airfield. The pilot pushed back the canopy but did not kill the engine. A ground crew of one waited beside a white utility truck. Without delay, he positioned a ladder against the fuselage and helped Jonathan unbuckle and descend from the cockpit. The pilot slotted the canopy, pushed the plane through a tight 180-degree turn, and took off to the south. The ground crewman climbed back into his truck and drove away. Sixty seconds after setting foot on the tarmac, Jonathan stood alone, wind peppering his face with dust and grit.

And then, in the distance, a glint of blue beneath the midday sun. An automobile approached and stopped next to him. Two men got out.

"Welcome to Israel," said the driver, who was short and stocky and had curly black hair.

The other man was short and stocky and bald, and reminded Jonathan of an artillery shell. He held open the rear door.

"Are you Frank Connor's friends?" Jonathan asked.

The answer was an incline of the shaved head toward the open door. Jonathan got in.

They drove for an hour, climbing out of the desert on a series of long switchbacks, and then descending toward the coast and the Mediterranean Sea. Road signs read, "Tel Aviv," "Haifa," and "Herzliya." Jonathan tried several more times to engage the men in conversation, but neither responded.

The car left the highway at the town of Herzliya. Five minutes later they pulled into the forecourt of a small, whitewashed building. A sign on the facade advertised it as the Hotel Beach Plaza, but there was no beach to speak of, rather a stone promontory plummeting into the sea and below, at water's edge, a jetty of sharp, inhospitable rocks.

They passed through the lobby and went directly to the elevator. No one at the front desk uttered a word, or even glanced in his direction. Check-in had been taken care of. Jonathan's room was on the third floor. In the hall, the men handed Jonathan the card key. The driver stood with crossed arms, looking Jonathan up and down. "Suit, forty-two long. Pants, thirty-four by thirty-four. Shoes, size twelve."

"Thirteen," said Jonathan.

"Boats," said the artillery shell.

The men left without another word.

Jonathan noted that the door to his room was ajar. He knocked and pushed it open. "Hello?"

A cleaning maid was dusting the night table. "One moment," she said in accented English. "Almost done."

Jonathan entered the room, feeling strangely shy without any bags. "It's fine," he said. "You can go. I'd like to get some rest."

The maid smiled and promptly ignored him, returning her attention to an already immaculate desk and countertop.

Jonathan sidestepped her and opened the glass doors that fed onto a narrow balcony. The temperature was a balmy seventy degrees. A few hundred meters up the coast, the rocks gave way to sand and he could see several sunbathers lying on colorful towels. A gull swooped by, *cai*-ing lustily. The wind was steady, and he observed a line of sailboats tacking against the current. He closed his eyes, enjoying the sun, and realized that he didn't know what day it was. Friday? Saturday? The last week of his life had woven itself into a violent tapestry. He saw Amina stretched out on the table and Hamid drawing his blade across Abdul Haq's throat. He saw the top of the

Ranger's head blown clean off and the hardened captain named Brewster shuddering as the machine-gun bullets stitched his chest, and then Hamid again, as he dropped from Jonathan's grasp. Jonathan jolted, as if awakening from a nightmare. Opening his eyes, he saw that his arm was extended, his hand still searching for Hamid's. Yet even as he stared out at the diamonds sparkling on the ocean, the pleasant breeze ruffling his hair, he felt a pair of black kohl-lined eyes challenging him from beyond the horizon, silently declaring him a coward and vowing revenge.

Jonathan walked inside, closing the doors behind him. Happily, the maid had left. He checked that the thermostat was set to low, then drew the curtains. The air conditioner rumbled to life, and he raised a hand to check that the air pouring from the vent was cool. His time in Afghanistan had accustomed him to sleeping with a cold head and warm body. He took off his watch and laid it by the bed. He had no idea what the agenda was, but no doubt Connor had everything planned out. For the moment, he was too tired to care. Still standing, he removed his pants and his underwear. He thought about taking a shower, then decided against it. The bed was too inviting. He pulled back the sheets.

Without warning, a sharp blow pounded his kidney. He gasped, feeling the presence of someone close behind him. He spun and saw a flash of powder blue, but before he could turn halfway, iron hands clutched his arm and threw him to the ground. He landed belly down, his left arm wrenched behind him in a police armlock.

"Never turn your back on a stranger."

"Let go," grunted Jonathan, his face mashed against the carpet. "You're breaking my arm."

"Did you see me leave the room?"

Jonathan recognized the accented English. "No," he managed out of the side of his mouth.

"Did you notice if there was a service cart in the hallway? See my nametag?"

"No."

"What about downstairs? Many guests milling about? Lots of cars in the parking lot?"

"Uh-uh."

"Any reason why I should be servicing your room so late in the afternoon if the entire hotel is empty?"

"Ummm . . . no."

"So are you *naive* or just plain *stupid*?" A twist of the arm emphasized each adjective. "Never trust anyone."

"Get off of me."

"Make me. You're a strong man. Go ahead. I weigh one hundred and twenty pounds. Surely you can free yourself."

Jonathan struggled to flip her off his back. Then he tried to get his right arm beneath him and raise himself to his knees. He was no martial arts expert, but over the years he'd picked up a little jujitsu here, some Krav Maga there. And he was strong. Yet his every attempt was stymied with a hold more painful than the last. "Enough," he said, his cheek wedged against the floor once again.

"Look around you. Ask yourself why, where, how, what if. Don't just look but see. Observe."

His eyes focused on the carpet less than an inch away. He *observed* that it was blue, with green speckles.

The armlock relaxed. The weight on his back lifted. Jonathan lay still, catching his breath. The maid walked to the curtains but, true to her advice, never completely took her eyes from him. "Get up and put something on."

Jonathan pushed himself to his feet and limped into the bathroom. By the time he returned with a towel wrapped around his waist, the maid had removed her apron and let down her hair. She was tall, more handsome than pretty, maybe thirty-five years old, with weathered skin, blue eyes, and black hair as straight as straw.

Often Jonathan was able to guess a person's nationality at first glance. Not her. She could be American or French, Argentine or Swedish. The perennial wanderer in him sensed a kindred spirit. Like him, she was at home anywhere in the world. She wore little makeup, and her lips were chapped. Her arms were toned, with the veins running down chiseled biceps. She didn't need to be a black belt to hold him down—she had enough raw strength. Her nails were trimmed, her fingers thicker than most women might like. It was no wonder the jab to his kidneys had hurt so badly. He also sensed that, like him, she preferred life away from the madding crowd, and that time spent in cities was a down payment against the next foray into the wild. His flash of perception troubled him. He'd felt the same way about Emma.

"What happened to the lei and a welcome cocktail?" he asked.

"This isn't a holiday, Dr. Ransom. School is now in session. We don't have much time, and from what I just saw, we have far too much work to do. Now get some rest. I'll be by at six to take you to dinner. Your clothes will be here by then."

"Do you have a message for me from Frank Connor? He told me I'd hear from him."

"Who?" The blue eyes bore down on him. It was not a name to be said aloud.

"No one," said Jonathan, backpedaling. "I was mistaken."

"I thought so." The woman came closer and extended her hand. "I'm Danni. I'll be your trainer."

18

It was called "the Bubble," but the official name for the soundproof chamber on the third floor of the Rayburn Office Building, one block from the Capitol, where testimony graded classified or higher was given to the House Subcommittee on Intelligence, was a SCIF, or Sensitive Compartmented Information Facility. The Bubble looked no different from a large, windowless office. It had four walls, a ceiling, and the usual painful fluorescent lighting. But the differences were there. The floor, walls, and ceiling were constructed of three-inch-thick cement and lined with soundproof acoustic tiles. To enter, one passed through a double set of alarmed doors and stepped up a half foot, the distance necessary to separate the Bubble from the original floor. A low level of white noise played constantly to frustrate any eavesdropping device. Finally, the Bubble benefited from its own power supply, connected to an independent generator in the building's basement. Once the Bubble's door closed, no sound could get in and no sound could get out.

"Hello, Joe," said Connor, ducking his head inside the door of the SCIF. "Got a minute?"

The Honorable Joseph Tecumseh Grant, representative of the eleventh district of Nebraska and chairman of the House Subcommittee on Intelligence, stopped putting the day's testimony into his satchel. "Frank? That you? What are you doing out of your coffin? I thought you spooks only came out at night."

"Must have me confused with someone else." Connor stood by the door as the last few stragglers left the chamber. "I'm a mortal like anyone else. Haven't you heard? We do things aboveboard now. In daylight."

Joe Grant crossed the room with alacrity, one hand extended for the shake. His birth certificate stated that he was sixty-five years old, but the combination of his lopsided grin and the thatch of shoe-polish black hair hanging over his forehead gave him the air of a man half his age. "By golly, it's been a while," he said, gripping Connor's hand as if he were the last voter in a tight contest. "I think it was March, after that blowup in Zurich. Your confirmation hearing, right?"

"That sounds about right," said Connor.

It was a memory he could do without. The hearing was a referendum more on Division than on who should head it next. The level of sanctimonious bullshit had reached historic heights. Never again could a covert agency be allowed to overstep its boundaries so grossly (true, thought Connor), or meddle in the political affairs of another nation (false), or take human life without a two-thirds majority vote of Congress (pure and utter nonsense). Yet when presented as the man to best repair Division's tattered reputation, Connor had been met with a barrage of disbelieving stares. Despite his sterling service record, the portly man in the wrinkled gray suit with his ruddy cheeks and cascade of chins did not meet expectations. For all the talk about reining in Division, it was painfully apparent that the august members of the House subcommittee wanted a carbon copy of the square-jawed, blue-eyed, uniform-wearing patriot who had nearly taken the world to the brink of nuclear conflagration. Or, at the least, they didn't want Connor. The final vote had been 5–4 in favor, and had required considerable arm-twisting behind the scenes.

Still grinning, Grant put his hand on Connor's shoulder and guided him to the tables at one end of the room.

"You know, I saw a line item tucked away in that last defense spending bill that looked like it might have had your signature," said Grant, perching himself on the edge of the table. "A fifty-million-dollar request for a Counterintelligence Resource Analysis Program. C-R-A-P. That you?"

"I'm not that clever, Joe."

"The heck you're not."

The last staffer left the room, closing the door behind her. Without bidding, Grant flipped a switch under the table, activating the lock. A subtle hum was instantly audible. The Bubble was secure.

"So, Frank," said Grant, losing the smile, "why do I get the impression that I should not be happy to see you?"

"Broken arrow," said Connor. "You remember what that means, don't you?"

"The signal a pilot gives if he loses a nuke. Everyone knows that. You don't need me to tell you."

"How often has it been given?"

"Luckily, not very often. That's not an incident you can hide. It's a matter of public record."

"I know about the public record."

In fact, Connor had memorized the details of each incident.

March 10, 1956. A B-47 bomber carrying two nuclear cores, or detonation devices containing fissile uranium, vanished during a routine flight over the Mediterranean. A thorough search turned up no trace of either of the weapons.

June 25, 1957. A C-124 transport flying off the eastern seaboard jettisoned two nuclear weapons without their radioactive material after experiencing mechanical problems. Neither weapon was found.

February 5, 1958. Following a midair collision between a B-47 bomber and an F-86 Sabre fighter, a nuclear weapon without its fissile core was lost in the waters of Wassaw Sound near the mouth of the Savannah River, not far from Tybee Island, Georgia. Again, no trace of the weapon was found.

January 24, 1961. A B-52 bomber carrying two fully operational nuclear weapons broke apart in midair over Goldsboro, North Carolina. Both bombs were equipped with parachutes for this eventuality. Only one parachute opened. The second bomb broke apart on impact. After it was retrieved and examined, the military determined that five of six safety switches had failed. A single switch prevented the hydrogen bomb from detonating its twenty-kiloton fissile core.

The most famous occurred above the town of Palomares, Spain, when a B-52 collided with a KC-135 tanker during midair refueling. Four hydrogen bombs plummeted to the ground. The high explosives in two exploded on impact, resulting in a "dirty bomb" that spread radiation across a two-square-kilometer area. A third was recovered safely, and the fourth fell into the Mediterranean Sea and was recovered intact after a two-month search.

"I didn't come all the way up here to talk to you about something on the books," said Connor. "I was hoping you might be able to shed some light on any incidents that didn't make it into the public record."

"Why are you asking me? A lil' old congressman from Nebraska?"

"I think you know the answer to that question."

Grant leaned back in his chair, pushing the hair off his forehead. Prior to seeking elected office, he had spent thirty years in the air force. He'd started off flying B-52s and ended up a major general assigned to the Strategic Air Command, or SAC, as it was better known. One important element of SAC's mandate involved overseeing the nation's airborne nuclear arsenal, including interfacing with NEST (the Nuclear Emergency Search Team), which was tasked with locating and retrieving lost nuclear materials.

Connor went on: "Anything you want to tell me about? You have my word it'll stay between us."

"Sure, there have been unrecorded incidents," said Grant. "We just called out one of our squadron chiefs for allowing a few of his planes to overfly the States with nukes aboard. But have we lost a nuke since the seventies? No sir, we have not. You have my word."

"Scout's honor?"

Grant gave the three-fingered Boy Scout salute. "Cross my heart. Now it's your turn, Frank. Spill."

Connor helped himself to a glass of water sitting on the table. He was obliged to give Grant something, but he didn't want to tip his hand. "Got wind of something turning up on the black market," he began cautiously. "Just a rumor, mind you, but one of my operators thought enough of the source that he passed it on."

"Go on."

"There may be an American cruise missile for sale."

"What kind? Tomahawk? ALCM?"

"A big one. An air-launched cruise missile. Swept-back fins. Whole package."

"You said it was a rumor. Has your operator seen this thing?"

"There's a photo making the rounds. Who knows if it's real?"

Grant appeared unfazed by the disclosure. "If it is real, then the missile will be carrying a conventional warhead. I wouldn't worry."

"So it's not the other thing?"

"A nuke? Are you kidding me?" Grant laughed as if this were the most far-fetched notion he'd heard in years and Connor was a damned fool for even considering it. "No way we'd lose a nuclear-tipped cruise without all hell breaking loose."

"That's what I thought," said Connor. "Apparently it's an old one. Maybe twenty years or so. Still, word is that the broker is claiming it's a nuke."

Grant began to tap his foot. "He's bullshitting. There is no way on God's green earth that anyone could get ahold of a nuclear-tipped ALCM. "

"Glad to know it, Joe."

"Where did you say this thing's for sale?"

"Pakistan," said Connor. "Right on the Afghan border. Apparently someone stumbled across it high in the mountains. We're talking very remote. It had been buried for years."

At the mention of the word *Pakistan*, Grant froze. His foot stopped tapping, and the animated face turned waxen. "Now hold on, Frank. Your story's changing awful fast. Are you telling me that some-one actually has this thing? I mean, physically possesses it?"

Connor took his time answering, observing the steady blanching of Grant's ageless features. "Not that I know of," he said finally. "Like I said, there's a photo, that's all."

"Just a photo?"

"Yeah."

Grant regained his color. "Sounds like quite some story."

"That's why I'm here. You were a B-52 pilot. You used to fly around with those things in your payload every day. It's impossible, right? We couldn't lose a nuclear-tipped cruise missile and just forget about it?"

Grant sat forward, his jaw raised to defend his impugned integrity. "This is the United States of America you're talking about, Frank. Not one of them 'stans or banana republics or African dictatorships where you boys conduct your dirty business. We do things the right way."

"Good to know." Connor put down the water glass, stood, and walked to the door. "You've taken a lot off my mind. I'll be able to sleep better tonight."

"Hey, Frank," called Joe Grant, his smile back in place. "You still in contact with this operator?"

"Sure thing. Why?"

"Tell him not to believe everything he hears."

19

The Toyota pickup rocked to a halt on the muddy track.

Sultan Haq clutched the dashboard, grimacing as pain racked his body. "Dammit," he said, staring out the windscreen at the dense foliage pressing in on all sides. "I was here two days ago. Where has it gone?"

Haq threw open the door and stepped outside, fighting back the tangle of branches that threatened to envelop the truck. He sniffed the air, and his eyes watered with the scent of ammonia and wood smoke. He was close. He stepped to the front of the truck and gazed ahead. The track continued for a brief stretch, then curved to the right and was swallowed by forest. According to the route marker on his handheld GPS, he was in the right place. Yet no matter how hard he looked, he could see no sign of the security fence or the long wooden building or the corrugated tin roof and chimneys that carried away the toxic smoke.

Haq forced his way to the driver's window and punched the horn three times. Not ten meters away, a swatch of foliage rustled and, as if by magic, disappeared. Two men clutching Kalashnikovs waved him forward. Haq saw the fence and the guard dogs, and behind them the abandoned lumber mill housing a refinery to convert raw opium into morphine paste. He signaled for the truck to advance, and followed it into the clearing.

Immediately the fence was secured. The foliage slipped back into place. The refinery was once again hidden from the outside world.

A haggard old man wrapped in black robes stood on the sagging landing, smoking an opium pipe. "How much?" he asked, his mouth a toothless, black hole.

"Five hundred," said Haq, meaning five hundred kilos of raw opium.

"Bring it in."

Sultan Haq ordered his men to unload the truck and leaned against the body as they carried bag after bag of raw opium into the building. Normally he would help, but his injuries prevented it. Bandages on his neck, shoulder, and forearms covered third-degree burns left by the American bombs.

A week had passed since his father's murder at Tora Bora, seven tortured days during which he'd endured the blistering of his seared flesh. Seven days during which he'd mourned his beloved father, who had been his closest friend and most trusted counsel. Seven days during which he'd thought of nothing but the American healer, Ransom, and his treachery, and how he might one day meet him again and kill him. He knew that such sweet revenge would not be granted him. No matter. He would make do with punishing those who had sent Ransom. America would pay dearly.

Haq climbed three steps and entered the building. The first room was for intake and storage. Transparent plastic bags filled with raw opium crowded every wall, rising past the rafters. The process of refining the raw opium into morphine base began in the next room over. Haq looked on as men emptied bag after bag of the resinous, tar-like opium into great rusted oil barrels filled with boiling water and lime. The raw opium quickly dissolved into a clear brown liquid. Shreds of poppy plants, dirt, and residue sank to the bottom. The morphine alkaloid in the opium reacted with the lime slake to form a white rind of morphine paste on the surface. The boiling water was filtered and the morphine paste separated and taken to the next room, where it was placed in another barrel and reheated with concentrated ammonia.

As the paste solidified, it settled to the bottom of the barrel, becoming large brown chunks of morphine base. The rule was that ten kilos of raw opium made up one kilo of morphine base. The morphine base was taken into a separate room and wrapped into brick-sized blocks. It was now ready for sale and shipment to heroin laboratories.

The economics of the opium business were impossible to dispute, mused Haq as he walked through the dark, humid, foul-smelling rooms. One hectare of land under poppy cultivation yielded twenty kilos of raw opium. The market price for one kilo ran between $250 and $300. A farmer cultivating a single hectare could earn nearly $6,000 for his crop, a princely sum in a country where the average annual income barely reached $800. Haq and his clan controlled over 2,000 hectares of land suitable for poppy cultivation. This year's harvest had brought in over 40,000 kilos of raw opium and would end up yielding nearly 4,000 kilos of morphine paste.

Haq sliced open a plastic-wrapped brick with his long curling fingernail and scooped out a pile of the brown base. One snort confirmed that the quality was exceptional. The pain from his burns subsided, and a sense of contentment took hold. He was tempted to take more, but discipline forbade him. He must ration the drug carefully, lest he become an addict like the production master. He would not shame his father so.

Haq chopped the block into quarters and slipped one into the folds of his jacket. It would provide useful in the coming days. A balm for his pain, so he might concentrate on more important matters.

A television was playing in a corner. Three addicts sat on the floor, entranced. Haq approached. "What are you watching?"

"Gangsters in America," said one.

Haq picked up a DVD cover off the floor. "*Scarface,*" he said aloud. "Good?"

"Very. The Americans like drugs."

Haq stared at the screen. A man was chained to a curtain rod in a shower. Another wielded a chain saw. The opium in his system combined with the violent sound and images to transport him to another place. He was not home, but far away. He was at Gitmo. The room at Camp X-Ray was hot and smoky and smelled of sweat and vomit. A circle of anxious, well-fed faces surrounded him. A television blared in one corner. The same film always played. Three happy sailors cavorting across Manhattan, singing and dancing in their white uniforms. The volume was turned up very loud to drown out the unpleasant noises.

The questions began.

"Tell us what you were doing in Kunar Province during the months of July through November 2001."

"I sell carpets. Persia. Isfahan. Very good quality."

"Horseshit, Muhammad. You couldn't tell a good carpet from a used shit rag."

"Yes, sell carpets in Kabul."

"Then why did we pick you up two hundred miles north of Kabul along with five hundred soldiers fighting for Abdul Haq?"

"Abdul Haq? I do not know this man. I travel. I sell carpets. I with him for safety. I no fighter."

"A big strong brute like you, not a fighter?"

"I sell carpets."

"Horseshit."

"We heard you're his son. Admit it."

"No. Only sell carpets."

And then the hood fell over his face and he was tipped backward and the water flowed into his face and he could not breathe.

And always when the hood was removed, there was the television blaring down at him, mocking him, mocking his culture. The three sailors singing and dancing merrily across New York.

He saw this forty-seven times.

Finally the red-faced men from the CIA believed him. By then he knew New York City well. *The Bronx was up and the Battery down.* And he despised it.

Haq felt someone nudge his shoulder, and the old, frightening images fled from his mind. He turned and looked into the toothless face of the production master. "Well?"

"Two days to finish," said the production master.

Haq eyed the ziggurat of bricks stacked in the center of the room. He calculated there were approximately four thousand kilos, wrapped, weighed, and ready for shipment. With shrewd negotiation he might sell the lot for as much as $10,000 a kilo. Forty million dollars was not a princely sum. It was a conqueror's sum. And he would use it to drive the crusaders from his land.

"Have the entire supply ready by then. I will be back the day after tomorrow."

20

"How high up is it?" asked Emma.

"Six thousand meters," said Lord Balfour.

"How was it found?"

"A local came across it."

"What?" asked Emma with irritation. "He stepped outside his hut and tripped over it? You're not talking to one of your toadies anymore. I need specifics."

Balfour started out of his chair, only to catch himself. "He was traveling home from his father's village on the other side of the pass. He made camp and came across it as he was collecting snow to melt for water. There had been an avalanche, and he saw the guidance fins protruding from the icefall several hundred meters up the slope. People here are ignorant, not idiots. He knew that something of that nature might be worth a lot of money. When he returned home, he told his brother. They took a picture of the missile and brought it to the regional boss of Chitral. The man is a friend of mine. He knew I would be interested."

"That's more like it," said Emma.

"I'll thank you to watch your tone."

"I'll thank you to answer me properly."

It was midafternoon. The day was clear and warm, the air dry as a bone, the kind of day that the north of Pakistan produced in abundance in late fall. She sat in a high-backed leather armchair in Balfour's study, with a cup of Darjeeling tea to keep her awake and a bottle of Vicodin to kill the pain. Balfour had other, more potent remedies should she need them. If weapons were his first love, narcotics came a close second.

He called his estate Blenheim, and Blenheim it was. Oriental carpets covered the parquet floor. There were Regency desks and Gobelin tapestries and life-sized oils of long-deceased (and surely unrelated) ancestors staring down from walnut-paneled walls, pretending to be Sargents or Gainesboroughs. Every time she glanced out the window, she expected to look upon the rain-swept hillocks of Oxfordshire. Instead she was granted a breathtaking view of the violet-hued mountains of the Hindu Kush.

"So no one else knows about the find?" Emma continued.

Balfour shook his head.

"You're certain?"

"This is Pakistan. Certainty is not a word to us. We make do with 'probably' and hope for the best."

Emma rose from her chair. "Show me the rest of the pictures."

Balfour laid a series of eight-by-twelve color photographs on his desk. They showed the missile fully uncovered from a variety of angles.

"Six four seven alpha hotel bravo." She read the identification number painted on the cruise missile's belly. "You know what this is?"

"It's an air-launched cruise missile manufactured by the Boeing Corporation circa 1980. Weapons are my business."

"I mean what these numbers denote." Emma pointed to a photograph showing a close-up of the missile where the identification number was clearly visible. "Designation 'alpha hotel bravo.'"

Balfour sipped tea from his Wedgwood cup. "It is the American designation for a nuclear-tipped weapon," he said, looking at her from under his brow. "Does that cause you any concern?"

"Why should it? Weapons are my business, too."

Balfour threw his head back and laughed richly, his theatrical laugh. "I knew I was right to come for you. You and I are a match made in heaven."

"Really?" said Emma. "I'd have thought it was more the other place."

Balfour laughed louder.

Emma nearly smiled, feeling something close to fondness for the man. A little more than a week earlier, she'd never been happier to see anyone in her entire life.

After her beating at the hands of Prince Rashid, she'd lain in the desert for hours, broken in body and spirit. It was not only the pain of her injuries that left her without hope, but the circumstances of her betrayal. Over and over she'd played Rashid's words in her mind. "Who do you work for? The CIA? The Pentagon?" It was Connor's doing. There was no one else to blame. It was anger that drove her to her feet, to deny the impossibility of her situation. She hadn't sacrificed so much to die alone in a foreign land. It wasn't right. Not for all she had done. Not for a woman in her condition. She'd made it fifty steps before Balfour arrived, and she didn't know if she could have made it one more.

He'd flown her to Pakistan aboard one of his jets. He'd seen to it that she received medical care and proper rest. But all the while she'd known there would be a price.

"Why do you trust me?" she'd asked when she'd recovered enough to ask why he'd come for her.

"Because you're like me," Balfour had answered. "You have nowhere else to turn."

"What makes you so sure?" she'd asked, a rebel despite her bruised ribs, second-degree burns, and the angry scabs that covered her hips and shoulders and back.

"Thanks to Prince Rashid, the Russians know you're a double. You can't go back there. It's obvious the Americans don't want you either."

"How do you know?"

Balfour had leaned close, so that she could smell the mint on his breath and note the long eyelashes that made his brown eyes glimmer. "The bullets, darling. Rashid told me that someone tipped him off."

"Who?"

"Does it matter?" Balfour's dismissive tone convinced her he knew more than he was saying. "Someone on your side wants you dead. You can't go home."

"Don't worry about me," she'd countered, turning her head away so he couldn't read the hurt in her eyes. "I can take care of myself."

"Of course you can. But first I need your help."

Emma had said nothing. She could refuse him, but he could as easily kill her as let her go. In the end, it came down to actions. He'd saved her life. The fact that he'd done so to further his own aims changed nothing. She owed him. It was only later that she began to fashion her own plan.

"Give me a map," she said, returning her mind to the present.

Balfour showed her to a round table in the center of the room where a detailed topographic map was laid out. For an hour they discussed the logistics of the operation—men, equipment, timing. And all the while she sensed his eyes on her, measuring, appraising, calculating. She had known that Balfour was in trouble, but she sensed a new impatience about him, a frisson of desperation that electrified his every movement.

She had more questions. To whom did he intend to sell the missile? How much did he expect to receive? Where would the transfer take place? But these were an intelligence agent's questions, and she knew better than to ask.

She remembered Rashid's shadowy associate, the solemn, robed man kept deliberately apart from the others. She realized now that his separation was not to prevent him from learning too much about Rashid's transaction but to keep Emma, and perhaps even Balfour, from learning too much about him.

"How soon can you go up?" Balfour asked, barely able to keep his ostrich-skin loafers in one place.

"How soon would you like?"

"Two days," said Balfour. It was a command, not a request.

"All right," said Emma, hiding her uncertainty about whether her still fragile body would be up to the task. "Two days."

It was then that Emma knew Balfour's troubles were worse than she'd realized.

Retrieving the missile was key.

For him and for her.

21

"**The first thing you need** to learn is how to move between two places without being tailed. This requires two skills, the ability to spot who's following you and the ability to evade them."

It was ten o'clock the morning after Jonathan had arrived in Israel. Standing next to Danni on the corner of Ramat Gan and Ben Gurion streets in the commercial heart of Tel Aviv, he leaned closer to hear her over the noise of the traffic. Around them, the sidewalk pulsed with activity. A multitude of shoppers passed in both directions, all of them appearing to be in an urgent rush.

"We're going to start with something simple," she went on. "I want you to cross the street and continue halfway down the block before crossing against traffic to the other side. When you get to the other side, keep on going in the same direction until you reach the traffic signal. We'll catch up to you there."

Jonathan scoped out the route. "It's less than two hundred meters."

"That's far enough," said Danni. She had abandoned the maid's uniform for jeans, a white tank top, and black designer sunglasses. "Four people are going to follow you. They're all in plain sight right now. Take a second to look around you and familiarize yourself with the people you see."

Jonathan stepped away from Danni, finding a gap where he had a clearer view of both sides of the street.

"What are you doing?" she asked, grabbing him by the arm.

"What you said. I'm looking around at everyone."

"And everyone knows that's what you're doing. You look like a virgin in a strip club. Your eyes are about to pop out of your head. Watch me."

Danni walked casually to the corner of the intersection, taking up position next to a squat middle-aged woman carrying two straw shopping bags. Danni said a word to the woman, then returned her gaze to the intersection, pausing only to scratch her head. The light changed. The pedestrians around her crossed the street.

"That's how you do it," Danni said, once more at Jonathan's side.

"Do what? You didn't look anywhere except at that lady and the pavement in front of you."

"Exactly." Keeping her eyes locked on Jonathan, she said, "There's a man across the road by the kebab stand, blue jeans, red shirt. Another guy is waiting to cross next to him, dark suit, sunglasses, cropped hair, can't keep from checking his watch. Kitty-corner to us are two teenage girls, I'd say fifteen or sixteen, who've been working their way through the same rack of T-shirts since we've been standing here."

Danni went on, pointing out men and women both stationary and on the move. Jonathan viewed each in turn, marveling at her ability to recall. "Which ones are going to follow me?" he asked.

"That's not the point. I'm saying you have to observe without looking. Keep your head still and let your eyes move. Use store windows. Reflections from passing cars. Use natural movements as an excuse to look. Stop to tie your shoe. This is about sensing as much as anything else. Clear your mind. Expand your listening. Feel your surroundings."

"I thought this was Israel, not Japan. I'm about to have a Zen moment."

"If that's what you want to call it, fine. Hone your senses. Right now they're about as sharp as a butter knife."

"How can you hone anything when you can barely hear yourself think or move without bumping into someone?"

As if to prove his point, a police car sped past, siren blaring. Jonathan stepped back from the curb, only to notice that he was the only one who had done so.

"Off you go," said Danni, arms crossed. "One hundred meters. Cross halfway along. Your job is to spot the four people following you. And don't give yourself away."

The light turned in his favor. The pedestrians surrounding him left the curb. A step late, Jonathan joined them. *Four people tailing him.* He started to turn his head, then yanked it back to center. *Let your eyes move.* He looked out of the corner of his eye. The teenage girls who'd been examining T-shirts were mirroring his progress on the opposite side of the street. The businessman in the dark suit was there too, talking on a cell phone. Jonathan locked onto a pregnant woman and a boy wearing a Lakers cap. It might be them, too. Danni probably thought he wouldn't suspect a guy wearing an American basketball hat. Jonathan stepped onto the curb, just avoiding a collision with two Hassidim barreling right at him, and realized he'd been craning his neck.

Foot traffic slowed. Ducking his shoulder, Jonathan angled through the crowd, keeping a steady pace. He lost sight of the teenage girls. The businessman was long gone, too. He was unable to spot one familiar face. Overwhelmed, he gave up trying to locate his tails. He concentrated instead on not barging into anyone. He reached the midway point and stepped to the edge of the sidewalk. Automobile traffic cleared, and he jogged across the street.

This opposite side of the road was less crowded. He kneeled to tie his shoe, then realized he was wearing moccasins that didn't have laces. Giving himself to the illusion, he pretended, but when he looked to either side of him, he saw only knees and shoes and men with potbellies, all too close for comfort. Rising, he continued on toward the end of the block.

At a cell-phone store, he stopped to study the items on display, hoping to use the window to spot one of Danni's tails. But the sun was too bright, and he couldn't see anything except glare. He started off once more, and after ten steps reached the end of the block. Standing next to the traffic signal, he studied the faces of the people walking past. Nothing. No one looked familiar.

"And so? Who are they?"

Startled, Jonathan spun to find Danni behind him. "How'd you . . . ?" he asked. "When did you . . . ah, forget it."

"It was too easy, right?" she went on. "They were sticking out like sore thumbs."

Jonathan took a last look down the street. "Trick question, right? No one was following me."

Danni's eyes narrowed. "Not one?"

Jonathan averted his gaze, more embarrassed than he cared to admit. "Sorry."

"All right, then—I'll show you." Danni pointed to a blond woman in the doorway of a music store. A moment passed, and a woman walked up next to her. Something about them was vaguely familiar. The women casually took off their jackets, one let her hair loose from a ponytail, and Jonathan recognized them as the teenagers in the T-shirt shop. Next Danni indicated a trim man in a warm-up jacket and racing cap. The man removed the racing cap and turned the warm-up jacket inside out. Jonathan found himself staring at the frenetic businessman.

"I even pointed them out before you started," said Danni. "I couldn't help you more than that."

"But they changed clothing."

"Common practice. My girls put on jackets and threw their hair into ponytails. If you look closer, you'll see that they did not change their pants or their shoes."

Jonathan noted that one wore yellow shorts and Nike tennis shoes and the other white Capri pants and matching flats. He hadn't paid attention to their attire. Just their faces.

"Your job is to spot the consistent item. Don't look at faces. Faces change. Look at shoes or at belts or at anything you find distinctive."

"And the fourth?"

"I was the fourth. I was right behind you the entire time."

"Impossible."

"Inside of three meters, every step of the way. And I didn't even change clothes."

"But—"

Danni checked her watch. "Go again."

22

Frank Connor heard the kitchen door slam and a pair of vigorous feet charge up the stairs. The bedroom door opened, and Congressman Joseph Tecumseh Grant bounded into the room. He was wearing athletic shorts and a sweatshirt and he carried a basketball under one arm. Like half the other members of Congress, he was a late-in-life pledge to the fraternity of Phi Slamma Jamma. He saw Connor and drew up.

"Frank . . . What the—?"

"Why did you lie to me, Joe?"

Grant put down his basketball, then closed the door to the bedroom. The modest row house on the 300 block of C Street Northeast sat within sight of the Capitol and was home away from home for Grant and three other congressmen.

"I'm afraid I have to object to your presence in my home. Just what the heck gives you the right?"

"Sit down and shut up."

"I know all about you and your crew of 'operators.' Trained killers is what they are. Nothing but thugs and assassins."

"That's enough, Joe."

"Are you trying to intimidate me?" Grant advanced toward Connor, his finger raised in righteous indignation. "If you are, it won't work."

"I don't do intimidation, Joe. Otherwise, you'd be lying in an alley somewhere between here and the gym with that basketball shoved up your ass. I do results."

"You got your results yesterday. I answered all your questions to the fullest of my ability. If you don't mind, I'd like you to leave now."

Connor didn't move a muscle. He sat in Grant's swivel chair, as imperturbable as Buddha. "It's like this, Joe. I know you lied to me. I would have lied myself if I were in your shoes. The problem is that I don't have time to cut through a load of air force BS. This thing with the cruise missile—it's happening now. We both know that no one would ever admit to having lost a nuclear weapon unless I personally delivered the device myself to the Pentagon and plopped it on the desk of the chairman of the Joint Chiefs."

"I have no idea what you're talking about," protested Grant. "We have never lost a missile. I told you the whole truth and nothing but. Scout's—"

"Honor," said Connor, in unison. "I've heard that tune before." Frowning, he removed a manila envelope from his jacket and flipped it onto the coffee table. "Open it."

Grant stepped forward and picked up the envelope, his eyes widening as he read the name of the world-famous journalist to whom it was addressed. The envelope was not sealed, and its contents slid easily into his hand. He looked at the photographs first, his expression passing from bewilderment to anger to shame. Connor had seen it all before. Then Grant read the transcripts of the cell-phone intercepts and his expression collapsed entirely. He gazed up at Connor, then, seized with a notion, threw the papers down and began pulling books off the shelves, dumping them on the floor. Connor had seen this, too.

"Where is it, you sonofabitch? Where'd you hide it?"

"Don't bother," said Connor. "You won't find the camera. We don't leave stuff like that around."

Grant stopped. "Was it her?" he said. "Is she one of yours, too?"

"As I said yesterday, Joe. I'm not that clever. She really is a fourteen-year-old student at Sidwell Friends School."

Grant dropped to a knee and replaced the papers and photographs in the envelope. "Is this the only copy?"

Connor shook his head. "Of course not."

"Why?"

"Leverage. I won't lie and say I didn't enjoy putting you holierthan-thou blowhards in your place. But really it's more about efficiency. I need to be able to do my job without you interfering."

A terrible idea came to Grant, and his face darkened further. "You don't do this to everyone?"

"God, no," said Connor. "We don't have the resources. Besides, everyone isn't the chairman of the House subcommittee that oversees my activities. Ways and Means has nothing to worry about. Neither does the Banking Committee."

Grant paced the perimeter of his room, every so often looking at Connor and shaking his head. "Jesus Christ, Frank, you put your finger in it this time."

"I'm just collecting information, Joe. I think this one is in your court."

"It was twenty-five years ago."

"Last I heard, uranium had a half-life a wee bit longer than that."

"Frank, I just can't . . ."

"I'm waiting."

Grant sat down, as if he had an unbearable weight on his shoulders. "You know what a mirror mission is?" he said finally.

"That's not my bailiwick."

"Back in the day when Russia was still the big bad bear, we used to send out our aircraft on long-range runs mirroring the flight profiles we would follow in the event of a nuclear exchange. That's when it happened. One of our B-52s suffered a catastrophic engine failure and went down, carrying two nuclear-tipped ALCMs. Since the plane's flight was top-secret, we couldn't mount a full-fledged retrieval operation. There was also the embarrassment factor. We weren't going to admit to losing anything until we got them back. It stacked up as a disaster on ten different levels."

"So you just left them there?"

"Our tracking data showed that one of the devices broke apart on impact and was rendered useless. We figured we only had to worry about the one. We had a decent idea where the plane went down, but remember, this was back in 1984, before we had the kind of GPS system we do now. We were able to narrow down the crash's location to a one-hundred-square-mile perimeter. The problem was the terrain. Up there, a hundred square miles might as well be a million. For three years we put teams up that mountain. It was a monumental undertaking, more so because it's impossible to travel around without being noticed. When a place is absolutely deserted, even a single person stands out. It's not like you can zip in there at night, grab the thing, and zip back out. We're talking the tallest mountains on earth."

"What about satellites?"

"To reposition one of our birds in space required an order of Congress. You can't just flip some switch and move your footprint. At least, you couldn't back then. No one wanted to spill the beans. We were effectively blind."

"No one ever found it?"

Grant shook his head. "It was a miracle we were even able to locate the plane. We blew up all the pieces we found. There was sensitive equipment on board, and we wanted to cover our tracks. But we never did find hide nor hair of that last bomb. After a while we just forgot about it. It was no different from losing a bomb at the bottom of the Mariana Trench. Hell, if we couldn't get to it, who could?"

Connor absorbed the information without emotion. He had seen a lot of incompetence during his years. He knew about prevarication and self-deception and all the other white lies bureaucrats tell themselves to paper over their failures. "How big, Joe?"

"I swear we tried," said Grant. "We did everything we could. You of all people should know that some things have to remain secret."

"How big a bomb are we talking about?"

"It was Russia we were up against. How big do you think?"

"I'm waiting, Congressman."

"One-fifty."

"One-fifty what?"

"One hundred fifty kilotons. The biggest that we could fit on an ALCM."

"And Hiroshima was how big?"

"Ten."

Connor kept his liverish gaze on Grant.

"It can't be found," Grant pleaded. "It's above twenty-two thousand feet, two hundred miles from the nearest city. The goddamn thing weighs three thousand pounds. It's gone, Frank. Do you hear me? It's at the bottom of some prehistoric crevasse. No one can get to it. It's impossible."

23

The team numbered eight in all. There was the helicopter pilot, a rangy Pakistani who had flown rescue missions in the Hindu Kush for forty years. The guide, the farmer from the region who had found the missile and knew the approach like the back of his hand. Two nuclear physicists, both veterans of the A. Q. Khan network. Three porters to carry the equipment. And Emma.

Emma was the team leader, or, as Lord Balfour had informed her, "his personal ambassador to keep the others in line and focused on their task." She knew better than to rely on his imprimatur of authority. In her pack she carried an Uzi submachine gun, just in case.

It was eleven o'clock in the morning. Emma had put down at an airfield in Chitral, elevation twenty-six hundred meters, four hundred kilometers northeast of Islamabad and a stone's throw from the Afghan border. If, that is, one could throw a stone over the towering peaks that held the impoverished mountain village in their palm. She stood huddled with the pilot and guide on the tarmac, backs turned against a bitterly cold norther as they studied a topographic map of the region.

"Missile here." The guide pointed to a red dot inked near the peak of Tirich Mir.

"It's very high," said Emma, noting the altitude. "Seven thousand meters."

"No worries, madam," he continued in his crisply enunciated but broken English. "Missile not at seven thousand meter. Avalanche in spring. Maybe missile come down mountain. Maybe six thousand meter. No higher."

Emma considered this. Six thousand meters was over nineteen

thousand feet. With little time to acclimatize, the entire team would require oxygen. "You're sure you can find it again?"

"My brother there now. Lord Balfour pay."

Emma turned to the pilot. "How high can you take your chopper?"

"Five thousand meters."

"That's all? Surely you can take us higher."

"Not in my aircraft. The air's thin at that altitude. It's very difficult to get proper lift. To go higher, you need a military helicopter. I'm sorry."

"Any place to put down nearby?"

"There are no airfields, if that's what you mean. No one lives in the area. It's beyond hell and gone. I suggest we make a recce and hope to find a decent place to set down." The pilot caught Emma's eye. "Might I have a word?"

Emma said, "Of course," and asked the guide to give them a moment. Grudgingly, the guide moved a few steps away. The pilot glanced at the sky, taking in the thin cumulus clouds that raked it. "There's a front moving in. If you think it's windy here, wait until we get up high. The gusts will be blowing at gale force. It might be better to postpone the expedition."

A front meant snow. This late in the year, a significant snowfall would keep the missile buried until the spring thaw next May or June. Emma couldn't allow that to happen. "We'll manage," she said. "Let's finish fueling and get moving."

"So we go?" asked the guide, who'd overheard every word. The trip meant payment, and in his case an early retirement.

"We go," said Emma.

The guide smiled broadly and began barking orders at the porters and engineers to get to the chopper. Emma did not smile, though she had equally compelling reasons to get up the mountain. Her future survival would depend on it. She phoned Balfour and informed him that they were completing fueling and would be taking off again in minutes. All further communication would be conducted via radio.

Emma climbed into the copilot's seat and pulled the door closed. The helicopter lifted into the air, buffeted by the gusting wind. The town of Chitral passed below, a maze of mud walls and battered buildings laced with thousands of colorful prayer flags. The pilot pushed the stick to the left and the aircraft banked hard, leaving behind the high plateau and advancing into the towering, shark-toothed mountains.

Behind her, the guide and the engineers sat bunched together, looking miserable. The porters were crammed along with the equipment into the aft cargo bay. Emma shifted in the seat and stared out of the Perspex canopy. An infinite landscape of peaks and valleys beckoned. The wind calmed, and she felt as if she were floating into the jaws of a great white beast. The altimeter read four thousand meters, but already the mountains soared high above them. The broad, snowy faces threatened to graze the helicopter's skids, passing so close that she was certain she could reach out and scrape her palms against the exposed rock.

Emma roused herself from her daydream, reminding herself of the importance of the mission. It was a rare rebuke. Normally her single-minded focus was her strongest suit. And so she readily admitted to having been drifting for a while now. Days, if not weeks. Her destination never varied: it was the past that drew her. And now, looking at the mountains, feeling as if she were being swallowed whole by them, she heard its siren song more strongly than ever.

She knew only one person who loved the mountains more than she did.

"His name is Ransom. He's a surgeon. We think he's exactly the ticket to provide you the cover you require."

The photograph showed a tall, lanky man in jeans and a parka carrying a rucksack. Dark hair with a hint of gray, strong nose, sturdy lips, and black eyes that made her look twice.

"Rather on the intense side, isn't he?" said Emma as she slid the picture across the table. "He looks more like a student than a surgeon."

"He's finishing up a fellowship at Oxford in plastic surgery. Apparently he's the real deal. Has offers from hospitals all over England and the States."

"*Is he one of us?*"

"*Good Lord, no,*" said General John Austen, the air force two-star who had stood up Division several years before. "*And we don't want him to be. He just turned in his application to work for Doctors Without Borders.*"

Emma took back the picture. "*A do-gooder?*" she said, not entirely trusting.

"*Aren't we all?*" Austen opened a file on his desk. "*We want you in Nigeria. The deputy minister isn't playing ball. He's making noise about terminating some contracts with our friends in Houston. Thinks his country is more than capable of drilling their own oil and seeing it to market.*"

"*And I'm going to convince him otherwise?*"

"*Either that or kill him,*" said Austen.

"*Come now, General, you don't mean that.*" It was the other man in the room who spoke. The fat one who insisted on wearing short-sleeved shirts and was constantly perspiring. Emma remembered his name: Frank Connor. "*The deputy minister has been dipping his finger in the till for quite some time now. We'd like you to collect evidence of his greed and remind him where his true interests lie.*"

"*Or else I'll provide the information to the prime minister,*" said Emma, "*who'll string him up with piano wire and cut off his balls with a rusty knife.*"

Connor frowned. "*Accurate and persuasive.*"

"*I still say we kill him,*" said John Austen. "*But I will defer to Frank, seeing as how this is his operation.*"

Connor went on: "*We're putting you into Doctors Without Borders a month ahead of Ransom. We've wrangled you a job as a mission administrator. Basically, you'll run the whole show. Don't worry, we've got a few weeks to bring you up to speed. Get close to Ransom and we'll fix a transfer for him to Lagos. The Lagos mission is staffed by locals, so it's imperative that Ransom request that you accompany him. No one's going to be looking at a doctor and his trusted colleague.*"

Emma didn't like Africa. It was too hot, too humid, and had far too many creepy-crawlies. "*How long?*"

"Start to finish? Two months in Liberia. It's up to you to see how quickly you can get the job done in Nigeria. Best case, six months."

"And after?"

"The usual. You break it off with the doc. We pull you out. Take sixty days and go lie on a beach somewhere."

Emma looked at the photograph again, and she felt a current pass through her. Ransom was handsome, to be sure. But there was something about him that disturbed her. It was his eyes. Like her, he was a believer. And so he was dangerous. At once she warned herself to be wary of him. Six months was a long time. "Where did you find him?"

Austen took back the picture and slid it into his file. "None of your business."

The helicopter landed on a rock-strewn plateau at 4,500 meters. Emma shouldered open the door and jumped to the ground. The cold hit her like a hammer. To the east, a track of cumulus clouds streamed past the summit of Tirich Mir. During the hour's flight, the sky had turned a curdled gray. Heavy weather was approaching.

Emma dug the Magellan GPS out of her pack. The device put the distance to the bomb at twenty-two kilometers. But that did not take into consideration the 1,500-meter gain in elevation, the lack of a well-marked trail, or, most trying of all, the thin air. Alone, she might cover that stretch in six hours. She looked over her shoulder at the porters unloading the equipment. Each would carry a load weighing forty kilos. They would be fine. Near them stood the two engineers, batting their arms for warmth. One took a few steps, then bent double and put his hands on his knees. They would not be fine.

Emma walked to the guide. "Get those men some oxygen," she said. "And tell the porters to hurry. We move out in twenty minutes."

She watched the guide run off, then turned her attention back to the darkening sky.

Trouble.

24

"*You have thirty seconds to* walk into a room and commit everything you notice to memory," said Danni.

"Like what? The color of the curtains? Kind of bedspread? I don't get it."

"Both of those. But also the location and type of desk. Do the drawers have locks? What's on the counters? How do the windows open? Is there an alarm system? Anything that your instincts tell you is important."

Jonathan stood next to Danni on the front steps of a run-down villa in the hills above Herzliya. It was past two in the afternoon. The morning's robin's-egg blue sky had given way to sodden gray clouds. The temperature had dropped ten degrees, and raindrops had begun pelting his cheek. Mentally he prepared himself for the task at hand. Closing his eyes, he willed his mind to become a blank slate able to capture everything it saw. He drew a breath and ordered himself to be calm. But all the while a voice shouted in his head: "You have to do better!"

The morning's work had been an unmitigated disaster. Danni had run him through five more courses. The route varied, but the objective remained the same. Spot the four tails. Each time, he had failed. His senses weren't as dull as a butter knife. Sandstone was more like it.

Danni opened the door and led him into a foyer with concrete floors, a high ceiling, and paint chipping off the walls. They ascended a flight of stairs and stopped at the first room on the right. "Thirty seconds."

Jonathan opened the door and stepped inside.

The room was pitch black.

Panicked, he ran a hand over the wall until he found the light switch. The question was whether to turn it on. He decided he must, or what was the point? He flicked the switch, and a bulb hanging from a threadbare wire threw a weak light around the room. Should he move or stay still? He took a step, and the floorboard groaned loudly enough to be heard in Syria. There was a king-sized bed with a ratty cover and four filthy pillows. There were two night tables with several books stacked on each. A chintz sofa took up one corner, a standing mirror another. He took another step, and the ungodly floor creaked even louder. If he were being judged on stealth, he had failed already. For some reason he found himself staring at the curtains, which were purple with green polka dots. At the far end of the room sat an imposing desk with lion's paws for feet. He tried to see if it had locks, but the light was too dim, and the sensitive floorboards left him nervous about making so much noise. So far he'd seen nothing of the least interest to an intelligence agent.

Frustrated, he decided to forget about the creaky floor and set off on a circuit of the bedroom. He rushed to the desk and tried the drawers. All were locked with an old-fashioned key. There was a television with some papers on top of it, and next to it an electric fan. He kept moving and found a closet. The door was open. Inside was a safe, and on it another stack of papers. He reached for the papers just as a hand shoved him headlong into the closet. He hit the floor and turned in time to see Danni closing the door.

"I said, 'Look, don't touch,'" she said.

"How did you get across that floor without me hearing you?"

"Be quiet and tell me everything you saw."

The dark in the closet was absolute. Jonathan pulled his knees to his chest and tried to re-create the bedroom. "A king-sized bed, some dirty pillows, a desk that I couldn't open, and a stack of papers on top of a safe."

"What about the diamonds?"

"What diamonds?"

"And the Kalashnikov?"

"Come on."

"You didn't see the terrorist hiding behind those horrid curtains?"

"Danni, let me out of here."

"You're right, there were none of those. But did you at least notice something else by the side of the bed?"

Jonathan imagined the night tables bracketing the bed. He saw two stacks of books, three on one side, four on the other. There was more. A pair of glasses. A pack of chewing gum. Trapped in the dark, he was able to examine his memory as if it were a photograph. "Yes," he said. "On the right table, there's a box with a black button on it."

"That's a panic button. Balfour keeps one identical to it next to his bed. He is paranoid to a fault. And the television?"

In his mind's eye, Jonathan made a new circuit of the room. An old twenty-inch cathode-ray model sat in one corner. "Yeah, I see it."

"Anything on it?"

"Papers."

"Can you see what they say?"

"No . . . I mean yes." His mind's eye held a clear image of bold writing across the top of the paper. "'Weapons and Armaments Available for Immediate Sale,'" said Jonathan with surprise, reading from the picture in his memory. "There are lots of items under it, but I can't read them."

"Try harder."

"M4 automatic rifles. Grenades . . . ammunition . . . The rest is a blur."

The door opened, and Danni helped Jonathan to his feet. "Are the papers his?" he asked. "Do they belong to Balfour?"

"They're out-of-date. Otherwise they're authentic."

Jonathan walked directly to the television set and picked up the papers. His recall had been accurate. He looked at Danni, amazed. "Well?"

"Not bad."

25

Sometimes you had to pull in a marker.

Frank Connor tossed the piece of metal in the air and caught it in his palm. For a moment he gazed at the chunk of misshapen lead. The odds were fifty-fifty, no better. Fourteen years was a long time, and memory warped the past. Too often, people remembered events as they wished they'd happened. Still, Malloy was an honorable man, as most Navy SEALs tended to be. If he said no, Connor wouldn't blame him. After all, he was asking a lot.

Slipping the metal into his pocket, Connor turned up the collar of his coat against the rain and locked the door of his car. It was a secure government lot, but that didn't mean it was safe.

The National Geospatial-Intelligence Agency, or NGA, was situated on the grounds of Fort Belvoir in the rolling hills of northern Virginia, not far from Arlington National Cemetery. Its brief was simple enough: to provide imagery and map-based intelligence solutions to the U.S. defense establishment and private industry. The NGA was a jewel in the crown of the intelligence community, one of the sole agencies that produced an actual physical product that could be used to tangible effect by both public and private organizations, and as such, a moneymaker.

Connor entered the smoked-glass doors of the West Tower and presented himself to the security desk. "I'm here to see James Malloy. He's expecting me."

As he waited to be cleared, he looked around him. The complex consisted of three buildings. The West Tower and East Tower each stood six stories and were built like the two sides of a clamshell. In between them stood the Core, an eight-story glass cylinder that housed the NGA's Source Directorate, where all mission-critical operations were conducted.

"Go ahead, sir. Mr. Malloy's office is in the operations office on the sixth floor of the Core. Someone will be waiting for you on the landing."

Connor slipped a visitor's ID around his neck, passed through security inspection, and rode the elevator to the sixth floor. The doors opened and he stepped into the welcoming arms of six-foot-three-inch, 220-pound James Malloy. "Frankie, good to see you."

Connor stood awkwardly, briefcase in one hand, as Malloy hugged him. "Likewise, Jim. How's tricks?"

Malloy released him and ran a hand through his black hair. "Just made watch officer."

"Watch officer? Nice. You must be putting in the hours."

"Just doing the job," said Malloy.

"How many years now?"

"Five. You were right about me being a good fit. I owe you."

"Nonsense," said Connor, but his hopes rose a notch.

His relationship with Malloy dated to the '90s, when Malloy was an operator attached to SEAL Team Six working in Bosnia. During a hunter/killer mission targeting the rebel leader, Radovan Karadžić, Malloy and his team were caught in an ambush. Malloy alone survived and was taken captive. Connor heard the news and sent a Division asset to recover him. The affair got messy before it even began. There were gunfire and civilian casualties, along with a dozen or so Bosnian regulars killed. In the end, the asset's cover was blown. It was a disaster all the way around, except that Malloy had escaped with his life.

Malloy set off down the hall at a demon's pace, with Connor struggling to keep up. It was hard to believe the man had a prosthetic leg, but of course, that was the point. Unable to meet the SEALs' rigorous fitness standards, Malloy had left the navy and moved to the civilian side of things. He'd worked for a few of the bigger private contractors before Connor arranged for him to come back to the government. It was time to see if his good deed would pay off.

"Take a seat," said Malloy.

His office was an open desk on a raised platform in the middle of the operations center. From it, he surveyed an impressive array of computer monitors, video screens, and high-tech gadgetry running 360 degrees around him, allowing him to supervise all real-time collection of data carried out by satellites tasked to the NGA.

"I came to ask a favor," said Connor as he pulled his chair closer.

Malloy smiled uneasily. "I figured as much. I heard about your promotion, too."

Connor leaned closer and explained about the cruise missile that had been lost when an air force B-52 went down in the Hindu Kush in May 1984. "We believe that someone's found it and may be trying to sell it on the black market to a rogue nation or fundamentalist cell."

"How good is your intel?"

"Near-actionable. The problem is, I don't know exactly where the bomber went down."

"With all due respect," said Malloy, "why am I hearing this from you? Seems to me that if we're talking about a nuclear-tipped ALCM, I should be fielding calls from Langley, the Joint Chiefs, and maybe even the commander in chief himself."

"There are other issues."

"Such as?"

"The incident was hushed up by the air force. As far as they're concerned, the missile is sitting at the bottom of a thousand-foot crevasse. It's not something they're eager to see dredged up. Anyway, I'm not quite there yet. For all I know, the whole thing could turn out to be a wild goose chase."

"But you don't think so."

Connor shrugged. "I'm here."

Malloy considered this. "What is it you need from me?"

Connor started him off easy so as not to scare him away. "Historical data. I need you to check and see if you have any imagery for the area dating from May 1984. I'm looking for evidence of a plane crash."

"In those mountains? You're talking about a couple of thousand square miles. That's like looking for a needle in a haystack. You're going to have to give me something more specific."

Connor removed a folder from his battered satchel. The topmost sheet held the final map grid coordinates to which the air force had narrowed its search.

"Better," said Malloy. "So we're talking a fifty-square-mile search grid right smack on the border of Afghanistan. As I recall, there was something big going down in that part of the world in 'eighty-four."

"The Russian invasion was at its peak. The Red Army had a hundred and twenty thousand men stationed in the country. It was about then that the agency started supplying arms to the mujahideen. It pays to think we had at least one bird making a pass somewhere in the region every day."

Malloy typed a stream of commands into his workstation. "No go," he said, frowning.

"What's the matter?"

"Too long ago. In terms of satellite imagery, 1984 was the dark ages. We were transitioning from wet film to digital technology. Up to 'eighty-three, our birds would take pictures on good old Kodak film. There was no such thing as real time. The best you could hope for was a three-day lag. More realistically, you'd get your pictures in a week or longer. The pictures aren't here anymore."

"But someone did keep them?" asked Connor, who knew a thing or two about bureaucratic incompetence.

"Absolutely, but not here. We need to hit the archives. Time to get off that fat butt of yours, Frank, and do a little PT."

"Fantastic," said Connor, groaning as he pushed himself out of the chair and lumbered after Malloy.

Their destination was a suite of offices on the fifth floor. "Back in 'eighty-four, this place went by the name of Comirex—the Committee on Imagery Requirements and Exploitation," said Malloy as he powered up a workstation. "It was a black organization. Totally off the books. Since then we've changed names too many times to count. Now that we've got it down to three initials, everyone's happy. NGA sits at the top table with the CIA, DHS, FBI, NSA, and all the other big shots." He hit Enter and sat back. "Okay, here we are . . . Looks like we had four birds covering Afghanistan. Two were push brooms—they flew over the area with their apertures open wide and snapped pictures of everything. They won't help. We need to drill down further. This is better. The other two were in geostationary orbit, maintaining a static post above their targets twenty-four-seven." Malloy punched in some more commands. "Here we go. This bird was in your area. Looks like it was taking pics of a supply route over the mountains."

The picture on the screen showed a section of earth from a high altitude. He saw a few black rectangles in one corner and lots and lots of mountains. Malloy refined the grid coordinates and the picture zoomed in on a section of mountainous terrain. "Bingo," he said. "That's where the flyboys were looking. No wonder they didn't have any luck."

"And that photograph is from May thirtieth or thirty-first?"

Malloy studied the screen, then scrunched up his nose. "Strange. I requested a pic from May thirtieth, but it shot back to the twenty-eighth. Let me try again." Malloy repeated his commands and the same picture reappeared. He typed some more, then raised his hands over his head, blowing air through his teeth. "Every time I request a picture between May thirtieth and September thirtieth, it kicks me back to the twenty-eighth."

"Of May? Is that normal?"

"Hell no, it's not normal," retorted Malloy. "If that satellite was up in the air, it should have been sending back pictures every minute of every goddamned day."

"When do the pictures go current again?"

Malloy banged at the keyboard, his frustration mounting. "October first."

"October first? That's a long time for a satellite to be out of operation." Connor studied the image. Approximately 120 days' worth of photographic evidence was missing. He reasoned it was during that period that the air force had found the plane, or its debris, and destroyed it. "Snow," he said. "The crash site is entirely covered. I guess that somebody wanted to make sure that no one found that plane."

Malloy rolled back his chair. "Sorry, Frank. I can't help."

"Don't be," said Connor. "Now we know where to look. An area twenty square miles shouldn't be beyond our capabilities."

"But it's November. There's already a ton of snow up there. Even if the plane were still there, we wouldn't be able to see it."

"I don't expect to find the plane or the missile. I'm looking for the people trying to recover it."

Malloy turned to face him. "Are you asking what I think you're asking?"

"It will only take an hour's time."

"No, Frank. Absolutely not. I can't task a bird to cover that area."

"Actually, you can. You're the watch officer. You're the only person who can override any of the flight programs."

"Every satellite has been tasked out months ahead of time. Every minute of every day for the next two years of their flight time has been reserved and accounted for. We have clients who depend on these images. You're talking about compromising national security."

"I'd say my actions fall into the opposite category—ensuring our national security. Look, it'll only take a few minutes."

"And what am I supposed to say to the boys at the CIA or CENT-COM or whoever I steal a bird from?"

"Say it broke down. It does happen."

"All the time," said Malloy. "And afterward, about a dozen pencil-pushers from Lockheed Martin and DOD descend on the place like a bunch of screaming blue meanies to find out why. Listen to me, Frank. Every keystroke on every workstation in this place is recorded. It will take exactly five minutes for them to discover that it was me who issued the override commands and interrupted a defined surveillance program. This isn't taking your daddy's Ford out for a joyride. You're talking about hijacking a billion-dollar piece of equipment. Why don't you get a Predator and fly it up there? Hell, that'd be easier than this."

"I thought about it, but it wouldn't go. Like you said. A needle in a haystack."

"Goddamn it, Frank. This is a total nonstarter."

Connor kept his voice low, his tone even. "You were a SEAL, Jim. You did what you did to save lives. I'm only asking you to do what you've already trained for. The only difference is that this time it's without a gun."

"You're not just asking me to risk losing my job. We're talking possible jail time." Malloy logged off the computer and stood up. "Sorry, Frank—look around you. This is bigger than me."

Connor sighed and lowered his head. He sat like that for a minute, monklike, disappointed, contemplative. And then he pulled the nub of misshapen lead from his pocket and tossed it to Malloy. "That's the slug the doctors dug out of your back after my man rescued you."

Malloy examined the metal. "No, Frank . . . sorry."

"This isn't about me or you or any debt between us," Connor went on. "This is about what we swear to do every morning when we get out of bed. This is about protecting our nation. If there is a nuclear-tipped cruise missile somewhere in those mountains, I need to know about it. This is bigger than both of us. Bigger than this agency. It's bigger than anything I've ever come up against."

Malloy ran a hand over his mouth, all the while shaking his head. He muttered some choice words, and Connor knew what he was thinking. *Why me, God?* Finally he tossed back the old bullet and said, "Screw you, Frank."

"You'll do it?"

"Come back tonight. We have a bird due to make a pass at eleven. I can't alter the satellite's trajectory, but I can fiddle with the camera a little. You've got one chance—then we're even."

"Thank you, Jimmy. You're a good soul."

"Don't give me that good-soul nonsense. I'm an American, whatever that means."

Connor picked up his satchel and put a hand on Malloy's shoulder. "God bless."

Malloy shook his head. "And Frank," he said. "Don't ever ask me for a favor again."

26

The day's work was done. The countersurveillance exercises in downtown Tel Aviv had been followed by spatial recall and memorization drills. An abysmal beginning had been followed by a miserable second act and capped with a mediocre finale. Still, Jonathan could tell himself that his performances had improved over the course of the day. Progress was progress.

Danni steered the BMW sedan along the curving road leading down to the Mediterranean with finesse. It was raining harder now, a downpour that blurred the windows and made it difficult to see outside. Seated so close to Danni, Jonathan had the impression of being in a cell, and felt the cellmate's forced camaraderie.

"How do you know him?" he asked.

Danni shot him a sidelong glance.

"No one's listening," Jonathan went on. "It's just you and me. I'm talking about Frank Connor."

"I know who you're talking about."

"Well?" Jonathan's tone was insistent, bordering on insubordinate. For the past seventy-two hours he had been on the move, following others' instructions without question or complaint. To obey meant to survive. Connor's arrival on the scene changed nothing. His proposal of service was an order concealed as a request. Emma was Division's trump card, and Connor had waited to the end to play it. Jonathan had had no choice but to comply, as a husband and as a citizen singled out by his government as the sole individual capable of performing a service essential to his nation's security. It was his role as the reluctant operative that rose up inside him now and demanded an explanation.

Every minute in Danni's company magnified the peril of his assignment. "Need to know" didn't cut it anymore.

"We worked together," said Danni.

"Are you Mossad?"

"Names aren't important. Let's just say that most governments have their own equivalent of Division. I work for Israel's."

"How did you get into it?"

Danni looked at him, her blue eyes appraising him yet again. But instead of dodging the question, she smiled. It was Jonathan's first victory of the day. "Now we're getting personal?" she asked.

"Yesterday I was lying buck naked on the floor with your knee in my back and your mouth at my ear. I'd say we've gotten past the embarrassing part."

"In Israel, military service is compulsory for men and women. Turn eighteen and off you go. Two years in uniform. I guess I liked it more than most. Maybe I was just better at it. Does it surprise you to see a woman doing this?"

"Are you serious?" Jonathan began, realizing only then that Danni knew nothing about Emma. "Need to know" went both ways. "No," he said. "Not at all. I've climbed with lots of women who are stronger than me."

The blue eyes narrowed. "Only stronger?"

"Okay," said Jonathan. "Smarter, faster, safer. And stronger."

Danni nodded, her lips curling as if to say "That's better."

"You climb?" he asked.

"Me? No, thank you. I'm afraid of heights. It's my one phobia. I washed out of jump school because of it. I made it as far as the doorway of the plane, looked down at the ground a thousand meters below me, and had an absolute fit. I wrestled the jumpmaster to the floor and nearly knocked him out. That's when they decided I might have other skills they could use."

"Funny how things work out."

Danni chuckled, and for the first time all day, Jonathan felt as if he were seeing the real woman behind the carefully constructed facade. "My sport is orienteering," she said. "You ever do it?"

Jonathan said he hadn't.

"Map, GPS, running shoes, and off you go. It's good fun."

"I think I'd like that."

"No one's tailing you. You might just be good at it."

They both laughed. Jonathan allowed himself to look at her. For once, her mouth wasn't so firmly closed, the jaw not so rock-solid. Her eyes had softened, and seemed a lighter shade of blue. She brought her left hand to the steering wheel and he saw that she did not wear a wedding band.

"You're not married?" he said.

"No."

But when Jonathan was going to ask her why, he saw that the mouth had tightened and the jaw had resumed its combative stance. Her eyes were locked on the road ahead, as relentless as ever.

Jonathan rolled down the window. A gust brought a fresh wave of rain into the car. The air smelled strongly of salt and brine. Danni said nothing.

27

The satellite was a Lockheed Martin KH-14, a next-generation reconnaissance unit the size of the Hubble Space Telescope (or, in layman's terms, as big as a Chrysler Town & Country) weighing two tons and built at a cost to the American taxpayer of $1 billion. Recent advances in optical coatings applied to the satellite telescope's lenses multiplied their resolution tenfold. The KH-14 could not only read a newspaper headline, it could tell you the name of the reporter who'd written the lead story.

"We're looking at an area five miles by five miles from an altitude of fifty thousand feet," said Malloy, pointing at the monitor before him, which displayed an area on the Pakistani-Afghan border. "The broad, smooth swaths are the valleys, the sharper lines are the spines of the mountains."

"Take it down to a thousand feet," said Connor. "Look for any signs of human activity. This time of year, there shouldn't be any."

Malloy uploaded the commands. The camera zoomed in, and Connor was presented with a bird's-eye view of a snow-covered landscape. White, white, and more white, a monotonous vista interrupted by shadow, rock, and fields of crumbling talus.

"I'll start a search program," said Malloy. "It will break up the surveillance field into a search grid measuring five hundred feet by five hundred feet, roughly one city block. Every thirty seconds we move to the next location."

For fifty minutes they remained glued to the screen. Not once did they spot anything that might indicate human presence.

"How many more grids?" asked Connor.

"We're halfway done."

"Keep it going."

"Ten minutes, Frank. Then you're on your own."

Connor scooted closer to the screen, as if proximity to the picture might improve their chances of spotting Balfour or his associates. The grid moved over a particularly steep peak. A caption appeared giving the name as Tirich Mir (7708 m). The camera continued its sweep. More rock. More snow. A glacier.

"Stop." Connor's voice was a whisper as he pointed to a smudge of gray against the white panorama. "What's that?"

Malloy zoomed in and the gray smudge gained definition. There was a sharp line, and the line became a long metallic plane. The surface led to a larger, tube-shaped object.

"It's a chopper hidden beneath camouflage netting," said Malloy.

"At that altitude?"

Malloy manipulated the camera and the helicopter's tail numbers were visible. "Looks like it's a private aircraft. I make it an Aérospatiale Ecureuil."

Suddenly a figure appeared from beneath the netting. A man carrying a backpack walked twenty paces before disappearing.

"They've got shelters set up," said Connor. "How much closer can you get?"

Malloy took the camera down further, so that it was possible to see tracks in the snow. Transfixed, they studied the screen. Another figure emerged from the shelter. Someone slimmer, walking briskly. The figure stopped and lifted its head as if to study the sky.

"Closer," said Connor.

The camera zoomed in. The figure's face remained tilted toward the sky. Then it took off its cap and shook loose a mane of tangled auburn hair. Connor felt the world slip from beneath him. "My God," he said. "Emma."

28

"He's leaving the West Tower building now," said the man seated behind the wheel of the maroon Buick sedan.

"How long was he inside?" asked a voice in his earpiece.

The man watched Frank Connor walk across the dark parking lot and unlock the front door of his battered Volvo station wagon.

"Two hours."

"Same contact as earlier?"

"Security desk has him signed in to see James Malloy, watch officer, operations center." The man slid lower in his seat as Connor backed out of his space and drove directly past him. "Target is mobile. Permission to pursue?"

"Negative. Proceed to 3624 S Street, Northwest. Malloy residence. Have a heart-to-heart with Mr. Malloy when he gets home. Find out what Connor was so interested in. And be advised, Malloy was a SEAL. You can expect him to have firearms in the house."

The man, whose name was Jake Taylor, took note. He was ex-military himself. He'd enlisted in the army at seventeen and over a ten-year career had served with the 82nd Airborne Division, the first Ranger battalion, and the Green Berets in Iraq.

Faced with the prospect of returning stateside, First Sergeant Taylor put in his papers and signed up with a private contractor. He was back in Baghdad inside a month. The pay was outstanding, the chow well above army standards, and, best of all, he was back doing what he did best: killing.

Every night after his official duty was completed, he left the safety of his compound and trawled the back alleys of Baghdad. There was no part of the city he didn't frequent. With his wiry black hair, olive skin, and two-day stubble, he hardly looked different from a native. His targets were insurgents whose names had been posted on the watch list. He would locate them, track them, then gain entry to their homes and slay them, often as they lay in their beds asleep. He used his knife, because it was quieter and because he liked the taste of blood. News of the executions spread. The frightened citizens gave the stealthy killer a name. They called him "the Ripper" because of his propensity to cut open his victims' bodies from stem to stern.

In the course of three years, he executed 461 men and 37 women.

Jake Taylor had left Iraq. "Jake the Ripper" had come home.

"What's his status?" asked the Ripper.

"Married. Wife is thirty-five years old. A nonprofessional. No children. Be sure to clean up afterward. We don't want Connor knowing we're interested in him."

"Roger that."

The Ripper started the Buick and left the parking lot, driving north past Arlington National Cemetery and crossing Key Bridge into the District of Columbia thirty minutes later. He passed Georgetown University, turned onto Reservoir Road, and found a parking spot in the quiet residential neighborhood north of campus. During the drive over, photographs of Malloy's home as well as a floor plan of the residence had been sent to his phone, and he spent ten minutes committing them to memory.

At two a.m., he slipped on a pair of leather gloves and pulled a balaclava over his face. He retrieved a P40 semiautomatic pistol from his glove compartment and screwed on a silencer. He set the gun on the seat beside him while he stuffed several pairs of flexicuffs and a roll of duct tape into his pocket. He checked his calf to make sure the KA-BAR knife was in its sheath. His only other tool was a pair of needle-nosed pliers. He'd learned long ago that simplest was best. Fingernails were very sensitive.

There was one last thing to do. Taking a vial from his jacket, he shook two small blue tablets into the palm of his hand. The tablets were Oxycontin, a synthetic morphine known on the street as "hillbilly heroin." Using the vial, he crushed each tablet on a small vanity mirror, then snorted them rapidly. An arctic rush spread through his limbs and his eyes rolled back in his head.

"Time to rock 'n' roll," he whispered, and slid into the night.

The Ripper returned to his automobile a few minutes before three. He pulled off the balaclava and sat for a minute, gathering his breath.

"Raven, checking in," he said into the encrypted phone.

"What do you have?"

"Connor wanted to see about the location of a B-52 that went down in 1984 somewhere in Pakistan. He said the bomber lost a cruise missile—a friggin' nuke—and thought there might be some people trying to retrieve it."

"A nuke? Was he able to find this missile?"

"No, ma'am. The pictures of the crash site taken twenty-five years ago were missing. But Malloy borrowed a KH-14 making a pass over the area and the bird spotted a recovery team in the vicinity of the crash site."

"Real time?"

"Yes, ma'am. Malloy said the team had plenty of equipment and it looked as if they were getting ready to move out."

"And Connor saw all this?"

"Oh, yeah."

"Did Connor tell Malloy what he intended to do?"

"No. Malloy just said that Connor was real upset."

"And did he tell anyone else about what he'd discovered?"

"Not while he was with Malloy."

"Good."

"And so?" asked Jake the Ripper, wiping the blade of his knife back and forth against his trouser leg. "What about Connor?"

"That's the question," said his superior, and for a rare moment the Ripper caught her accent. Working for a woman was bad enough, but for a foreigner, too, was damned near unimaginable. "What about him?"

29

Ashok Balfour Armitraj, better known as Lord Balfour, sat in a cramped, untidy office on the second floor of the Ministry of Foreign Affairs, running his fingers along the razor-sharp creases in his trousers. He was hot and impatient and perilously close to losing a grip on his precious manners.

"The decision is final," said the colonel with the immigration police. "Your permit has been revoked. You have thirty days to leave the country."

"The entire matter is a misunderstanding," said Balfour, for the umpteenth time. "I'm sure if you review my paperwork, you'll see that I've received all necessary approvals. I was promised by the highest authorities that my stay was open-ended."

With care, he removed a linen handkerchief from his jacket and wiped his brow. It had been a difficult day from the start. He had arrived at the meeting punctually at nine a.m., only to be kept waiting an hour without explanation or refreshment. When the meeting did begin, it was not with the usual simpering functionary who faithfully executed his superior's orders but with a gold-frocked colonel who'd descended from his lofty perch on the top floor to deliver the bad news. For the better part of an hour, Balfour had been trying to talk sense to the man, all to no avail.

"I am the sole individual with the right to grant an open-ended residence permit," said the colonel. "And I've never seen your papers before."

"Be that as it may," Balfour countered, light as ever, "promises were made. Assurances were given. I've made a sizable investment in your country."

"And we're grateful," said the general, without the least sincerity. "But that does not change how things stand. You have thirty days."

Balfour sighed and raised his hands. He did not like to pull rank, but it was clear he had no choice. "Perhaps we need to speak with General Gul."

"General Iqbal Gul?"

"That's correct. I made my agreement with him. The general is a personal friend."

"That won't be possible."

"Why not?"

"General Gul is no longer with the ISI."

"That's ridiculous," said Balfour. "Of course he's with the ISI. He's deputy director. "

The colonel leaned across the desk. "So you haven't heard?"

"Heard what? Has something happened to him? Is he all right?"

"Oh, you needn't worry about his health," said the colonel. "General Gul is in prison. He was removed from his post one week ago."

The room rocked beneath Balfour's feet. "What for?"

"Bribery and corruption."

Balfour looked at the documents on the desk in front of him. The stack was encyclopedic and contained the official history of his stay in Pakistan, down to the receipts for every niggling fee he'd paid to the state. Nowhere in the overflowing dossier, however, was there a receipt for the $1 million he'd paid General Iqbal Gul to gain residency or the monthly retainer of $50,000 he wired to Gul's account in Liechtenstein to keep it.

Balfour leaned across the table and put his hand on the colonel's arm. "Perhaps you and I might discuss this matter between ourselves. I'm certain we can find a mutually satisfactory agreement. May I suggest dinner this evening?"

The colonel's stare did not waver. "Your status is no longer in my purview," he said. "It has been taken up by the federal police. There is nothing more to discuss."

Thirty days.

Balfour thought of his home and his operations at the airports in

Islamabad and Karachi. Arms trafficking was not a cheap business to get into. He owned seven aircraft and maintained an entire workshop full of spare parts. If he left, he would lose them all. Not counting the amount he'd paid to Gul over the years, the loss would total in the tens of millions of dollars. Yet it wasn't the money that upset him so and left his heart beating frantically. It was the thought of having to physically leave the country. Ashok Balfour Armitraj had nowhere else to go.

"Look here, colonel," he said amicably, "my visa is good for another year."

"Really? Valid for another year, you say?" The colonel met his smile with one of his own. "May I see your passport?"

Relieved, Balfour placed his Indian passport on the table. Finally he was getting somewhere. "I've another eleven months before it runs out."

The colonel thumbed through the pages. The smile had vanished as quickly as it had appeared. Finding the visa, he set the passport on the table, took a ruler from his desk, and, using it as a straightedge, ripped out the offending page.

"Hey!" shouted Balfour, rising from his chair. "What are you doing?"

The colonel crumpled the paper in his fist. "Your visa has expired."

Standing, Balfour took back the passport and stuffed it into his jacket pocket. "Do you know who I am?" he said, his face quivering with contempt.

"An embarrassment to the government of Pakistan. Good day."

30

Frank Connor eyed his deputy, Peter Erskine, with an unsettling suspicion. "We don't have any other choice," argued Connor. "We've got to run this op ourselves. No one else can act quickly enough."

"Division is an intelligence agency," replied Erskine, with the glacial cold that seemed to flow through his veins. "We are not a branch of the military."

"We are a clandestine agency whose one and only mission is to insert operators into foreign territories—"

"To gather intelligence—"

"To safeguard our nation's interest!"

The clock on the wall of Division's operations center gave the time as one minute past four o'clock in the morning. Though nothing to compare to the size or sophistication of the ops center on the sixth floor of the Core at the National Geospatial-Intelligence Agency, the room boasted enough state-of-the-art equipment to meet all of Division's needs and then some. Liquid crystal display monitors measuring sixty-two inches diagonally and only one-half inch in width covered one wall. A bank of sleek workstations lined another. A red telephone and a white telephone and a black telephone were embedded in the console, and each had its use. Connor and Erskine sat at opposite ends of the conference table in the center of the room.

"What you are proposing is a full-scale, overt, armed intervention outside a recognized theater of war," said Erskine. "The minimum force requirement is an entire special operations team with air support. You might as well be ordering an invasion."

"Less," said Connor. "I need a squad of operators. Ten men. And the missile is sitting in no-man's-land, the northwest tribal territories. No one has sovereignty over it."

"You're missing the point, Frank. We're not talking about black-mailing the dictator of Guinea-Bissau in exchange for some oil leases. This is a pressing national security issue."

"You're right. That's why we can't sit on our asses a second longer. This is actionable intel that requires an immediate response."

"But not the response you're thinking of."

Connor cracked a can of diet soda and drank a slug. "Let me tell you what'll happen once I breathe word of this up the official chain of command."

Erskine looked away, a child who'd heard this lecture too many times already. "Please, Frank, I know . . ."

"Maybe so, but let me remind you. The first person I'm going to call is SecDef himself. The secretary will need a few minutes to wake up and process everything I've told him. I guarantee you he'll call back an hour later and make me repeat the whole thing again. He's an SOB, so naturally he won't believe a word I say. He's going to call the air force and ask if it's in fact true that they lost a nuclear-tipped ALCM twenty-five years back. The air force will say, 'No. Frank Connor is full of malarkey. The whole thing is complete and utter BS.' But the secretary won't stop there. He's a politician from way back. To cover his ass, he'll ring up the National Security Council and pass along my warning. The NSC is paid to be suspicious, so they'll talk to the air force and yours truly before ringing up the chairman of the Joint Chiefs of Staff and running the scenario by him. You know what time it is by now?"

Erskine shrugged. "Noon."

"Tomorrow at five p.m., earliest," said Connor. "So anyway, the Joint Chiefs will call the air force themselves, and this time the flyboys will realize that we're onto them. They'll ask for time to conduct an internal investigation, which means everyone will start scrambling to see whose ass is in the ringer if they admit to losing the bomb. Finally they'll realize that too many people are in the loop to make this thing disappear, and they'll cough up some excuse about 'possibly having lost a weapon,' but being certain that 'if the weapon were lost, it was certain to be irretrievable.' That's another day gone by.

"At which point the Joint Chiefs will convene a crisis meeting in the Situation Room at the White House. The Oval Office will call me on the carpet and ask where in hell I came up with this information. I'll tell them about Emma and Prince Rashid and about Congressman Grant's confirming the missing bomb, and then we'll all look at the satellite imagery and someone will ask how I managed to task a KH-14 satellite without a written order. And finally, after all this crap, I'll have to identify Emma and admit that one of my agents has apparently lost her mind and is leading the team of bad guys up the mountain to retrieve the nuclear payload."

Connor unbuttoned his collar and stretched his neck. His heart was beating a mile a minute, and his face felt flushed as red as a beefsteak tomato. "Four days from now, the president will authorize a strike. A SEAL team will go in and find absolutely nothing, because Emma will already have removed the payload, and if she's smart—which we know she damn well is—she will have blown the rest of the missile to kingdom come. The president will call me over to the White House and personally fire me and shut down Division once and for all."

"That's a worst-case scenario," said Erskine.

"No," railed Connor. "The worst-case scenario is that Balfour gets the nuclear payload, the thing actually still works after all these years, and he sells all one hundred fifty kilotons of it to a group of blood-thirsty terrorists slobbering at the mouth to use it." Connor slumped in his chair. "You know, I don't even care if the president does fire me, but I'd like for him to do it after he authorizes a strike to stop Balfour from getting that WMD. She's there, Pete. She's up in those mountains making her way to the missile right this second."

"Tell me this. Why is Emma helping him?"

Connor pushed himself out of his chair and circled the table. Gazing through the glass panel that made up one wall, he counted seven men and women hard at work. With a flick of a switch, the glass wall grew opaque. He looked over his shoulder. "One word: revenge."

"For what?"

"Haven't you asked yourself how Rashid knew about the gun?"

"He didn't. He just assumed it was booby-trapped when the bullet backfired. We already know he's paranoid—and with good reason."

"Maybe," said Connor, softly and with conviction. "Maybe not. But tell me how Rashid knew that she was a double agent working for us. I've been getting an earful from the FSB ever since. They're threatening to expose the entire operation to the press unless we release two of their agents from custody."

Erskine pushed his glasses onto the bridge of his nose as his brow worked furiously. Finally he raised his hands in defeat.

"Emma's working with Balfour because she's convinced we betrayed her," said Connor.

"What you're suggesting is impossible," said Erskine. "Too few people knew."

"It's never impossible, Pete. If you start counting, at least twenty people knew of the op, one way or another."

Erskine's pale, boyish face grew flushed. Suddenly he flew out of his chair. "You don't think it's me?"

Connor let him hang for a good long time, all the while taking careful note of his deputy's reactions. Erskine was quaking. Not with fear, but with a heartfelt and entirely merited indignation. "No, Pete. I don't. But I've thought about it."

"I don't appreciate that, Frank," stammered Erskine. "Not one bit. I've given everything I have to this organization. Why, my grandfather worked for Franklin—"

"Yeah, yeah, I know about your grandfather." Connor waved him down. "And I know you didn't tip off Rashid. You're very good at a lot of things, but you're the lousiest goddamn liar I've ever met. You couldn't pull it off, Pete. You're too honest."

"Thank you, Frank. That's good of you to say—I think." Erskine spent a minute cleaning his scholar's horn-rimmed spectacles, and Connor saw that his hand was still shaking. It took real guts to spy on your own. No mole could be so easily rattled. Erskine replaced his glasses. "So who?"

"I don't know. But I'll find out. I'll find out for her, because you know what, Pete? Emma won't forget this. They always say that it's the ones who move to this country who are the most patriotic. No one was more loyal to us than Emma. But deep down she's Russian, born and bred. She'll get her revenge. I have no idea what's on her mind right now. But I'm scared. I truly am."

"So what exactly do you propose?" asked Erskine.

Connor rubbed a hand across the back of his neck. "Immediate action. We found it. We nip it in the bud. Keep this whole situation in-house. The quicker we clean it up, the fewer people will ever know about it."

"That's quite some mantle of responsibility. Even for you."

"Yeah, well. You do what you gotta do."

Erskine leaned forward, appraising Connor. "Are you all right, Frank? I mean, you sure you're up to this?" His concerned tone did not inspire confidence.

"If I drop dead, I'll make sure you're the first to know."

"You're immortal, Frank," said Erskine, much too smoothly.

"So they tell me." Connor finished up the can of diet soda and felt a little better. "You with me? As you said, it's quite some mantle of responsibility. I wouldn't mind sharing it."

"You know I am, Frank. It's my job to make you aware of our options."

"I understand. I just wish we had more of them in this instance."

"So what are you going to do?"

Connor sat stock-still for nearly a minute before answering. "I'm going to take her out," said Connor. "Right now."

31

Balfour walked the length of the hall and passed through the ante-room into his bedroom. The desk was too neat for his liking. The global arms bazaar was busier than ever, but his share of it was diminishing rapidly. The sum total of orders from Libya, Sudan, Malaysia, and Georgia reached a paltry $10 million. His commission was 10 percent of that. He leafed through the papers with growing disinterest. His days as an arms merchant were behind him. His clients could not follow him into his new life.

He flipped open his laptop and logged on to his account at a private bank in Geneva. The balance stood at $90 million. With disgust, he observed the red asterisk placed at the top of the page and the notice that read, "Funds in account are frozen until future notice, pursuant to Judicial Order 51223, Office of the Federal Prosecutor, Bern."

The Swiss government had slapped a freeze on his funds the day Interpol placed his name on its Red List. Accounts in other countries were likewise blocked. His only accessible funds were the commission he'd earned from Prince Rashid and the money he kept in his local accounts. It wouldn't last long. Monthly operating costs ran to $100,000 for Blenheim alone.

Balfour considered how his good fortune had run out, the fruits of his years of hard labor yanked out from beneath him. But he was a shrewd man. He had a plan. If all went well, in a few days he would be guaranteed years of anonymity and safety lived in the plush style to which he was accustomed, and which he so richly deserved.

Balfour pulled off his jacket and kicked his shoes onto the carpet. Two inches shorter, he crossed the room and opened the French doors. A sweeping vista of the foothills and mountains of the Hindu Kush greeted him. Somewhere up there was Emma Ransom. She had radioed that she was en route to the site of the weapon. In hours, she and her team would begin dismantling the missile.

Balfour returned to his desk and unlocked the top drawer. There, on top of his personal papers, lay the photograph of the American cruise missile. If the nuclear core could be successfully removed and brought down the mountain intact, its sale would earn him enough to live comfortably for quite some time.

One last deal and Ashok Balfour Armitraj, a.k.a. Lord Balfour, would disappear. His Swiss plastic surgeon would arrive shortly, and Count François-Marie Villiers would be born.

32

Connor had one avenue of attack and one only: CJSOTF-A. Combined Joint Special Operations Task Force—Afghanistan.

Traditional military units function according to a top-down hierarchy. A general at division level issues an order to a colonel commanding a battalion, who passes it along to a company commander, either a major or a captain, who with his men actually carries it out. In short, no one moves until his superior officer gives him an order.

Special Forces—Green Berets, Delta Force, SEALs, Air Force Pararescue, and Marines Special Operations Command—function differently. Unless specifically tasked, special operations forces deployed in a theater of war are responsible for generating their own missions. Instead of top-down, they work according to a bottom-up hierarchy. Commanders in the field, usually at the rank of captain, are given considerable discretion and latitude in planning the parameters and scope of their missions.

In Afghanistan, where Special Forces' primary goal was to seek out and destroy enemy combatants, teams of ten to twenty men established outposts at far-flung locations and used these as bases from which to locate, track, and kill the enemy.

Connor sat down at a keyboard and logged on to JWICS. Civilians had the World Wide Web. The military had its own dedicated networks, and civilians were not welcome. JWICS, or the Joint Worldwide Intelligence Communications System, was reserved for top-secret or classified communications. Information available included a listing of all U.S. forces deployed around the world, down to battalion level. Connor navigated onto the page for the Joint Special Operations Task Force—Afghanistan. A colonel was in charge, but it was enlisted men who drove special ops. One man in particular held sway. In this instance, he was Marine Sergeant Major Lawrence Robinson and he ran the Tactical Operations Center at Bagram Air Base, thirty miles north of Kabul.

Connor thanked the Lord for this piece of luck.

Smiling inwardly, he rolled his chair over to the red phone. A red phone for the red line, a secure, encrypted line linking intelligence agencies, military installations, and embassies around the world.

"This is Sergeant Major Robinson."

"Frank Connor at Division. You the same Robinson helped pull Saddam out of his spider hole a few years back?"

"You the same sonofabitch sent me to find him?"

"Hello, Larry. How they hangin'?"

"Two more years till I have my thirty in, then I'm coming to work for you."

"Any time. Just remember to tell the wife you're selling washing machines."

Robinson cleared his throat. There was precious little time for levity. "Why don't you give me your verification code, just for old time's sake."

Connor rattled off his ten-digit alphanumeric ID. He had visited the Tactical Operations Center at Bagram on more than one occasion. Waiting for his clearance, he envisioned Robinson standing at his perch on the raised platform that overlooked the rows of desks and wall-mounted video screens and the determined young men and women hard at work. At any one time, Robinson might be monitoring a Predator mission on one screen, a field interrogation on another, and a platoon engaged in combat on a third, all while signing off on the next day's duty roster.

"And what can I do for Division this fine day?" asked Sergeant Major Robinson.

"We have some HVIs"—high-value individuals—"in transit on the border of the northwest tribal region traveling with a team of enemy combatants. We've been after these guys for a long time. We're talking some extremely nasty individuals. Do you have a team in the area available for immediate dispatch?"

"Gotcha loud and clear, Frank. I have two Marine special ops teams working out of Korengal Valley. I'll have to speak with the ground commanders to see who's good to go. Hold for ten."

Connor looked at Erskine and crossed his fingers. He knew better than to mention the missile. An HVI in the company of enemy combatants was a mouthwatering target. At this point, retrieving the missile could wait. Liquidating Balfour's team was mission one. And that included Emma Ransom.

"I have Captain Crockett at Firebase Persuader patched in. Mr. Connor, go ahead."

Frank Connor outlined the story as he chose to present it. A group of enemy combatants, including at least one individual figuring on the Terrorist Watch List, had been spotted in the mountains of northwestern Pakistan. He had 100 percent visual confirmation as well as the precise coordinates where the targets had been seen a short time earlier.

"I've got a pair of Chinooks on the flight line powering up," said Robinson. "ETA to Captain Crockett is one hour."

The TOC was situated adjacent to the flight line at Bagram, and Connor imagined that Robinson could see the crews running to the large helicopters and the long twin rotors beginning to turn.

"One question, Mr. Connor," said the Marine captain. "Should any effort be made to capture and interrogate either the combatants or the HVI?"

"Negative. They are to be considered armed and dangerous and will resist capture. Shoot to kill, captain."

"Hoo-yah," said the Marine.

Connor ended the call and looked at Erskine.

No death warrant was ever worded more clearly.

33

It was morning, and morning was when they did memorization games. Danni pulled a white cloth off the table and said, "Go." Jonathan had ten seconds to look at and memorize as many of the objects on the four-foot-square table as possible. The first day she'd given him thirty seconds, the second day twenty. The amount of time he was allotted to observe and commit the items to memory kept decreasing while the number of items increased. Danni had a word for this method of training. She called it "elongating," and said it meant pushing the envelope at both ends. Jonathan, ruled by his secret mantra to do everything better than anyone else, either before or to come, called it "bullshit" and struggled to increase his scores.

Ten seconds.

Jonathan regarded the assortment of dissimilar objects, registering each in turn, assigning it a letter or a numeral. C for candle. N for notepad. *1* for cell phone, because there was always a cell phone, therefore it was a constant. (The other constants were an alligator billfold, *2*; a pair of sunglasses, *3*; and a pack of breath mints, *4*.) He estimated that there were twenty-five items on the table. Some were large and impossible to forget—a Colt .45 pistol, for example. But he had learned that these were put there to obscure his recollection of the smaller, more important things. It was these items he sought out first and branded into his memory: a flash drive disguised as a pen; a slip of paper with a twelve-digit phone number. ("Concentrate on the last eight digits," Danni instructed him. "We can figure out the country later.") A photograph of three men and a woman. (Two of the men were swarthy, with heavy mustaches, the third bald, with a birthmark on his left cheek. The woman was red-haired, with sunglasses, and, oddly, topless.) A business card with Arabic script.

There were other assorted items, ranging from a flathead screwdriver to a ring of keys. And these his mind registered in a fleeting, once-over sweep.

"Time."

Jonathan turned his back to the table, but not before Danni threw the cloth over the items, just in case he might have eyes in the back of his head.

The exercise was not over yet. To mimic real life as much as possible, Danni made him wait ten minutes to the second before he was permitted to recite the list he'd stored away. During that time, it was their practice to discuss the main stories taken from that morning's edition of the *Jerusalem Post*. "Compartmentalization," she called it. Carving up your mind into individual, hermetically sealed sections and putting a lock and label on each.

Today's headlines were stolen from a world at war. The Israeli navy had boarded and seized a cargo ship under foreign flag in the eastern Mediterranean, which was carrying a devil's arsenal of Iranian weaponry destined for Hezbollah in Syria and Lebanon.

"Name the ship and the country of registry," said Danni.

Jonathan had the reply at his fingertips. "*Faring Rose.* Norway."

Riots had broken out again on the Temple Mount. More than two hundred policemen had been called to quell the violence.

"What's everyone so damned mad about?" Danni asked.

"Access to the Temple Mount by Palestinians."

"Who's for or against?"

"People's Party for . . ." Jonathan gave up. Israeli politics had always confused him. He found it no easier to follow now that he was in the country. "Next."

The routine required that they stand face-to-face and maintain eye contact so that Jonathan could not engage in any mental gymnastics that might make recall easier. As Danni continued her tour of the headlines, Jonathan couldn't help but notice a weariness tugging at her features. He'd read his share of similar stories and had become inured to them, yet the mournful cast to her eyes suggested that she'd lived them. He looked into those eyes and noticed the specks of green sprinkled on the blue irises. It was a warm morning, and she was dressed in shorts and a black tank top that matched the raven's black of her hair. Her one concession to makeup was a coat of balm to heal her cracked lips. She smelled faintly of French perfume. For these observations his mind had no compartment, no lock or label. He experienced them wholly and without effort, even if he might have cared not to.

Danni continued. In Peshawar, on the border of Pakistan and Afghanistan, three car bombs had exploded simultaneously near a military base. It was a story to which Jonathan had paid special attention. "How many dead?" she asked.

"Sixty confirmed. Three hundred injured. Both figures are expected to rise."

"Who took responsibility?"

"A Taliban warlord."

"Name?"

"Sultan Haq. He claimed the bombing was in retaliation for the murder of his father. I was there in the cave when he was killed. I saw him die."

Danni looked up sharply. "You know Haq?"

"That's where I was before I came here."

"Haq was a prisoner in Guantánamo," said Danni with hatred. "You released the wrong man."

"Looks like it."

Danni went back to her paper. "And who supplied the explosives?" she asked.

"I don't know," said Jonathan. "Do you?"

"No, but it doesn't matter. If it wasn't Balfour, it was someone like him. Another cockroach that needs to be crushed. Balfour's your focus. Let's not forget why you're here."

Jonathan noted that his heart was beating faster, and he felt as if he'd taken a step closer to his target.

"Ready?" said Danni. "Begin."

Still looking into her eyes, Jonathan recited the list of objects on the table. It ran to twenty-one items. He forgot only the fountain pen, the business card with Arabic script, and a tangerine. He also transposed the last two digits of the telephone number written on the slip of paper.

"Not bad," said Danni. "Take five minutes, then we're going back to the street. Maybe you can finally pick out someone who's following you. I'm not optimistic."

Jonathan spotted the first tail almost immediately. He was young and rangy with a mop of curly black hair and tattered jeans, and he was trying too hard to appear captivated by each store's varied offerings. A sportsman might look closely at a display of fishing rods and boating equipment, but the same man could hardly be expected to find anything of interest in the fashion boutique next door. As proud as Jonathan was of having spotted the tail, he was prouder still of how he'd managed it. Looking around for ways to see behind him, Jonathan had caught the tail's reflection in the window of a taxi stalled in the midday traffic. No look over his shoulder, no stopping to tie his shoe and glance surreptitiously behind him. Just a casual flick of the eyes to the taxi's window—as clear as a mirror—and Jonathan had him. When Jonathan walked briskly, so did Curly Black Hair. When Jonathan slowed, his shadow slowed, too.

Number one down.

The time was half past twelve, and on this sunny afternoon, the Haifa waterfront was a hive of activity. Sidewalk cafés, curio boutiques, and thriving markets attracted a cross-section of the Israeli populace. Young, old, natives, Palestinians. It was a mix of ancient and modern, a slice of contemporary Israel. Danni knew how to pick her spots.

Jonathan passed the old clock tower as it rang the half-hour. On the corner, a bent vendor sold soft drinks and shawarmas from his cart. Jonathan bought a Coke, making conversation with the old man. As he did, he turned slowly and gazed up and down the street. Danni had instructed him to let his eyes do the walking, and Jonathan fought to keep his head still.

He picked out his second tail a block later. She was a thin middle-aged woman mirroring him on the opposite side of the street. She wore an orange smock and a straw sun hat, but they were camouflage. Five minutes earlier she'd been wearing a blue sweater and had her hair in a braid. It was her shoes that gave her away: clunky brown Mephisto hiking shoes that he'd picked up two blocks back.

He was learning.

Number two down.

He heard rather than saw the car approaching at speed to his rear. The engine revved high enough to hurt his ears, the noise growing louder each second. Still, he refused to yield to his curiosity. It was only when the black BMW nearly brushed against him that he jumped to one side and gave it his full attention.

The sedan pulled to the curb and the front door flew open. Danni jumped out and motioned for him to approach. Jonathan broke into a jog. "What is it?" he asked. "Did I do something wrong? It was the guy with curly hair and ripped-up jeans and the straggly lady in the straw hat."

"That doesn't matter," said Danni. "Get in."

Jonathan was slow on the uptake. "But I got 'em," he said proudly. "I actually figured out who was following me."

"Congratulations," said Danni, without joy. "Get in the back. We're late."

Jonathan climbed into the rear seat and Danni slid in next to him. "Late for what?" he asked. "What's going on? Did something happen?"

The car accelerated into traffic and Danni slapped a passport into his hand. "Change of plan. Things are moving faster than expected. We're leaving the country."

"When? I mean, where to?"

"The plane leaves in two hours," said Danni, throwing up a tanned forearm and checking her watch. "Don't worry. You'll like where we're going. It's cold and there are mountains."

34

Emma pulled the hood of her anorak further over her head and cursed the weather. The front she'd observed approaching from the east when taking off from Chitral had moved in more quickly than she'd expected. The temperature had plummeted twenty degrees, and for the last hour snow had been falling.

Burying her ice ax into the slope, she watched the members of her team lumber past. "Oxygen working okay?" she asked, patting one of the nuclear physicists on the back.

The engineer grunted but did not slow.

"Not much farther," she said. "Just up this slope."

It was a pardonable lie. Ninety percent of climbing was mental. It was easier to break down the route into short, accomplishable segments. She stood in place, allowing the others to pass: the guide; the porters with their forty-kilo loads carrying tents and rations, and of course the toolboxes of sophisticated equipment that would be required to open up the missile and dismantle the payload; and finally the second physicist. She looked at him more closely. His face was knotted in pain, his stride wobbly. He was a thin man, and earlier she'd judged him fit by the sparkle in his eye and his serious manner. Now she saw that she was wrong. He was in bad shape.

They had been marching for six hours, with a respite every sixty minutes. From base camp at 4,500 meters, the trail had assumed a gentle grade across a firm snowfield. The first test came at the three-kilometer marker, where the snowfield abutted a massive icefall. Emma stopped the team to rope up and attach crampons and to say that if she saw anyone treading on the rope, she'd personally throw him off the nearest ledge. After that, all conversation died and the climb began in earnest.

The icefall resembled a gargantuan, fractured marble staircase and rose 250 meters over a couple of kilometers. The abject fear that comes when jumping over a crevasse or hearing the loud, godlike groaning of ice shifting below your feet sharpened everyone's concentration. Thankfully, all managed to make it up without incident. From there the route led across the flank of the mountain, as if following the hem of a skirt, the snow once again firm beneath their crampons.

At noon they stopped for a lunch of lamb jerky, rice, and beans. Emma had forgotten the tedium of cooking at altitude. It took water thirty minutes to boil. Minute rice also needed half an hour. It was then that the complaints had started. The stocky engineer had blisters. She lanced them and put on antifriction salve and moleskin. The other engineer complained of a persistent leg cramp, which Emma massaged away by pressing her thumbs so deep into his calf muscles that she brought tears to the man's eyes.

The engineers weren't the only ones with issues. The guide began to make noises about stopping unless he was paid the remainder of his fee. Emma had a solution for that kind of problem, too. Leading him out of earshot, she grabbed him by the unmentionables and squeezed very hard.

"You'll take us to the missile directly," she said, ignoring his gasps and bulging eyes. "You will not tarry. You will not pretend to be lost. Because if you don't, not only will I see to it that Balfour doesn't pay you"—and here she released her grip, drew her pistol, and pressed it against his forehead in a single quicksilver motion—"I will personally put a bullet into your greedy little skull."

She replaced the pistol in her holster and patted his cheek with a little mustard. "Balfour didn't put me in charge of this expedition because he likes my tits and ass. Are we clear?"

"Yes, ma'am."

Emma freed her ice ax and motioned toward the line of climbers.

"Even the porters are getting tired," she said. "I can keep everyone going for another two hours, three maximum."

"We are close," said the guide, one hand placed protectively in front of his family jewels. "Over this crest there is a small valley. The object is at the far side."

"Can we reach it before dark?"

"If we hurry."

"What about shelter?"

"There are caves nearby."

Emma grabbed a fistful of his parka. "And you do know precisely where we are going, yes?"

The guide nodded vigorously.

"Off with you, then," said Emma, releasing him.

She stared at the darkening sky and the snow, heavier now, and wetter. Three hours was an eternity when you were fatigued. The whole expedition was much too ambitious. Two days was hardly enough time to plan a day hike, let alone an eight-man trek at altitude. Then again, she hadn't had a choice. Balfour had insisted on moving the weapon immediately and she was eager to share in his urgency. Connor's betrayal was still foremost in her mind. Recovering the warhead was the only means to ensure her survival beyond the next few days.

She stood a moment longer, observing the team's slow ascent. At lunch she had laced their tea with a mild amphetamine, but soon the extra zip would wear off. She checked her watch, then set off.

Three hours.

Nearly impossible.

The skinny engineer petered out first. Emma allowed him an extra ten minutes' rest. She removed his boots and massaged his feet. She brewed more of her special tea and forced him to drink a cup. None of it made a whit of difference. He was done. His eyes had the forlorn, far-away look she knew too well. She gazed at the high mountain valley, a vast bowl of white, unadorned by rock or tree. The flanks of Tirich Mir rose defiantly from the distant side, disappearing into the cloud.

Emma looked back at the engineer and the others, waiting patiently, the porters not bothering to remove their packs. They had just reached the crest, and anything resembling a route had disappeared beneath the new-fallen snow, leaving them all to make their own paths. Wind slapped at their faces. Emma tightened her jaw. The storm was worsening.

The guide lifted an arm and pointed at an outcropping of rock shaped like a horn in the distance. "Five kilometers," he said.

Emma handed her pack to the strongest porter, then told the ailing engineer to stand up. Kneeling, she ordered him to climb onto her back. She stood, adjusting her arms beneath his spindly legs. She guessed he weighed about sixty-four kilos. The team looked at her oddly.

"Last one there's a rotten egg," she said. Then, to the guide, "Go!"

It was 4:50 and night was descending when they reached the horn-shaped rock. She put down the engineer and collapsed onto her back. She allowed herself two minutes to rest, then stood. Her vision faltered, and she realized that she was perilously close to exhaustion. In response, she ordered herself to move faster and checked on each of the team members, telling them to hydrate, helping find energy bars in poorly packed rucksacks, offering words of encouragement. When she saw that everyone had a snack, she dug out some trail mix for herself and drank a liter of water.

After ordering the porters to make a fire in a cave, she gathered the engineers and the guide together. "It will be dark soon," she said. "But I want our friends here from Dr. Khan's workshop to have a look at the prize before the light goes."

"One hundred meters," said the guide. "I will show you."

It was larger than she'd imagined. She'd downloaded the specs from the Net, but she hadn't expected it to be so imposing, so martial. Its full name was a Boeing AGM-86 Conventional Air-Launched Cruise Missile. It measured twenty-one feet in length and four feet in diameter and weighed 3,250 pounds.

The guide brushed away a layer of snow and removed the tarpaulin he and his brother had brought to protect it. The missile was a shark's gray and had an angular snout that resembled that of a commercial jetliner. The long, thin wings that aided it in flight had not deployed and were tucked beneath its body. A circular air intake valve sat at the base of its tail fin. The words "U.S. Air Force" were painted on its skin, as were the serial number and other operating information. But all eyes were glued to the yellow-and-black radiation symbol stenciled at three places along its long body, and the words "Danger: Radioactive material contained inside. Failure to follow instructions may result in physical injury or death."

There was an understatement, thought Emma.

The heavier engineer produced a Geiger counter from his pack and held it to the center of the missile, where the payload section was located. The needle danced wildly before coming to rest in the red.

"Uranium-235," he said, studying the isotope chromatograph. "Hasn't degraded a bit."

"What about the tritium?" asked his colleague, referring to the concentrated gas necessary to produce the chain reaction.

"Ninety percent."

"My God."

"What is it?" asked Emma.

"The bomb is still live. It can be detonated at any moment."

35

Swiss International Airways Flight 275, originating in Jerusalem, landed at Geneva's Cointrin Airport on schedule at 1645 local time. The weather was gray and leaden, with ground temperature measuring thirty-three degrees Fahrenheit, or one degree Celsius, and humidity at 80 percent. Jonathan walked the long corridor to baggage claim alone, feeling more anxious than he would have liked or would ever admit. Danni was somewhere ahead. She'd traveled business class while he sat in the last row of economy. The separation was intentional. Training was over. The operation had begun. Nothing made it clearer than the American passport he carried in his left hand, issued in the name of John Robertson of Austin, Texas. Jonathan had been granted his first alias. It was official. He was a spy.

At immigration control, Jonathan watched with anxiety as his passport was scanned and whatever information its security strip held was displayed on the official's monitor. Five seconds passed—an eternity by Jonathan's newly calibrated soul.

"The purpose of your visit?"

"Business," said Jonathan.

The official compared Jonathan to his picture, then brought down his stamp. "I wish you a pleasant stay."

Jonathan accepted the passport in return, then stood for a moment like an idiot before realizing that the passport was good and he had been cleared to continue.

As instructed, he waited five minutes after seeing Danni pick up her luggage and clear customs before following suit. It was easier said than done. With typical Swiss efficiency, his bag was already on the carousel when he arrived, and he had to force himself to stand still and watch it go past again and again.

Suitcase in hand, he left the terminal and crossed the street to Parking Structure B. A gray minivan was parked at the farthermost recesses of the third floor. He opened the door and saw Danni in the rear seat, cloaked in shadow. "Get in," she said.

"Now, please, Dr. Ransom," said the driver. "We have a bit of a drive ahead of us." English with a hard Swiss-German accent. The driver was a compact man with sloped shoulders, a stern countenance, and gray hair cut to a commando's stubble. Jonathan's breath caught.

"You?"

"Hello again," said Marcus von Daniken, director of the Service of Analysis and Protection, Switzerland's counterespionage agency. "Please shut the door. I have the heat on."

Jonathan climbed into the middle seat and pulled the door closed. "How's your arm?"

"I won't be playing tennis anytime soon, but at least I can still watch it on television."

Von Daniken had been wounded helping Jonathan and Emma thwart the attack on the Israeli jetliner ten months before.

"So you know Connor?" asked Jonathan.

"Frank and I are colleagues of long standing. The affair last February brought us into closer contact and enabled us to recognize our mutual interests. I help when I can."

"It's good to see you," said Jonathan.

"Really, Dr. Ransom, politeness is not a requisite of this profession."

"I just mean—"

"Yes, I know what you mean." Von Daniken met his gaze in the rearview mirror. Something close to respect pulled at his steadfast eyes. He nodded gravely, then said, "I am disappointed in one thing."

"Oh?"

"I see you're still hanging around with the wrong kind of woman."

"Shut up, Marcus," said Danni, but she didn't mean it. Von Daniken laughed and Danni joined him, and Jonathan had the feeling of being odd man out in a shadowy, ever-shifting fraternity.

Von Daniken put the van into gear and steered them out of the parking structure and onto the superhighway. For a while they drove along the outskirts of Geneva, which in the gathering dusk was as faceless and depressing as any other central European city. Then the buildings fell away, the highway climbed a rise, and the vast expanse of Lake Geneva stretched before him, an anthracite-colored sea guarded to the west by the imposing peaks of the French Haute-Savoie.

The heat was too much, so Jonathan cracked a window. Bitterly cold air redolent of fallow farmland rushed in, stinging his nostrils. Instantly he was awake, his senses keen. He looked at Danni, her eyes closed, dozing. A flash of anger passed through him. She knew everything—why he was here, what he was to do, how he was supposed to do it—yet she refused to tell him. *Need to know.* The three words drove him crazy. If anyone needed to know, it was Jonathan. And he needed to know now.

The highway followed the shore of the lake, past Lausanne and Montreux and Vevey, until finally the lake narrowed to its confluence with the Rhône River and the mountains drew closer on both sides, their shadows pressing in on the valley like sentinels of the gods.

"Dammit, where are we going?" Jonathan demanded.

Danni opened her eyes. But instead of telling him once more to mind his own business, she yawned and said, "Marcus, Dr. Ransom wishes to know where we're going. Would you be so kind as to tell him?"

"We're going where every couple should go when there is plenty of snow and they are rich and in love," said Von Daniken. "Gstaad."

The Palace Hotel sits atop its own hill at the north end of the village of Gstaad, a fairy-tale castle presiding over a sugarcoated kingdom. Strands of sparkling white bulbs danced over the road leading toward it through the village. Von Daniken turned sharply right and shifted into lower gear as the van began a steep, winding climb. For a moment the hotel disappeared from view, replaced by a hillside of snow and barren birch trees. Another curve and it was there again, much larger

than before, a symphony of lights and red carpets. Frock-coated chas-
seurs waited beneath the porte cochere to open the door.

"Help me with this, would you?" Danni extended her wrist, and
Jonathan clasped the diamond tennis bracelet. She wore an emerald
on her right hand and a canary yellow diamond the size of a Brazil nut
on the other.

"Are they real?" he asked.

It wasn't until the last hour of the drive to Gstaad that she'd
finally briefed him on the details of his mission. According to their
cover, they were Mr. and Mrs. John Robertson of Austin, Texas. He
was something big in real estate. ("If they ask, say 'land,'" Danni had
advised. "In Texas, that says it all.") And they'd come to Gstaad for a
restorative holiday. Sun, skiing, and a little nip and tuck courtesy of
Dr. Michel Revy. Revy was the target, the Swiss plastic surgeon Lord
Balfour had contracted to travel to Pakistan to alter his appearance.

"Of course," she answered, eyes fluttering like a debutante's.
"Baby loves her ice."

For a moment Jonathan didn't answer. He wasn't shocked by the
quality of their passports or the explanation of why they'd come to
Gstaad and what he was to accomplish. He'd been waiting for hours,
if not days, to find out, and his responsibilities weren't as demanding
as he'd expected. What shocked him was Danni's voice. All trace of
her accent had vanished. She spoke English as if she'd been brought
up in the shadow of her daddy's oil well on the great Permian Basin.

"Baby?" Jonathan looked to von Daniken for support, but the
Swiss policeman was already climbing out of the van and instructing
the bellmen that he would not be staying.

Check-in proceeded without a problem, if one didn't count
Jonathan's need to consult his passport to ensure that he spelled his
name correctly, "Robertson" being exotic to the novice operative's eye.
A credit card was on file, and when asked, Jonathan replied that yes,
all expenses were to be placed on it. The resident manager guided
Jonathan and Danni to their room and spent no less than ten minutes
describing the various features controlled by the bedside panel.

Room 420 was a junior suite, with a small salon leading into a spacious bedroom. The carpet was the color of honey and decorated with patterns of the fleur-de-lis. The furniture was lush and modern. A liter of Passuger mineral water was cooling in one sterling silver ice bucket and a bottle of Veuve Clicquot in the other.

"Shall I open the champagne now?" asked the hotelier.

"No, that won't be—" began Jonathan.

"Of course, Herr Ringgenberg," interceded Danni, who somehow had remembered the man's name. "We're parched, aren't we, darling?"

Herr Ringgenberg poured the champagne with ceremony and wished them a marvelous stay. When he loitered at the door, it was Danni who slipped a fifty-franc note into his palm and thanked him ever so graciously. The door closed. She turned and raised her glass. "Cheers, darling."

"Cheers," said Jonathan, lifting his glass in return. "But weren't you putting it on kind of heavy?"

"You've got to have some fun with it," said Danni, without any fun at all, her Israeli accent knocking the frivolous, diamond-loving Texas gal flat on her behind. She set down the glass without drinking. "Get changed. You'll find a suit in the closet. White shirt and necktie, please. We're rich and conservative. This is no place for flannel shirts and boots."

Inside the closet Jonathan found three suits, one charcoal, one navy, one black. "I'll look like an undertaker," he said.

"Undertakers don't wear Zegna."

Jonathan didn't know what or who Zegna was, but knew better than to ask. "What about you?"

Danni entered the bathroom, a garment bag slung over her tanned arm. "Wait and see."

The door closed and Jonathan stood for too long gazing at the strip of light beneath it. He was thinking of another luxury hotel where he'd had no business being, another foreign city, and another woman. A longing stirred inside him. Something stronger than desire. He took a step toward the door, then stopped, unsettled by his actions.

———

As instructed, Jonathan dressed in the navy suit, white shirt, and midnight blue tie. The clothing fit as if tailored, and when he looked in the mirror, he saw the doctor his father had always wanted. Or, as Frank Connor might have said if he were present, "the doctor he was going to become."

The door to the bathroom opened. Classical music drifted into the room, strains of Beethoven's "Emperor." The scent of French perfume.

"Ready to go?"

Jonathan turned from the dressing table and something inside him locked up. His first thought was that the woman standing in the doorway couldn't be Danni. Someone had exchanged the fit, handsome woman with whom he'd spent the last four days for a raven-haired knockout who'd just stepped off the runway in Paris. The woman staring at him wore a black sheath that left no room for imagination. Her curves were more prominent than he'd suspected. Thanks to her heels, she was taller, too. Her face was expertly made up, with lipstick to put fire engines to shame and eyeliner to make Cleopatra blush. She wore her hair up, the better to show off her diamond stud earrings. More ice for Baby.

"What is it?" asked Danni. "Is something wrong?"

Jonathan rummaged through his store of sarcastic comments for something to explain away his awestruck expression. He found only the truth. "You look . . . *nice*."

Danni's eyes grew liquid, and she rushed back into the bedroom. She returned a minute later, holding a black leatherette box. Jonathan stood from his chair as she removed a men's wristwatch with a brown crocodile strap. "An IWC Portuguese Chronograph," she said, turning over his wrist and buckling the timepiece. "White gold, because you're not flashy."

"Unlike you."

Danni lowered her eyes, and Jonathan tried not to enjoy the touch of her fingers, the rapt attention she paid to her task, the nearness of her. When she'd finished, he pulled back his sleeve and whistled. "Not exactly a Casio G-Shock."

"This is Switzerland," said Danni. "Watches matter. Oh, and one last thing."

"What's that?"

Danni took his hand and slipped a wedding band on his finger. "Now it's official," she said.

Jonathan looked at his hand, remembering that once he'd worn a ring. He was a man who admired permanence. "Good evening, Mrs. Robertson," he said.

Danni glanced up, and all levity had fled her gaze. "Good evening, Mr. Robertson. Ready to head out?"

Jonathan nodded, and they stood for much too long, looking at each other.

36

Firebase Persuader was located at the head of a narrow mountain valley in the northern Afghan province of Korengal, five kilometers as the crow flies from the Pakistani border. The firebase was home to fifteen United States Marines, the members of Special Operations Team Alpha, Third Battalion, First Marines. The firebase's footprint ran twenty meters by thirty and was surrounded by a waist-high HESCO wall, the successor to sandbags, and a three-meter-tall fence topped with coils of razor wire.

For four months, Special Operations Team Alpha had combed the valleys that ran like a witch's fingers through the mountains. They had set up ambushes and constructed hides and humped up and down more hills than Sisyphus. Their mission was simple: interdict the flow of weapons and matériel from the ungoverned tribal regions of neighboring Pakistan and stop the traffic of foreign fighters slipping across the border to join their Taliban brethren. There had been some successes and some defeats. They'd lost two of their own, but they'd killed a hundred times that number. It was a painful trade-off, but no one would argue it wasn't fair. In the war, Special Operations Team Alpha was a single barb in the country's defensive perimeter. But it was a sharp barb.

Captain Kyle Crockett heard the flutter of the helicopters before he could see them. It was dusk and a purple haze hung in the air, obscuring the view down the valley leading from the northern plain. In a war zone, helicopters always flew in pairs. If one was shot down, the other was there to ferry the survivors, if there were any, and to provide cover for their rescue. Grabbing his rifle and his ruck, he left the CP and crossed the muddy ground to his men. The team going out this evening numbered twelve in all. They were well trained, disciplined, and fit. Under fire they kept their cool, and when called upon, they could be as vicious as a pack of wolves.

The team was dressed in winter gray camouflage utilities with anoraks covering their Kevlar vests. Ten of the men carried the standard-issue M4 automatic rifle, a look-alike of its predecessor, the M16, along with ten clips of ammunition, a total of 270 bullets per man. Four had mounted M203 grenade launchers under the barrel of their weapons, and two had the more accurate M79 launcher. The eleventh man was a sniper, who carried an M40 rifle, essentially a souped-up Remington 700. The twelfth was the team gunner, who carried the M249 Squad Automatic Weapon, a heavy machine gun capable of laying down 2,500 rounds of ammo a minute. Tonight's fighting would be done with machine guns set to full auto.

The radio crackled and the helicopter told Crockett to clear the LZ. "Landing in two minutes."

"Oscar Mike," called Crockett to his men. On the move. "Two minutes to deploy."

The Marines threw their rucksacks on their backs and headed down the hill to the LZ.

The Chinooks barreled through the valley and landed, one after the other. The crew chiefs jumped to the ground and waved the Marines aboard.

Crockett drew his men close for a final word.

"We can expect some fight from these guys," he shouted, straining to be heard above the rotors. "Once we engage, you are to shoot to kill. These are enemy combatants. We don't have any room for prisoners on the ride back. Are we good?"

"Hoo-yah," shouted the Marines as one.

"All right then," said Crockett. "Let's go get us some."

37

The lecture was titled "Advances in Aesthetic and Cosmetic Treatments: A Clinical Perspective," and the speaker was to be one Dr. Michel Revy, diplomate of the Swiss Board of Plastic Surgery, FACS, member of the International Society of Cosmetic Plastic Surgery, and recipient of a half-dozen awards and fellowships that Jonathan had never heard of. The venue was not a university or a hospital but the second-floor private dining room of the Restaurant Chesery, at the southern tip of the village. A plaque by the door indicated its membership in the Chaîne des Rôtisseurs as well as a score of 18 of 20 as awarded by the *Gault Millau*. Jonathan needed only a single whiff of the richly scented air to tell him he was in culinary heaven.

A man waited by the stairs to relieve them of their overcoats. Jonathan took Danni's arm. "Which one of us is the patient?" he asked.

"Me," she said, as she slipped her hand into his and interlocked their fingers. "I need a nip and a tuck."

"Not likely," replied Jonathan, with a surgeon's outrage.

"Why, thank you, John. That's the nicest compliment I've received in years." Danni dropped her voice. "Keep your eyes on Revy. Look for any habits or mannerisms. Engage him in conversation. Turn on the recorder as soon as you get close. We're here to listen and learn. He and Balfour have been exchanging calls three times a week for a month, but that's all we know. We have no idea what Revy may have told Balfour about himself."

The dining room was already full. Jonathan's fellow guests comprised a cross-section of the international elite. In the course of twenty minutes, he shook hands with a German Graf, an Argentine cattle baron, and a Norwegian oil magnate. Jonathan was unfailingly polite. He smiled. He made small talk. But all the while he kept his eye trained on the animated form of Dr. Michel Revy as he held court in the corner, talking to a succession of pinched, pulled, and primped matrons.

Revy was of medium height, stocky, with thinning blond hair and avuncular eyes hidden behind wire-rimmed spectacles. He wore a dinner jacket and black tie. According to Connor, he and Balfour had never met. Revy's website did not offer any photos of the doctor himself, only the usual before-and-after shots of his patients. A thorough search of the Internet confirmed Revy's preference for anonymity.

At eight-thirty, the lecture began. Revy spoke for an hour about the latest procedures to halt and reverse the aging process. He began with the necessity of better nutrition, moved his way to the latest dermatological advances in acid peels and laser treatments, and finally delved into his own specialty, the field of cosmetic surgery. Each body part was covered, from the ass to the eyebrows, with plenty of before-and-after slides to make his point. Jonathan had a sense for a doctor's skills, and he didn't for a moment doubt Revy's competence. The man was a gifted surgeon, no question.

"He's a gambler," Danni had explained. "He's made a fortune and lost it ten times over. He's in debt up to his eyeballs. The banks took his homes and his toys. He owes the bad boys big-time. A few years ago he operated on the head of the Corsican Mob, and since then he's gotten a name as a knife for hire."

Revy concluded his remarks, saying, "I'm happy to speak with you personally after our dinner."

The guests applauded politely, then turned toward their place settings to await their meal. White wine was poured, a local Fendant, followed by an *amuse-gueule* of terrine de foie gras with fig and pistachio. A first course of Bouillon mit Mark, or beef broth with marrow, was followed by Kalbgeschnetzeltes nach Zürcher Art, morsels of tender veal and thinly sliced mushrooms bathed in a white wine cream sauce, accompanied by a side dish of rösti (which Jonathan had always considered to be hash browns with an attitude). A green salad was served. Waiters bearing countless bottles of Dole des Monts made sure no glass remained empty. Fruit and cheese came next. And finally, a dessert of Apfeltorte mit Schlagrahm, warm apple tart with whipped cream. Cognac and eaux-de-vie were offered. Conversation grew louder. Finally Revy rose, signaling that dinner was at an end.

"Now's your chance," said Danni. "Go get him. And don't worry about asking personal questions. You're an American."

Jonathan pushed back his chair and made his way to the front of the room. A group of fawning women had formed a circle around the doctor. Arms crossed, Jonathan waited until the women cleared away and he was face-to-face with the physician.

"Restylane," said Michel Revy.

"Pardon me?" Jonathan looked over his shoulder, thinking that someone else was the target of Revy's outburst.

"You need Restylane." Revy raised his chin as he examined Jonathan's face. "Yes, yes, yes—one syringe for your nasal labial folds and another for those terrible frown lines. You'll be amazed how refreshed you'll appear."

"Refreshed?"

"Mm-hmm. It will take off ten years. I insist you come and see me. Yes, yes."

"I will," said Jonathan. "I wanted to ask—"

Before he could finish, Revy turned his attention to a more promising client, a flat-chested woman in her fifties with flaming red hair and skin so sun-damaged it had the texture of the Dead Sea Scrolls.

Jonathan stayed close, watching and listening as the doctor poked and prodded the woman's deflated bosom with his pen and went on about the merits of silicone versus saline implants. Jonathan noted that Revy had the habit of saying "Yes, yes, yes," that he constantly ended sentences with "isn't it?" and that he couldn't let someone speak for more than five seconds without a "Hmm, hmmm, hmmm." And all this with his thick Suisse Romande accent.

"What did you learn?" Danni asked when Jonathan broke away.

"Nothing. He's too busy drumming up business. He's lined up two facelifts, a boob job, and a tummy tuck inside of ten minutes."

"Not good." Danni touched Jonathan's sleeve and led him to the stairs. "I'm leaving."

"Where are you going?"

"To Revy's hotel. Maybe I'll find something there."

"How do you know where he's staying?"

"Von Daniken told me. Grand Hotel Park. Room 333."

"Did he give you the key, too?"

"No," said Danni. "I got that all by myself." And she brushed his leg with the card key.

"How did you—"

"We didn't have time for the class about picking pockets. Maybe when you get back." She gave him a peck on the cheek and whispered, "If anyone asks, say I'm indisposed. Don't let him go until I get back. I'll need an hour."

"What if I can't delay him?"

Danni put a finger to his lips. "Shh," she said. "In this business, there are no what-ifs."

38

It was an excavation site. They had erected a large tent to protect them from the snow and the howling wind and to guard against unwanted eyes gazing down from high above. A pair of sodium floodlights cast a harsh light on the missile. The porters stood up to their knees in a ditch next to it, swinging their pickaxes in rhythmic succession. The men had been digging for an hour, and despite the cold, they had stripped down to sweaters and their dark faces shone with sweat.

"How much deeper?" asked Emma, standing with her arms crossed at the edge of the pit.

The snow had come away easily. The soil, hardened to a diamondlike permafrost, less so. The ditch was a meter deep and twice that in length, but still it wasn't large enough.

"Another half meter," answered the stocky engineer. "Or I won't be able to open the access panel."

The Boeing AGM-86 was divided into three sections. The rear third of the missile housed its power plant, a Williams F107 turbofan jet engine and fuel. The nose and forward section held a terrain contour-matching guidance system, the predecessor to GPS-based navigation systems. The payload, in this case a 150-kiloton nuclear weapon, sat in the center of the missile. Access to it was gained through a panel in the missile's underbelly.

Emma envisioned the panel swinging open, releasing the dangerous cargo. "Will it fall out?" she asked.

"I don't believe so," said the engineer. "The weapon is bolted to the interior wall. Anyhow, you needn't worry. The bomb cannot detonate until a high-explosive charge drives a pellet into the uranium core, initiating a chain reaction."

"What kind of charge are you talking about?"

"Approximately one-half kilo of plastic explosives."

A half kilo of Semtex was more than enough to obliterate everyone standing within seven meters of the missile. "And could that explode if it dropped?"

The engineer lost his smug expression.

Emma hopped into the ditch and lay down on her back. Steel rivets held the rectangular access panel in place. The rivets wouldn't be a problem. All the equipment needed to open up the missile and free the weapon sat in one of three duffel bags. There were drills and wrenches and power saws and even an acetylene torch. Earlier she'd asked the men if they'd ever worked on this kind of missile.

"Of course not," came the unworried reply. "Our expertise is in ground-based ballistic missiles. But we've studied the schematics."

The crackle of the satellite radio echoed through the tent. Emma climbed out of the ditch and answered it. "Yes?"

"How are you progressing?" asked Balfour.

"About to open it up."

"What does that mean, *about*? When will work be completed?" There was an urgency in Balfour's voice that hadn't been there an hour before.

"What is it, Ash? What's wrong?"

"You must hurry. You don't have much time."

Emma turned her back on the porters raising the picks over their heads and the engineers staring transfixed at the missile. "What do you know?" she whispered.

"Your presence has been noticed. The U.S. military is sending a team to investigate."

Emma held her tongue. The implications of Balfour's words were too complex, too far-reaching to absorb at once. Who had spotted them? How had they known where to look? And, most important, who had passed along the information to Balfour? Emma had no doubt that he knew more than he was telling, but now was not the time to press him. It was imperative to focus on matters at hand. "How long do we have?" she asked.

"The order was passed down to a special operations unit in northern Afghanistan a few hours ago. I suppose it depends on how quickly they can get a team to you."

Emma had worked with members of special operations units in the past. She knew firsthand that they could mobilize very fast. "So they could be here any second?"

Balfour offered little consolation. "I suggest you get the weapon out now."

"We're trying."

"You'll have to do better than that," said Balfour. "The Americans have an order to shoot to kill. They don't want anyone to learn about their lost nuke."

The line went dead. Emma paused to bridle her anger before rejoining the others. "Gentlemen," she said. "There is a new development. We need to accelerate our efforts. Balfour expects us back by morning. Accordingly, he is doubling your fees."

Fifteen minutes later, the porters had finished digging and both engineers had taken up position beneath the missile. The panel came off. More time passed as they exchanged wrenches for screwdrivers and back again. Bundled in oversized parkas and down-lined pants, with oxygen masks covering their mouths, they worked with agonizing slowness.

Emma stepped outside the tent. Snow like goose down fell from a low-lying cloud cover. She scanned the sky, seeing nothing, knowing all the time that when they came, it would be with lights doused. Then she heard it—the distinctive rhythmic batting of a helicopter. And a second, with the same signature. Twin rotors. Probably Chinooks. That meant a large team, at least ten operators. The Americans were loaded for bear. No prisoners, indeed.

Emma squinted, seeking out a shadow among the clouds. It didn't matter that the pilots could not make visual contact or that they were flying with night-vision goggles. The helicopters carried sophisticated infrared scanning devices that would spot their heat signatures through the densest cloud.

Dum . . . dum . . . dum . . . dum . . . dum.

The throbbing grew louder. Just then the wind gusted and she could no longer hear it. She stood stiller than she ever had, waiting for the gusts to pass, fearing that when the wind quieted, the helicopters would be upon them. But a moment later the gusts calmed and the sky was silent. The pilots had flown up the next valley.

Emma stepped back inside the protective tenting and dimmed the floodlights. "Can you get the device out in the next ten minutes?"

"We need more light."

"Out of the question."

One of the engineers frowned. "There are still seven bolts attaching it to the wall of the fuselage, and then—"

Emma grasped him by his shoulders. "Just a yes or a no."

"If I must, yes."

"You must."

The engineer went a shade paler, then barked a few commands to his thin colleague, and the men attacked their task with renewed vigor. Emma took up position half in, half out of the tent. One eye kept watch on the engineers while the other scanned the sky. She heard a yelp and saw that one of the engineers lay on his back and that a stainless steel projectile had dropped halfway out of the missile's belly and landed on his chest.

"Careful!" she shouted, nerves getting the better of her. She put her head back outside and heard the helicopters again. This time there was no mistaking it, nor the fact that the helicopters were approaching. The moment the Americans turned their infrared cameras onto her location, their screens would light up, showing red human forms against a black background.

"Anyone who doesn't need to be here, leave now. Get back to the cave and go as far inside as you can. Hurry."

The porters and the guide took note of her voice and fled.

If I sound as scared as they look, thought Emma, we're in deep trouble.

She hurried to the missile. "Get the payload clear."

"It's stuck," the engineer said. "I can't free the last bolt."

Emma hopped into the pit. "Give me the wrench."

The engineer thrust the tool into her hand and pointed to the recalcitrant bolt.

Emma tightened the wrench on the bolt and gave a tug. Nothing. Then another. Still nothing. Above the wind, she could hear the batting of the helicopters. "Get out of here," she said, motioning for the engineers to scram. "I'll take care of this myself. And make sure you go at least twenty meters inside the cave. Those helicopters are looking for us. And they don't plan on asking us too many questions."

The engineers ran from the tent.

Emma lay on her back, staring into the guts of the missile. It looked like a souped-up Chevy, she thought. One of those cars that Jonathan always dreamed of having. A '68 SS Camaro with a racing stripe down the hood. She laughed grimly. This was hardly the moment to be reminiscing. She tried the wrench again, to no avail.

"Sod it all." Drawing her pistol, she placed the barrel a few centimeters from the bolt, shielded her eyes, and pulled the trigger. The bolt shattered as the bullet passed through the steel skin. The warhead dropped from its carriage onto her chest, crushing her. Gasping, she rolled it one way while rolling her body another. The warhead slid onto the dirt.

The nuclear weapon was encased in stainless steel and measured one meter in length. It was shaped like a bullet, rounded at one side and wider at the shoulders. A litany of serial numbers ran along the side, but there were no warnings except a small yellow-and-black radioactivity symbol. Anyone who got this close to a nuke didn't need to be reminded to be careful.

Emma slid from beneath the missile and hefted the bomb onto the lip of the ditch. It weighed at least forty kilos, and she needed all her strength to maneuver it to the door of the tent. The helicopters were closer, and though the wind was driving the snow horizontally and the Gore-Tex was snapping wildly, she could make out the pitch of the two aircraft. It was impossible to tell where they were. Noise traveled strangely in the mountains. Close enough, thought Emma.

Still her feet did not propel her out of the tent toward the cave. She felt the weight in her hands dragging her down. She considered carrying the warhead outside and sitting down on top of it to wait. She wouldn't feel a thing when the machine gun bullets struck her. Existence would simply end. Death was not always the worst tragedy. The bomb would be discovered and whisked to safety. Her last act would be seen as having spared thousands of lives and forestalling untold misery.

Then she thought of the crimes committed against her, the individuals who had perpetrated them, and what they would do to others. She thought about Balfour and the money he owed her. Finally she thought about herself and the future.

With a grunt, she lifted the weapon and carried it through the snow toward the safety of the cave. She couldn't help but look at the sky. The helicopters were so close she could feel the concussion of their rotors.

39

The Grand Hotel Park sat on a wooded knoll, a giant's chalet built of dark pine with fairy lights dancing below its eaves and loaves of snow weighing down the roof. The Park was another of Gstaad's five-star ultra-luxe hostelries. The nouveaux riches chose the Palace. The filthy rich chose the Park.

"You're certain he's alone?" Danni sat in the passenger seat of the van, staring at the hotel's festive facade. "I don't want any surprises."

Marcus von Daniken handed her a copy of the registration form. "Dr. Michel Revy. Party of one. No wife. No consort. No dog."

Danni pulled a black sweater over her dress and exchanged her heels for crepe-soled shoes. "You're sure it will hold?" she said, slipping on a pair of climbing gloves.

Von Daniken shot her a glance.

A last flurry of activity as Danni tucked her hair beneath a watch cap. "Wait here."

"I'm a policeman, not a taxi service."

"Do as you're told, Marcus. There's a good boy."

Without another word she climbed out of the van and ran through the woods toward the hotel. Security at luxury establishments was stringent. With only ninety-nine rooms, the Park's clientele was not large. Staff members were trained to recognize their guests. Danni couldn't risk being questioned.

Reaching the south side of the building, she grasped a drainpipe and gave it a tug for good measure. Solid. This was Switzerland. No doubt there was a federally licensed drainpipe inspector. She climbed to the first floor. There was no terrace, just a large twin window overlooking the forest. Von Daniken had promised it would be unlocked. Wedging a foot between the pipe and the building, she leaned to her right and slipped the blade of her work knife into the seam. The window swung open. With the grace of a gymnast, she reached a foot to the sill, then a hand, and a moment later she was standing safely inside the hotel.

"There are no cameras in the guest halls," von Daniken had told her. "The clients like their privacy. But watch out for the cleaning staff. They're like hawks."

Danni found the emergency staircase and ran up two flights to the third floor. She ducked her head into the hall and observed that it was empty. Room 333 was a corner suite. She walked briskly to the door. Voices echoed in the hall behind her. Guests? Maids? She kept her head down and slid the card key through the reader. A woman laughed drunkenly. Guests—maids didn't drink. The door opened and Danni stepped inside.

From her fanny pack she took a penlight and commenced a survey of Revy's quarters. Turn-down service had been completed. A terrycloth robe lay on the plump duvet, a pair of slippers on the floor below it. Instead of a chocolate on the pillow, there was a trio of miniature pastries on the nightstand. Classical music played softly. She moved from dresser to closet to desk, searching for papers and personal documents. A laptop sat open on the desk. She hit Enter. The screen blazed to life, and she noted that the computer was connected to the Internet.

A check of the browsing history showed that Revy had been perusing the society pages for background information on his guests. Every man a spy, she thought. She continued past addresses for online poker, the Bellagio Hotel sports book, and English off-track wagering, stopping when she saw instructions for Web searches on "Ashok Armitraj" and "Lord Balfour" and "tourist risk in Pakistan."

The last address was for Emirates Airlines.

Double-click.

A reservation for Dr. M. Revy from Zurich to Dubai. First class, seat 2A. Onward connection via Pakistan International Airlines to Islamabad. She memorized the details as her heart beat faster and a voice protested inside her head. *Too soon.*

Danni exited from the browser and surveyed the desktop screen. In the search window, she typed "Balfour Armitraj." A list of files appeared, including one titled "Armitraj Medical History." Slipping a flash drive into the laptop, she copied all files relating to the Indian arms merchant. She wasn't done with Revy's laptop yet.

The transfer completed, she opened a spyware program called Remora. Remora was the real reason for her late-night visit. Like the fish it was named after, Remora latched on to its host and followed it wherever it went. In this case, that meant piggybacking Revy's every use of the computer—word processing, Web browsing, and, most important, e-mail—and transmitting the information via the computer's wireless hardware to Division. Each time he wrote a letter or consulted a document, a record of the changes he made would travel to Washington. Each time he logged on to the Internet, Connor would know what sites he visited and for how long. Every time the good doctor wrote or received an e-mail, Connor would know that, too.

The program downloaded in ten seconds, and ten seconds after that, Danni ejected the flash drive and slipped it into her pocket.

She stood for a moment, listening. The hotel was as quiet as the grave. She checked her watch. She needed to hurry.

There was one paper she'd yet to find.

Danni returned to the closet and went through Revy's jackets and pants. Nothing. She checked behind the bathroom door. Again nothing. She discovered his briefcase beneath the bed. She slid it toward her and defeated the spring locks without difficulty. The briefcase was filled with papers, files, and brochures, all arranged neatly. Revy's passport peeked from a pocket. She slipped it out and laid it on the floor, open to the personal information page. She attached a biometric scanner to the power slot of her phone and ran the passport's security strip through it, stealing Revy's vital data, a nifty little trick known as "cloning." Page by page, she photographed all the immigration stamps. Finished, she turned to the papers and files in the briefcase and reviewed them methodically as the clock ticked in her mind.

She found what she was looking for in a manila folder marked with a crisp white label: "Pakistan: Travel Documents." Inside was a tourist visa with one passport-sized photograph attached. She slid it into her pocket.

She replaced the briefcase and stood, checking to make sure that she'd left no trace of her visit. Satisfied that the room was exactly as she'd found it, she went to the door and peered through the spyglass. The corridor was empty.

Three minutes later she was sitting next to von Daniken as he drove the van down the hill.

"Trouble," she said.

"What is it?"

"He's leaving sooner than we expected."

"When?"

Danni told him and von Daniken frowned, understanding the problem instantly. "Is Ransom ready?" he asked, with skepticism.

Danni shrugged and gave him a look that professionals understood the world over. It said that there was never enough time for training. "Right now he needs a Swiss passport," she said, handing him Revy's Pakistani visa. "*Schnell.*"

"*Einverstanden,*" said von Daniken.

Understood.

40

The CH-47 Chinook helicopters navigated the narrow mountain corridor with difficulty, advancing side by side through snow and clouds like two lost brothers. Visibility was down to thirty meters, with intermittent whiteout. Traveling at a forward ground speed of 180 knots, the pilots were essentially flying blind. Night-vision goggles did not help. The pilots relied on their instruments and their training, and hoped to God that there was an angel on their shoulders.

Captain Kyle Crockett sat alongside the crew chief, his eyes glued to a monitor showing a view of the ground below as translated by the infrared cameras situated beneath the helicopter's nose. A second screen displayed a detailed topographic map of the same area, with an icon indicating their current position.

The pilot spoke in Crockett's headphones. "We're passing over the coordinates where the bad guys were spotted this morning. See anything?"

"Nothing," said Crockett, staring at a field of black.

The chopper hit an air pocket and dropped ten meters in a millisecond, jarring the Marines sitting on their rucksacks and sending Crockett's stomach into the roof of his mouth.

"Weather's getting ugly," said the pilot. "I can give you twenty minutes on-site, then we're out of here. Landing is out of the question. You spot the enemy combatants. We've got to take them out from the air."

Crockett consulted the map. The valley below ran in a northerly direction for another ten klicks, then split into two branches, one running east toward the Afghan border, the other west into Pakistan.

"Stay on this bearing, then follow the valley to the east," he said. "If they're heading into our neck of the woods, that's their best route."

Crockett wrapped his fingers around the cargo netting as the helicopter banked to the left. For ten minutes he stared at the black screen, his heart jumping at the slightest flash of color. Never once did he see anything that resembled a human being, or any other living creature for that matter. It was a wasteland on top of the world.

"End of the line," radioed the pilot. "We've got some monster peaks blocking our way. Ready to go home?"

"Negative," said Crockett. "Try the other valley. They can't have gotten far in this storm."

"Ten minutes, captain."

"Roger that."

The helicopter banked hard to port as it executed a 180-degree turn. Simultaneously, a strenuous crosswind took the chopper in its grip and threw it violently up and down. Crockett clenched his stomach. He felt like a fly in a jam jar. Worse than the turbulence was the ungodly noise. The turbine engines shrieked as they fought to maintain lift in the thin air, while the fuselage groaned in accompaniment. A helmet got loose and rolled across the cabin. His men were battle-tested and airworthy, but none had experienced a ride like this. Several of his operators had already tossed their cookies. The cabin reeked of vomit and nerves. Going down in a helo was a Marine's worst nightmare. Crockett watched his gunnery sergeant buckle and let go into his barf bag.

"You okay, gunny?"

"Fuckin' A. Got to love it."

"Hoo-yah," said Crockett. "I'm gonna extend my tour as soon as we land."

"Right behind you, cap. I can't get enough of this shit. Semper Fucked."

The CH-47 flattened out and commenced its run up the neighboring valley. Crockett leaned closer to the monitor, as if by sheer will he could force a heat signature to appear. The topographic map indicated they were overflying an icefall before traversing a relatively flat stretch of ground.

A red speck lit on the screen, indicating a heat signature.

Crockett's heart jumped.

"North by northwest," he radioed the pilot, his voice dead calm. "Give me all you got."

"Ramming speed," said the pilot, as he increased the flight speed to 220 knots per hour. "You find our bad guys?"

"Too soon to tell."

Crockett didn't blink as the dot grew larger, and before long it was the size of a peanut. He noted that the shape was moving, but he was too far away to know if it was a human or an animal. The shape grew larger, and he was guessing it was one of their high-value individuals. God knew what manner of beast would be out in this weather.

And then the dot disappeared.

"What the—?" Crockett turned to his chief. "Did you see that?"

The chief shrugged. "Gone."

"What's our distance?"

"Two klicks."

Crockett relayed the coordinates where he'd last seen the heat signature to the pilot. "Take me down low."

Sixty seconds later the Chinook was hovering over the position.

"I got nothing," said the chief, scanning his monitor.

"Hit the lights," said Crockett.

"You sure?" The captain's concern was merited. Illuminating the five-thousand watt searchlight would be akin to painting a bull's-eye on the Chinook and inviting any enemy combatants in the area to take a shot. Hovering at a standstill thirty meters above the ground, the helicopters would have no time to evade even the most rudimentary shoulder-launched missile.

"We didn't come this far to go home empty-handed."

"Your call." The pilot radioed his intention to the second chopper, allowing it time to climb three hundred meters. "Lights, camera, action," he said.

A circle of light fell from the helicopter. The rotor wash combined with the storm's swirling winds to raise a blinding eddy. Even this low, Crockett had difficulty glimpsing the ground.

"Take her up a little."

The helicopter rose swiftly. The eddies died down, leaving only the falling snow to contend with. Then he saw it: a corner of pale fabric flapping madly in the wind. Looking closer, he made out the form of a large rectangular tent.

"Any warm bodies in there?" he asked the chief.

"Negative. No one's down there, unless they're dead."

"Drop an abseil line."

The crew chief tapped the exterior temperature readout. "Minus twenty Celsius without wind chill. You sure?"

Crockett nodded.

"This is gonna hurt." The crew chief opened the sliding door, and a torrent of subfreezing air invaded the cabin. He positioned the winch assembly out the door and attached a rope. "You're good to go, sir."

Crockett slung his M4 over his shoulder, wrapped his feet around the rope, took hold with gloved hands, and slid to the ground.

Ten steps took him to the tent. He pushed aside the flap with the barrel of his rifle. He scanned the area, taking in the floodlights, the pickaxes, the ditch, and the cruise missile. He placed a hand on the nearest lamp and noted that it was still warm. In an instant he registered what had taken place.

Laying down his weapon, he jumped into the pit and ran his hand along the missile. His eye quickly found the yellow-and-black symbol for radioactivity. He was a ground-pounder and proud of it; all the same, he knew what he was looking at. A motherfuckin' nuke. Sliding under the missile, he gazed up at the empty belly. The payload was missing.

Crockett left the tent and observed where the snow had been disturbed. He spotted a boot print sunk deep into the snow and another a few meters along.

"Time to exfil," said the pilot in his earpiece. "We're running low on fuel."

"No way. These guys are here. They're close."

"Two minutes, then we're leaving. Your choice."

Crockett followed the tracks a short way and stopped. The wind howled, buffeting him and making it difficult to stand upright. The topographical map indicated his position to be on the lower slope of the mountain, but visibility was so limited he was unable to see more than ten paces in any direction. He considered ordering his men to the ground to commence a search. He was certain that the bad guys could not be far away. If they were in possession of what he thought, they could not be allowed to escape the area.

Multiple factors weighed against a search: lack of fuel and oxygen, deteriorating weather, unfamiliarity with the terrain, and finally uncertainty about the enemy. He had no idea how many combatants might be near or how heavily they were armed. For all he knew, he might be leading his men on a wild goose chase or straight into an ambush.

Against that, he considered the prospect of interdicting a terrorist cell in possession of a WMD.

"That's it, captain," said the pilot. "Time's up. Shit or get off the pot."

The decision came more easily than Crockett expected. In the end, it was too dangerous. He couldn't risk the lives of fourteen men or the downing of the two Chinooks.

"I'm on my way," he said. "Just got to snap some pics for the record. The boys in D.C. are going to want to see this. Mark these coordinates and call for another team to get up here ASAP."

Crockett hustled back into the tent and began firing off pictures with his digital camera. He concentrated on the missile itself, and was sure to get close-ups of the serial numbers on the tail and the belly. Finally he crawled back into the ditch and lay on his back staring into the guts of the missile.

Inside, pressed to the wall, was a square packet the size of a pack of cigarettes wrapped in green plastic. A slim aluminum baton was inserted into the packet, with wires running to an LCD timer. He'd worked with similar devices before and knew at once what he was looking at, and that he was in danger. He hit his helmet light and twisted his head to read the display.

The numbers on the LCD timer attached to the half-kilo charge of C4 plastic explosives read 0:00:06.

Six seconds.

"Evac immediately," he radioed the pilot, amazed at how calm his voice sounded. "I'm fucked."

Captain Kyle Crockett did not try to get away. Eyes open, he watched the timer count down to zero. There was a flash, then darkness.

He felt nothing.

41

Frank Connor took the news stoically and, except for a sudden and nearly unnoticed grimace, with no outward show of emotion. He was a veteran of too many campaigns to fear that all was lost. One battle did not a war win—*or lose*. Sitting in his office, Peter Erskine at his side, he listened dispassionately as the helicopter crew chief relayed the facts of the failed mission.

"Captain Crockett radioed that he believed enemy combatants were in the vicinity just before he was killed by an explosion on the ground."

"Mine? IED? Grenade?" asked Connor. "Can you give me any more detail?"

"It wasn't no mine or grenade," said the crew chief in a slow Texan drawl. "We were hovering directly above him, telling him to get his ass back into the wagon. The flight conditions were horrendous, Mr. Connor. Half the guys had already thrown up, and Major McMurphy, our pilot, wanted to get the hell out of there. We'd used up more than half our fuel just trying to find the bad guys. Anyway, there I was yelling for Crockett to exfil and suddenly he radios back for us to get the hell out of there. He must have seen what killed him, 'cause three seconds later the place went up. Ask me, it was C4. Had that bright orange color to it. The friggin' blast nearly took us out of the sky, I kid you not."

"What do you mean, the place? Was he inside something?"

"Yessir. A tent. Didn't I tell you? That's why he went down there in the first place. There was some dang tent right there on the mountainside."

Connor shot a glance at Erskine and said, "He found the damned thing." Then, to the crew chief, "Did he tell you what was inside the tent?"

"No, sir. Didn't say anything, just that he was sure the bad guys were close by."

"Did you have any indication that the combatants were in the area beforehand?"

"We caught a blip on the infrared screen for about twenty seconds, but when we got closer it was gone. We turned on the spotlight and Captain Crockett saw the tent flapping in all that wind."

"Were you able to confirm that the heat signature belonged to a human?" asked Erskine.

"No, sir. Like I said, it was just a blip. Coulda been anything, but you tell me what kind of animal might be out in that kind of blizzard. Only a goddamned Marine's crazy enough. I'll tell you that for free."

Or my best operative, bent on retrieving a WMD, thought Connor. "Did you see anything on the ground afterward?"

"Nothing but fire. Crockett was gone, too. But there must have been something inside that tent. Our helo took a hard shot on our belly. When we landed I found a piece of steel three inches square dug into our skin. If it had hit the rotor, we would've been toast."

"Shrapnel, maybe?" asked Erskine.

"No, sir. Wasn't shrapnel. This was heavy milled steel, least an inch thick. That's all I can tell you."

Connor requested that the crew chief remove the steel and send it to Division by courier, then sat up in his chair. "How soon can you mount a mission to get back up that mountain?"

"That's up to Sergeant Major Robinson, but the weather has to clear first. Ask me, I don't see the need. Whoever was up there is long gone by now."

Connor ended the communication. It was late in the afternoon in northern Virginia. He looked out the window and noticed for the first time that it was a lovely day. He stood, thinking of Crockett and wondering what the Marine had found.

"She's got it," he said.

"You can't be sure," said Erskine. "We have no idea what was in that tent."

"I'm not in the mood for the devil's advocate routine, Pete. I haven't slept in thirty-six hours, and that boy's death is weighing on my conscience. If there was a tent on that mountainside, then Emma put it there while she was retrieving the nuclear warhead from that missile. She blew the evidence to kingdom come, just as I expected she'd do. Sometimes I think we trained her too well."

"Would you like me to call the secretary?"

Connor turned on Erskine. "And say what? One of our agents has been turned by terrorists and is in possession of a WMD? Because if I do, that is the day this agency ends. No, Pete, this is still our play. We made the decision to handle this thing. We'll do it to the end or until someone takes it away from us. I don't trust anyone else with this."

Erskine frowned sourly. "Frank, I think it's time we took this to someone higher up. Someone with more resources."

"We already had this discussion," said Connor. "Resources take time, and that's the one commodity we do not possess."

"But—"

Connor silenced Erskine with a liverish glance. "We can still get this done."

Erskine slumped in his chair. "So what's the next move?"

"Get me a plane to Zurich. I want to talk to Jonathan Ransom."

42

Seated in the passenger seat of Chief Inspector Marcus von Daniken's Audi sedan, Jonathan was immediately aware of a heightened tension in the air. It was eight o'clock in the morning, and von Daniken was driving out of Gstaad, down the valley toward Saanen. The sky was blue and cloudless. A bold sun turned snow-covered meadows into fields of sparkling diamonds. Yet one look at all the stony faces and Jonathan could be forgiven for believing he was headed to a funeral.

Von Daniken was taciturn even by his usual curt standards. He spoke to Jonathan with looks, not words. Get in. Buckle up. Sit still and be quiet. A rainbow-striped hot-air balloon lifted off from the field next to them, joining two others drifting over the peaks. No one said a word. Jonathan glanced at the rear seat. Danni met his gaze, then looked away. Like him, she was dressed in jeans, a fleece jacket, and a parka. Her jewelry was a memory. The earrings, bracelets, and wedding rings had all been packed away and left at the hotel, along with the ghosts of Mr. and Mrs. John Robertson. It was just Danni and Jonathan again, teacher and pupil, and he wondered if he'd been incorrect about her and if the attraction was not mutual.

The first indication of a change in the atmosphere had come upon her return to the restaurant the evening before. Jonathan had noticed immediately that her face was slightly drawn, her acting skills nowhere on display. Without explanation, she'd insisted they leave immediately, saying only that he needed his rest. Things were no better at the hotel. If anything, her demeanor cooled from icy to glacial. Attempts at conversation were met with monosyllabic responses. He'd woken at three a.m. to find an empty space in the bed next to him. Rising, he'd found her at the salon window, staring at the crescent moon.

The Audi left the highway and climbed a narrow country road into the forest. The asphalt gave way to hard-packed snow. Pine trees closed around them. Shadows replaced the sun. The interior of the car cooled immediately. Ahead, a steel barrier blocked the road. A sign next to it read, "No Trespassing. Property of Swiss Defense Department. Rifle Range and Storehouse."

Von Daniken left the engine idling and unlocked the barrier, needing both hands to push it out of the way. When he returned, he looked more morose than ever. For the first time that day, Jonathan felt anxious.

"I'm supposed to be taking the place of a plastic surgeon," he said. "What do I have to practice shooting for?"

"Who said anything about shooting?" Von Daniken put the car in gear and drove another kilometer before stopping in a gravel parking lot fronting a long concrete building that resembled a barracks. Another car was parked close to the entry.

"Out," said von Daniken.

Jonathan opened the door. "You coming?" he asked Danni, who hadn't moved a muscle.

"I know this part," she said. Then, softening, "Go ahead, Jonathan. I'll be up in a few minutes."

Two men stood inside a large multipurpose room. Fluorescent lights shone overhead. Some chairs were stacked in one corner. Gym mats covered half the floor. Someone had forgotten to turn on the heat. The room was chill and damp.

"This is Mr. Amman and Mr. Schmid," said von Daniken. "They're going to teach you some useful skills."

Amman was slight and blond, and his ruddy, wind-burned skin marked him as an outdoorsman. Schmid was taller and more muscular, his head shaved, the circles under his eyes accentuated by his pale skin and heavy stubble.

"He won't have a gun?" said Amman, turning to face von Daniken.
"No."

"Or a knife?" added Schmid.

"Only if he finds one," said von Daniken. "Otherwise he's going in naked."

"It is more interesting this way." Amman's eyes darted to Jonathan, and Jonathan knew that his instincts had been accurate. He was right to be afraid.

There was a table in a corner, and they had put the tricks of their trade on it. There was a ring of house keys, a ballpoint pen, a credit card, a hardback book, and several other equally innocuous objects. Jonathan looked at them and for a moment thought he'd been brought here to continue his memory work. But across the room, Schmid was pulling protective pads over his forearms, and Jonathan knew this had nothing to do with memorization.

"Catch!"

Jonathan spun, snatching the keys out of the air a split second before they struck him in the face.

"What do you have in your hands?" asked Amman.

"Keys."

"Incorrect. You are holding a deadly weapon. Take one and grip it between your index and middle finger so that the teeth extend away from your fist."

Jonathan looked down at the set of keys in his palm. "Is this necessary?" he asked, his gaze moving to von Daniken.

"I would do as you're told," said the Swiss policeman.

Jonathan gripped the key as instructed. Amman motioned him onto the mat. "You must always strike as if you have only one chance to inflict injury. One blow with maximum force. *Klar?*"

"*Klar,*" said Jonathan.

Schmid raised his padded forearms and circled Jonathan.

"One blow," repeated Amman.

Jonathan tightened his grip on the key. He struck out tentatively, and Schmid batted his fist away, knocking the keys to the ground.

"With a bit more oomph," said Amman.

"Er ist wie ein Mädchen," said Schmid, cracking a smile.

Jonathan picked up the keys and gripped the largest one between his fingers. Schmid left his arms at his sides and puffed out his chest. He shot his colleague a smug look that said, "What are we doing here with this turkey?"

Amman shrugged, resigned to his task, the more professional of the two.

Jonathan took all this in. Raising himself on the balls of his feet, he cracked his neck and rolled his shoulders. Fair warning, he thought, as Schmid stepped closer, arms still dangling at his sides, chin lifted arrogantly.

The first blow connected just under the ear, Jonathan turning the key vertically so as to shave as little skin as possible off Schmid's cheek. Before the instructor could react, before he could raise his arms even halfway to his face, Jonathan sent a left crashing into his jaw. Schmid crumpled.

"Wie ein Mädchen," said Jonathan, standing over the dazed man. Like a little girl.

"So you fight?" asked Amman as he helped his colleague to his feet. "Chief Inspector von Daniken neglected to inform us."

"You should have asked me, not him."

"You are right." Amman spoke sharply to Schmid, who grudgingly handed over his pads, then hurried to the bathroom to stanch the blood flowing from his wound. "I think we are done with the keys. Pick up the pen."

Amman showed Jonathan how to hold the pen. "Not like a knife, but like a dagger." And how to strike with it as an extension of his fist. "No slashing. Jabbing. In, out. In, out. The force coming from inside." Amman pointed to his chest, meaning his core muscles.

And when it was Jonathan's turn, he jabbed so fast that only Amman's reflexes saved him from having an eye poked out.

The credit card became a razor to cut a throat. The book, an instrument to bludgeon the victim's temple and cause irreparable brain damage.

At some point Danni entered the room. Jonathan saw von Daniken speaking to her, and for a moment she nearly smiled.

"I think it is Danni's turn," said Amman when they had finished working through the objects. "Good luck. We are amateurs. She is a pro. Be careful."

Amman and Schmid left the room. Von Daniken exited immediately afterward. Danni kicked off her shoes and walked onto the mat. "So, anything else you're hiding from us?" she asked as she pulled her hair behind her head and bound it in a ponytail. "You're a natural."

"Hardly," said Jonathan. "There was a while way back when I liked to mix it up a little. I got pretty good with my fists. The one benefit of a troubled youth."

"You, *troubled*? I don't believe it."

"Yeah, well, luckily, we all grow up." Jonathan sat down cross-legged and wiped his forehead with a towel. "So what's next? Arm wrestling?"

"Not exactly." Danni sat down next to him. "All these techniques that Mr. Amman and Mr. Schmid were showing you were primarily for self-defense. Ways to protect yourself when nothing else is at hand. That's not my specialty."

Jonathan was caught off-guard by her reticent tone. "What is?"

Danni stared straight ahead. "It turns out that I'm very good at killing."

"Killing? Like an assassin? For real?"

"We don't use that word," she said coldly, looking him in the eye. "I can do the things I trained you for. I can make dead drops and spot a tail and pick just about any lock on the planet in under two minutes. But that's not how my government chooses to use me."

"And that's not why we're the only ones in the room?"

"No."

"You're here to . . ." Jonathan allowed her to finish the sentence.

"I'm here to teach you how to kill quickly and silently."

"I'm going to Pakistan to gather information. Connor never said anything about killing."

"It wasn't an issue at that point."

"And now it is?" asked Jonathan.

"Think of it as a precaution," said Danni, but something in her eyes told him the lesson was more than that.

"Has he found out something about my wife? Is she being held against her will? Is she in danger?"

"I don't know anything about your wife."

"Then what? Come on, Danni. I mean, get real. Connor can't ask me to kill somebody. Self-defense is one thing. This is another ballgame."

Jonathan jumped to his feet and strode across the room. Danni was by his side in an instant, stopping him, taking him by the hands. "Just listen to me."

"What's there to say? The whole notion is ridiculous. I'm a doctor. I don't take lives. I save them."

"You've done it before. Connor told me."

"To protect myself."

"And in Zurich? General Austen? You shot two men dead. That wasn't just self-defense."

"I didn't have a choice."

"And what if you don't have one now?"

"It was different. There was a plane. They were going to kill hundreds of innocent people. It was happening at that instant."

"It's easier that way, isn't it? Not having time to think."

Jonathan dropped her hands and walked to the far side of the room. He needed space. Room to figure things out. He rubbed his forehead, feeling as if he were seeing things clearly for the first time. "What was I thinking? Why did I even tell Connor that I would help? I must have been out of my mind. PTSD or something. All of this— the training in Israel, the marching up and down the streets looking over my shoulder for you and your buddies, the memory games, shadowing Dr. Revy. Who am I kidding? I'm not one of you. I'm not an operative or a spy or whatever it is that you call yourselves."

Danni approached in measured paces, her eyes locked on his. She was no longer pleading. Her speech to convince had ended. She spoke slowly and calmly, as if he were a criminal who needed to be talked out of his gun. "What if we're talking about more than that? Not hundreds but thousands."

"I don't care how many people you're talking about. If he thinks I'm going to kill someone, he's lost his mind."

"And if there is no one else?"

"That's not my concern."

"Isn't it all of ours?" asked Danni. "You think this is something I like to do? I felt the same as you when I first learned my trade. I was a twenty-one-year-old woman. I knew how to shoot machine guns and run an obstacle course. But killing? The only thing I'd ever harmed in my life was a duck I shot hunting with my uncle, and I felt sick to my stomach for a week afterward. I thought, How dare they ask me to do such a thing? I'm not evil. But my teachers saw something in me. Not something bad, just something unyielding—maybe something rather cold and uncompromising. I always completed a task, no matter how difficult. I was able to remove myself from the equation and do what needed to be done. Too often it's your mind that gets in the way. You're the same as me, Jonathan. You can't leave a job undone. It's why you're here."

"I'm here because a man tortured my wife and I have a chance of doing something to prevent him and his colleagues from hurting anyone else again."

"No, that's not the reason why. You're here to see if you are as good as she is."

"That's ridiculous."

"Is it? You want to find out for yourself if you are capable of doing everything she does. If you measure up."

"No. Not true."

Danni put a hand to his cheek. "You're here because you still love her."

Jonathan pulled her hand away. He wanted to deny her words, to shout at her that she was mistaken. He couldn't. He looked away, then sat down. Danni sat cross-legged next to him. "If you have any questions, you can ask Connor yourself."

Jonathan looked at her, surprised. "He's coming?"

"He'll be here later today to give you your final briefing. You're leaving tonight."

"Tonight?"

"Eight-thirty."

"But . . ." Suddenly there was nothing more to say, and Jonathan wondered if the fear showed on his face.

Danni slid a long, slim knife from a hidden pocket in her pants. Its blade was the color of mercury. "Let's get started," she said, offering him a hand so he could get to his feet. "We don't have much time."

43

The kidnapping of Dr. Michel Revy took place at two in the after-noon on that same picture-postcard day and was orchestrated and executed by Chief Inspector Marcus von Daniken, with assistance from members of his own Service of Analysis and Prevention, the wing of the federal police concerned with counterterrorism and the monitoring of all espionage activities within Switzerland's borders.

The operation was hurried from the start, but this was nothing new. Time was rarely a policeman's ally, and von Daniken had long ago made his peace with rushed operations. Perfection was not a word in his vocabulary. He'd had twelve hours to draw up his plan, assem-ble a team, and put them into position. He would have liked another day in order to stage at least one rehearsal, but Michel Revy's sched-ule forbade it. In von Daniken's business, you worked with what you were given, not with what you wished for.

"Mobile One, pull off. Mobile Two, get in position."

Von Daniken sat parked in a shaded lay-by in the densely forested foothills on the outskirts of Bern. An insistent breeze was blowing from the north, kicking snow off the hillsides and sending it spinning and twirling in the fractured light. On his lap was a handheld tracking monitor, and he kept his eyes glued to the red dot moving along the A1 motorway in his direction. The red dot was Revy (transmitted from the homing beacon von Daniken himself had installed in the bumper of Revy's Porsche Panamera, the outrageously expensive, out-rageously beautiful sports sedan for which the surgeon owed three months' back lease payments). The three blue dots trailing the Panamera belonged to von Daniken's men. He was running a standard "three-car swing," slotting a new driver behind Revy in a seven-minute rotation.

"He's exiting the motorway," said Mobile One.

"Hang back until he gets through the village. Once he turns on Dorfstrasse, set up the roadblock. No one gets through."

In fact, the surveillance was a precaution. An e-mail sent from Revy's computer the night before and intercepted by the Remora software indicated that he was planning to drive to his mother's home that afternoon for a short visit prior to boarding a jet later that evening for Pakistan. There had been discussion about how and where to abduct him and what to do with him afterward: whether to grab him at his mother's house, whisk him from the hotel before he checked out, or, finally, kidnap him somewhere en route between the two. Some suggested drugging him and placing him in an induced coma for the duration of his captivity, others locking him in a safe house near the Gornergrat where only the crows would see him. Any option had to meet two imperatives. No one could witness the capture, and Revy could never know who had kidnapped him or where he'd been held.

In the end, they decided on the third alternative—kidnapping Revy en route to his mother's home—after field reconnaissance located a stretch of road von Daniken could commandeer and ever so briefly make his own. Afterward, Revy would be taken to an abandoned air-raid shelter in the Engadine above the town of Pontresina and be looked after by a revolving team of two guards. The coma was deemed too risky.

Von Daniken rolled down the window and turned his head toward the van with Swiss Telecom markings parked next to him. "Five minutes," he called.

The driver flicked the ash from his cigarillo to the ground, then started the van and drove up the road.

Von Daniken shifted in his seat. As was his habit before a take-down, he was suffering from a case of nerves. The fact was, he was no field man. He'd made his name investigating financial crimes before moving laterally to counterterrorism and espionage. Despite his dislike of guns and violence and all things martial, he'd found that he had a propensity for the work. It turned out that he was a sneaky bastard who could outthink and outmaneuver even the best-trained agents. But thinking was one thing and acting another. At this moment, von Daniken would have much preferred to be seated at his desk, sipping his second espresso of the afternoon and listening to his department chiefs deliver their daily reports.

The red dot veered right at the fork of Lindenstrasse and Dorf-strasse. Dorfstrasse was a two-lane road winding through forest and foothills for exactly 3.8 kilometers before reaching the nearest inter-section.

"Mobile One, what's the status of your roadblock?"

"Roadblock up," said Mobile One.

"Mobile Four," radioed von Daniken to the driver of the Swiss Telecom van. "Any traffic?" Mobile Four was charged with blocking traffic coming from the far end of Dorfstrasse and placing a repair crew in the middle of the road. The goal was to force Revy to stop without making him suspicious.

"No one in sight."

"Close down the road."

The red dot glided around a turn, with the first of the blue dots a short distance behind. Craning his neck out the window, von Daniken caught the silky howl of Revy's Porsche.

"Get on his tail," he said. "I don't want him thinking he has any place to run if he gets nervous."

Von Daniken's vantage point offered a view of the road as it curved and climbed through the forest. He caught a patch of silver among the trees and knew it was Revy.

"Mobile Four, are your men in place?"

"Road closed. No one in sight."

Von Daniken tightened his fingers around the steering wheel. Now it was up to Revy to follow the script.

The Porsche rounded the nearest bend and von Daniken was granted an unobstructed view of his prey. He was happy to observe Mobile One directly on his tail. Von Daniken started the engine and edged toward the road. Revy whipped past, followed by Mobile One. Von Daniken was astounded by how fast Revy was driving. Then again, he reminded himself, Revy knew the road perfectly. Von Daniken gunned the engine and shot into the road.

"Thirty seconds," he radioed.

"Thirty seconds," confirmed Mobile Four.

Von Daniken watched the Panamera pass the first of a series of orange cones running down the center of the road. He waited for the Porsche's brake lights to flare, the car to slow. If anything, the Porsche seemed to accelerate, its tail sliding to the left as it negotiated the sharp curve. *Verglas*, thought von Daniken. Black ice. A thin sheet of impossibly slick ice invisible to the eye. A second later, Revy had disappeared round the bend.

Von Daniken hurried to catch up. He knew what lay a few hundred meters ahead. A three-man crew dressed as laborers in grimy pants and orange safety vests gathered in the center of the road. A fourth man directed traffic. The Telecom van blocked the oncoming lane. In a country obsessed by the condition of its roads, it was a sight every Swiss could count on seeing once a day.

He came around the bend, but Revy was already out of sight, and he saw only the rear of Mobile One's sedan. *You're driving too fast*, von Daniken admonished Revy from afar, as if the doctor were purposefully disobeying his instructions in an effort to defeat his planning. *Slow down. That's an order!*

Von Daniken rounded the next curve in time to witness the accident. There were some things one could not plan for, or for that matter even foresee. And in that never-ending instant, as he watched the disaster unfold and saw his carefully wrought plan quite literally go up in flames, he knew that later, when they would meet at headquarters in Bern, some smart-ass would say that he should have known that the area was a wilderness preserve and that all kinds of animals were roaming the woods.

But for that moment, all he could do was watch.

The stag was the biggest he'd seen since he was a child in the mountains near Zinal. The deer bounded off the hillside and into the center of the road not ten meters in front of Revy's 200,000-franc sports sedan. Seeing the oncoming car, the animal froze, its head raised proudly, its magnificent rack (eighteen points at least) silhouetted against the waning afternoon sun. It was a testament to Revy's reflexes that he did not hit the buck. The Porsche veered crazily to the left, and von Daniken was certain he did not see the faintest glimmer of its brake lights as it careened off the hillside and seemingly took flight before slamming nose first into the trunk of a century-old pine and plummeting twenty meters to the stream below.

Revy didn't stand a chance, even with airbags and a safety belt. The Porsche landed flat on its back, buckling the roof. Von Daniken was out of his car in time to hear the shattered windshield tinkle onto the rocks, watch the splintered treetop spear the wreck, and spy the first flames lick from the gas tank. The explosion came a second later, enveloping the automobile. He prayed that the fall had broken Revy's neck.

Von Daniken looked on for ten seconds as the flames danced in and out of the passenger compartment. He lamented Revy's death. Maybe he even felt sorry for him. By now his men had gathered beside him. They stood like mourners gazing into the ravine, their pale, impassive faces shadowed by the specter of death. In a few minutes a police car would arrive, then a fire truck, and afterward an ambulance. Someone would call a reporter from the local newspaper. The crash was spectacular enough to merit a half-page article with color photographs in *Blick*, the country's daily tabloid. Von Daniken could not allow that to happen.

"Keep the roads blocked," he said to his colleague. "Get a cleanup crew over here on the double. This never happened."

44

The final briefing of Dr. Jonathan Ransom, newly minted operative, by Frank Connor, director of Division, took place in a sterile conference room on the fifth floor of the Executive Business Center at Zurich Flughafen. The time was six o'clock in the evening. A floor-to-ceiling window offered a view toward the piers of Terminals A and B and, five hundred meters away, like an island rising out of the tarmac, Terminal E. Planes from a dozen nations sat parked at gates, awaiting departure. Most were from Far Eastern lands and being made ready for night flights to the Orient: Thai Airways, Cathay Pacific, Singapore Airlines. Barely visible at the farthest corner of Terminal E was a Boeing 787 with the green, black, and red tail markings of Emirates. Emirates Flight 221, service from Zurich to Dubai, was scheduled for 8:30 departure, with a full complement of 248 passengers and crew.

"Here's my boy," said Connor as he entered the room and spied Jonathan standing by the window. "Christ, I hardly recognize you. What did they do to your hair? Is it blond? Glasses, too, and a suit. You clean up nice."

Jonathan smiled tightly. The only thing Connor had missed was the blue contact lenses. "Hello, Frank. How're the legs?"

"Hurt like the dickens. You're a doctor. Can't you do something about it?" Connor laughed to show that he was in good spirits, and the two men shook hands, Connor keeping Jonathan in his grip a long time and looking him up and down. "Danni taking good care of you?"

"I guess you can say that."

"She tells me you've done marvelously. Exceeded all our expectations. One of her best ever. I'm just sorry I didn't find you earlier."

"You did, actually. At least, Emma did. Isn't that the same thing?"

Jonathan sat down and crossed his hands on the table. There were bottles of mineral water at all eight seats, along with blocks of papers and pens. A sign outside the door read, "Reserved for Atlantic International Consultants."

Connor sat next to him, pulling his chair out so the two could look each other in the eye. "I apologize for the hurry. No one expected things to develop so quickly. But that's the way things are in the business."

"Is Balfour in trouble?"

"Not any more than before. Pakistanis want him out a little sooner than he expected. That's all." Connor sat down with a huff and pulled a stack of files from his satchel, making a show of checking his watch. "Two hours until boarding. We've got some time." He rapped his knuckles on the topmost file. "So, you know all about our boy?"

"Balfour?" Jonathan nodded. "I think I've got him down. Details are a little sketchy."

"He likes to keep them that way. Everyone knows he's from the slums, but he doesn't like to admit it. He's got a chip on his shoulder the size of Mount Everest. Anyway, we were able to dig up about a hundred e-mails exchanged between him and Revy. I've brought you a summary of the important stuff. Read it on the plane. When you're finished, tear it up and flush it down the toilet, page by page. Are we clear?"

"Yes, sir," said Jonathan, responding to the martial patter of Connor's instructions and discovering that he was no longer bothered by the military lingo. "We're clear."

"Apparently Balfour's set up the Taj Mahal of surgical suites over there. What he didn't know was that Revy was taking a fat commission from the medical equipment companies." A wry grin between accomplices to gauge the new operative's nerves. Jonathan chuckled, and Connor relaxed a notch. "And here's a list of Revy's recent trips: Sardinia, Rome, Paris, Athens, Kiev, Berlin. The man gets around. Memorize it. Finally, we were able to draw a set of plans of Balfour's home from the city surveyor in Islamabad. Balfour calls it Blenheim. The main building is twenty-two thousand square feet on three floors. There are several outbuildings and stables. Balfour likes to ride.

Apparently Revy served in a cavalry unit in the Swiss army. You'll see a few exchanges about Hanoverians and Warmbloods and all manner of bullshit relating to matters equestrian. How are you in the saddle?"

"I know how to get on and off a horse," said Jonathan. "But that's about it."

"You're not a rider, then?"

"Give me a saddle with a horn and I'll be fine. Otherwise, things might get ugly."

Connor frowned. "Say you've got a bum knee. Hurt it skiing. Whatever you do, don't get on the horse. We don't want to give him any reason to think you're not who you're supposed to be. Clear?"

"Crystal."

"Good." Connor spread a reduced blueprint of Balfour's home on the table. "Let's get down to brass tacks. The guest suite is on the second floor, right here. The master suite, where Balfour conducts his business, is on the third floor, directly above you. That's the nerve center of his operation. Everything we need to know, we should be able to find in there."

Jonathan studied the drawings. "Does he have guards inside the house?"

"Not guards per se, but plenty of underlings, including a six-foot-six-inch Sikh named Mr. Singh who's his majordomo, personal assistant, and hired gun."

"Sounds like he'll be hard to miss."

"He's the muscle, and he'll be keeping an eye on you. Be careful." Connor gave Jonathan a look of warning before going on. "Balfour's also got his own little harem of between eight and twelve girls. He ships them in and out every six months. Russians, English, even some Americans, I've been told. If he offers, accept. Revy's a bachelor, and Balfour's asked him a few times about what his preferences are."

"Preferences?"

"Blond, brunette, or red. The answer, by the way, is young, blond, buxom, and smooth. Don't ask me anything more about it. I'm an old man and I embarrass easily."

Jonathan caught sight of his reflection in the window. Or rather, Revy's. He was beginning to develop an intense dislike for the Swiss plastic surgeon. "Did you get him?" he asked.

Connor's eyes shot up from the papers. "Revy? Oh yeah. We got him. Not to worry. Von Daniken didn't harm him in the least. The good doctor is resting comfortably and shall do so for the immediate future."

Jonathan said he was glad, but he was markedly less concerned about the doctor's well-being than he had been a few days ago.

"We did have one setback," Connor went on. "Revy's phone was broken in the hand-off. We've got a new one for you. It has his same number, but we weren't able to transfer the information from his SIM card."

"Will that be a problem?"

"We don't think so. You shouldn't be contacting anyone once you're in Pakistan anyway. You can count on the fact that Balfour will block all calls into and out of his compound. His run-in with the Indian government has made him more than a little paranoid about people spying on him."

"So how do I pass on any information I find?"

"If at all possible, use your laptop and send it to my secure mailbox. Even better is if you get out of the compound and call. If you can't, we've got a nifty little toy that should defeat his jamming signals and allow you to place a call. Only use it if you've got important information or if you need help. We should have a team to you within a day."

"That sounds like a long time. What about Danni?"

"What about her?"

"Is she coming?"

"'Fraid not. I used up that favor. She's due back in Israel. Pressing business. I told you from the beginning you'd be hanging out there pretty far. It's no different from one of your big climbs. Once you get past a certain point, you're on your own. You've still got a chance to back out. I won't hold it against you."

"What about Emma?"

"I'm afraid I can't tell you any more about her unless you commit."

"So you've learned something?"

"We have."

The room had suddenly gone still. For once, Connor had stopped shuffling his papers and banging his fingers for emphasis and speaking in his overly loud voice. The table shook minutely as a jet took off, and Jonathan was once again reminded of being back on the USS *Ronald Reagan*. "Do you have any more idea about the information you'd like me to find?" he asked, testing the waters.

"We're still talking about a munition and the identity of the man to whom Balfour plans to sell it."

Something in Connor's voice sounded an alarm. He sounded too matter-of-fact, too coy. Or maybe it was something that Danni had said earlier in the day. *What if it's more than hundreds of lives?*

"What *kind* of munition?" asked Jonathan.

Connor held his eyes. "In or out? I think we've reached the Rubicon."

Jonathan rubbed a hand over his mouth. He thought about Danni and what she'd said about his motivation for helping Connor. He decided that she was right. He was trying to see if he could do his wife's job. But the root of his desire was more nuanced than that. It was not competition that drove him, but an ingrained sense of responsibility, maybe even guilt. Willing or not, he had helped Emma carry out too many missions to be a simple spectator. A husband had a duty to know his wife's business. Once he'd learned her true profession, his own actions had changed markedly. The past eleven months had seen his role grow from pawn to participant—in Switzerland, France, and finally Afghanistan. He'd been a fugitive from justice. He'd witnessed terrible crimes. He'd killed with his own hands in self-defense and with malice and forethought. Somewhere along the way, he'd stopped being just a husband or a doctor or a civilian and become something else. It was a testament to his own skills that Connor had recruited him. Jonathan had never known the weight of being asked to serve your country. Looking at the portly, ruddy-cheeked man in the rumpled suit seated an arm's length away, he felt something close to honor. There was a conviction in Connor's eyes that Jonathan wanted to be his own.

I save lives, he told himself. This is just a different way.

"In."

"You're sure?"

"Yes."

Connor nodded momentously, and a great sigh sent a shudder through his shoulders and his back, right down to his thick working-man's hands. "We believe Lord Balfour to be in possession of a nuclear weapon. A warhead from one of our cruise missiles lost in the mountains near Afghanistan about twenty-five years ago, to be specific."

Silence followed, as only silence could.

"A WMD?" asked Jonathan, finally.

"A nice little one-hundred-fifty-kiloton WMD in a stainless steel warhead not much bigger than a ripe summer watermelon."

Connor was still leaning forward, still staring at him a little too hard. Jonathan sensed that there was more, and that it was going to be awful. "And Emma?" he asked.

"Emma helped Balfour bring it down from the mountains. A peak called Tirich Mir."

"Tirich Mir?"

"Name mean something to you?"

"Never mind." It did, but this wasn't the time to bring up the past. Jonathan looked away, a curtain of horror falling over him. He didn't ask if Connor was sure. They were past the bullshit. Past the untruths and the posturing and the deception. This was the real deal. This was "operational," as Connor might say.

"When I learned where the missile was lost, I tasked a spy satellite to give me a close-up view of the area. I saw her with my own eyes. She was leading a recovery team to the site. I tried to get a special ops team there in time to intercept her, but the weather didn't cooperate. One of the Marines leading the mission was killed."

"By Emma?"

"She set a charge to blow up the remnants of the missile. She knew that without proof, I couldn't raise much of a hue and cry. Captain Crockett didn't get out in time."

Jonathan sat up straighter, forcing himself to speak in a measured voice. It was his doctor's voice, the one he used when delivering the worst of news. He'd learned long ago that professionalism was the first refuge of shame. "But why would she help Balfour? You told me he was present when Rashid tortured her."

"We're guessing that Balfour rescued her from the desert and this is some sort of way she's paying him back. It's my fault. We got her wound so tight she didn't know who she was any longer. The torture pushed her over the edge. If I hadn't seen her myself, I wouldn't believe it either."

"Is she there?"

"No idea. We're surmising she brought the weapon down from the mountain and delivered it to Balfour. There's no reason for her to stick around, but I wouldn't have said she'd jump ship to Balfour either."

Jonathan returned his eyes to the blueprints. He needed to focus. For the mission and for his sanity. "Any idea where on the premises it might be? The warhead, I mean?"

"I doubt Balfour will keep it in the main house. It's not the kind of thing you tuck under your pillow. My experts tell me there's no way the bomb is still functional after all these years. If Balfour wants to sell it for top dollar—and we're certain that is his intention—he's going to need to bring it back up to working condition. For that, he'll need a secure workshop away from prying eyes."

Jonathan pointed to the two outbuildings and suggested they might serve as acceptable spots. And for the next ten minutes he and Connor discussed the other places where the bomb might be kept, general security at Blenheim, and Balfour's working habits.

Then Connor fished in his jacket and came out with a small razor cartridge cradled in his palm. "See this? As far as you're concerned, it's the crown jewels, and you will guard it accordingly. Looks like a razor blade, but it's really a flash drive. All you need to do is put this in Balfour's computer for ten seconds—laptop or desktop, doesn't matter as long as it has wireless or Ethernet connection. It will install spyware on the computer and send us the entire contents of his machine and every machine it makes contact with. If Achilles built the Trojan Horse today, it would look like this."

Jonathan held the compact flash drive in his hand. He felt relatively comfortable with the parameters of his mission. He knew Pakistan fairly well from his salad days climbing in the Hindu Kush and the Himalayas. He was a doctor impersonating a doctor, so that wouldn't be a problem. Even the thought of inserting himself into Balfour's inner sanctum didn't scare him much. He'd been in arduous circumstances before and kept his cool. As a surgeon, he was constantly operating under a microscope, so to speak.

There was only one wild card.

"What if I see her?" he asked.

Connor leaned forward, making a steeple of his fingers. "Talk to her. Find out why she's doing what she's doing. See if you can get her to tell you where the bomb is. Try to bring her back."

"And if she threatens to expose me?"

Connor wrinkled his brow. "I suppose you'll have to kill her."

Jonathan said nothing. Surprisingly, no protest welled up inside him. There was no cry of indignation. Instead, he remembered the feel of the blade in his hand, the cold, heavy heft of it. Now he knew why Danni had been so insistent on teaching him how to use the knife.

But it was Connor who had the last word. "If, that is, she doesn't kill you first."

45

The two stood side by side watching Emirates Flight 221 climb into the sky. The observation deck was deserted except for an elderly woman standing at the far end of the concourse. All the same, they spoke in hushed tones. For Connor, it was habit. For Danni, it was necessity. There was no other way to mask her feelings.

"How'd he do?" asked Connor.

"What kind of question is that?" Danni snapped. "We'd hardly even begun."

"And?"

"Not bad, but not good, either. He's got a mind like a steel trap. The memorization came easily to him. He's got a fine eye indoors. If he gets into Balfour's office, he'll do a good job finding what he needs. But he's no field agent. Not by a long shot. He needs another month at least."

"Too late for that."

"It's not right. He's a rank amateur."

"Don't underestimate him."

"I'm not. You're underestimating Balfour. All those good manners and fancy clothes—it's a disguise. He's a cold-blooded killer from the worst streets you can imagine. My people tried to put a man into his organization two years ago. He lasted a month before his corpse turned up in a Pindi slum with his throat cut and his testicles stuffed into his mouth. And he was good, Frank. Sayeret. You're putting a novice with no operational experience into a gangster's household in a foreign country without any backup. How long do you think he's going to last?"

"Long enough to tell us where Balfour is keeping that warhead and who he intends to sell it to."

"Did you tell him about Revy?" asked Danni.

"I didn't think it was necessary."

"Can von Daniken keep it quiet?"

"He's working on it. So far, so good, but he's not as confident as I'd like."

"You owe Jonathan the truth."

"The truth will ruin his nerves."

"And Emma?"

"He knows what to do if he sees her."

"Think she's there?"

"I honestly don't know."

"He won't do it. She's his wife, for God's sake."

"He's killed before. I've seen that look in his eye. He's not as averse to it as you think."

"Not like this, he hasn't. You're asking too much."

"All the same, it needs to be done."

Danni put a hand on Connor's arm. "Don't make him go through with it. You can reach him in Dubai. He has a six-hour layover."

"That's not an option. You of all people should know that."

"He isn't ready."

Connor heard something in her voice. Something that he'd never heard before. "I'm sure you did a fine job, Danni."

"He needs backup. You can't just send him in there alone. He'll never get out."

Connor looked at her. The job had never sat so heavily upon him. Suddenly he felt very old and very tired. He sighed. "I never expected him to."

46

The sale took place in a one-room shack in a settlement one kilometer from the Tajikistan border. Sultan Haq's annual production of morphine paste would finance the final piece of the transaction. Outside the shack, rolling hills the color of red alkali dust stretched to the horizon. A postcard of desolation.

Inside, the atmosphere was formal but without tension. The parties had done business with one another for too many years to count. If they still did not trust each other, they had long ago settled on a grudging respect. The arrangement was far too profitable for either side to risk anything but the utmost professionalism. To make sure, each had brought a private militia of fifty men armed to the teeth.

Sultan Haq's counterparty was a man named Boris, chief of the Islamic Movement of Uzbekistan, an organization as intent on ridding its country of despotic rule as Haq and the Taliban were of their own. The two men sat facing each other across a low round table with an ornately inlaid brass serving tray, sharing tea and sweet pastry. Boris had dressed as slovenly as usual, with a sweat-stained T-shirt and a leather jacket concealing his hog's belly. Haq wore his best robes and had smeared extra kohl beneath his eyes for the occasion. He kept the Kentucky hunting rifle slung over his back as a reminder to all that, unlike Boris, he was a warrior first and foremost and a businessman only second.

"I can offer six thousand dollars a kilo," said Boris. "It is the best I can do, my friend. The market is saturated. Your country is producing twice the product of last year. It is a question of supply and demand."

Haq sat without moving, a fierce sphinx clad in black. Six thousand dollars represented exactly 60 percent of what he had earned the year before. Boris's offer was low, but he could not in good conscience consider it insulting. Production of raw opium had skyrocketed in the past year. Despite the American invasion, total opium production in Afghanistan equaled 6,100 tons, an amount so mammoth that it exceeded global consumption by 30 percent. Countering this, Haq knew that Boris had a growing market on his hands and needed every last ounce of Haq's morphine paste if he were to satisfy demand. It was Boris's practice to transport the morphine paste to his own laboratories and refine it into heroin no. 4, after which his organization would smuggle the product into Russia, where drug use was expanding at an astronomical pace.

"Nine thousand," said Haq, after much deliberation.

Boris scowled and ran a hand with bitten nails over his unshaven jowls. "Seven."

"Eight," said Haq, and thrust out his hand.

Boris grabbed it immediately. "Eight."

The deal was struck.

Boris snapped his fingers and a younger man entered, holding a BlackBerry. Instructions were given to transfer $32 million to Haq's account at a family-controlled bank in Kabul. Ten minutes later all formalities were concluded.

Haq stepped outside and placed a call. "Hello, brother."

"And?" said the deep, familiar voice.

Haq related the details of his business with Boris. "Was it enough?" he asked.

"After we pay off our tribesmen, we will be left with twelve million. That should more than suffice."

"I am pleased," said Sultan Haq. "Is everything in place?"

"The transfer will take place in two days."

"And the rest?"

"Our friend has seen to our every need. You will leave for the target directly from Pakistan. Are you ready?"

"As ready as anyone can be to become the enemy."

"Your language skills will allow you to blend in perfectly. They will not know a viper is among them."

"There are many things the Americans do not know."

"And have you chosen the final target?"

Haq looked out across the dun-colored hills of his native land. "In America, there is only one."

47

The drive to Kabul took twelve hours over tortuous roads. Haq rested in a safe house overnight. In the morning he rose and made his prayers, then prepared for the journey. A folder had been left for him. He studied its contents: maps of the target, timetables, schedules, and travel documents, including a British passport bearing a photo taken ten years before, when he was still a young man.

In the courtyard, he took a sponge bath and gingerly bathed his burns. Finished, he soaked his hands in a basin of warm water, allowing his fingernails to soften. Each represented a lesson learned on his life journey, and he clipped them with care.

Helplessness, from the younger brother who had died at three of an unknown illness.

Tragedy, from his mother, who had died a year afterward giving birth to the son who would have replaced him.

Surrender, from the boy who had died with her.

Honor, from his oldest sister, raped by the Russian invaders when she was pure; knowing herself to be dirty and unworthy of marriage, she had thrown herself into the river rather than disgrace her clan.

Grace, from his wife, the mother of his six children.

Wisdom, from his father, who had shown him how to lead men.

Humility, from the Prophet, peace be unto him.

Self-respect, from his clan, the noble Haqs, who had resisted invasion for a thousand years.

And finally, hope, from his young only son, whom he loved with a heart as wide as the Afghan sky, and who he prayed would fight for another thousand years.

He did not clip the last nail, for this represented courage, and courage was a lesson he would learn only at the very end.

Afterward, he sat in a chair while a young girl cut his hair.

"Short," he said. "But leave enough to comb."

The girl worked quickly, and in fifteen minutes her task was complete.

He shaved his beard and mustache himself, and this took longer. He had difficulty managing a comb. He had never before established a part in his hair. Inside his room, he dressed in the clothing left for him: a dark suit with a white shirt and a necktie. The leather shoes were constricting and painful.

Finished, Haq viewed himself in a mirror. It was then that he saw what he had forgotten. Dampening a cloth, he scrubbed the kohl from beneath his eyes. He stared at the reflection in the mirror, and a Westerner stared back.

Worse, an American.

He wanted to vomit.

He placed a call to Ariana Afghan Airlines. "I'd like to make a reservation on a flight this morning," he said.

"May I ask your destination?"

"Islamabad."

"Will it be round-trip?"

"No," said Sultan Haq. "One way only."

48

He had two days to live.

Lord Balfour bounded through the kitchen door and crossed the stone motor court. His stride was long and purposeful. In one hand he carried a mug of chai, and in the other a black leather crop. He was dressed for leisure, in linen pants and his favorite polo shirt, from the Highgrove team (on which Wills and Harry were regular players, along with their father, Prince Charles). Such was his buoyant mood that he'd permitted his hairdresser to straighten and part his coarse hair and to trim his mustache. He had a guest arriving, and guests were rare indeed, especially Europeans. And as he walked, he airily whistled the "Colonel Bogey March." He did not look like a man at death's door.

One half step behind followed Mr. Singh. His stride was longer and more purposeful. He did not carry a mug of chai or a leather quirt. Instead, he gripped an AK-47 assault rifle with an elongated banana clip. He was dressed for work in his everyday attire of white shalwar kameez and a Sikh's turban. He did not whistle. He grimaced. And no one had combed his hair or straightened his beard or mustache. If they'd tried, he would have killed them.

The Range Rovers had been pulled from their bays for their daily wax and detailing. They sat in the morning sun, one next to the other, an imperial fleet of gleaming white destroyers. A team of attendants stood at attention nearby. Balfour handed his mug to Mr. Singh and, straight-backed, inspected the vehicles, circling each and pointing out areas that required attention. Seeing an errant water spot, he grabbed a chamois cloth out of an attendant's hand and polished it himself. The punishment was a lash to the offending boy's cheek with his crop.

Balfour inspected the interiors as well. Remnants of polish were found on the backseat of one vehicle, a trace of ash in the ashtray of another. He made it a policy to find fault. It was the only way to keep the staff on their toes. The crop flashed through the air and found its target twice more.

Finished, he called over the chief attendant. Make no mistake, he told the young Pakistani, the work was of low standard. He was lucky he didn't have to clean the cars all over again. Balfour expected a marked improvement next time. He raised his crop, then smiled and handed the lad a $100 bill. The chief attendant bowed at the waist and spoke as he'd been taught. "Thank you, m' lord."

Only Balfour knew that there would be no next time. In two days he would be dead.

Leaving the motor court, he walked to the end of the drive and crossed Runnymede, the cricket pitch–sized meadow, to the stables. Currently he owned twelve horses. Six were Arabians, and too skittish for his taste. Two were Hanoverians and three Belgian Warmbloods. The last, his favorite, was a paint quarter horse named Sundance, given to him by the local CIA station chief six years ago as thanks for ferrying supplies for the United States military from Kazakhstan to Bagram. The grooms were lunging Sundance in the large ring, and Balfour stood on the railing to admire the fleet gelding.

"Will you be riding this morning, m' lord?" the groom asked.

"Not today," said Balfour. "But I have a guest arriving who is an accomplished rider. Have Inferno tacked up and ready tomorrow morning at ten. We may have time for a quick cross-country ride."

Inferno was a Hanoverian charger, the stable's sole stallion.

Balfour walked through the stable, rubbing the noses of his favorite steeds. In a month's time, after the authorities had given up searching for him and declared him dead, the horses would be quietly shipped to the estates of several Pakistani generals with whom he'd made arrangements. He'd miss the horses dearly.

Looking across the meadow, he spotted his girls finishing their morning jog. First came the Americans, Kelly and Robin, then Anisa,

Ochsana, and Greta. Pulling up the rear as usual was Petra, the former Miss Bulgaria and runner-up in the Miss Universe contest.

"Pick up the pace," he shouted. "Your bottom's as big as an elephant's."

Women were no different from animals. They required proper exercise, feeding, and discipline. He acquired his girls from the agency in London that supplied the sultan of Brunei. Salaries ranged from $10,000 to $15,000 a month, and the usual stay was ninety days. Food, accommodation, and gowns were provided. And the women had plenty of opportunities to earn bonuses in the form of jewelry, drugs, and cash.

Petra gave up altogether and slowed to a walk. The sight incensed Balfour. He wasn't paying her good money to turn fat and lazy. He had half a mind to use his crop on the Bulgarian laggard.

An idea came to him.

"Mr. Singh, provide our lovely Miss Bulgaria with a little motivation, if you please."

Singh lifted the machine gun to his shoulder and fired off a two-second burst. The grass behind Miss Bulgaria erupted into the air. There was a scream, and Miss Bulgaria broke into a sprint.

"That's more like it!" Balfour shouted. He jogged a few paces to lend moral support, but grew winded and stopped.

Returning along the path they'd come on, Balfour and Mr. Singh entered the security shack located at the entry to the motor court. Two guards sat before a multiplex of monitors broadcasting live pictures from inside and outside Blenheim. Since the ISI had pulled their protection, Balfour had upped all security measures. Visiting vehicles were to be parked thirty meters outside the front gates. A two-man team was stationed on the roof with Stinger shoulder-launched ground-to-air missiles. Perimeter patrols were doubled.

"They could come at any time," he announced, patting the guards on the shoulders. "Keep a sharp eye."

"They" was the RAW, the Indian intelligence service, who had sworn to repatriate their most infamous son and make him stand trial for supplying weapons to the terrorists who had stormed Mumbai, killing almost two hundred people. Rumors were swirling about a planned commando raid.

Satisfied that all was well in hand and his safety assured for the next few hours, Balfour left the security shack and walked to the maintenance building. Two guards stood by the front door. He checked both their weapons, making sure a round was chambered, the safety on, then entered the building. A second pair of guards stood by the door at the end of a long corridor. Again, he checked their weapons before opening the door.

He stepped into a large, open room with a concrete floor and high ceilings. There was no furniture, only a long steel workbench running the length of the wall. The warhead sat in a cradle hanging from chains attached to a strut in the ceiling.

"And?" asked Balfour.

The two nuclear physicists stood beside the warhead, beaming. "It works."

"You were able to successfully arm it?"

"We were."

"Outstanding."

Balfour left the workshop, returned to the main wing, and climbed the stairs to his office. He motioned for Singh to shut the door, then placed a call. "Yes," said a voice he now recognized and instantly disliked.

"Hello, Sheikh," he said to the man he had first met as Prince Rashid's guest at the Sharjah airfield, his newest and final client. "The carpet will be ready for delivery as promised."

"And it is in good condition?"

"Like new."

"I'm pleased."

"We will make the exchange at my warehouse at the Pindi airfield tomorrow at twelve noon. The price is as discussed. Will your brother be arriving as planned?"

"Yes. And he thanks you again for the invitation to stay with you.

Regarding the exchange," the sheikh continued, "have you made the arrangements we discussed?"

"Of course. Your brother will have no problem taking the carpet with him. I've seen to every contingency."

"Very good. Until tomorrow."

Balfour hung up. He checked his watch and grew worried. "It's almost ten," he said, turning to Mr. Singh. "You must leave at once. Dr. Revy's flight arrives at noon."

49

"We believe Lord Balfour to be in possession of a nuclear weapon."

Jonathan Ransom drank the vodka in one long draft. Seated in the first-class compartment aboard the Emirates flight, he stared out the window as the desert metropolis of Dubai rose to greet him. The spirits burned his throat wonderfully, and he closed his eyes, allowing its warmth to spread across his chest. It was his second flight in three days. Geographically, he was backtracking. Nonetheless, he had the real and discomfiting sensation of moving toward his quarry.

Until now, everything had been a rehearsal. Not just the past five days with Danni, but his entire life. The youth in conflict, the climbing to escape it, his redemption as a doctor, and his marriage to Emma, which was not a marriage at all but eight years of aiding and abetting a Russian-born, American-trained spook. All of it one long march, culminating in this moment. The birth of an operative.

"We believe Lord Balfour to be in possession of a nuclear weapon."

Connor's words hadn't left his mind since he had heard them eight hours before. It was quite a step up from sorting through desk drawers to find a man's name or searching dark closets for a few hand grenades. Before leaving he'd asked a hundred questions about why the government wasn't pursuing this at a higher level, why Delta Force or the Navy SEALs weren't going in instead of Jonathan, and why they didn't just drop a bunker buster or a daisy cutter or whatever they called the bombs that obliterate everything within a mile of where they hit right smack on Balfour's compound and be done with it. And Connor had answered firmly and with a rationale that Jonathan wholly understood: "Because we don't have time."

The surgeon had been called on to perform a lifesaving procedure on his nation's behalf.

Jonathan ordered a last vodka. The stewardess, a stunning, dark-hued girl from Wales dressed in her tan Emirates uniform and red pill-box hat, bent at the knee to serve him, supplying him with a fresh dish of warm smokehouse almonds.

"Will you be staying in Dubai?" she asked.

"No," said Jonathan. "I'm continuing on to Islamabad."

"Pity." She smiled, then returned to her duties.

50

No stewardess inquired if Frank Connor wanted a second glass of vodka or a dish of warm smokehouse almonds. Seated alone in the darkened cabin of a borrowed Lear, Connor stuffed the last of a Baby Ruth candy bar into his mouth and washed it down with the remnants of a Diet Coke. Below, the runway lights of Dulles International Airport lit a stripe across the black Virginia countryside. The time on the ground was two a.m.

By rights he should have been exhausted. He had been on the go for thirty-six hours and hadn't slept more than four consecutive hours in two weeks. Instead he was wide awake, as jittery as a case officer running his first Joe. It wasn't nerves, however, that made him rush down the stairs upon landing and hurry to his car without thanking the pilot. It was a growing sense of failed responsibility, a tardy realization that he had become too cynical, too jaded by half, and that he was endangering his Joe because of it.

Connor didn't doubt his decision to put Ransom into Balfour's household, ready or not. There was no other choice. The job needed to be done, and Ransom was the only asset available. Even now, he gave Ransom only a 20 percent chance of uncovering information leading to the location of the WMD Emma had brought down from the mountain and identifying Balfour's mystery buyer. Twenty percent was betting odds in Connor's game. Mostly, though, he chastised himself for having given up on his agent. Jonathan Ransom wasn't dead yet. He deserved Connor's best shot.

Connor slid into the front seat of his Volvo and steered the car onto the highway toward D.C. Traffic was light, and he immediately placed a call.

"Desk officer," said the man at the NGA.

"I need Malloy. Tell him it's Frank Connor on the horn."

"Hold on a sec."

Connor tapped the wheel, thinking how he might persuade Malloy to help him out. He knew full well that two favors were one too many. Still, if he could convince Malloy to position a bird on Balfour's estate, he just might get a picture of the warhead as it was being transited from one location to another. And that picture would be all the evidence he needed to bring in the big boys. There would be no waiting around for approval from the secretary of defense or the boys in the Situation Room. This one would go operational ten minutes after it hit the commander's desk at CENTCOM.

At last count, Pakistan possessed over seventy nuclear missiles, and the thought that one might somehow get into the wrong hands was ever-present in military planners' minds. A rogue WMD on Pakistani territory was a scenario that had been gamed a hundred times over. It was a not-so-well-kept secret that a Delta Force rapid reaction team was stationed permanently at a Pakistani base in Rawalpindi, not thirty minutes from Balfour's estate, to deal with such a scenario.

"Yeah, Mr. Connor, Malloy isn't here. Can I help you?"

"He told me he was on shift tonight."

"He was, but he didn't show. Actually, he missed coming in yesterday, too. He must be pretty sick, because he didn't phone in. Sure there isn't anything I can help you with?"

"No," said Connor. "Thanks anyway. It was a personal matter. I'll try him at home."

Connor yanked the car into the right lane and took the next exit, onto the George Washington Parkway. His night vision was poor and he was preoccupied with the job at hand. Neither condition excused him from missing the late-model sedan that had been following him at a safe but obvious distance since Dulles, which now mimicked his reckless maneuver.

Connor crossed the Potomac on Chain Bridge and drove along Canal Road, the spindly, bare limbs of the oak trees spreading a skeletal canopy above him. The sedan followed. Arriving in Malloy's neighborhood, Connor found a place to park up the street from his home.

He approached the house with measured steps, hands digging into his trench coat. The lights were out, which he thought typical for the dead of night. He rang the bell and stepped away from the door. No one answered. He heard no voices, no steps moving around inside. After two minutes, he walked to the end of the block and cut through the alley running behind all the homes. Malloy's car was parked in the space in back, along with a second car which Connor assumed belonged to his wife. A sturdy flight of steps led to the back porch. He tried the door and to his surprise found it unlocked. This was not typical for the dead of night. For a former Navy SEAL working in a classified position, it was downright unthinkable.

Connor kept his hand on the doorknob, listening for any sounds from within, but it was impossible to hear anything above the thumping of his heart. He tightened his fingers around the knob and pushed open the door. The smell hit him as soon as he stepped inside. He rushed to cover his mouth, steadying himself on the kitchen sink. It was a smell like nothing he'd known before, sour and rank and evil and altogether overpowering. He gazed out the kitchen window. Under the half-moon, the alley was as still as a grave.

"Malloy!" he called.

No answer.

Connor stepped tentatively toward the swinging door that led to the living room. He carried no weapon. There was normally little need, and he knew himself well enough to realize that he'd probably end up shooting himself instead of his assailant. The swinging door opened with a creak, and he passed through the living room. A can of soda was on the table next to a bowl of popcorn. He climbed the stairs to the second floor, wincing as the odor grew stronger.

"Malloy! It's me, Frank Connor. You okay?"

The voice bounced off the walls, and Connor felt like a rube for talking. He paused before the bedroom and took a moment to fold his handkerchief properly and place it over his nose and mouth. On the count of three, he opened the door.

"Oh Christ," he said as he caught sight of the two bodies and the smell hit him full on. He stared at the bodies for a second, maybe less, before his eyes began to water and he had to turn away. It was plenty long enough to see that it was Malloy and his wife, and that their chests had been carved open from sternum to pubis and their organs ripped out and flung on the floor. It was long enough to see the maggots writhing in the offal and to confirm what he'd known since he'd stepped into the house.

Malloy and his wife had been killed, and he was responsible.

Jake "the Ripper" Taylor stood at the entrance to the alley, keeping watch on the Malloys' rear stoop.

"He's inside. What do you want me to do?"

"Nothing for the moment."

The Ripper stared at the upstairs bedroom window. He knew that Connor was finding the bodies now, admiring his handiwork. He had a sharp, nearly uncontrollable desire to add Connor's body to his canvas. The fat man would squeal when the blade opened him up.

"You sure? I can go in and take care of things real quick. No one's gonna know."

"He's too valuable in place. Kill Connor and we upset the apple cart."

The Ripper didn't care about the apple cart. He cared about thrusting his knife deep into Connor's belly, feeling that first bit of resistance before the muscle gave way.

"See where he goes and get back to me."

"Yeah, boss. You got it."

The Ripper hated taking orders from a woman, especially a dark-skinned hottie like her. One day he was going to have his way with her. His knife would enjoy that.

51

Jonathan passed through immigration control without difficulty. The Swiss passport von Daniken had provided matched that used to obtain Revy's Pakistani visa. Asked if he had anything to declare, he shook his head and was waved through. A skyscraper of a man wearing a black turban towered among the sea of people waiting beyond the cordon outside customs control. Seeing Jonathan, he raised a hand. "Dr. Revy?"

"Yes," said Jonathan. "Good morning."

"My name is Singh. Mr. Armitraj sends his regards. He looks forward to greeting you at Blenheim. Come with me."

Singh lifted Jonathan's Vuitton suitcase as if it were a feather and carved a wide path through the milling crowd. Jonathan followed close behind. Singh's assumption that the tall, blond Westerner had to be Revy suggested that he didn't know precisely what the Swiss surgeon looked like. It was a momentary reprieve. The real test would come when Jonathan met Balfour.

Four men in identical tan suits accompanied Singh, and they formed a loose phalanx as they made their way out of the airport building. The security men weren't the scrappy, unshaven sort Jonathan was used to seeing hanging around street corners all over South Asia, looking for their next mark. They were young, fit, and neatly shaven. A jacket flapped open, and Jonathan caught sight of a compact pistol.

Twin white Range Rovers idled at the curb with an honor guard of airport police. Singh opened a door and Jonathan climbed in, the Sikh pressing in close behind, his bulk crowding the backseat, his perfectly wrapped turban brushing the roof. One of the bodyguards jumped in front and offered Jonathan a warm towel and a bottle of water.

The car left the airport and joined the highway, crossing a dun plain dotted with ramshackle huts and plots of tilled land. Smoke from a hundred solitary fires curled into the air, like a legion of genies escaping their bottles. Closer, foot traffic crowded the shoulder— farmers leading goats, merchants bearing baskets of goods, children hawking soft drinks as automobiles passed at a hundred kilometers per hour. The fallow plain gave way to asphalt. The city sprang up in fits and starts, until all at once he was engulfed in a teeming urban center, part colonial, part modern, all of it laced together by the din of extreme poverty.

The air conditioning was blowing, so Jonathan cracked the window. The scent of exhaust and open sewers and charred meat and wood smoke invaded the car. The smell was the same everywhere in the third world and Jonathan felt himself slipping into the landscape, growing at ease. The farther away he journeyed, the more at home he felt.

And then they were leaving the city, climbing into the Margalla Hills. A long, brown, unlovely lake appeared on their right. It was Rawal Lake, whose shores were the desired area of Pakistan's rich and famous, and even more of their infamous. They drove past a succession of mansions set on the lakeshore, all done in the Mogul style, smaller, drabber cousins of the Taj Mahal. The road swung to the north. The vehicles left the highway and started up a razor-straight road advancing deeper into the rolling hills. A tall chain-link fence rose in the midst of grassy fields. The vehicles drove faster. The gatehouse passed in a blur, but not so fast that Jonathan failed to glimpse the guards carrying automatic weapons or the machine-gun nests on either side of it. Farther along he spotted a black jeep bounding across the terrain, a .30 caliber machine gun mounted on its back, the men driving wearing folded safari hats. The Rat Patrol had left North Africa and come to Pakistan. There was another fence, this one electrified, according to a warning sign, and topped with barbed wire. He wasn't visiting a home but an armed encampment.

A final burst of acceleration. The vehicles crested a ridge. The road dropped down the other side, and Blenheim came into view. Connor had provided photographs, but nothing could prepare Jonathan for the scale of it, the sheer weirdness of seeing a replica of the Duke of Marlborough's famed estate six thousand kilometers from England. They rumbled over a wood plank bridge and entered the gravel forecourt. A slim, small man stood by the front door, waving exuberantly. He wore a white suit and white necktie and a red carnation in his lapel, and the wattage from his smile could light a small village.

Don't be fooled by his behavior, Connor had warned. *One minute he'll hug you and swear to you that you're blood brothers. The next he'll have his man, Singh, put a kukri to your throat and slice it clean through with a single stroke. And he'll be smiling all the time. Manners are his armor. They shield him from his enemies and protect him from his past.*

The Range Rover came to a halt. Singh opened the door and Jonathan stepped out. Balfour remained where he was, not making a move. The waving stopped and he stared hard at Jonathan, the smile still plastered to his face. *He's seen a picture of Revy,* thought Jonathan. *He knows I'm a plant. Any second he's going to tell Singh and that will be that.* But instead of panicking, Jonathan relaxed. This was what Emma had done for eight years. Never once had he caught her acting. He could do it, too.

Selecting a smile to match Balfour's, he approached his host. "'Allo, Mr. Armitraj. A pleasure!" he said in his best Suisse Romande accent.

Still Balfour didn't move. He gazed at Jonathan gravely, then signaled to Singh and spoke to him sharply. The Sikh shot Jonathan a glance, and Jonathan struggled to guard his smile. He remembered Connor saying that the good news was that he wouldn't spend time in a Pakistani prison and the bad news that Balfour would execute him on the spot. He caught a shadow from above and observed a sniper on the rooftop, a rifle pointed at his chest. Balfour's voice rose, and the security men came closer, like jackals scenting a kill. The smile grew excruciating.

Balfour shouted a final exclamation, and Singh turned and walked directly to Jonathan, halting a body's width away. "Please do not move," he said.

Jonathan readied himself, loosening his shoulders, feeling an electric jolt in his fingertips.

And then Singh reached into his side pocket, withdrew a carnation similar to Balfour's, and placed it in Jonathan's lapel. "My apologies. M' lord requested I give you this on your arrival."

"A carnation," added Balfour, striding toward Jonathan while glaring at Singh. "Symbol of Blenheim." He grabbed Jonathan's hand. "Welcome to my home, Dr. Revy, and call me Ash. None of this Mr. Armitraj nonsense. That's what the police put on their warrants. I thought we'd already gone over that."

"It is difficult for a Swiss to avoid formalities," said Jonathan, amazed that he'd found any words at all.

"One more reason why I love your country." Balfour took his arm and guided him toward the front door. "This way. I want to show you the operating theater. Everything is exactly as you specified. I hope you don't mind if we get started right away."

"Of course," said Jonathan. "But I am here for two weeks."

"My schedule has been advanced."

"No problem at all. We can have everything ready in a few days."

"Not in a few days, Dr. Revy. I'd like to undergo the procedure tomorrow evening."

"Not possible," said Jonathan, brooking no retort. "I operate in the morning. I'm freshest then. As for you, it's essential that your stomach is empty. You're not to eat a thing for twelve hours before receiving general anesthetic." The actor in Jonathan wanted to bang a heel on the ground for good measure, but the ground was gravel, and he didn't want to be melodramatic. "Besides," he said, less forcefully, "that doesn't even give us time to complete your blood work, let alone complete our consultations."

"The blood panel is already back from the lab," said Balfour. "The results are in your room."

"Oh?" Jonathan hadn't read anything about Balfour's blood work being completed ahead of time. One of the last notes exchanged between the men suggested that Revy would oversee a blood panel upon his arrival. "Excellent, yes, yes, yes," he said, summoning the verbal repetition that was Revy's trademark. "Hmmm, it's clear we don't have any time to lose."

Balfour guided him through the portico and into the foyer. As the heavy wooden door closed behind him, he saw the first of the armed men standing inside the cavernous minstrel's gallery, and Jonathan knew he had just stepped into a prison.

52

Before the surgical suite came the tour of the estate.

Balfour had dropped Jonathan's arm and strode a pace ahead through the long hallways, dropping tidbits of information about the rooms and decorations like a distracted docent. There was the library, where every book had been imported from the Duke of Bedford's residence at Woburn Abbey. There was the living room, with a portrait by Sargent and a landscape by Constable. There was the study, and in it Winston Churchill's desk from the office in Whitehall where he had written his "Nothing to offer but blood, toil, tears, and sweat" speech at the beginning of the Second World War.

He's an inveterate liar, Connor had told Jonathan. *You'll catch him out a dozen times, but don't say a word. It's his fantasy world, and he doesn't like it disturbed.*

As they continued through the house, Balfour pointed out those areas that Jonathan was free to visit and those that were off-limits. The media room was open territory, and Balfour stopped long enough to demonstrate his prowess at Call to Duty on a ninety-six-inch wall-mounted plasma screen and to boast about the ear-splitting surround-sound system.

The disco likewise was his to roam freely. It was barely one in the afternoon, but house music was blaring and three blondes dressed in beaded evening gowns and sipping flutes of champagne stood in the center of a black marble dance floor, moving their hips and trying hard not to appear bored. Balfour introduced them as Kelly, Robin, and Ochsana and told them that Jonathan was his most important guest and was to be shown every conceivable courtesy. The women offered soft handshakes and glances that left little to the imagination.

For his part, Jonathan said he was delighted and estimated that the combined work done on the three of them exceeded $100,000 worth.

But when Balfour came to a staircase leading to the third floor, he stopped cold and addressed Jonathan in a singularly inhospitable voice.

"My office is upstairs. It's where I conduct all my business and handle my personal affairs. You are to consider the entire third floor off-limits."

Never kowtow to him, said Connor. *You're everything he aspires to be. Wealthy, educated, European. He'll be looking to trump you any way he can, but don't let him. It's weakness he hates.*

"But perhaps I may wish to view some more of your exquisite art collection," said Jonathan. "Another Constable, perhaps?" ·

"All the art is downstairs."

"And if we need to speak?" continued Jonathan, knowing he'd reached a boundary and was testing its strength.

"I can find you whenever necessary," said Balfour. The smile returned, but this time to cloak a warning. "If I see you anywhere upstairs, I will have Mr. Singh kill you. Do I make myself clear?"

The outburst shocked Jonathan, and he could do nothing to conceal it. His eyes narrowed as he searched for a response, and for that instant he and Revy were one. His first reaction was to grab Balfour by his spiffy white lapels and threaten to kick his teeth in if he ever spoke to him that way again. *Cover,* urged Emma from a distant corner of his mind. *Dr. Revy doesn't get into fistfights.* Jonathan followed his wife's advice, but reluctantly. The novice spy was already chafing at the collar. So in the end he chose humor. A wealthy, educated European didn't lower himself to a South Asian bastard's level.

"But then who will there be to make your face even handsomer than it already is?" he asked.

Balfour considered this. Deciding to accept the diplomatic way out, he threw his head back and laughed much too loudly.

The two left the main wing through a back door and Balfour led the way along a garden path through a topiary of bears and deer and foxes. At the end of the topiary, the path forked. To the left was a low-slung concrete building with a shingle roof and no windows. A map of the premises had labeled the building a maintenance shed, but to Jonathan's eye it looked more like a bomb shelter. Two guards with AK-47s held at their chests stood by the door. Another Range Rover was parked nearby, doors open, and four more security men stood at the ready. There was a hubbub as two men in white jackets rolled in a piece of mechanical equipment.

"What's in there?" asked Jonathan.

"My future," said Balfour.

"Looks dangerous," said Jonathan, still smarting from their earlier exchange.

Balfour glanced over his shoulder. "Mind your own business."

It was the surgical suite Jonathan had always dreamed of. Every time a ventilator clogged and a pulse oximeter failed, whenever there were not enough clamps or even a rudimentary crash cart in the OR, he would swear to himself, close his eyes, and imagine operating in a place like this. There was a Stryker operating table and a Drager anesthesia machine as big as a dryer. There was a brand-new crash cart and a defibrillator. There was a suction machine and monitors to measure cardiac function, pulse, blood pressure, and CO_2 levels. And then there were the instruments. Arrayed on a tray was a rack holding scissors, needle holders, clamps, forceps, and hemostats, all polished to an exquisite gleam. At least one hundred in all, if not more.

"Adequate," said Jonathan, as arrogantly as any spoiled surgeon to the rich and infamous should. "I think I can make do. Yes, yes, yes."

Balfour's brow knitted in concern. "Did I miss anything? I ordered everything you suggested."

Jonathan recalled the shopping list taken from Revy's computer. "Ventilator with a HEPA filter?"

Balfour rushed to a corner of the room. "A Guardian 400."

"*Very well,*" said Jonathan. "And my assistants? You've found a trained anesthesiologist and a surgical nurse?"

Balfour explained that he had hired the chief of anesthesiology from the National Institute of Health and that the surgical nurse was the doctor's daughter. Jonathan replied that he thought that was fine. "I am a little tired," he said. "And I'll need time to read the results of your blood work. Shall we say three p.m. for our initial consultation?"

"Three is fine," said Balfour. "If you'd like, we will take a ride afterward. I told my grooms to have my favorite stallion ready."

Jonathan saw the challenge in his eyes. He thought of Connor's excuses and discarded them in a bunch. "I look forward to it," he said. "It will build our appetite for dinner."

Suddenly Balfour checked his watch and hurried from the room. "Excuse me," he said. "There's someone else I must meet."

Jonathan kept himself from following too closely. He had not yet seen Emma and was nearly insane with curiosity that it might be her.

53

Frank Connor climbed the stairs to his third-floor retreat slowly—
one step, rest, one step, rest—so as not to give his heart another reason
to expire at an inopportune moment. Reaching his bedroom, he did
not lie down and rest for his customary twenty minutes before entering his study. When the people spying on you were already inside, any
further deception was useless.

Connor poured himself three fingers of bourbon and quaffed it in
a long, desperate swallow. He was not a field man, nor had he ever
been. He was an operations man: a planner, a persuader, an organizer,
and at times a procurer. So it was with difficulty that he drove the
blood-soaked image of Malloy from his mind. The bourbon helped,
carving a soothing course down his throat, leaching his anxiety. Collapsing in his captain's chair, he forced himself to focus on the events
of the past two weeks, moving from one day to the next in an effort to
spot the mole's tracks and put a name to a traitor.

First there was Dubai and Emma's unmasking as his agent at the
hands of Prince Rashid. Peter Erskine was correct in establishing that
a handful of people had been privy to the manufacture of the booby-
trapped rifle, but fewer still knew of Emma's status as a double agent.
That number was four. There was Connor, Erskine, Sir Anthony
Allam, director of Britain's MI5, and Igor Ivanov, the Russian director
of the FSB, who was Division's most highly placed asset and the man
to whom Emma, or Lara Antonova, reported.

Connor could take himself out of the running. Likewise, Igor
Ivanov was beyond suspicion. He could not risk outing the one agent
who could out him. Allam was a possibility, but only if the leak had
stopped there. It hadn't.

The mole had likewise known about Connor's visit to Malloy at the National Geospatial-Intelligence Agency. The question was how. Had he followed Connor to NGA headquarters? If so, how had he discovered that he had visited Malloy? Or had someone told him about Connor's destination and the object of his interest?

Connor replayed his conversation with the Marine helicopter crew chief. If he dared read between the lines, he could imagine that Emma had been forewarned to expect the Marine special operations team. Only one person other than Connor had been witness to his call to Bagram Air Base and had sat with him during every agonizing minute of the operation. Peter Erskine.

The number of suspects dwindled to one.

But here Connor's exercise in deduction hit a wall. Erksine knew every detail of Connor's trip to the NGA. There was no reason for his counterparts to torture Malloy for information he himself could provide his handlers. Unless, of course, Malloy was privy to information that even Connor didn't know.

Connor rose and poured himself another measure of bourbon. No matter how compelling the evidence, he could not bring himself to believe that Peter Erskine was a spy in the pay of a foreign power. The man was a newlywed, a scion of blood so blue it was practically black, and, Connor had to admit, a damn good guy. To distrust Erskine was to distrust himself. But what other answer was there?

When you have eliminated the impossible, whatever remains, however improbable, must be the truth.

Thank you, Mr. Sherlock Holmes.

It was Erskine, whether Connor wanted to admit it or not.

And if Erskine had told his handlers about Emma and about Malloy, there was no reason why he hadn't told them about Jonathan Ransom.

Connor put down his glass and went to his desk, where he accessed his secure line and dialed a foreign number. To his frustration, no one answered. By now she was back in Israel, no doubt taking some well-deserved leave. The voicemail was a mechanical prompt.

"Danni," he said. "It's me. It's Frank. Get to Islamabad as quickly as you can. Our boy is in trouble. Call me as soon as you get this. No matter what, call me."

He hung up and called her superior at Mossad headquarters in Herzliya. He was put through immediately, only to be disappointed that his suspicions were correct. Danni had signed out for a week's leave prior to leaving Zurich. She had not left any word on her whereabouts.

Despondent, Frank Connor hung up.

He could not lose another one.

54

Jonathan unpacked his clothing with care, placing socks and underwear in one drawer, shirts in another, and hanging his suits in the
closet. The room was enormous. A tartan carpet covered the hardwood floor. The canopy bed was big enough to sail across the Atlantic,
and the ceiling was high enough for a regulation basketball net. Connor had instructed him to act as if he were being watched every second of every day. There was no need to act. A bulky surveillance
camera perched high in one corner dispelled any doubt about his privacy. Taking a towel from the bathroom, he leaped and managed to
drape the cloth over the camera's lens.

The blood panel lay inside a folder on the desk. Standing,
Jonathan studied the results, but not before starting the chronograph
on his wristwatch. A cursory study showed Balfour to be in moder-
ately good health. His cholesterol was high. Enzymes indicated a
problem with his liver. Maybe he had an ulcer. Still, there was nothing
to prevent him from having reconstructive surgery.

Jonathan put away the blood panel and crossed to a sash window
that looked down on the rear of the house. The motor court was
directly outside, and to his right lay the stables and a large grassy
meadow. To his left he could see the maintenance shed that had been
the hub of so much activity. A van pulled up to the far entrance, and
workers in blue coveralls unloaded a piece of machinery and dollied it
into the shed.

He observed this for a minute. The activity, combined with the
presence of so many armed guards and Balfour's agitated behavior,
convinced him that the arms dealer had taken possession of the
nuclear warhead and that it stood at this very moment barely fifty

meters away in the maintenance shed. He could also conclude that if Balfour wanted to move up the surgery to tomorrow evening, he expected his official business to be terminated by then, and that therefore he meant to deliver the warhead to his buyer sometime tomorrow.

An icon on Jonathan's phone indicated that there was no wireless service. Connor had been correct in assuming that Balfour maintained a strict digital net over his home, jamming all incoming and outgoing calls. Cell phones were an intelligence agency's preferred tracking system and could be hacked to act as a microphone or a homing device, or, more simply, just eavesdropped on.

Jonathan lifted the window and ran a hand over the exterior wall. The surface was rough and pitted, with smooth grooves cut horizontally into the stone a meter apart. According to the floor plans, Balfour's office was directly above Jonathan's room. The windows farther along the house looked to be about four meters, or twelve feet, above his own. He ran his fingers inside the grooves and judged them to be five centimeters deep. That was fine for his toes, but precious little for his fingers to work with.

A knock at the door interrupted his impromptu recon. "Yes?"

Before he could close the window, the door opened and two of Balfour's tan-suited security men stepped into the room. Immediately Jonathan checked his watch. It had taken security six minutes and thirty seconds to notice that the camera in his room had gone black and to arrive to investigate the cause. "Is there something you need?"

One of the men marched directly to the obscured surveillance camera. He tried twice to jump and snatch the towel, but he was too short. "Sir, you will please remove," he said.

Jonathan stood with his arms crossed. "Tell Mr. Armitraj that the only way he can watch me all day and all night is if he moves in here with me. Otherwise, the towel stays."

The security men exchanged words. One placed a call on his two-way radio, speaking in Hindi, a language Jonathan did not speak or understand. The man frowned, then bowed and left the room with his colleague, closing the door softly behind them.

"Nice meeting you, too," said Jonathan as he walked to the bed and lay down.

Just then he heard a horse neigh from the stables. The animal did not sound happy. He closed his eyes for a nap, but sleep would not come. He was thinking about his ride with Balfour and what a big mouth he had.

Balfour was dressed to ride to hounds in a guard's red blazer, white jodhpurs, and knee-high leather boots. A groom held his mount, a tall dapple-gray mare with a calm disposition. "This is Copenhagen," he said. "You'll be riding Inferno."

"The stallion," said Jonathan. "Let's have a look at him."

A groom emerged from the shadows of the stable, leading an imposing black horse with a broad chest and fiery eyes. Jonathan swallowed, and approached the animal. "Hello, Inferno," he said, touching its nose.

The horse bared its teeth, backing away nervously.

"Do you think you can handle him?" asked Balfour haughtily.

Jonathan grabbed the halter with something he hoped approached authority. "I shouldn't see why not," he said.

"Excellent," said Balfour. "Shall we?"

It was four p.m. The physical was over and done with. Balfour had passed, as Jonathan knew he would, but he was far from the model of health. His blood pressure was elevated. He carried fifteen pounds too much weight. His flexibility was terrible, and his resting pulse hovered at eighty beats a minute, hinting at below-average conditioning. He admitted to drinking two cocktails a day, but the first rule any doctor learns is to double whatever a patient tells you about booze. One look at his liver panel suggested that the two drinks a day might really be four. Still, with the right mix of statins and beta-blockers and all the other wonder drugs available for those who squandered their health, Balfour would probably live to see eighty.

A cosmetic consultation followed the physical, and Balfour was specific in his demands. In one hand he had a picture of Alain Delon and in the other a picture of Errol Flynn, and he made Jonathan swear to do his best to make him look like both of them. With the help of the latest software, Jonathan was able to create a digital facsimile of Balfour's face-to-be. It was decided to narrow his nose, place implants in his cheeks and chin, slim the lower lip, and perform a mini-face-lift. With the help of hair dye and contact lenses, Balfour would be another person entirely—at least in the eyes of the law and the increasingly sophisticated facial recognition software deployed to identify wanted criminals the world over.

The stallion, Inferno, whinnied and backed away, and Jonathan was aware of the animal's strength. "Be a good boy," he said, rubbing the horse's neck. Inferno calmed. A groom made a step with his hands. Jonathan put his left foot into it and threw his right leg over the saddle. He took the reins in both hands and squeezed his legs. Inferno followed Balfour on Copenhagen out of the stable and into the field. The stallion walked calmly, and Jonathan grew more at ease. He let his hands fall onto the saddle, but there wasn't a second he didn't wish to God there was a horn he could grab.

"I'm glad you could come," said Balfour as the two rode side by side. "I realize it was an imposition."

"Not at all. It's what I do, after all."

"You have no idea the relief. After all these years—the running, the hiding, the constant worrying if you've paid someone off or haven't, or if they're even the right person to begin with . . . Frankly, I'm glad to be leaving it all behind."

"What will you do?"

"Relax," said Balfour. "Enjoy life. Read. Maybe I'll take up golf."

"Nonsense," said Jonathan. "You're like me. You've never relaxed in your life. You couldn't if you wanted to. Your brain is too busy. You have to have something going to feel alive. For me, it's my work and gambling. I'm good at one and a disaster at the other. But do I stop? No. Stopping isn't the answer. I only work harder."

"You're right, of course. I already have a venture set up."

"Really? Are you free to talk about it?"

"Not guns this time, but chemicals. Bioweapons are the next big market. Sarin, ricin—those are just toys compared to what chemists are cooking up these days. The genius is that even a small amount of these new substances can wreak tremendous destruction. And no one has the faintest notion how to look for them. The profit margins are incredible."

"Are you working alone?"

"As always," said Balfour. "I don't have partners. Too difficult to find someone you can trust. I only have clients. You'll meet one of them tonight. We're dining together—if you don't mind."

"It would be a pleasure," said Jonathan, anxious to learn the identity of Balfour's guest.

"Just be glad you're not an American," said Balfour as he broke into a canter. "He wouldn't like that one bit."

Jonathan dug his heels into Inferno's sides, but the horse didn't respond. "Come on," he said. "Giddyup! Let's move it." Still the horse maintained its leisurely walk. Jonathan squeezed his legs hard against the flanks and dashed the reins. "Come on. Go."

Inferno stopped altogether, and Jonathan sighed. He'd been worried about falling off the powerful stallion, not it falling asleep. He kicked the horse again. The horse lurched forward and broke into a headlong gallop. Jonathan held the reins tightly, struggling to stay in the saddle. *Heels down*, Emma had taught him. *Never hug the horse if he breaks out of control. He'll only go faster.*

Inferno sped past Balfour and Balfour pushed his horse into a gallop, too, thinking it was a challenge. The gray mare came alongside and Jonathan saw Balfour standing comfortably in the stirrups, grinning at him. Inferno raced even faster and Jonathan bounced hard in the saddle, falling to one side, losing a stirrup. He righted himself and yanked the reins, but the horse was too strong for him. Inferno ran.

"He's a strong boy," said Balfour, catching up again. The mare's flank rubbed against Inferno's shoulder. The black stallion juked to the right, then regained its mad forward stride. But Jonathan continued horizontally, leaving the saddle and Inferno behind and flying through the air. He met the ground unceremoniously, landing on his shoulder and toppling onto his side.

"Quite a tumble," said Balfour, who had stopped his mount on a dime. "Are you all right?"

Jonathan stood and dusted himself off. "Yeah," he said gruffly, before catching himself. "Yes," he added in his accented voice, the Swiss doctor once more. "Fine."

"You're lucky you didn't break your neck." Balfour dismounted and helped to brush the grass and dirt off Jonathan's fleece jacket. "Inferno can be difficult to control," he added. "Especially if you haven't ridden in a while."

Jonathan met Balfour's eye but didn't respond. He rubbed his sore shoulder, finding the spot where he'd bruised the muscle.

"It has been a while, hasn't it?" asked Balfour.

"A long while," said Jonathan, as if admitting his guilt.

Balfour laughed, and Jonathan realized that Balfour couldn't care less that he'd lied about his riding skills. He was happy to have demonstrated his superiority over the European doctor in at least one domain. For a moment he could consider himself Dr. Revy's equal.

Lord Balfour whistled, and Inferno trotted back. Offering a friendly pat on the back, Balfour helped Jonathan into the saddle and suggested they walk home.

As Balfour set off, he looked over his shoulder and shook his head in disbelief. "Who ever heard of a Swiss horseman anyway?"

55

It was a thing of beauty.

Sultan Haq stared in awe at the cylindrical stainless-steel object set on the table in front of him. The device measured eighty centimeters in height and had a maximum diameter of thirty centimeters, tapering slightly at either end. A faint line barely a finger's distance from the top indicated where the device could be opened. "That is it?"

"Indeed," said Balfour. "Impressive, isn't it?"

"May I?" asked Haq, gesturing toward the reconfigured warhead. Balfour nodded, and Haq picked it up in his hands. The device was heavier than it looked but weighed no more than twenty kilos.

"Just don't drop it," said Balfour.

Haq quickly set the device back on the table.

"Actually, I'm told it's quite sturdy," Balfour went on. "Nearly indestructible, in fact. My men will instruct you in its use. Just promise not to blow us all up. I must run, but I will see you this evening, yes?"

Haq nodded, never taking his eyes off the nuclear warhead as Balfour left the workshop. "And so?" he asked, more gruffly, addressing the physicists dressed in lab coats. "How does it work?"

Haq listened intently as the scientists educated him in the use of the weapon. For all its devilish complexity, the warhead was simplicity itself to activate. The control panel was accessed by flipping open the cover. Inside were two keypads, each set below an LCD display. To arm the weapon, the user must correctly enter a six-digit code. Once the bomb was armed, it could be detonated by means of a timer or manually, with a small red button protected by a plastic casing.

"How large is the yield?" he asked, the technical vocabulary awkward on his tongue.

"Twelve kilotons," answered one of the scientists.

"How large is that?"

"Large enough that everything within one kilometer of the detonation will be instantly obliterated by a fireball with a core temperature of over ten million degrees. Within three kilometers, say twenty-five city blocks, the blast wave will ravage every structure and annihilate almost every living creature. No building will be left standing. Those that aren't killed by debris will be consumed by the firestorm. Within five kilometers, fatalities will fall to seventy percent, with those surviving sure to die from radiation poisoning within a short time. I can go on if you like."

Haq shook his head, regarding the warhead with new respect.

"Perhaps you would like to learn how to operate the timer," inquired one of the men.

"That won't be necessary," said Haq.

56

Dinner was served in the great hall. White linen napkins blossomed from crystal goblets. There were pewter plates and sparkling cutlery. A pair of candelabra supplied the intimate lighting, helped by an enormous iron chandelier overhead. Entering the room, Jonathan counted sixteen place settings. He was dressed in a blue suit and necktie, his blond hair rich with pomade and parted neatly. Dr. Revy wore his black-framed glasses for the formal occasion.

A waiter in a white waistcoat approached, bearing champagne on a silver tray. Balfour intercepted him, taking two flutes and offering one to Jonathan. "I've decided to follow your advice," he said. "We'll wait till the following morning for the surgery rather than force things tomorrow. Better safe than sorry. Cheers."

"Cheers," said Jonathan, lifting his glass in salute. "I didn't realize it was open for discussion."

"Isn't everything?" Balfour polished off the champagne and availed himself of another. "And the shoulder? Not going to keep you from operating?"

Jonathan noticed a glazed look to his eyes and wondered if he'd already ingested something stronger than champagne. "It's fine. Just a little sore. Remember, no food after six o'clock tomorrow evening. It's best to rest the day before major surgery. I hope you don't have anything taxing planned."

"Just business," said Balfour. "I'm afraid I'll be absent most of the day. You'll be on your own."

"Nothing too strenuous, I hope."

"Not unless cashing a large check falls under that definition."

Jonathan smiled. "Do you think I might have a tour of the city?"

"You'll remain here," said Balfour sternly. Then he softened, the smile arriving a moment late. "But do stay off Inferno. I can't risk anything more happening to you."

The guests arrived in a bunch, as if all let off the same tour bus. Balfour insisted that Jonathan remain at his side as he introduced them in turn. There was Mr. Singh, dressed in a white Nehru jacket and matching turban, followed by three Pakistanis named Mr. Iqbal, Mr. Dutt, and Mr. Bose, all of whom were visiting Blenheim to help with a "special project." The women came next. There were the lovelies he'd met earlier and four more whose names he forgot as quickly as he heard them. As for himself, Jonathan was introduced as "Mr. Revy from Switzerland," with no mention made of his medical diploma.

Jonathan counted fourteen bodies, but there was no sign of Emma.

A waiter whispered something in Balfour's ear, and Balfour cast a long look around the room, apparently searching for someone, before saying, "Shall we sit?"

Jonathan was placed at Balfour's right, with a blond woman named Yulia from Ukraine as a buffer. ("Young, blond, and buxom," just as Balfour had promised. As for "smooth," he would have to leave that to his imagination.) The guests took their places, and Jonathan observed that two seats remained empty, one at the end of the table, the other directly across from him.

"Ah, there you are," said Balfour, shooting from his chair and striding toward the entry. "I was beginning to wonder."

She's here, thought Jonathan, and, panicking, he realized that he didn't know what he was supposed to say. He turned his head to see the late arrival, but it wasn't Emma. It was a tall foreign man dressed in a gray suit, and Jonathan guessed that he was Balfour's client. Balfour seated the gentleman to his left. "Michel, meet my friend Shah. Shah, Michel is from Switzerland."

Jonathan said hello and the man nodded back. He was not Pakistani or Indian—his skin was too pale, his cheekbones too high. The man stared at Jonathan and Jonathan stared back, but just for a moment. There was something familiar about him, something vaguely disconcerting.

Balfour addressed his client in Dari, while the beautiful Yulia from Ukraine touched Jonathan's arm and asked if he had ever visited her country. Jonathan said that he had not and did his best to maintain a conversation while eavesdropping on Balfour and his client, whose words had quickly grown hushed and urgent.

Waiters arrived with a first course of potato-leek soup. Wine was poured by a sommelier wearing a tasting cup around his neck. Balfour took a sip and gave the wine his benediction. The sommelier moved to Balfour's guests and made ready to pour. The man named Shah raised a hand to cover his glass. Jonathan saw the long fingernail extending from his pinkie, and he feared his composure would evaporate on the spot. He knew why the face had seemed familiar.

Mr. Shah was Sultan Haq.

"Michel, have you tried the wine?" asked Balfour. "In your honor, I chose a Swiss Dézaley."

"Excuse me?" Jonathan snapped his eyes away from the curling, yellowed fingernail.

"The wine—a Dézaley. I'm sure you'll enjoy it."

"Merveilleux," said Jonathan after he drank from his glass. His accent was too thick, his response too exuberant. Any second, Haq would recognize him. He would spring from his seat and expose Jonathan as an American agent and execute him on the spot.

Putting down the glass, Jonathan anxiously resumed his conversation with the striking Ukrainian girl. He had no real idea what they talked about. He was too busy snatching glances at Haq from the corner of his eye. It was nearly impossible to recognize him without his towering headdress and beard and the kohl smeared beneath his eyes. Time passed. Haq said nothing, but Jonathan felt no relief. He was certain that Haq had shared his initial flare of recognition and was struggling to place the dimly familiar face.

"Michel, Shah recently lost his father," said Balfour. "I told him that you were a doctor and that his countrymen would do well to train more physicians."

Jonathan had no choice but to gaze at Haq. "I'm sorry for your loss," he said, seeking refuge behind his Swiss accent. "Where are you from?"

"Afghanistan," said Haq, in the same unaccented English that had so impressed him two weeks earlier. "Just across the mountains, actually. To tell you the truth, my faith in doctors does not match Mr. Armitraj's."

"Oh?" said Jonathan, staring directly into Haq's dark eyes. "Why is that?"

"A doctor killed my father."

"I'm sure he did not do it intentionally."

"What else would you call a knife across the throat?"

"Do you mean that there was an error during surgery?"

"I mean that the doctor I trusted to care for my father cut his throat."

Jonathan looked to Balfour for support. "I'm not sure I understand."

"My father was a *warrior*," continued Haq, emphasizing the word so as to leave no question about whom he was fighting against. "The Americans wanted him dead. They sent a doctor to do their dirty work. You'll excuse me if I don't share Mr. Armitraj's respect for the profession."

"I cannot comment on that, except to say again that I am sorry for your loss."

"Are you?" asked Haq, leaning closer, the eyes honing in on Jonathan's. "You are Swiss. A European. I'm sure you have the same one-sided views of my people as the rest of the West."

"I try to keep out of politics," said Jonathan.

"Even worse," said Haq, dripping with contempt. "You are without principles."

"I promise you that I have principles," retorted Jonathan. "I simply choose not to force them on others. Especially those I've just met."

"Gentlemen, please," said Balfour, a hand to either side to calm the waters.

"It is all right, Ash," said Jonathan. "Mr. Shah is entitled to his anger. Clearly he is still grieving for his father."

"My grief has nothing to do with my hatred for a people who have invaded my country on the pretext of guaranteeing their freedom when actually they seek to enslave my sisters and brothers."

"The only thing that enslaves your people is ignorance and poverty, which, from what I understand, are both conditions you promote enthusiastically."

"Really, Michel, must you . . ." said Balfour, pained.

Haq threw down his napkin. "You, sir, do not know my country, and so you have no business commenting on our policies."

"I do know that until you build schools and educate your young, both boys and girls, your country will not progress from its current lamentable state."

Haq stood, glaring at Jonathan from behind a pointed finger. "My country's welfare is none of your concern."

"Unfortunately, it is," said Jonathan. "If your politics bring chaos and ruin to your neighbors and thus instability to the world, it is everyone's con—"

Somewhere outside there was an explosion and the house shook. The chandelier swung and the lights flickered. Balfour froze, his eyes wide. The sound of gunfire crackled from outdoors. There was a second explosion, this one either bigger or closer. A window shattered in the next room and a painting fell from the wall. A heavy machine gun opened up, assaulting the eardrums, and Yulia screamed. The assembled guests abandoned the table, some running toward the door, others dashing this way, then that, and still others just standing and staring. Jonathan was back on the hilltop in Tora Bora.

"Bloody Indians," said Balfour, calmly placing his napkin on the table. "They've finally come, the cheeky bastards."

"Is it safe?" Haq was on his feet, addressing his host from a distance too close to be anything but confrontational. Any interest he'd had in Jonathan was replaced by a more pressing concern.

"It's me they want," said Balfour. "But if you'd like, I'll have Mr. Singh accompany you to the maintenance building. You can keep watch yourself."

Mr. Singh led Haq from the room as a new cascade of gunfire broke out. Balfour's two-way radio buzzed. "From Runnymede? You're certain? How many are there? Five? Ten? What do you mean you don't see anyone? Call me when you know." He hung up and turned to Jonathan. "Dr. Revy, I suggest you go to your room and lock the door. Stay away from the windows. I'll be in the security shed. Don't worry. I'm sure this will all be over in time for us to enjoy our dessert."

Another explosion rocked the house, and the lights went out.

57

Now was the time.

Jonathan stood with his back to the door, listening as footsteps pounded through the hallways and the jeeps peeled out of the motor court and the heavy machine gun he'd seen on the roof continued its basso profundo assault. He ran to the window in time to make out Balfour and Singh climbing into a Range Rover, machine guns in hand, and roaring through the portico. Balfour was no coward. Jonathan had to give him that.

Jonathan opened the window and poked his head outside. The estate was cloaked in darkness. No lights burned in the main house or the maintenance shed. Even if the security system was operational, there were more pressing concerns than keeping tabs on the visiting doctor.

And then he was moving. Jacket off. Shoes off. In the bathroom, he snapped the blade off his razor and slipped it into his pocket. Talcum powder for his hands, extra on the fingertips. He was out the window and standing on the sill thirty seconds later. The motor court was deserted. In the stables, the horses neighed frantically as the sound of small-arms fire punctured the night sky.

Extending his right foot, he wedged his toes into the groove cut into the building's stone facade. Testing his weight, he found he could support himself. He lifted his left knee and placed the ball of his foot on the lintel above the window. The lintel was ten centimeters wide, practically a stair step for someone of his skill. He stood tall and, reaching up, grasped the ledge outside Balfour's office window.

Another toehold. Right hand extended. Fingers on sill. He pulled himself higher until he could peer into Balfour's office. His toes found the next groove and he was able to support himself as he checked whether Balfour's window was open. It was not.

Jonathan struggled to lift the sash, to no avail. The motor court remained deserted, but he couldn't count on its staying that way. The next window was three meters to his left. He shimmied across the wall. This time the window opened easily.

Relieved, he hauled himself inside the house. For a moment he remained stock-still, his shirt clinging to his back. The door to the hall was closed, and he sensed that the room was empty. He slid a penlight from his pocket and activated the beam.

He was not in Balfour's office but in a bedroom decorated similarly to his own. A suitcase stood open on a luggage stand near the armoire. Inside were men's clothes—shirts, underwear, socks. On the ground was a pair of men's loafers. Very large men's loafers. He examined the clothing and noted that the labels were from foreign brands he did not know.

A Quran sat on the desk, and below it a manila folder stuffed thick with papers. A ticket jacket for Ariana Airlines lay to one side. He opened it and saw a reservation from Kabul to Islamabad. He was standing in Sultan Haq's room.

Aware that he had little time, Jonathan rummaged through the folder. There were papers downloaded from Islamic websites and others written in Pashto. There was a map of Islamabad Airport, with some numbers and letters written across the top. A letter written in a child's hand on pale blue paper demanded his attention. Though it was in Pashto, he was able to understand a few words here and there: "Dearest Father, I miss you already . . . I am sorry you will not see me grow up . . . I hope to make you proud . . . Your loving son, Khaled."

Peeking out from beneath it was a paper bearing some kind of logo: METRON, and below it HAR and NEWHA.

Footsteps pounded down the hallway. Hurriedly Jonathan closed the folder and went to the door. The footsteps faded. After a moment he cracked the door. The hallway was empty. He stepped out of the room, walked to the door leading to Balfour's office, opened it, and stepped inside.

Back pressed to the door, he directed the penlight's beam around the office. An imposing mahogany desk ran the length of one wall, with three monitors arrayed side by side taking pride of place. To one side was a rattan basket filled with used mobile phones, and above it shelves stacked with new ones still in their boxes. Cabinets occupied the other walls. And everywhere paper. Reams of paper, bundled and tied and stacked high. Balfour's records, made ready for the shredder.

Placing the penlight in his mouth, Jonathan studied the papers arrayed on Balfour's desk. Connor had told him to act as if he were a reporter. He must look for the where, when, who, and how. Names, places, dates, times. Connor had suspected Balfour had the bomb, and Jonathan now knew that suspicion was correct. Somewhere there was information regarding the buyer and the time and place of the exchange. Was Sultan Haq the end user, or was he passing it along to someone else? Was the exchange to take place at the airport?

One stack contained banking confirmations, another telephone bills, and a third credit card bills. The problem wasn't too little information, it was too much. He remembered Danni's instructions about opening his mind to see everything at once and trusting his memory to mine the valuable nuggets later. He scanned the information, committing accounts and phone numbers and transfer instructions to memory, assigning each an individual locker in his mind and ordering it to remain there until needed.

An explosion lit the sky, rattling the windows and furniture. Jonathan crouched and protected his head instinctively. Rising, he spied a large blotter on a side table. The blotter was covered with notes, but they were written in Urdu and thus incomprehensible.

He hit Enter on the computer keyboard. The monitor remained dark. Power was still out, and it seemed that the IT system did not benefit from its own auxiliary power supply. If he couldn't find anything, he'd let Connor have a try. He slipped the blade he'd taken off his razor from his pocket and held it between his fingers. It wasn't in fact a blade at all, but a flash drive encoded with the Remora spyware. The operating instructions were idiot-proof: insert the flash drive into a USB port for ten seconds and withdraw. Remora would copy the computer's hard drive and send its contents via the computer's own Ethernet connection to Division. There was only one problem. Jonathan could not find the computer's central processing unit. Wires extending from the monitor dove behind the desk and disappeared beneath the carpet. He scanned the wall to both sides but saw nothing.

Another dead end.

More footsteps sounded in the hall. The same pairs of boots. Two men, at least. Jonathan froze, and the footsteps continued past. He breathed again.

He moved back to the desk. The top drawer was locked, but a side drawer was not. In it he found a brochure for Revy's surgical practice, a matchbook from Dubai, pens, a calculator, and little else of interest. He tried the top drawer again, but it still didn't budge. The desk was old enough to have a conventional lock. No doubt Mahatma Gandhi himself had signed the declaration of India's freedom on it. He looked around for a key but found nothing. He tried a letter opener, but the blade was too wide. He trained the light across the desk. Something glimmered. It was a pair of surgical scissors. Inserting the pincers into the lock, he felt for the tumbler. This was one class Danni had forgotten. He angled the scissors up and down. Feeling resistance, he pressed harder and the tumbler fell.

Gingerly he slid the drawer open. An agenda lay on top of a raft of papers. A ribbon marked today's date. He opened to the page and read, in English, "M. Revy—Emirates Air 12:00." And on the next line, "Haq arrives. Prepare for transport to EPA. H18." He turned the page. "UAE6171. 2000. PARDF Pasha." A phone number followed with the initials M.H. He recognized the country code as Afghanistan.

He turned the page and read more details, this time about flights to Paris and onward to St. Barts. He read names and places: hotels and banks, government officials and corporate bigwigs, the entire itinerary of Balfour's new life.

His eyes strayed, and the trained observer saw something else in the drawer. A knife. Dull and gray as a shark's skin. He picked it up. An army issue KA-BAR, one side of the blade honed, the other serrated.

Another explosion shook the windows, and for an instant the office lit up. In that moment he spotted the computer tower behind a glass cabinet door. He returned the agenda to its place and closed the drawer just as an engine roared into the motor court. Car doors opened and closed. He looked out the window to see Balfour and Singh climbing out of the Range Rover.

"They can't be phantoms," Balfour was saying. "Someone is shooting at us. If it's not Indian intelligence, it's the ISI trying to scare me into leaving. Don't tell me no one's there. I want them found, do you understand?"

Jonathan rushed to the computer and, falling to a knee, ran his hand behind the unit. One USB slot remained empty. Fingering the flash drive, he struggled to slip it into the slot, but the space behind the tower was too narrow. He set the drive on the table, then leaned over and dragged the tower away from the wall.

Still kneeling, he ran a hand blindly across the table.

The flash drive was gone.

"Looking for this?"

Jonathan froze.

The voice.

It was her.

Slowly he rose from his knees and turned to face his wife. "Hello, Emma."

58

They stood face-to-face in the dark. For a long moment, neither of them spoke. Jonathan needed the time to take her in. He noticed the hair pulled back into a sleek ponytail, the windburned cheeks, the chapped lips. There was a scar on her jaw that hadn't been there before—a laceration that had required stitches. She wore a loose-fitting black blouse and jeans, and he knew they were not her clothes. He met her eyes, and the shock of seeing her hit him like a gale-force wind. Yet there was no surge of lost love, no overwhelming desire to take her in his arms. Some time ago he had forbidden himself to consider her his wife. He loved her, no question, maybe something deeper than that. Even now, her outlaw beauty thrilled him. With no distance separating them, the sound of her breathing slow and shallow, the warm smell of sandalwood rising from her skin, he was as overwhelmed by the animal force of her personality as he had been the day he met her.

"What in God's name are you doing here?" asked Emma, her whisper strangled with rage.

"I should ask you the same question," said Jonathan.

Emma tossed the flash drive onto the desk. "So Connor finally got to you. He must be very proud of himself. What did he tell you?"

"That you helped Balfour bring the cruise missile's warhead down from the mountain. That was enough."

"That must have surprised him."

"Why, Emma?"

"You mean Frank forgot to tell you? He betrayed me, Jonathan. He wanted to have me killed."

"I don't know about that."

"Then what do you know?"

"I know that you're helping a half-crazy arms dealer deliver a nuclear warhead into the hands of a very rational, very capable terrorist who will not hesitate to use it against the United States."

"Then you really don't know a damn thing at all."

"I know that Prince Rashid tortured you."

"Is that how Frank convinced you? 'Save your poor wife'?"

Jonathan's hand touched hers. "Are you all right?"

"I'm alive. Only a few new scars. Practically beauty marks in our trade, *darling*. Now, why don't you mind your own business?"

"You are my business."

"I was never your business," she flared. "It was the opposite way around. Get that through your head once and for all."

"I don't believe that."

"Believe what you want," she said, as if suddenly too tired to convince him otherwise. She shifted her weight, and her expression changed. On a dime she changed from beleaguered to ice-blooded operative. "I am curious as to how he got you inside Balfour's armed camp."

"The Pakistani government wants Balfour out. He hired a Swiss plastic surgeon to alter his features so he can disappear after he sells the warhead."

"And Connor swapped you in for him?"

"Something like that."

"So now you know what it's like to be someone else. How does it feel?"

"I don't like it much."

"Neither did I." Emma dug her chin into her throat and adopted Connor's sincere baritone. "Buck up and take one for the team, Dr. Ransom."

"Stop it." Jonathan grabbed Emma by the shoulders. "Why are you still here?"

"It was part of our deal. He saved my life. In return I helped him bring down the warhead, and now I'm teaching him how to live under the radar. I've been doing that for almost ten years. Who better?"

"Balfour's handing over the bomb tomorrow. We can't let that happen. Where is the exchange taking place?"

Emma smiled coldly, eyeing him from across their personal no-man's-land. "You're out of your depth, Jonathan."

"You didn't leave me much choice."

"You could have said no."

"That wasn't a possibility."

Emma stepped out of his grasp. "Go back to your room. Go to sleep. And when you wake up tomorrow, you'd better have a damned good reason for leaving. In fact, I'll give you one. You don't do well under gunfire. Your nerves are shot. All this excitement tonight got to you."

"I can't do that, Em."

"You're nothing to Connor. He knows you'll never make it out alive. Do you really think Balfour's going to let you walk away from here after you've altered his appearance? You—a Westerner? The color of your skin marks you as a permanent liability. You still have a chance if you go now."

"There's a nuclear warhead in that building right there. I'm not going anywhere until I get that information to Frank Connor. Where is Hangar 18? What does EPA stand for?"

Emma didn't answer.

"We can do this together," he said. "We can make it right."

"I'm not on your team, Jonathan."

At that moment he caught a look in her eye that frightened him. It was a fanatic's regard, a militant anger that had never been there in the past. Once she'd been his lover, his wife, his confidante, and his closest friend. In the space of an instant, he realized he no longer knew her. She was a stranger, and if he wanted to live, he had to consider her the enemy.

"I won't let you help him, Emma."

Her eyes dropped to the knife in his hand. "Be careful," she said. "You could hurt someone with that."

"Where is the exchange taking place?"

Quick as a cobra, Emma locked her iron grip around his hand and raised the knife to her throat. "Did they teach you where to insert the blade so I won't be able to scream? It's right here. Just below the collarbone." Jonathan tried to pull the knife away, but she was too strong. "One downward thrust," she continued. "The blade pierces the heart. Do it quickly enough and there's no time to react." She dropped her hand and raised her jaw, leaving herself open and vulnerable. "There," she said.

Jonathan yanked the knife away. In the dim light, her eyes shone like blown glass. He could smell her hair, see the beads of perspiration on her cheek. She raised her face to his and kissed him, her lips lingering on his. "Leave or I'll tell Balfour who you really are."

"No, you won't."

"Try me."

"And if I tell him you're my wife?"

Emma pushed her body against his. "You don't have the balls."

Jonathan stepped back, regarding her with horror. "What happened to you?"

Their eyes locked, and something in Emma softened. Her shoulders dropped, and she sighed. "I'm—"

The words were cut off by Balfour shouting from the motor court. "How could it be only one person?" he demanded as doors opened and slammed and boots pounded the bricks. "And we couldn't even catch him! I should have all of you shot at dawn! No blindfolds. No last cigarettes. You're all worthless! How are my guests?"

Emma glanced out the window. "He's coming inside. Go back to your room. Do as I told you. It's your only chance."

Jonathan checked the motor court and saw that it was empty. He turned back to Emma. "You're what?" he asked.

But that Emma had disappeared at the first sign of danger. Any trace of vulnerability had vanished as if it had never been. "Nothing," she said. "You'd better be gone tomorrow or I'll keep my promise. Do you understand?"

Jonathan threw a leg over the windowsill and found a foothold. Carefully he climbed down the wall.

It was only when he was back in his room and the window was closed and he was feverishly writing down all the information he'd gathered that he remembered he had left Connor's flash drive on Balfour's desk.

59

Balfour opened the door to Jonathan's room without knocking. "You are all right?" he asked. "No phantom intruders came to snatch you?"

Jonathan rose from the desk, where he had been studying Balfour's medical records. "I'm fine," he said, the picture of overwrought concern. "Is it over? What exactly happened?"

Balfour entered the room with a reticent swagger, like a warden preparing to search a jail cell. His hair was mussed, his jacket open, and a pistol dangled from one hand. "That is what we are endeavoring to discover."

"You said something about its being the Indians."

"That was my first thought. I seem to have been wrong. They would never mount such a scattershot operation. Anyhow, my problems with the Indian government are not your concern. The compound is secure. Two of my men are dead, but I am safe. There is no need to change our plans."

"Two dead? That is terrible. So it was an attack."

"An attack, yes," said Balfour. "Quite definitely an attack. We are still working out its aim."

"And it is finished?"

"Do you hear any more gunfire?" asked Balfour sharply.

"No."

"Then it is finished."

"And the surgical suite is all right?"

"Intact," said Balfour, making a slow, steady circuit of the room.

Mr. Singh entered the room behind him, his eyes locked on Jonathan.

Jonathan didn't question the intrusion. He played the frightened guest who refused to be mollified. "But there were so many explosions. Isn't this a matter for the police?"

"The explosions were only hand grenades and an RPG that took out my men on the roof. Mostly it was small-arms fire. The police do not intercede in this kind of thing. It is an army matter, but frankly, the army has no interest in protecting me these days."

Balfour skimmed the desk with his pistol, pushing aside a copy of his medical records and tilting his head to read Jonathan's notes on the pad of paper beneath it. Jonathan heard Emma telling him to find a good reason to leave. If he chose to follow her advice, the time was now. He could feign battle stress, admit that the tumult was too much for him. He could say he was a doctor, not a soldier, and ask to be put on the next plane home. Then he remembered that Revy had operated on a Chechen warlord in Grozny and a Corsican gangster under a death warrant from the national police. The Swiss doctor had logged too much time in stressful conditions for a few hand grenades and an RPG to shatter his nerves. But Revy's history was beside the point. Jonathan had committed to the mission, and he never backed out on his word.

"And you stayed here the entire time?" asked Balfour, sliding open the closet door and admiring the suits.

"Of course," said Jonathan. "I wasn't about to leave."

Balfour murmured, "Of course," while Singh maintained his baleful glare.

"So we are still on for the morning after next?" said Jonathan.

"Certainly." Balfour had moved into the bathroom and stood rifling through Jonathan's shaving kit, pretending not to be interested in what he found. "I came to tell you that Yulia is quite distraught," he called. "She will not be able to accommodate you. You would like another, perhaps?"

"No, no," said Jonathan. "I've had more than enough excitement for one night."

"No condoms," said Balfour quizzically, poking his head into the bedroom.

"Excuse me?"

"I would think that a doctor would know well enough to bring sheaths."

But Frank Connor was every bit as smart as Ashok Balfour Armitraj. He had read the correspondence between Revy and his client enough times to master the details of Jonathan's cover. Sex, he knew, was foremost on the single male traveler's agenda.

"If you need to borrow one," said Jonathan, "look in the drawer."

Balfour slid open the vanity's drawer and picked up a silver packet.

"Help yourself," said Jonathan. "I hope it's not too big."

For once, Balfour had no response.

"Good night, Ash," said Jonathan. "I'm glad that you're safe."

Balfour dropped the condom back into the drawer and walked from the bathroom.

60

Peter Erskine greeted Connor as he walked through the door to Division. "Frank, am I glad to see you. The phone's been ringing off the hook from Islamabad for the past hour. Where have you been?"

"Busy," said Connor as he made a beeline through the operations center to his office. "What's the big news?"

"The ISI is talking about a firefight at Balfour's estate."

"At Blenheim? Close the door behind you. Go on."

Erskine shut the door to Connor's office and leaned against it, arms crossed over his chest. "The ISI has been keeping a man on Balfour even though it withdrew protective custody. He said all hell broke loose about forty-five minutes ago. Small-arms fire. Grenades. RPGs. He wasn't inside the compound perimeter, but from what he saw, it was a fierce little battle."

"Any clue that it was Indian intelligence trying to snatch Balfour? The RAW's had a hard-on for him since that Mumbai thing. They probably got wind he was blowing town and finally got up the guts to make their move."

"No word. It's too early to tell."

"So that's it? Small-arms fire? A couple grenades? How long did this 'fierce little battle' last?"

"A short while, maybe twenty minutes."

Connor set down his satchel on his desk. "Hell, it was probably Balfour showing off some of his weapons."

"I don't think so. Two ambulances reportedly went to the estate."

Connor snapped to attention. "Oh? Well, did they or didn't they?"

"It's Pakistan. What looks like an ambulance might be a repair truck. Anyway, they didn't leave in a hurry."

"Meaning whoever they went to look after was dead."

Erskine approached the desk. "Have you heard from Jonathan Ransom?"

"He only arrived at the compound eight hours ago. I told him to keep quiet until he has something concrete. Find Colonel al-Faris and get him on the line. If it's our boy who was killed, I want to know it. Try him at his home, and if he's not there, at his mistress's place."

"Do you have her number?"

"It's on file," said Connor. "She works for us."

Erskine turned to go, pausing at the door. "Oh, I almost forgot to tell you. We got a response from the Brits about the picture of Prince Rashid's associate we sent over to them—the creepy guy we couldn't identify at Balfour's hangar in Sharjah."

Connor looked up sharply. "What about him?"

"They think he's Massoud Haq. Sultan Haq's older brother."

"Can't be. Massoud Haq is in Gitmo. They picked him up back at the beginning. He was a general in the Taliban army. Led a cavalry charge against a battalion from the 82nd Airborne Division. He's a crazy one, all right. He's as hardcore as they come." Connor shook his head, shuddering at the possibility. "Nah, no way it's him. He's in custody for the duration."

Erskine pushed his glasses up on the bridge of his nose. "Massoud Haq was released six months ago," he said. "I checked. The Department of Justice wrote a brief clearing him."

"What?" Connor dropped into his chair, uttering a rare expletive. "Not another one. Half the guys we're targeting these days spent time in Gitmo. Doesn't anyone realize we're fighting a war? Last time I checked, you didn't release the enemy until they surrendered." He paused and studied Erskine. "When exactly did you find this out, Pete?"

"It came in while you were gone."

Connor considered the answer evasive but said nothing. He signaled that they were done, and Erskine left the room. Connor watched him return to his desk, wondering just how long ago that had really been. Demoralized and thoroughly pissed off, he opened his satchel and took out his legal pad and his BlackBerry. He scrolled through his messages but saw nothing from Danni. He called Mossad headquarters in Herzliya and this time demanded to speak to the director of the service.

"Frank, if I knew where Danni was, I'd tell you. She's on leave. She could be anywhere. She has lots of miles racked up, you know what I mean? She's due back in six days. The girl needs her rest."

Connor hung up the phone, then placed a call to a closer destination: Fort Meade, Maryland, home of the National Security Agency, or NSA. The NSA was responsible for gathering signals intelligence from around the world. Essentially, this meant eavesdropping on every known mode of telecommunications, both terrestrial and satellite-based. His conversation was brief. He read off four telephone numbers and requested a log of all calls made to and from them for the past thirty days. The numbers belonged to Peter Erskine's private cell phone, his company BlackBerry, his home landline, and his home fax.

Treason was a serious matter, and Connor was not about to point any fingers before marshaling his evidence. Until then, he'd have to do his utmost to restrict Erskine's access to any and all information relating to Ransom's search for the warhead. There was more to it than that. Erskine was only a pawn, a single node in a larger operation. Connor was more interested in discovering whom he worked for and breaking down the entire operation. Arrest Erskine now and his handlers would shut down and go into hiding. In six months' time they'd be back, using new names and new aliases, with the same devilish intent of corrupting Division and its sister agencies within the intelligence community.

Connor followed the call to the NSA with one to an organization on his side of the Potomac, the Financial Crimes Enforcement Network, or FinCEN. FinCEN was one of the unsung heroes in the fight against terrorism. Created to investigate financial misdeeds within the United States, it had seen its portfolio increase significantly since 9/11 and was now the foremost actor in the international battle against terrorist finance.

Connor greeted his contact, supplied Erskine's Social Security number, and requested a full workup on his financial history. He was most interested in Erskine's bank accounts and asked that statements from the past six months be scrutinized with a view toward determining the identity of any person or party who might have transferred monies into the accounts. Requests like this were FinCEN's bread and butter. Information would be forthcoming within twenty-four hours.

The office phone rang. Connor finished with FinCEN and picked up. "Yeah?"

"I've found Colonel al-Faris."

"Thanks, Pete," he said. "Put him through."

A pause as the call was transferred.

"Frank—it is Nasser. It is very late here. Please tell me how I can be of assistance to my American friends."

"Hello, Nasser," began Connor. "I was interested in—" He stopped speaking in midsentence. Something had caught his attention.

A red cursor flashed on the screen of his computer monitor. A window opened, and a prompt read, "Remora 575 Active. Currently downloading 1 of 2,575 files." An IP address followed. "Time remaining: two minutes."

"Frank . . . are you there?"

"Holy mother of God," said Connor, his eyes glued to the screen. "I gotta call you back."

Remora 575 belonged to Jonathan Ransom. With amazement verging on disbelief, Connor stood motionless, watching as the files from Lord Balfour's hard drive were copied and transferred onto his own.

And sometimes your prayers are answered even as the world is falling apart around you.

61

Sultan Haq woke, alarmed.

Bolting upright, he stared into the darkness. A face stared back. Blue eyes. Blond hair. Heavy black-rimmed glasses. It was Revy, the Swiss doctor who had so freely insulted him and his country this evening.

Haq met the man's regard, despising him, as he viscerally despised all men of the West. For his privilege and arrogance, but mostly for his false, ingrained superiority. The face stared back, saying nothing, yet demanding something of him nonetheless. Haq looked more closely at him, frustration welling up inside him. And more—a nagging certainty that he was being deceived. He looked past the glasses and studied the blue eyes.

His chief interrogator at Camp X-Ray had had blue eyes, and the same blond hair. Looking into Revy's face, Haq felt himself drawn back into the interrogation room. He remembered the fluorescent lights, his captors' greedy, dissatisfied faces, the rank breath and insistent questioning, and then the hood, the abrupt tilting of his head, the last desperate breath before the torrent of water. Water in place of breath. Water in place of light. Water coming as death to carry him away on its fluid, relentless waves.

And there, high in the corner, taunting him when the hood was removed and he could breathe again, the undying television, blaring on and on, playing the same dreadful images, the dancing sailors crossing New York City, belting out cheery, hopeful songs. American songs.

Haq closed his eyes to ward off the memories, but they persisted.

Images from a different world. A barbarous, deceitful world. A world Haq swore to end.

The interrogator was a soft, weak man, but the blue eyes staring back at him in the darkness were neither soft nor weak. They were formidable adversary's eyes. And so Haq asked what it was that Revy demanded of him. For what purpose had he lured him from his sleep?

Haq believed in the power of dreams.

Revy didn't answer, and Haq knew he was baiting him, daring him to guess his secret.

Sultan Haq stared into the darkness until the face receded and there was nothing but black, and a terrible gnawing settled on his soul.

62

Emma came to him in his sleep. He felt her warmth beside him and his body responded. He touched her and she moaned. Jonathan was dreaming, of course. It was only there that he could see her as she was, or perhaps as he wanted her to be. He ran his hands over his wife's body, and he stirred as if discovering her for the first time. He saw her lying on the grass beneath him. It was night in the green hills of West Africa where they'd first met and he'd fallen irrevocably in love with her. He undid her belt buckle, yanking the leather strap free, and slid her jeans over her strong, eager hips. She parted her legs and whispered his name. *Jonathan. Love me.* A warm breath caressed his ear, his neck. His heartbeat quickened. He met her eyes, and as he entered her, she nodded to say it was all right. More than all right.

"Jonathan."

He woke with a start. Emma sat on the bed beside him, her hair down, shirt unbuttoned to the waist. "Shhh," she said as she removed her clothing.

She pulled back the sheets and climbed on top of him, back arched, eyes locked on his as he pushed into her. He gasped, and she covered his mouth with animal swiftness. She said nothing but shook her head, always watching him, her breath quickening. Light from the approaching dawn fell over her breasts, which appeared fuller than he remembered, her nipples exceptionally pert. Grasping her hips, he drove into her and she fought back, their tempo growing more rapid, more violent, Emma lowering her head, letting her hair fall on his chest, sweating now, her breathing labored, hard fought, her motions unrelenting, urging him on, demanding his attention, until he could match her no more and he surrendered and allowed himself release.

A moment later her body began to tremor and a languorous moan issued from her clenched teeth and she buried her face in his neck and expelled a long, hot breath.

"Come with me," she said, still gasping. "I'm leaving first thing in the morning. I can get you out."

"No."

"You'll die here."

"Maybe."

She pushed herself off him. "For me?"

"I'm not on your team, Emma."

"And for your child?"

Jonathan pushed himself up on an elbow. "What? You're—"

"I'm pregnant."

"How far?"

"Four months."

Jonathan sat up, stunned. "London?"

Emma nodded.

"You're sure that's when it happened?" The words came of their own volition, a reminder of his distrust. Emma slapped him very hard and slid to the edge of the bed. Jonathan stared out the window. His room faced east, and he saw the first sliver of the sun edge above the horizon. "Then why are you here? Why are you doing all this?"

"To save myself."

Jonathan caught something in her voice, an intimation of a task yet to be accomplished. "What does that mean?"

Emma met his gaze and held it. "Come with me and you'll find out. But you have to trust me."

Jonathan looked at her belly and saw that it was round where before it had been flat. Her breasts *were* larger, fuller. He reached out to touch her cheek, but she clutched his hand and turned it away. Joy and sadness filled him in equal measure. "I can't," he said. "I'm sorry."

"Then you're a fool."

And she rolled off the bed and left as silently as she had come.

63

It was eight a.m. and Blenheim was in full swing. In the motor court, the Range Rovers had been pulled from their garage bays and were being washed and waxed. The sound of horses being led to and from the stables carried in the sunlit air. The house trembled with the comings and goings of its many residents. Strangely, the area by the maintenance building was lacking any activity. There were no trucks nearby. No sign of the armed guards Jonathan had observed yesterday keeping watch on the entrance.

At first Jonathan surmised that the warhead had been moved. The previous evening's attack had spooked Balfour, and he'd wasted no time in spiriting his crown jewel to a safer location. Then another idea came to him. It was precisely because the attack had spooked Balfour that he would not risk moving it. The calm was a facade, Balfour's effort to avoid drawing attention to the shed. Something moved at the corner of his eye, and Jonathan gained proof that his hunch was correct. A pair of snipers lay flat on the garage roof, keeping an eye on the shed's perimeter. Snipers did not guard an empty building.

All this Jonathan took in from his second-floor window. Freshly shaved and showered, and dressed in shorts and a T-shirt for a morning run, he felt himself in the grip of a feeling unlike any he'd known. Part call to action, part thirst for revenge, a manic desire stirred inside him to do whatever was necessary to see his job through. His own safety and well-being did not come into play. He would pass along the information he had gathered to Frank Connor. It was that simple. He wasn't sure if it was a fool's courage or a father's first and last duty to his unborn child. He knew only that actions defined a man, and that waiting was not an option.

It was Emma, of course. Her visit had awakened feelings he'd thought dead. Or maybe he had preferred them that way. The ego's almighty and seductive trickery. No matter the scope of her betrayal, the enormity of her crimes, he could not rid himself of his love for her. She was poison, yet he tasted her incautiously. He was a man of discipline, yet she defeated his will. Her essence tormented him. Her competence inspired him. And now he had learned that she was the mother of his child. For that, he swore allegiance to her forever. Allegiance, but not assistance. If he could not defeat her in love, he would defeat her in war.

Turning, Jonathan strode to the dressing area and removed a platinum American Express card from his wallet. The card bore Michel Revy's name but it was not a credit card, nor had it ever belonged to him. The card was one of Frank Connor's neatest tricks. Embedded in its skin was a powerful counterjamming device capable of defeating the wireless cage Balfour had erected over his estate.

Connor's instructions were clear. As soon as Jonathan came into possession of information relating to the warhead's location and its sale and transfer to Balfour's client, he was to transmit it to Division. This could be done in one of three ways. If Jonathan was able to free himself from Balfour and get liberty outside Blenheim, he could simply call the secure line programmed into the phone. If that were not the case (and Connor had been plainspoken about his belief that Balfour would not permit Jonathan to leave the compound), Jonathan could transmit the encrypted information to a secure site via his laptop. As there was no wireless service and no Internet connection in his room, the laptop was also out.

The last option involved activating the counterjamming device in the credit card. Once activated, the card possessed sufficient power to defeat the most robust jamming system for five to eight minutes. During that time Jonathan would be able to place a call to Division, transmit his information, and receive instructions as to his further actions. There was only one catch. Connor had been up front in explaining that Balfour's security team would immediately notice the disruption in the jamming system, and, as important, would be able to triangulate the location of the counterjamming device within sixty seconds. Use of the credit card meant certain detection, and thus certain death.

Jonathan slipped the card into his shorts along with his phone and quietly left his room. He paused in the hallway, looking left and right, and decided to use the back stairs, which passed adjacent to the kitchen. The hallway was empty, and with every step his confidence grew. Once outside, he would jog past the stables and across the meadow Balfour had named Runnymede to the farthest corner of the estate. The farther he was from the jamming signal, the greater the counterjamming device's ability to defeat it. He passed the reproduction of *Blue Boy* and the framed collection of medieval fighting irons and wondered what was going to happen to all of Balfour's possessions.

To his right a door opened and Mr. Singh stepped out, blocking his path. Jonathan offered a polite good morning and walked around the man-mountain, not slowing his stride. Mr. Singh's phone rang, and Jonathan heard him say in the queen's English, "Good morning, m' lord."

Reaching the stairs, Jonathan put his hand in his pocket, fingering the credit card for reassurance. As he descended the stairs, he was met by the smell of sausage and eggs and all the wonderful scents of a country breakfast. The chef stood by the stairs, clutching a basket of muffins. Jonathan was forced to engage her in conversation, politely declining the offer of a muffin, French toast, and eggs Benedict. He secured his escape by accepting a red apple from the fruit bowl and promising to return after his run. Mollified, the chef attended to her stove and he crossed the last few meters to the door.

"Ransom."

His name was spoken, not shouted, in a faultless American accent that he had once admired. Danni had trained him how to spot a tail and how to memorize a roomful of objects. But she hadn't said a word about how to react when someone unexpectedly called your

name and you were thousands of miles from home and surrounded
by the enemy.

Jonathan froze, his shoulders stiffening, and at that moment he
knew that all was lost. He looked over his shoulder. Sultan Haq stood
at the opposite side of the kitchen. Their eyes met. The spark of
recognition passed between them and an image flashed in Jonathan's
mind of Haq standing on the mountain plateau surrounded by flames,
the Kentucky hunting rifle in his hands, crying out for revenge.
Jonathan remembered Hamid and the brave soldiers who had died in
the complex of caves at Tora Bora, and for a glorious moment he considered killing Haq then and there.

Footsteps approached from the stairs behind him. Mr. Singh and
Balfour.

Jonathan bolted out the door and slammed it behind him. He ran
past the line of Range Rovers, the car attendants shooting him confused looks, past the garage and toward the stables.

"Ransom!" shouted Haq.

"Stop him!" ordered Balfour.

A security guard astride an ATV motored in his direction, standing tall on his pedals, trying to make sense of the situation.

Lowering a shoulder, Jonathan knocked him headlong off the
four-wheel vehicle and jumped into his seat.

"Shoot him!" Balfour was saying.

Jonathan spun the ATV in a tight turn and accelerated out of the
motor court and past the stables. There was a shot and the ATV
jumped as a bullet struck the chassis. Jonathan hunkered low over the
handlebars, keeping the throttle full out, building speed. Another bullet struck the fender. He bounded into the meadow, putting distance
between himself and the main house. A look behind him showed that
no one had followed. He slowed enough to pull the credit card out of
his pocket and activate the counterjammer. Trading the credit card for
his phone, he hit the speed-dial for Frank Connor. There was a hissing
sound, and the call failed.

"Dammit."

It was then that he saw a black shadow advancing over the terrain.

Looking again, he saw that it was Sultan Haq on Inferno, the black stallion, galloping in his direction. Jonathan hit the speed-dial again. The hissing erupted and Jonathan swore. Abruptly the white noise died and the call went through. Jonathan revved the throttle and the ATV hurtled over the grass, rocking considerably, lifting him out of his seat. He could not control the vehicle and hold the phone at the same time.

Behind him, Haq was gaining ground. Jonathan returned his left hand to the grip, clutching the phone in his palm. An ATV appeared at the far end of the meadow, blocking his escape. Jonathan veered right, cutting a diagonal path away from it, then braked to a full stop.

"Frank, it's me, Jonathan. Can you hear me?"

"Jonathan . . . yes, I can, just barely. What the hell are you doing?"

"Frank, it's here. The warhead is at Blenheim. You have to get here fast. They're moving it today. The buyer's Sultan Haq."

"Say again? You're cutting out . . . can't quite pick you up . . ."

Jonathan glanced over his shoulder. Haq was charging at him, the horse breathing furiously. Jonathan grabbed the handlebars and squeezed the throttle, steering the ATV toward a spot in the fence where he'd glimpsed a jeep and some workers. He willed the all-terrain vehicle faster, but it could not outpace Inferno. The black stallion neared, close enough for Jonathan to hear his hooves thudding the ground, to feel his presence. He looked over his shoulder. Haq was five meters behind and closing fast. Jonathan searched the field ahead, observed that there was a tear in the fence, and aimed the ATV toward it.

Suddenly Haq was beside him, leaning off the horse and striking him with an enormous fist. Jonathan yanked the handlebars to the right, but Haq stayed with him, one hand clutching the horse's mane, his legs wrapped around the beast's flanks. Again his fist connected with Jonathan's cheek. Jonathan lashed out with his left arm, hitting the side of Haq's head. The horse slowed, and Jonathan was clear.

Fifty meters separated him from the fence.

He leaned low over the handlebars, eking out every ounce of power from the throttle.

A blur appeared to his right. A jeep barreled in front of him, blocking the fence. Mr. Singh was at the wheel, and Balfour stood in the back, manning the .30 caliber machine gun.

Jonathan spun the ATV to avoid colliding with them. The ATV bucked at the violent change of direction, two wheels lifting off the ground. Jonathan shifted his weight, but he was traveling too rapidly and the meadow's soil was too soft. The ATV flipped, and Jonathan tumbled headlong through the tall grass.

Spitting out a mouthful of turf, he pushed himself to his knees, only to see Balfour swing the machine gun around and cock the firing pin.

"Don't shoot!" shouted Haq as he dismounted and approached Jonathan. "Hello, Dr. Ransom. I hoped that we would meet again, but didn't dare believe it. This time I don't think you can rely on the cavalry to rescue you."

"Probably not," said Jonathan.

Haq kicked him in the ribs, and Jonathan fell to his side. The tall Afghan reached into the grass and picked up Jonathan's phone. He pressed several buttons but drew no satisfaction. "Who did you call?"

Jonathan remained silent.

Haq looked at Balfour.

Balfour said, "I have the world's most sophisticated jamming system. No one can make a wireless call from anywhere within five kilometers unless I clear the number beforehand. This man—Revy, Ransom . . . whatever his name is—could not have placed a call."

Haq appeared unconvinced. With mounting anger, he turned toward Jonathan. "Who were you calling?"

"I was trying to reach your father in hell. I wanted to tell him I was sorry I didn't cut his throat myself."

"I'll let you deliver the message personally, but first I must know if you are telling me the truth. Mr. Singh, hold him."

The Sikh wrenched Jonathan to his feet and locked his arms around his chest, imprisoning him.

Haq pulled an instrument from his pocket. It was a knife, but no ordinary one. A short, crescent-shaped blade extended from a scarred bulbous wooden handle. It was a poppy knife, used by farmers to slice grooves into the ripe poppy bulbs from which the precious opium could flow. "You have dark eyes," he said. "I remember."

Jonathan blinked several times, realizing then that the fall had knocked the colored lenses from his eyes. Haq raised the blade to the soft flesh just beneath his eye. "A surgeon cannot perform his duties if blind."

The cold metal pressed harder.

Jonathan struggled to break free, but Singh only tightened his grip.

"So, my friend," said Haq, moving the blade slowly back and forth, "as we do not have enough time for you to answer all my questions, I shall ask you to answer only one. Tell me the truth, or it will cost you an eye. And if you think I will kill you afterward, you're mistaken. I have other plans. Did you tell your masters about our plans?"

"The call didn't go through."

A flick of the wrist and the blade ripped his skin. Jonathan flinched but did not cry out.

"I will ask one more time, and then I will feed your eye to the horse."

Jonathan steeled himself. Emma, he knew, would not yield.

If not in love, then in war.

"Did you speak to your masters about our plans?" asked Haq.

"I did not."

Haq looked at Balfour, who offered no expression. "I'm sorry," said Haq, pushing the blade into the fold of skin. "But I can't believe you. Not yet."

"Try it," gasped Jonathan. "Try the phone yourself. Hit the number seven and press Call. You'll see."

Haq lowered the knife. He thumbed the seven and called, bringing the phone to his ear. Jonathan watched, asking himself feverishly if five minutes had passed since he had activated the counterjamming device. Haq's eyes opened wider, and Jonathan's heart sank. But a moment later the Afghan put the phone into his pocket.

"Well?" asked Balfour.

"The call could not go through. Your jamming system was effective."

"Move away, then," said Balfour. "I'll finish him."

Haq stretched out a hand to stop him. "Not yet. I would like to take him to my brother. Dr. Ransom has much to answer for."

Balfour considered this, then aimed the barrel of the machine gun toward the sky. "As you wish. I will make him my gift to you."

64

H18.

Slumped in the rear of Balfour's Range Rover, Jonathan read the large white letters painted on the wall of the hangar at Islamabad Airport and knew that they had arrived. Mr. Singh sat next to him. Ever-vigilant, the Sikh had not shifted his eyes off Jonathan for a moment during the hour's drive from Blenheim. Sultan Haq occupied the front seat, while Balfour himself drove. Another vehicle led the way. Two followed behind. But the most important cargo sat in the rear compartment, barely an arm's length from Jonathan. It was an unmarked olive-drab crate the size of the footlocker he'd taken to Boy Scout camp, inside which rested a nuclear warhead.

Built to accommodate large jets, Hangar 18 sat alone at the far corner of the airport. The words "East Pakistan Airways" ran above the closed doors. *EPA.* Another clue from his visit to Balfour's office. There was no sign of activity, but as Balfour approached, a door built into the hangar slid open. Balfour didn't slow as he maneuvered the car over the steel tracks. Shadow replaced the sun. There were no planes, but there were crates. Mountain after mountain of olive-drab crates piled to the sky. Stenciled on the sides in English, Cyrillic, and Arabic were words like "Ammunition: .45 caliber. 5,000 rounds. Grenades: Antipersonnel. Rifles: Kalashnikov AK-47." And there were other words, like "Semtex" and "C4" and "Bofors" and "Glock." It was the United Nations of weapons.

Balfour navigated a winding path through the stacks. A welcoming committee waited at the far side. Jonathan counted ten men dressed in traditional shalwar kameezes, and one, an older, darker figure, wearing the black robes of an imam. Several vehicles were parked behind them: a Hilux pickup, two jeeps, and a van.

The Range Rover halted and Singh hauled Jonathan out of the car. At the same time Balfour's men decamped from their vehicles and formed a perimeter. There were no fewer than twenty of them, all wearing identical tan suits, all carrying identical Kalashnikovs. Singh barked a command, and two of the men unloaded the crate and carried it to a large table.

Haq approached Jonathan and handed him a damp cloth. "Clean yourself up."

Jonathan dabbed at his eye, and Haq patted him on the shoulder. It was the gesture of victor to vanquished, and Jonathan pushed his hand away. "I'm done," he said, tossing the cloth back.

Haq walked to the man in the black robes and kissed him three times on the cheek. The men exchanged words and Haq pointed at Jonathan. The older man approached. "You are the healer who killed my father?"

Jonathan didn't answer. The truth embarrassed him. He had been an unwitting pawn when he should have been an active participant. His fingers itched for a knife to plunge into the man's gut.

"My name is Massoud Haq. I am the head of our clan. You will return with me to our tribal lands. We have a particular punishment for murderers. We bury them to the neck and allow the wronged family to cast stones until they are dead. I will cast the first in my father's name."

"I look forward to it," said Jonathan, acidly.

"As do I."

Two of the scientists Jonathan had seen at Blenheim supervised the removal of the warhead from the crate. The weapon did not resemble the pictures Connor had showed him. It had been reduced in size. Instead of an artillery shell, it resembled a larger version of a stainless-steel thermos. The scientists unscrewed one end of the device and performed a series of tests for the benefit of Haq and his brother. English was the lingua franca, and Jonathan heard the words "twelve kilotons," "undetectable," "timer," and "detonation code." Sultan Haq carefully punched six digits into a keypad. The device was resealed and placed in a second crate. Looking closely, Jonathan noted the words "U.S. Department of Defense" stenciled on the side.

Massoud Haq placed a phone call and issued a succession of instructions in Pashto. Jonathan understood enough of the language to know that a bank was involved and the subject was the transfer of $10 million. Massoud Haq hung up, and immediately thereafter Balfour made a call to his banker, speaking an account number that Jonathan recognized as one he'd memorized the night before. Balfour smiled broadly, and Jonathan knew that the transfer had been successful.

Balfour walked to Jonathan and extended his hand. "By the way, you wouldn't happen to know of a good plastic surgeon?" He laughed loudly, showing his perfect white teeth, his eyes smiling with the knowledge that even though his chosen surgeon had been exposed as a spy, no harm had come from it, and he could still take pleasure in knowing that his retirement was gilded and that surely it would not be too difficult to find another physician to provide him with a new face and a new identity.

"Bastard," said Jonathan, ignoring the outstretched hand, at which Balfour cocked his head and laughed even louder.

There was a harsh, slapping sound, and Massoud Haq's face dissolved in a miasma of gore. Like a rag doll, he collapsed to the ground.

Machine-gun fire broke out from all directions. There was a terrific explosion, and a pack of Humvees roared into the hangar.

The smile vanished from Balfour's face. Cowering, he ran to a stack of crates draped with webbed netting and fell against them.

Jonathan hit the ground and crawled toward the safety of the nearest stack of crates. Looking to his left, he saw the word "Semtex" stenciled ten centimeters away.

The exchange of gunfire devolved into a pitched battle. Balfour's men, along with Mr. Singh and Sultan Haq, held position at one end of the hangar, taking cover behind their vehicles. Soldiers in assault gear advanced from among the crates of guns and ammunition at the other end. Jonathan was caught in between.

A grenade sailed over his head and rolled toward Sultan Haq. One of Balfour's guards jumped on it, his body lifting into the air a second later, the blast inaudible in the cacophonous gunfire. Another grenade followed. Haq caught it on the bounce and threw it back. But he did not throw it at the attacking troops. Instead, he turned toward the stack of crates where Balfour had sought protection and lobbed it expertly into its center. Jonathan read the words ".30 caliber ammunition" stenciled on an exposed section of pine. The grenade bounced once, and Balfour scrambled to pick it up, fumbling with the ovoid canister. Jonathan watched as he cocked his arm to throw it. The grenade exploded, Balfour disappearing momentarily inside a blossom of orange and black.

The explosion died and he was still standing, half his arm obliterated, bone and muscle dangling, his face sheared off by the force of the blast. Dazed, he spun and saw Jonathan looking at him. His one eye opened wider, as if he were confused at how this might have come to pass. Another grenade landed in the webbing. There was an explosion, and the .30 caliber rounds began to cook off. Balfour's body jerked as the bullets tore into his body, hurling him to the floor.

The hangar shuddered. Overhead, the lights flickered.

The assault troops pulled back, and Jonathan spotted an American flag sewn to one man's shoulder. It had to be Connor who'd sent them, but how had he known the site of the exchange when Jonathan himself hadn't?

Nearby a fire broke out among the crates. In seconds, flames were shooting into the rafters. More ammunition began to cook off. Tracers arced above his head. Explosions grew more frequent. Shrapnel whizzed through the air like bottle flies. A girder broke from the ceiling and fell to the floor, crushing a soldier.

Desperate to escape, Jonathan lifted his head and peered around him. Ten meters away, Haq stole the warhead off the table and carried it to the flatbed of a jeep. Jonathan rose to a knee. A bullet slammed into a crate above his shoulder and he fell back to the floor, watching as Haq closed the tailgate and ran to the passenger seat. A man climbed into the driver's seat, was shot, fell, and was replaced by another.

"Get him!" Jonathan waved his arms and pointed at Haq, but his voice was a whisper among the murderous symphony. Fed up, he climbed to his feet and dashed across the floor toward the truck. Bullets sizzled past, one shaving off the top of his ear, upsetting his balance and toppling him to the ground. He pushed himself up. "Haq!"

A body slammed into him, knocking him to the cement floor, winded.

Mr. Singh threw himself on top of him, rammed a pistol into his jaw, and pulled the trigger. The gun fired empty. Jonathan kneed him in the groin and heaved him off. Jumping to his feet, he managed one step before Singh grabbed his ankle and dropped him. In place of his pistol, the Sikh held the long curved kukri in his hand. He slashed, but the blade missed Jonathan's calf and struck the floor. Jonathan kicked at him, striking his cheeks, knocking his turban loose. Another blow landed squarely on his nose, breaking it, and a third connected with his chin.

Singh shook off the blows, matted braids of hair falling about his face, blood streaming from his nose. Rising to his feet, he held the blade high, a killing blow. In vain Jonathan threw up an arm to protect himself. But the blade did not fall. Singh shuddered time and time again, geysers of blood and fabric erupting from his chest. The Sikh fell to his side, his chest rising spasmodically.

A soldier pulled Jonathan behind a crate and helped him sit up.

"Get him," said Jonathan, disoriented, gesturing toward the jeep. "Get Haq! He has the warhead!"

"He can't go anywhere," the soldier shouted in Jonathan's face. "The place is sealed tight as a drum."

A female voice. So familiar. "Emma?"

The soldier pulled the black balaclava off her face. "Are you okay?"

Jonathan looked into the woman's face. Blue eyes, not green. Hair a raven's black. "Danni? You're here?"

"I tried to alert you last night."

Jonathan blinked, recalling the assault on Balfour's estate. "Connor sent you?"

"No," she said. "I came on my own. This morning I found out he'd been trying to reach me ever since you left. He hooked me up with Delta. My orders were to keep an eye out for you and make sure none of the good guys took you out by accident."

"But Haq," said Jonathan rolling to one side, seeking out the jeep, no longer seeing it.

A monstrous blast rocked the foundations of the hangar. Giant pan lights fell from the ceiling. A second rafter broke loose, crashing to the floor.

"We have to get out of here," said Danni. "Before the whole place goes up."

Before he could protest, she grabbed his collar and hauled him to his feet. Together they ran back through the canyon of crates and boxes until they emerged into the daylight, coughing and sputtering.

An American officer directed them to an aid truck at the side of the hangar, but Jonathan was still too amped up to worry about himself. "Haq," he managed, bent double and clearing his throat. "Did you get him? Black jeep . . . he has it . . . he has the bomb."

"Sir, you need water and medical attention."

Jonathan ignored the offer of assistance, forcing himself to stand upright and confront the officer. "Did you get him?"

"Sir, we're handling this operation. Right now you need aid. Corpsman! Take this man to the aid truck."

"I'll do it," said Danni.

"Didn't you hear me?" shouted Jonathan. "He's a got a WMD. I saw it—it's in there!"

"Get him out of here! Now!"

"Cool it," said Danni, restraining Jonathan. "There are over a hundred troops here. They've got the perimeter sealed. Haq isn't going anywhere."

Danni guided Jonathan around the side of the hangar to a spot fifty meters across the tarmac where two Humvees and a half-ton truck were parked. A Pakistani soldier offered them water and tea and energy bars.

"Who are they?" Jonathan asked, eyes glued to the hangar doors. "Where did they come from?"

"Delta Force and regular Pakistani army," said Danni.

"How did they know where to be?"

"The information you forwarded to Connor. He contacted U.S. Central Command and they called out Delta."

"The information I forwarded?"

"The files started coming through soon after my diversion. It was smart of you to take advantage of it to break into Balfour's office."

"And Connor told you all this?"

"He said he'd gotten the files you sent from Balfour's. He called them a goldmine."

"But I didn't . . ."

Jonathan left his words unsaid. His world had momentarily divided into parallel tracks. While one part of his mind replayed the events in Balfour's office last night, another watched in fearful surprise as a dozen soldiers ran out of the hangar en masse, heads bowed, followed by a Humvee reversing at full speed. At the same moment that Jonathan recalled Emma holding the flash drive in her open palm and realized that it could only have been she who had sent Connor the information, he spotted the obdurate American officer at the head of the fleeing soldiers, waving his arms furiously and shouting, "Get back!"

The words were slammed to the ground by a flash of orange, a burst of light so bright it eclipsed the midday sun. And in that instant before the shock wave struck him, Jonathan saw the Humvee rise up on one end, as if standing on tiptoes, and a soldier suspended in midair, and he thought, This is what it is like to see a nuclear weapon explode from two hundred meters away.

Jonathan blinked and opened his eyes. Stunned that he was alive, he rose to an elbow and watched as huge sections of the corrugated iron roof tumbled from the sky amid coils of black smoke and plummeted into the fire and debris.

"Stay down," shouted Danni, knocking the elbow out from under him. "It's a hellstorm. The whole place went up."

Jonathan ignored her. He had seen something else, something besides the fire and the debris and the Humvee traveling end over end. Lifting his head, he stared across the tarmac, squinting to see into the distance.

There, beyond the flames and smoke and mayhem, two jeeps were driving rapidly away from the hangar. A fireball blossomed from the carnage, obscuring his view. When the flames receded and the smoke cleared, the jeeps had disappeared into the airport's busy ground traffic.

65

"Jesus, Mary, and Joseph."

Frank Connor sat on the edge of a desk in the middle of the op center, jaw agape and not giving two shits about it, as he watched Hangar 18 disintegrate before his eyes. The screen blinked repeatedly, then went black, and he knew he'd lost the feed from Islamabad Airport.

"Get me hooked up with the on-scene commander," he said to his telecom tech.

"Audio is intact, sir. We just lost the picture."

"Well, get it back."

The room was packed with Division's senior staff. Victories were few and far between, and it was doubtful that any person present, Connor included, would ever again witness one of this magnitude. He had followed the operation from inception via a camera attached to the assault commander's shoulder harness. He had witnessed the breaching of the hangar, the killing of Lord Balfour and Massoud Haq, and the subsequent firefight. And now he was having a very difficult time remaining calm as he waited for the boys from Delta Force to bring him his prize.

"Have you retrieved the package?" he asked the commander.

"No, sir. We can't get near the place. The way that ammo is still cooking off, it's a war zone. Right now I've got to look after my men. I've got two seriously injured and one KIA."

The news sent a sobering chill through the assembled viewers.

"Keep me posted," said Connor.

It had been a long day. Upon receiving Balfour's files, he'd immediately run the batch through a keyword search. The results yielded a mountain of information about Balfour's various businesses and over a hundred articles about cruise missiles and the American nuclear arsenal, but precious little about the nuts and bolts of his operation to retrieve the warhead from Tirich Mir.

After three hours of sifting through thousands of individual files and letters, Connor chanced upon an e-mail retrieved from Balfour's trash addressed to Massoud Haq, agreeing upon a time and place for the exchange of the weapon. Again there was no overt mention of a WMD, just a cryptic and oft-repeated reference to a "carpet for sale." This e-mail, coupled with inquiries to a team of Pakistani nuclear physicists about traveling to Blenheim to examine "an object that required their expertise," was all Connor had to go on. Disappointingly, there had been no photographs or other concrete evidence of the weapon.

Connor looked to his side, where Peter Erskine stood, arms crossed, a glum expression aging his boyish features. "See, Pete, we did it. We took a risk and it paid off. If we'd sent this info upstairs, that WMD would be in Times Square by now and New York City would be a smoldering ruin."

"I agree, Frank," said Erskine. "It looks like your gamble paid off."

"Gamble my ass. It was a calculated endeavor. It was us or nobody."

"If you say so."

"I do, Peter. I say that and more."

Connor stood, keeping an eye on the screen. He would have enjoyed confronting Erskine about his treasonous activities, here in front of all his colleagues, but Connor hadn't received sufficient proof. The NSA's probe of Erskine's telephone records showed nothing more interesting than a propensity to call his wife at any and all hours of the day, whether at home or at her work at the Justice Department. No unlisted numbers. No overseas calls to unknown individuals or organizations. The Financial Crimes Enforcement Network had yet to report back one way or the other about Erskine's financial situation. For all his certainty about Erskine's divided loyalties, Connor was hamstrung without hard evidence to back up his claims.

There was a commotion at the entry to the ops center. Connor saw his executive assistant, Lorena, speaking to three men he didn't recognize and one he did: Thomas Sharp, national security adviser and a former deputy director of Division.

Sharp pushed past Lorena and made his way through the gawking crowd to Connor's side. "You've gone too far this time," he said, loud enough for all to hear. "I've been on the horn with CENTCOM for the past hour. They were pretty damned curious about why I wasn't in the loop on this op. You didn't think they'd give me a call?"

"Frankly, Tom, I didn't give a shit. If I'd wanted your opinion on the matter, I would have told you myself."

Sharp rode out the insult like the professional he was. Tall, sleek, and cunning, he was the perfectly evolved bureaucratic animal. "Luckily," he said coolly, and with a victor's confidence, "Mr. Erskine felt differently."

"Mr. Erskine?" Connor shot Erskine an incredulous glance, but Erskine refused to meet his gaze. "Peter called you?"

Sharp stepped closer, moving in for the kill. "You suspected Ashok Balfour Armitraj was trafficking a WMD—one of our own cruise missiles, no less—and you didn't see fit to inform me, or anyone else, for that matter. Are you out of your mind?"

"It was time-critical intel. I didn't tell you or the boys at the Pentagon because you would have screwed the pooch."

"How long have you known about this?"

"Days. A week, tops."

"Mr. Erskine said it's been two weeks."

"Two weeks since we began working the lead. If you want to get out the stopwatch, we only got confirmation that he has the thing a few hours ago."

"So you have proof that this weapon exists?" asked Sharp.

"The proof is in that hangar."

"Two weeks. And you sent in a rank amateur who hasn't even received an official security clearance to do the job?"

"It's that rank amateur who got us the information about where the exchange was taking place."

"Who is this man Ransom, anyway?"

"A doctor we've used in the past to help us execute our operations."

"A doctor? Well, I'm glad he's had some formal training, even if it has nothing to do with covert activities. Where is he now? I'd like to speak with him."

"I don't know," said Connor. "He tried to contact me several hours ago, but the connection was broken."

Sharp took a step back, hands on his hips, shaking his head. "Jesus Christ, Frank, you're not just off the reservation, you've left the entire planet. I don't even know where to begin."

"Then don't." Connor turned away from Sharp, despising him. "Just shut up and wait with the rest of us."

Five minutes passed, and Connor spoke to the commander again. "Can you get in there yet?"

"Not a chance. The whole damned hangar collapsed. There's enough ammo to arm a Marine division in there, and all of it's cooking off. It's raining shrapnel out here. No one's going near the place until it stops."

"And Sultan Haq?"

"Sir, no one got out of there but my men. If Haq was in there when it went up, he's in there now."

Connor looked at Sharp. "The bomb is in there," he said. "We had a visual confirmation."

"You saw it with your own eyes, did you?"

"We saw the crate it was packed in."

"The crate?" Sharp's skepticism was apparent.

"Yeah. What do you think—they carry it around on their belt like a BlackBerry?"

"For your sake, I hope so, Frank. But this looks like it's going to take a while to clear. In the meantime, you're removed from your post. President's orders. These men are federal marshals. They're here to escort you from the premises and take you to your home, where you are to consider yourself under house arrest until further notice."

With disbelief, Connor looked over Sharp's shoulder at the two men behind him. "House arrest? On what charges?"

"Gross dereliction of duty, for one," said Sharp. "Also, a man named James Malloy was found murdered in his home last night. I understand you paid him a visit the other night. I'm sure we're going to find plenty more violations as soon as you tell us exactly what you've been up to."

Connor pointed at the screen. "There is a WMD in that building."

"If it's there, we'll find it."

"I have an operator on-site. Her name is Danni Pine. I want to talk to her."

"One of ours?"

"Mossad."

"Another irregular? Good to know. I'll see that we get in touch with her immediately."

A marshal approached, and Connor backed away. "I need to know if Ransom is all right. We've got to get him out."

"I will be sure to ask her," said Sharp. "It's over, Frank. You're done. Goodbye."

A marshal took Connor's arm. "This way, sir."

Connor held his head high as he was led out of the building.

"I'm sorry," said Peter Erskine. "You left me no choice."

66

Jonathan and Danni commando-crawled one hundred meters to the safety of the repair shed where the troops had staged before the raid. The air continued to thunder with exploding mortars, artillery shells, grenades, and bullets, the tarmac shuddering with each blast. A mountain of smoke rose into the sky. But all Jonathan saw was the image of the jeeps driving at full speed away from the hangar. Winded, he stood and rushed to find the nearest soldier.

"I need to speak to your commanding officer," he said. "It's an emergency. I may have seen Haq driving away from the hangar."

A Pakistani soldier crouched on a knee before him, one hand on his helmet. "That would be Major Nichols," he said, looking around and not seeing him. The soldier hailed Nichols over his radio and passed along Jonathan's message. "He's coming around the hangar— he'll be here as quickly as possible."

Two minutes passed, and a soldier approached from the left, running, his head down.

"I'm Nichols," the man said. He was Delta Force all the way. The beard, the Oakley sunglasses, the neck thicker than an oak. "Who are you?"

"Ransom. I work for the government. I was with Balfour. Listen to me, the man you're looking for is—"

"Hold it!" Nichols raised a hand for Jonathan to shut up. "You're Jonathan Ransom? And you, lady, you're Pine?"

Danni nodded.

"You're both to come with me. I've been ordered to take you into custody."

"Custody?" said Danni warily. "What for?"

Major Nichols consulted a scrap of paper in his hand. "I'm to tell you that Frank Connor has been removed from his position as director of Division. Pending a debriefing and investigation, you're to consider yourselves under military confinement."

"Removed? Why?" asked Jonathan.

"Sir, I'm telling you everything I know. Now let's get moving."

"Hold it," said Jonathan earnestly, one smart, well-intentioned man speaking to another. "All this stuff can wait. A second before the hangar went up, I saw two jeeps driving out the far side, heading toward the cargo terminals. One of the jeeps looked like the vehicle Haq was loading the warhead into."

At the mention of the word "warhead," Nichols stiffened. "Did you see Haq with your own eyes?"

"The jeeps were too far away," said Jonathan. "Why? Have you found him inside?"

Nichols studied Jonathan's bruised face, the cut beneath his eye, the notch in his ear. "You the maniac that I saw running around in there trying to get at Haq?"

"Yeah."

Nichols stuffed the paper back into his breast pocket. "No," he said, after a moment's consideration. "We didn't locate Haq or the warhead. There wasn't time before everything started cooking off."

"He got out the back," said Jonathan. The images of the jeep were clearer now. He saw uniforms in the front seat and a hunched silhouette in the rear. A man covered by a blanket. He closed his eyes, willing himself to see more, to clear his mind and let his memory do the work, as Danni had taught him. The pictures grew more detailed, and with a jolt he opened his eyes. "It was Haq. He was in the jeep. I spent time with him in Afghanistan. I know the guy. He has the warhead. I saw him loading it into the jeep inside the hangar."

Nichols leaned in closer. "You saw him loading the warhead into the jeep? Alone?"

"Balfour had a couple of physicists reduce it in size. I heard them say it was twelve kilotons. The whole thing looked like an oversized stainless-steel thermos."

"Either way, we have the building surrounded. There is no chance Haq escaped."

"Do you have his body?" Jonathan asked again.

"I already told you that we don't," said Nichols, growing irritated. "No one's going near that hangar for a day to recover it. But take my word for it, there's no way out except through the main doors."

"Who told you that? The same Pakistani officers who are driving Haq in that jeep? Don't you know what they say about these guys? 'Not for sale, but always for rent.'"

The major bristled at Jonathan's tone but was savvy enough to take his words to heart. "Colonel Pasha, come in," he said into his two-way radio on his shoulder harness. "Your boys have the rear of the hangar covered, right?"

"Of course," answered the Pakistani officer.

"And no one drove out of there?"

"Negative."

Nichols looked at Jonathan and Danni. "You're a hundred percent certain on that? We have a report of a couple of jeeps leaving the rear of the hangar prior to the explosion, possibly with Haq and the WMD."

"Jeeps? No, nothing at all like that."

"He's lying," said Jonathan.

"Shut it!" said Nichols. Then to Pasha: "Anything at all? I thought I saw a jeep trailing out the back."

"Those were friendlies," said Pasha.

"The guy's lying," said Jonathan, getting into the major's space. "I saw them leaving. It was Haq. He had a blanket over him. You can't believe him!"

"Listen here, cowboy," said Nichols, clutching a fistful of Jonathan's shirt. "I've trained up close and personal with that man for a year. He's had my back more times than I can count. He tells me no one got out, then no one got out. Are we clear?"

"No, we're not clear," retorted Jonathan, not backing off an inch. "I'm telling you I saw Haq in a jeep. Are you willing to risk that he got away with the WMD?"

Nichols glared at Jonathan and at Danni, all the while shifting his ammo belt. "Fuck," he said. "You'd better be goddamned sure."

"I am."

Nichols released his grip on Jonathan's shirt. "Come with me." The major stalked off to an open Humvee and climbed behind the wheel. "You said it was heading east?"

"Toward the freight terminals. A black jeep. Two Pakistani military officers in front."

Jonathan and Danni climbed into the back and Nichols floored it, taking a wide arc around the burning hangar. As they drove, Nichols radioed for his subordinates to join in the search. "Mount up and follow me to the east side of the airport. Freight area. I got a report that one of the bad guys made it out the rear with the package. Call General Zoy and have him lock down the airport."

"He'll never do that," came the response.

"Tell him it's a direct order from United States Central Command."

"Hey, chief, aren't you forgetting something? This is their country."

"The hell it is. Tell him he's got a rogue nuke on the loose, and then see what he says."

Nichols checked his watch, then turned and shot Jonathan the most threatening look he'd ever received. "That sonofabitch Haq has been gone ten minutes. Why didn't you come to me earlier?"

67

"You're late," said the pilot as he shoved the forward door closed. "Find a place to sit and buckle up. We're leaving."

Sultan Haq started down the cavernous fuselage, squinting in the dim light as he made his way past jeeps and armored personnel carriers and various crates of military equipment. The jeeps belonged to the United States Army, as did the personnel carriers and every last piece of equipment loaded and secured aboard the Starlifter.

It was the greatest exodus of military matériel in history.

For seven years the United States military had sent its sons and daughters to the country of Iraq to free Iraq's people of a tyrannical dictator and sow the seeds of democracy. Along with the soldiers, a constant stream of matériel poured into the country. Day in, day out, planes landed at airbases across the country. C-141 Starlifters carrying tanks, artillery pieces, and up-armored Humvees. Boeing C-19s filled with heavy trucks, mobile kitchens, and Kevlar vests. Great cargo ships docked at ports in the Arabian Sea delivering jeeps, ammunition, and pallet upon pallet of MREs.

Now the war was winding down. The American military was moving on. And it was taking its war-making apparatus with it. A total of 3.3 million pieces of military equipment was to be repatriated or sent onward to Afghanistan, where American troops were engaged in a fierce conflict. M1 Abrams tanks, Bradley Fighting Vehicles, Stryker armored personnel carriers, howitzer cannons—the list went on ad infinitum. The task was too great to accomplish solely with its own equipment, so the masters of logistics looked outside the military for ships and planes available to assist them. One of the firms contracted to help was East Pakistan Airways, owned and operated by Ashok Balfour Armitraj.

Collapsing into a makeshift seat halfway down the interior, Haq leaned his head against the bulkhead and drew a deep breath. He was sweating profusely, the fear and adrenaline and terror of survival and escape still gripping him, leaving his hands trembling. He yanked at the sleeve of his jacket to get at his watch, hating the Western clothing. It was almost seven o'clock. Reflexively, he touched the crate placed on the webbed seating next to him for reassurance. Takeoff was scheduled for 1900 local time. Military transports did not wait for unlisted passengers and cargo.

One after another, the Starlifter's Pratt and Whitney turbine engines powered up. The plane gave a mighty shiver, then began to move. It taxied for several minutes, and Haq felt his anxiety lessen. Only then did he acknowledge the pain in his leg. He pulled up his pants leg and gazed at the chunk of shrapnel embedded in his calf. He saw that his shoe was filled with blood. He thought of his beloved brother Massoud lying dead on the hangar floor, his face shot away. And, less respectfully, of Ashok Balfour Armitraj, killed by his own ammunition.

The plane came to a halt. Time passed. Still they did not move. A full five minutes elapsed. Haq looked around for a window, but the plane was not configured for passengers. Worried, he rose and hurried to the cockpit. "What's going on?"

The pilot shot him a nervous glance. "All departures have been halted. The army is demanding to search every plane."

"Why?"

"You tell me." The pilot climbed out of his seat. "Get in the back and hide in one of the trucks."

Haq selected a truck near the rear of the aircraft and climbed inside. The wait was excruciating. Minutes stretched on, until an hour had passed. Finally he felt the plane shudder slightly and heard voices echo in the cabin. Crouching behind the backseat, he waited for the door to open, a flashlight to shine on his face. But the voices were gone almost immediately. He rose, looked out the windshield, and saw the pilot walking toward him alone.

Haq jumped down from the truck. "And?"

"We're an American military aircraft. They took one look at my cargo and left."

Haq breathed easier. "Will we be leaving soon?"

"As soon as the airport is reopened, we are number seven in line for takeoff."

"How long to our first stop?"

"Seven hours."

Haq winced, looking at his wounded leg. "Get me a first-aid kit and some pliers."

"I'll be back after takeoff," said the pilot before heading back to the cockpit.

A few minutes later the plane began to move. It made a series of turns, paused, and the massive engines revved loudly. The plane gathered speed. The jeeps and personnel carriers and crates began to shake violently, dust rising from them as the plane thundered down the runway. And then the nose lifted and the wheels rose off the ground and the shaking ceased.

Closing his eyes, Sultan Haq prayed. He prayed for his father's wisdom and his brother's cunning. He prayed for his son's respect and his family's courage. And when he was finished, he swore to make his clan proud.

A melody came into his mind. It was a bouncy, carefree melody, too smug by half, full of ridiculous promise, sung by men who wore their country's uniform too proudly, who instinctively mocked cultures different from their own. Men with small, ignoble noses who considered foreigners to be inferior by definition and were happy to kill them on general principle. Men who believed it was their birthright to rule the world. Americans.

Against his will, Sultan Haq hummed a few bars. If possible, his hatred grew. Suddenly he knew that he had been headed this way his entire life.

West.

Toward the setting sun.

68

The search was called off after two hours.

Over twenty vehicles and one hundred men combed the airport. All departing flights were delayed while manifests were checked. A description of Haq was sent to the airport police and given to every officer on duty. Every hangar was inspected. But no sign of the jeep or Sultan Haq or the warhead was found. For all intents and purposes, he was declared dead, his corpse a mass of superheated bone and ash buried beneath several tons of corrugated iron. And the bomb with him. Both would be found in due time. Colonel Pasha swore it. In the meantime, a formal perimeter had been established around the still smoldering hangar. The first preliminary cleanup was scheduled for the following morning at eight o'clock.

"It's too soon to stop," said Jonathan as he pulled to a halt with Danni and Major Nichols at the staging area where they had begun. "Haq may have boarded a plane. We need to pull everyone off all the flights."

"I can't do that," said Major Nichols. "That authority lies with the civilians. Colonel Pasha is adamant that no one got out of the hangar in the first place. Maybe he's right."

"I saw him," said Jonathan.

"Look, there was a lot going on. You're shaken up, you're bleeding . . . Maybe it wasn't Haq you saw. It wouldn't be the first time someone mistook what they saw."

"Dammit," said Jonathan. "Didn't you hear me?"

"I heard you loud and clear," responded Nichols. "This airport ain't LAX. There's only so many places he could have gotten to. We didn't find a trace of him or the jeep. Maybe it's not perfect, but it's as good as you're going to get today."

"Haq is alive. He is in possession of a nuclear warhead and he means to use it. It can't stop here. There's got to be something more we can do."

Nichols climbed out of the Humvee. "Look, Ransom, I don't know if you're right or you're wrong, but we've done all we can. You got an issue, talk to your superiors in Langley, or wherever it is you're tasked out of. Right now, you're coming with me. I've got to transfer you to the proper authority."

Jonathan followed at his shoulder. "You're the only guy I've got—"

"That's enough," said Nichols, spinning to face him. "Now, am I going to have any problem with you two?"

"No, Major Nichols, you're not," said Danni, stepping between the two men. "We thank you for giving us the benefit of the doubt. It's clear you did everything in your power to find Haq. It's been a difficult day."

"Yes, Ms. Pine, it has."

Danni smiled consolingly. "Do you have any idea where they're taking us?"

"Embassy. This is an intel matter. You spooks can sort it out among yourselves."

69

An hour later Jonathan was with Danni in the rear of a Pakistani Army Humvee, two Delta Force operators at the wheel, as it made its way along the sun-bleached streets of Islamabad. A bandage covered his ear. Arnica salve had been applied to his bruised forehead. Butterfly stitches closed the laceration from the opium knife.

"What's going on?" asked Jonathan. "Connor was 'removed from his post.' What's that supposed to mean?"

"It means that his colleagues found out what he was doing and objected to it," said Danni. "Frank was never one to follow the book. It may finally have caught up to him."

"The timing couldn't be worse."

"Forget about it. Right now our priority is Haq. We have to assume that he's alive and at large and that he has the weapon. Nothing else matters."

The two sat facing each other on opposite benches, heads close, whispering. There were no handcuffs, no restraints of any kind. After all, as Danni had assured Major Nichols, they were all professionals.

"Haq's hair was cut short," said Jonathan. "He'd shaved his beard and cut his nails, all except one. He's going somewhere where he has to look like us. Like an American or European."

"You mean like a Westerner," said Danni. "Yes, I agree. Do you know anything else about him? Something that might give us a clue as to his intentions?"

"He was in Gitmo for a long time. I don't think he's too fond of doctors or Americans. Oh, yeah, and he likes movies. I'm afraid it's not much help."

"It's a start. Like you said, he didn't cut his hair for nothing. It means he's delivering the WMD somewhere he has to blend in and he's delivering it now."

"How soon is now?"

"We have to assume he'll either hand off the bomb or detonate it himself within the next twenty-four hours."

"I saw it," said Jonathan. "It was so small. You can hide it anywhere. At least we can pass on what we know about the bomb to the people at the embassy. I'm sure they can do something."

"What bomb?" said Danni. "The only person besides you and me who knows about it is Frank Connor, and he's gone missing."

"What are you saying? That no one will believe us?"

"Would you? I mean, look at yourself. You're an untrained, untested operative being run by a disgraced spymaster."

"Except that I'm telling the truth."

"Granted. And eventually you will convince the men and women in Washington who'll debrief you of that. They're not stupid. They'll listen to what Connor tells them and what you tell them, and they'll put two and two together. But that will be four weeks from now. A bit late, by my calculations."

"What about you?"

"What about me? I'm not here in an official capacity. My people think I'm on leave. Once they learn of my participation in this fiasco, I'll be fired." Danni cracked a smile. "What did Major Nichols say about Connor? He was 'removed from his post.' Yes, that is what they will do to me. They will 'remove me from my post.'"

"I didn't think they fired people like you."

Danni considered this. "Actually, you're right. They don't. They're too cruel for that. Instead they'll transfer me to a guard post overlooking the settlements in the West Bank. I'll only wish I'd been fired."

The Humvee rattled over a pothole and Jonathan bounced off the bench, touching Danni's knee for support. He held her eyes, struck again by the depth of their blue, and he found himself unable to look away. Soot streaked her cheek; sweat beaded her upper lip. She'd ditched her vest and web belt and rolled up the sleeves of her black utilities. With her tunic casually unbuttoned and her tangled hair hanging across her face, she looked a far cry from the crack commando who'd grouped four shots in the center of Mr. Singh's chest.

"Danni, why did you come?"

"Because you weren't ready. Because you were my student and I was responsible for you. Because I don't send people I like out to be killed."

"Thank you."

Danni looked away, uncomfortable. "I'll have a word with my people," she said. "They'll pass along a warning to Interpol and the IAEA. They have measures in place to deal with the traffic of WMDs."

"What will happen?"

"The threat level will be raised at all ports of entry in Europe, Canada, and the States—airports, harbors, border crossings. They'll send out a description of Haq."

"Will it do any good?"

"No. But it's the best we can do until we get a bearing on exactly where he's headed." Abruptly Danni sat up, pressing her back against the bench. "Jonathan, I have to ask you something. If you didn't send the information from Balfour's computer, who did?"

"Emma."

Danni could not conceal her shock. "She was there?"

Jonathan nodded. "She tried to get me to walk away. She said she could take me out of Blenheim with her when she left this morning."

"Why? Did she know you were in danger?"

"She thought I was in over my head."

"What was she doing there?"

"Coaching Balfour on how to live his new life without drawing attention to himself. I guess she was teaching him to live like a spook."

Danni narrowed her eyes, bothered. "But why would she send Connor the information? If she was helping Balfour sell the bomb, why do something to endanger the sale? I take it he was paying her."

"Probably."

"Is she helping Haq?"

"I don't think so. In fact, I had more of the impression that Balfour was keeping the two of them apart. Last night he threw a big dinner for his guests—myself, Haq, and the nuclear physicists who'd reconfigured the warhead. Emma wasn't there."

"I don't like it," said Danni.

Jonathan sighed. "You asked me why, so I'll tell you. Because she's up to something. I just wish I knew what it was."

"Let's concentrate on what you do know," said Danni. "What did you see in Balfour's office?"

"I read over a lot of his papers. There were telephone numbers, bank accounts, stuff written on his blotter."

"Like what?"

"A few names. A lot of words in Urdu or Dari that I couldn't understand. I wrote down everything I could remember as soon as I got back to my room."

"Do you have the paper?"

"Not anymore. They took all my belongings after Haq recognized me."

"Can you remember some of it?"

"Some. Not all."

"That will have to do."

Jonathan looked out the forward windscreen. They had entered the diplomatic quarter. Wide green berms ran down the center of the road. High walls surrounded large, ornate residences. Private security guards manned every gate.

"You up to running a little?" Danni asked.

"You have someplace to go?"

"Maybe."

Jonathan inclined his head toward the front seat. "These guys aren't National Guardsmen. They're Delta Force. That means they're sharpshooters."

"I know," said Danni, and she slid closer to the rear door.

Against his better instincts, Jonathan followed suit. "What do you mean, you know? If you know, why are you planning on running?"

Danni didn't answer. At that moment the Humvee braked to a

halt at a traffic light. Immediately she threw open the door and jumped out. Jonathan followed her, hitting the ground running.

"Hey, what the— Stop! Both of you! Get back here!"

Jonathan heard the shouts of the soldiers behind him, but he refused to look back. He stayed a half-step behind Danni, zigging when she zigged, zagging when she zagged. They negotiated the mid-day traffic as if threading their way through an angry, smoke-belching maze, dodging cars and bicycles, flying past bewildered vendors, sprinting at full clip. At some point the sound of the combat boots thudding the pavement behind them receded, and then it died off altogether.

Danni took a sharp right at the next crossroads. The side street was narrower and only half paved. A deep, wide ditch ran down one side of the road. It was a *nullah*, used to capture water during the monsoon season and keep the streets from flooding. Danni hopped into it and climbed out the other side. A low wall bordered the ditch, and behind it was a slum of corrugated tin shacks and slapdash hovels. Danni vaulted the wall and motioned for Jonathan to keep up.

They ran down alley after alley, turning right and left, until finally Danni stopped, pushing her back against a kiosk selling European magazines two years out of date.

"See?" she said, peeking her head around the corner to verify that no one had followed. "I told you they wouldn't shoot."

Jonathan bent double, fighting for breath. "How'd you know?"

"This is Islamabad—the capital. An American soldier opens fire here, he'll have half the population swarming over him inside a minute and a full-fledged diplomatic scandal an hour after that. Officially, American soldiers aren't even supposed to be on Pakistani soil. The raid at the airport—there were no Americans there. For the record, it was a Pakistani job all the way."

"Call Connor. Now. We've got to tell him what happened. He has to know that Haq has the warhead."

Danni's mouth tightened, then she nodded and dialed the number. The call went directly to voicemail and she hung up. "He's not answering."

Jonathan stood and wiped the sweat from his brow. "You know where we are?"

"No idea," said Danni. "Islamabad isn't high on my list of vacation hot spots."

"Great. Now we're lost, too."

Danni set off down the road at a determined pace. "But I know where to go."

70

The house belonged to a wealthy Jewish merchant of English extraction whose family had lived in India and, more recently, Pakistan, since the Raj. The faded glories of a lost empire decorated every corner of the colonial mansion, from the marble foyer to the teak-paneled den: carved elephant tusks, ornate copper teakettles, a miniature replica of Zamzama, the "fire-breathing" cannon made famous in Rudyard Kipling's *Kim*. The merchant's position in the trading community granted him access to the highest levels of the Pakistani government and made him privy to the government's economic secrets. As his father had done before him, he passed along information he deemed would be of interest to his ancestral homeland. The Mossad had a word for men like him the world over: *sayyan*. Friend.

The merchant, a short, gray-bearded man, showed Jonathan and Danni to his study and without a word closed the door behind them.

Jonathan sat at his desk, with Danni close beside him. He set to work immediately, writing down the information he'd memorized in Balfour's office. Some numbers came back easily; others proved maddeningly elusive, slipping from his grasp like a morning dream. He had no problem recalling a batch of six-digit alphanumeric sequences which Danni recognized as SWIFT codes for wiring funds between international banks. He had more problems with longer sequences, and it was decided that these could not be relied upon. After fifteen minutes, he was spent.

"That's it," he said. "That's all there is."

And for the first time Danni did not prod him for more. "It's enough."

Besides the SWIFT codes (which Danni wrote down on a clean

sheet of paper, folded neatly, and placed in her shirt pocket), several notations stood out as being worthy of scrutiny. The first was the phone number he had recognized as having an Afghan country code, the initials MH inscribed next to it.

"MH has to be Massoud Haq," said Jonathan.

Danni agreed and said she would pass the number to the technical services branch of the office, "the office" being professional's shorthand for her own intelligence service. "It may take some time, but they'll be able to create a network of his associates from the calls placed and received."

"How quickly?" asked Jonathan.

"That's always the question," said Danni with exasperation. "With a little muscle, I think we can count on sooner rather than later."

Jonathan's finger rested on a grouping of letters he recalled seeing on Sultan Haq's desk. The first line read "METRON," and the successive lines below it "HAR" and "NEWH." "Ring any bells?"

Danni said the words aloud. "It sounds like it's only part of each word."

Jonathan tried sounding out additional syllables to form a word, but came up with nothing. "Let's move on."

"What interests me is this name." And here Danni pointed to where Jonathan had written "Pasha" and "PARDF." "Wasn't Pasha the name of our American major's most trusted colleague?"

"It's common enough."

"PARDF stands for Pakistani Army Rapid Deployment Force," Danni went on. "How many Pashas do you think they have?" She pushed back her chair. "Pasha was on Balfour's payroll all along. He was there to look after Haq and make sure he got the warhead to its destination. If Haq escaped through the back, it was with Pasha's help."

Jonathan returned his attention to the pad where he had written down "N14997." "I recognize this. It's an N number—an aircraft registration code. Every country has its own code. G is for England, F for France."

"And N?"

"N is for the United States."

"Are you a pilot?"

"No, but when I was working with Doctors Without Borders, Emma used to ferry medicine from one country to another. We were required to list the registration code of the aircraft flying the supplies on our customs declarations."

"I see," said Danni. "So I imagine there's a central registry that keeps track of these."

"Absolutely," said Jonathan.

"Let me run it by the office." Danni placed a call to Israel and rattled off a series of instructions in Hebrew. Jonathan listened patiently as Danni fought her position with her colleagues in Herzliya. Unable to understand a word, he found himself thinking once again about Emma.

There was not a moment since he'd arrived in Pakistan that he had not felt her invisible hand lurking above him, guiding events to her advantage. He had no doubt that it was she who had placed the spyware-encoded flash drive into Balfour's computer. Working under Connor for so many years, she would have known that his response would be to immediately dispatch the special ops boys stationed in Pakistan. But why would she want to thwart Balfour's plans after she had risked her life, and the life of her child—no, *their* child!—to help bring them to fruition?

"Jonathan, we've got a hit."

"Let's hear it."

"N14997 is a C-141 Starlifter registered to Blenheim Cargo Corporation of Miami, Florida, which in turn is owned by East Pakistan Airways, Balfour's private airline. Apparently the plane is being leased by the United States Army Materiel Command to transport military equipment back from Iraq to the States."

"Do they know where it is?"

"According to Plane Tracker, the aircraft landed in Islamabad this morning."

"A cargo plane," said Jonathan. "It figures. The last I saw Haq, he was headed toward the freight terminal."

"Hold on," said Danni, picking up her conversation where she'd left off, jotting notes furiously on her pad. "Okay, shalom. Thanks."

"And?"

Danni's eyes were wide. "The plane took off at eight p.m."

Jonathan looked at the ornate clock on the wall: 10 p.m. "Did the pilot file a flight plan?"

"Yes," said Danni, much too softly for Jonathan's liking. "It's flying to Ramstein Air Base in Germany."

"That's it?"

"No, Ramstein is only a refueling stop. It's slated to continue on to McGuire Air Force Base in Wrightstown, New Jersey. Do you know where that is?"

"Yeah," said Jonathan. "It's a little more than an hour from New York City."

71

In Georgetown, snow fell as Jake "the Ripper" Taylor approached the three-story gray-brick town house at the corner of 34th Street and Prospect Street. A Ford Grand Victoria sat parked directly in front of the stairs leading to the front door. The car was unoccupied, and he assumed that the federal marshals to whom it belonged were inside, minding their prisoner. A second Grand Vic waited around the corner, two officers in the front seat, drinking their afternoon coffee. The feds were not winning points for being inconspicuous, thought Taylor, and he was sure to make a full and complete stop at the intersection before continuing on. In that time he cracked his window and looked to his right. The alley was right there behind the town house, just as the boss lady had said it would be, and there, poking its head above the fence, was the old wooden shed.

"There's a back entry that's accessed through a shed in the neighbor's yard," she had informed him. "You can see it from the alley behind his home. Mr. Connor is a sneaky fellow, and he uses it when he thinks someone's checking up on him."

A sneaky fellow. The boss lady using that upper-class accent he knew so well from the university-educated camel jocks he'd met over in Iraq and Afghanistan.

And how the hell did she know that about the shed and the alley? Taylor wondered with grudging admiration. Probably the same way that she knew Connor was under house arrest and had just returned from questioning at FBI headquarters. The same way she'd known about his visiting Mr. Malloy at the NGA. The boss lady had someone inside Division. *Someone deep inside.*

"Take out Connor," she'd said. "Not your usual way. It must appear natural. He has a heart condition. It shouldn't be too hard. But be careful. He's a cornered animal, and cornered animals are dangerous."

He's also pushing sixty and has a belly the size of a boulder, retorted the Ripper silently. Frank Connor would not be a problem.

The Ripper turned left up 33rd Street, then left again at P Street, taking his time to circle round and eventually finding a parking spot two blocks from Connor's place. Opening the glove compartment, he removed a chamois cloth, balled it up, and shoved it into his pocket. For good measure, he took his carpet cutter, too.

Exiting from his car, he pulled his navy workman's cap low over his forehead and dug his hands deep into the pockets of his pea coat. Setting off up the brick sidewalk, he looked no different from any undergraduate en route to the Georgetown University campus, a few blocks away. He turned right on N Street and spotted the address of Connor's neighbors. He let himself in the side gate and came upon the shed at the back of the garden.

Though the shed abutted the back fence and appeared to belong to the neighbor's home, it was in fact linked by an underground passage to Connor's house. The Ripper jimmied the shed's lock and slipped inside. The beam of his flashlight shone on an old stone stairwell leading steeply downward to a low, damp tunnel redolent of the Potomac River, which flowed barely fifty yards to the south. A door blocked his way at the far end of the passage.

"No alarm," the boss lady had said. "The tunnel is Connor's secret. If he doesn't acknowledge it, no one else will."

The Ripper defeated the double-action bolt lock inside thirty seconds. With infinite patience, he turned the knob and opened the door. He stepped inside, his feet landing on a hardwood floor. His hand withdrew the carpet cutter from his pocket, and he advanced the triangular razor from its metal sheath. He wasn't disobeying orders. As far as he was concerned, suicide was a natural cause. Disgraced spymasters killed themselves all the time.

Step by step, he climbed to the third floor. Step by step, his heart beat faster as he closed in on his kill.

The Ripper marveled at how much blood spilled out of a wrist when you cut the vein properly: vertically, long and deep; never horizontally.

72

Frank Connor paced the floor of his secret study like a condemned man. His phone had been confiscated and his landline restricted. Likewise, technicians had disabled all Internet access, both Ethernet and wireless. Even his cable TV had been cut off. His isolation was complete. He might as well be in prison already.

Pouring himself a glass of bourbon, he threw off his jacket and loosened his tie. His initial interrogation by the FBI had been brief and to the point. He'd decided up front to tell the truth. Piece by piece, he'd revealed the operation. The unauthorized attempt on Prince Rashid's life with the explosive bullets was the first strike against him. Nine innings' worth more followed. There was no point in lying. If he hadn't already, Erskine would offer up his own version of the events. Connor's every action of the past six months would be put under the microscope—every phone call, every e-mail, every meeting. His only hope was for the WMD to be found inside the hangar. Results meant exoneration. Failure meant punishment. Frank Connor was a big boy. He knew the drill.

Connor pulled up the section of floorboard and unlocked his private safe. Inside was a stack of virgin BlackBerries. Terrorists weren't the only ones who didn't want the government eavesdropping on their calls. He chose a phone and called his assistant, Lorena.

"Did they find it?"

"I have no idea," she said. "Mr. Sharp made me leave right after you."

"What about Ransom and Danni? Any word?"

"I don't know, Frank."

"And Haq?"

Lorena started crying. "I'm sorry," she said. "I couldn't find out anything."

Connor hung up, walked through the closet to the bedroom door, and opened it an inch to make sure none of the marshals were nearby. Satisfied that he was alone, Connor called his colleague at the Financial Crimes Enforcement Network. "Got anything?" he whispered.

"As a matter of fact, I do."

Connor's spirits lifted. "Shoot."

"I checked Erskine. He's clean."

"I thought you said you had something for me."

"Hold on to your pecker. I'm just getting started. It's our policy not only to check the primary suspect but to look at everyone around him. So anyway, Erskine has a home equity account linked to his payroll account. That's normal. I do, too. But Erskine's always taking money out of the home equity account and never putting anything back in."

"That sounds about right," commented Connor.

"Here's where it gets interesting. There's a second account linked to the home equity line of credit—Erskine's wife's. Check this out: it's his wife who's making the occasional repayments, keeping the line of credit at a manageable level."

"I know her. They just got married six months ago. She's a nice gal. Lina."

"Lina Zayed Erskine."

Connor felt the floor shift beneath him, and a sharp pain radiated from his chest. "Go on."

"Except that she's putting in twenty, thirty, forty thousand at a time."

"That seems kind of steep for an attorney over at Justice."

"A GS-12. Annual salary of $74,872 before taxes. Obviously, that nugget got my attention, so I decided to look a little closer, see where she might be getting all that disposable income if it wasn't courtesy of Uncle Sam."

"And?"

"Turns out the money was wired into her account from a certain bank domiciled in the Cayman Islands that we here at FinCEN are very familiar with. This establishment turns up much too often in connection with some of our shadier targets—drug dealers, arms traffickers, even the occasional link to our friends in Islam, if you get my drift. Naturally, it was a numbered account. No name, no nothing. Knowing that this might be important, I gave the head of the bank a call myself. He was none too happy to hear from me. When I mentioned the account in question, he practically had a coronary. *One of my best clients, a man of unrivaled reputation, a humanitarian.* If I didn't know better, I'd think he was talking about the Good Lord himself. Finally this jerk tells me that if I knew what was good for me, I would never mention this account again. End of discussion."

"The client sounds more like Pablo Escobar than Jesus Christ."

"Bingo. First thing I did after I hung up was put this numbered account through our tracking system."

"Any results?"

"Big time! We got a dozen hits right off the bat, all of them linked to some very questionable characters."

"All right, I've still got my pecker in my hand, and you'll be happy to know it's hard as a rock. A real diamond cutter. Just tell me who the account belongs to."

"I don't have a definitive, but there's one name that keeps popping up."

"Who?" Connor listened to the name and felt his chest tighten. It was suddenly difficult to breathe.

"Frank . . . you there?"

"Yeah," said Connor, finally drawing a breath. "Forward what you've got to my BlackBerry. I've got a new number. Here it is."

There was a knock on his bedroom door and Connor hung up, hurrying from the study and stuffing the phone into his pocket. He unlocked the door, and one of the marshals peered inside. "Would you like something from your kitchen before bed, sir? I know chow down at the J. Edgar Hoover Building ain't so great."

"How 'bout a tuna sandwich and some coffee," said Connor.

"Yes, sir."

The door closed and Connor locked it. Hurrying back to his safe, he withdrew $50,000 in neat packets of hundreds, and with them two clean U.S. passports in the names of Donald Maynard and John Riggins. Connor was a Jets fan from way back, but he drew the line at Emerson Boozer. Finally, reaching deep into the safe, he withdrew a polished oak box. He unclasped the lock and removed a sleek stainless steel semiautomatic pistol, a Ruger .380. The sight of guns made him nervous, and he handled it clumsily, struggling to insert the clip and chamber a round.

Satisfied that he had everything he needed if circumstances forced him to become a permanent fugitive, he closed the safe, turned off the lights, and walked across his bedroom to fetch his gloves and overcoat.

It was then that he felt the icy breeze skirt his ankles and send an ache through his bad leg. He turned to find a trim, dark man standing ten feet away. The man wore a pea coat and a longshoreman's cap, and he held a very large, very sharp carpet cutter in one hand.

"Hey, Frankie."

A picture of Jim Malloy and his wife flashed through Connor's mind. Fear gripped him. Still, he reacted as taught. Reaching into his pocket, he drew the compact Ruger .380 and unlocked the safety with a flick of his thumb. He raised the pistol and took aim. But suddenly his eyes wouldn't focus. His arm began to waver as the pain in his chest worsened. He tried to squeeze the trigger, but his hand would not obey.

And then it was too late. The man was on him, knocking his arm away, flinging the pistol to the ground.

"Just you and me here, Frankie," he said, his face inches away. "Time for a little fun."

The intruder grabbed Connor's arm and drew it toward him, ripping back the shirtsleeve. "Soft as a baby's belly. We're not going to have any problem at all."

Connor tried to talk, but his breath wouldn't come. His entire body felt as if it were being crushed inside a vise.

"This won't hurt a bit," said the intruder.

Connor watched the blade touch his wrist.

There was a sound like someone spitting and something tore into Connor's shoulder and the man stopped what he was doing. His eyes widened, and he said, "What the . . . ?" Connor looked down and saw that his own shoulder was bleeding, and he knew that somehow he had been shot. And then blood streamed from the man's mouth and he fell to the floor and didn't move.

Emma Ransom stood at the top of the hidden stairwell, a silenced pistol in her extended hand.

"Hello, Frank. How long have I been telling you to put a proper lock on that shed?"

73

"I didn't betray you," said Connor.

"I know that now," said Emma, hurrying forward and kneeling at his side. "Sit down. Take a deep breath."

Connor collapsed into a chair. "How did you find out?"

"I've been a busy girl. All those dirty tricks you taught me came in handy."

"What the hell's going on? Did we get the bomb? Was Haq inside that goddamned hangar? Is Jonathan alive? They haven't told me a thing."

Emma opened his shirt and examined the wound. "Yes, Jonathan's alive. He's on a flight to New York right now."

"What about the warhead and Haq?"

Her eyes rose to his for a second, no longer, then skipped back to his shoulder. "I'm sorry about this, Frank. I didn't have any subsonic rounds. Usually I would have gone for a head shot, but I couldn't afford a miss. One of the rounds went right through the bastard." Emma pulled a wallet from the corpse's back pocket. "Jacob Taylor," she said, reading from his driver's license. "Know him?"

Connor said that he didn't, but he knew who had sent him.

Emma found the killer's phone and scrolled through the numbers. "You're right," she said. "Goes to show you never can trust lawyers."

She texted a short message and sent it.

"What did you do?" Connor asked.

"I told the bitch you were dead. Now stay put." Rising, she went to the bathroom and came back with hand towels. She folded one neatly and pressed it against the bullet wound. "You shouldn't have used Jonathan."

"He was the best choice."

"Even so."

"He did a good job."

"He always does."

Connor tried to sit up, but a wave of pain overwhelmed him. "Why are you here?"

Emma sat back and stared at him. Her cheeks were still wind-kissed from her trek in the mountains, and her eyes shone as if lit from within by an eerie green light. "Insurance," she said finally.

"What does that mean?"

"You'll figure it out."

"You think saving my life is your ticket back?"

Emma shook her head, smiling earnestly. "It's not about work. We both know I'm not coming back. I saved your life because I like you."

"I can fix things."

"Not this time, you can't. Besides, I want out. I have to stop while part of my soul is still alive." She stood, handing Connor a clean towel to hold against his shoulder. "You need to get to a hospital. I don't know where that bullet went, and I think you've had a wee bit of a heart attack."

Connor worked it all through in his mind, and a new and terrible knowledge imprinted itself on his features. If Emma was here, it could be for only one reason. "Haq," he said. "God, no—you won't let him do it. You'll stop him?"

Emma leaned down and kissed Connor on the cheek. "I'll always be your girl, Frank."

"Yeah," said Connor. "That's what I'm afraid of."

Emma headed to the concealed stairwell. "You'll give me a few minutes?"

Connor nodded. He wanted to say "Good luck" or "Godspeed" or even just "Thanks," but he knew that something had changed. Emma was no longer a prize to be fought over, an asset coveted by every side.

She had broken too many rules to go back. She knew that, and her actions said she no longer gave a damn. She had turned her back on all of it. From here on out, Emma Ransom was on her own.

A rogue.

And this, Connor realized with a chill, made her more dangerous than ever before.

74

The information passed to the air force attaché at the United States Embassy in Jerusalem originated from a small but respected department within Mossad. An agent had knowledge that a certain wanted terrorist, currently the target of a top secret operation run out of the U.S. Department of Defense, had boarded an aircraft in Islamabad belonging to the United States Army Materiel Command inbound to Ramstein AFB, Germany. Tail number N14997. Said terrorist was reported to be in possession of a small-yield nuclear warhead. The information was graded high: actionable.

From Jerusalem, the information was forwarded to the commander of United States Air Forces in Europe, and then on to USAF intelligence at Headquarters Air Force, Washington, D.C., the Central Intelligence Agency, the Office of Nuclear Energy of the U.S. Department of Energy, and the International Atomic Energy Agency in Vienna. Four hours elapsed before the information reached the hands of the commander of Ramstein AFB, Germany. By then it was almost too late.

Ten vehicles swarmed the C-141 Starlifter as it began its takeoff at the head of runway 29. The condor-winged aircraft braked violently, smoke billowing from its tires. Military police hit the ground with weapons raised, ready to fire at the slightest provocation. A mobile staircase was pushed against the fuselage. The forward door opened, and the police rushed inside.

All this Sultan Haq watched with tense detachment from a separate aircraft parked a good distance across the tarmac. Sitting back in the plush seats, he sipped from his glass of ice-cold Coca-Cola and swallowed another painkiller.

"How is your injury?" asked the handsome, elegantly dressed man seated across the cabin.

"I've had worse," said Haq. "It will not affect me."

"I am pleased to hear that," said Prince Rashid. "I imagine there will be a delay until we are allowed to take off. Get some rest. Tomorrow promises to be an eventful day."

75

Pakistan International Airlines Flight 333 outbound from Islamabad and Karachi to New York City cruised at an air speed of 590 knots at 39,000 feet over the snow-covered plains of central Europe. Arrival was foreseen at seven a.m. Eastern Standard Time, fifteen minutes ahead of schedule, with weather in New York forecast to be in the mid-thirties with snow flurries.

Seated in row 22, Jonathan relaxed with a Dr Pepper. PIA was a Muslim airline and carried no alcohol on board.

"Where do you think he was going?" he asked Danni, his head lolling against the seat.

"Haq? It's always New York City. They all want to top 9/11. Did he give you any clue as to his final target?"

"None." Jonathan sipped his lukewarm soft drink. Not only was there no alcohol, but there was no ice either. "Who gets custody of him?"

"It's your cruise missile he stole. I imagine he's in the hands of the military right now. I hope they put him in a black hole and let him rot."

"Amen," said Jonathan, a little frightened by the depth of his conviction. "All my life I've tried to keep out of politics. My dad was a bean counter for the General Accounting Office—those are the guys who figure out how much money the boys in Washington are really spending—and he was always complaining about the government. But for all his arguing, he never did anything about it. He just bellyached. He used to say that you couldn't do a darned thing to change Washington. I chose to study medicine for exactly that reason. I wanted to do something where I could make a difference. For a long time it's made me happy. Maybe it's made me feel important, too. But now, working with you, with Connor, I feel differently. It's like I was dodging my responsibility." Jonathan frowned, contemplating the bullet the world had dodged. "It's scary to think what one determined man can do."

Danni nodded in agreement. "I don't know Haq or his politics. I don't blame him for hating the West, though. It's his country. He wants you out. Just like the Palestinians want us out. After a while, you see both sides of the story."

"But that's no excuse for getting hold of a bomb," Jonathan protested.

Danni smiled wryly. "My, but you're sounding very political."

"I've changed. Or maybe the world has."

Jonathan looked toward the head of the aircraft and saw the captain advancing down the aisle. He walked purposefully, his eye on the row numbers, and stopped beside Jonathan.

"You are Ms. Pine?" he asked, kneeling and speaking in a low, confidential tone.

Danni returned her seat to the upright position. "Yes."

"I've been asked to pass along a message to you." The pilot looked at Jonathan, then back at her. "Would you prefer to accompany me to the rear of the aircraft?"

"No. You can talk freely."

The pilot leaned closer. "The message is from a Colonel Yaz with my country's Directorate for Inter-Services Intelligence. He says to tell you first that he is a friend of Benny's."

Danni nodded, indicating that she understood.

"He said that there seems to have been a miscommunication. The party you wanted met in Germany was not on board the plane. Nor was his luggage. He asked if you had any idea where your friend might be heading, and if so, that you tell me, so I may forward it along."

Jonathan looked at Danni as all his muscles tensed. "My God," he said. "It can't be."

76

The Gulfstream G-V landed at Westchester County Airport, thirty
miles northeast of Manhattan, at six-thirty in the morning. There
were no customs formalities to attend to. The pilot had killed his primary transponder shortly after takeoff. Nearing the tower, he'd turned
an alternate on and identified himself as a private jet incoming from
Boston, Massachusetts. The air traffic controller was curious about the
sudden appearance on his radar, but not enough to cause a problem.
He had a student pilot veering into commercial airspace to deal with.
Permission to land was given without further questions.

Prince Rashid's Maybach limousine waited on the tarmac. Sultan
Haq slid into the backseat, clutching his black leather overnight case
to his chest. Rashid sat next to him.

"The train is ready?" the prince asked his chauffeur.

"Yessir. At North White Plains Station."

The Maybach drove five miles to the North White Plains Station,
a sprawling rail yard. Prince Rashid's train sat on a remote siding, lost
among strings of cars waiting for repair and service. The train numbered four cars: a locomotive followed by storage car, galley, and the
passenger car. The cars appeared like any others, silver with blue-and-
red striping running below the roof. On closer examination, the
words "HRH Prince Rashid al-Zayed" could be seen in ornate gold
script written in the blue striping.

A steward ushered the men inside. The interior did not look like
any other passenger car. In place of torn leatherette seats and sticky
linoleum floors were plush couches, sleek chairs, coffee tables, and
wool carpeting. Haq sat in an overstuffed recliner, the leather bag in

his lap. Two beefy, well-dressed men stood at the opposite end of the car: Rashid's praetorian guard.

The train began to move, and the steward brought a platter of steaming eggs, croissants, jams, and fruit. Rashid poured two flutes of orange juice.

"To us," he said, toasting. "We shall be more famous than Muhammad."

Sultan Haq raised the glass.

No drink had ever tasted sweeter.

77

Jonathan stepped off the aircraft and walked briskly up the skyway into the terminal at JFK International Airport in New York City. He was happy to be back on solid ground. The remaining hours of the flight had passed with maddening slowness. He'd had too much time to question what steps he might take to find Sultan Haq and precious little success in coming up with the answers. The fact was, there was little he could do. He was traveling on a false passport. He was wanted for questioning by U.S. intelligence. He could hardly approach the first policeman and say, "Hello, I'm an operative working for Division and I believe that someone is trying to smuggle a nuclear weapon into the United States." Without Frank Connor to vouch for him, he could count on his warnings being met with arrest and incarceration.

Danni walked beside him. She had her cell phone out and was checking her voicemail. She pulled at his elbow and mouthed for him to wait while she listened to a message. Immediately her eyes narrowed and her shoulders tightened. "Here," she said after what seemed like a while. "It's Frank."

"Connor? What did he say?"

"Listen for yourself."

Jonathan raised the phone to his ear. "Hello, Danni. You know who this is." Connor's voice sounded thin, unsteady. It was obvious the man was in pain. "Haq got away. He's here in the States, or will be soon. My guess is his target is on the eastern seaboard, probably Washington or New York. Prince Rashid is helping him. I don't know how or why or anything else, just that Haq is on his way. I talked to Benny. He's setting something up. That's all I know for now. I've got some issues of my own. Oh, and be careful, both of you. Emma's here, and she's after Haq, too."

"Who's Benny?" asked Jonathan when the message was finished.

"My Frank."

They walked to the end of the long, featureless corridor and descended a flight of steps. A sign on the wall read, "Welcome to the United States." They proceeded to the end of another corridor. The passport area opened to their left. They stood in the line reserved for non-Americans. It advanced slowly.

"Excuse me, Dr. Ransom? My name is Bob. I'm with DHS—the Department of Homeland Security. Mind coming with me?"

Bob was fifty, balding, and avuncular and wore a black leather jacket over a turtleneck and jeans. Another man stood next to him, also in jeans and a leather jacket, but taller and lean, with gaunt cheeks and sunken black eyes.

Unexpectedly, Danni stepped forward and kissed him on both cheeks. "Hello, Benny," she said.

"Looks like you got yourself into trouble," said Benny, reprovingly.

Danni didn't flinch. "I did what I did."

"So you're not arresting me?" said Jonathan.

"Not yet," said Bob. "Come with me."

He led them through a series of doors and hallways to a shabby, windowless office. Posters and pamphlets advertising the various ways of getting around New York adorned the walls. They sat down at a table littered with empty Styrofoam cups.

"Benny tells me that we have the possibility of a nuclear device being smuggled into the United States. Is that correct?"

"We think so," said Jonathan. "Unfortunately, we don't have much of an idea where."

"Tell me what you know. If you can give me some details, I'll do my best to alert the proper authorities. I take what Benny tells me very seriously."

Jonathan gave a summary of what he had learned and witnessed the past few days at Balfour's estate. He drew a picture of the reconfigured warhead and offered a description of Sultan Haq. "Frank Connor believes the target area is either Washington or New York," he said in closing.

"That doesn't help us much," said Bob.

Danni leaned forward. "He also mentioned that Prince Rashid of the UAE is involved."

"We're trying to track him down now," said Benny. "I have a call in to the American Secret Service to see if he's due for a visit soon."

"A sketch artist is on the way," added Bob. "It will help to have a portrait to get out to all ports of entry. You want some coffee while we wait?"

Jonathan stood. Suddenly the room was too small, the lights too bright. "Is that it?" he asked. "We're just going to sit and wait for the bomb to go off?"

Bob opened his hands. "You're not giving us much to go on."

"Haq is here," continued Jonathan, unable to contain his frustration. "If Emma's looking for him, you'd better believe this is happening now."

"Who's Emma?" asked Bob, searching the faces around him for clarification.

Danni spoke swiftly to Benny, and Benny said, "Don't worry about it. We don't talk about her."

Jonathan stopped his pacing. His eye had landed on a cluster of pamphlets drooping out of a plastic holder attached to the bottom of a poster for the Metropolitan Transportation Association. The pamphlets had a blue border across the top, and there was something about the logo that looked familiar.

"Jonathan? Are you all right?" Danni stood and laid a hand on his shoulder.

"Yeah." He took a pamphlet giving the train schedule for White Plains, Chappaqua, and Mount Kisco. "Are there more of these?"

"Don't worry about taking a train," said Bob, irritated. "We have cars at DHS."

Jonathan pulled out all the pamphlets and started leafing through them. Then he saw it. On one of the pamphlets, the border read, "Metro-North Railroad." *M-E-T-R-O-N.* "Haq had one of these," he said. "Not an original. It was something he'd downloaded off the Net. Are there lines that begin with H-A-R?"

"Harlem Line," said Bob.

"And N-E-W-H?"

"New Haven Line."

"Where do they go?"

Bob looked at the faces staring at him. He shrugged, as if he'd been asked the dumbest question in the world. "Grand Central Station."

78

Sultan Haq removed the warhead from the leather bag and set it at his feet. Rashid sat across from him, eyes rapt. Haq flipped open the cover and studied the keypad. With his fingernail, he input the six-digit code to arm the weapon. A pinlight flashed from red to green.

The train rustled over the tracks and the device tipped to one side. Rashid caught it and set it back upright. "And so?" he asked.

"It is ready," said Haq.

"Where will we set it off?"

"It must be at street level for maximum effect."

Ahead, the skyline of Manhattan came into view.

79

It was her insurance.

She was done. She could not go on living life with one eye trained over her shoulder. She would never work again. Not for the Americans. Not for the Russians. Not for Division or the FSB. Not for anyone. She was finished. But still, she knew they would never stop looking for her.

Emma put a hand on her stomach. Recently the baby had begun to kick. It was a girl. She was sure. One task remained and she would be free. The bomb would keep the jackals at bay so that she could be a mother. They could never risk coming after her if she possessed such a deterrent.

Emma Ransom crossed the tracks and took up position near a wall that led to the special platform. The underground gallery was endless, with track after track receding into an eternal dusk. A steady mechanical humming filled the air, interrupted by the clumsy, cacophonous arrival or departure of a train. She checked her watch and squinted into the distance, thinking that it was time and that Rashid should have been here by now.

For a week she'd listened in on the prince's calls to Balfour and Massoud Haq. The process involved copying Balfour's SIM card, acquiring her own eavesdropping equipment on a day trip to Islamabad, and piggybacking on Balfour's impressive telecommunications system. She had followed the planning step by step, and so she knew that Rashid had picked up Sultan Haq in Germany and was headed this morning to Grand Central Station. She also knew that he had decided to offer his own life to further his goals, not for the glorification of Islam and the punishment of the West but for the elevation of himself as Godhead. Rashid wished nothing less than to take the place of the Prophet.

The track beneath her feet began to tremble. Craning her head, she made out the headlight of an approaching locomotive. She drew her pistol and checked that a round was chambered. She pulled her gloves tight and lowered the balaclava so it fit snugly about her face and did not crowd her eyes. Then she cracked her neck and drew a breath.

The train drew nearer, its brakes squealing as it slowed. The locomotive passed, then the passenger cars. The lights were illuminated and she saw Rashid and Haq, and two bodyguards standing at the door.

Emma ran behind the last car, grabbed hold of the railing with her free hand, and hauled herself onto the narrow observation terrace. The door handle turned easily and she threw open the door, raised the pistol, and fired twice, hitting the bodyguards in the chest, her arm already swinging the weapon toward Rashid as she advanced into the cabin. A hand chopped her arm and she fired early. Rashid spun from his chair, blood streaming from the graze at his temple.

It was Haq. He struck again, knocking the pistol loose and sending it to the floor.

The train braked hard, coming to a halt, and Emma allowed herself to go with it, moving away from Haq, bringing up her right leg to strike him in the chest. The blow landed squarely but did not faze him. Haq threw himself at her and she kicked again, deflecting him, following the kick with a closed fist to the head. Haq shuddered, then lashed out, a lightning-fast punch that connected with her jaw. Emma fell to the ground, her head spinning, blood filling her mouth. Throwing out her leg, she caught Haq's ankle and sent him tumbling against the window. Glass shattered. But the blow only angered him. He stood and took up position, face-to-face. Emboldened by his size advantage, he came straight at her. Emma kicked and he deflected it. She punched and punched again, the first blocked, the second landing on his cheek, stunning him. Then he had her in his arms. Massive, crushing arms. With a grunt, he hurled her across the cabin. She landed on her back on a low table, shattering the china beneath her. Her head struck the corner of the hard surface, and the world dissolved into a blizzard of white noise.

Slowly her vision returned. She sat up. Rashid lay near her, bleeding profusely, his eyes blinking, offering no fight. She heard a door slam and looked up sharply.

The back door of the car flapped on its hinges.

Haq was gone.

And so was the black leather bag.

Emma looked at Rashid. "I haven't forgotten what you did," she said. And then she climbed to her feet and left the car.

80

Manhattan was an island of commuters. Each day some 5 million people left their homes throughout New York, Connecticut, New Jersey, and Pennsylvania and crossed one of the major bridges and tunnels to reach their places of work. Access to the island was gained by automobile, bicycle, bus, and ferry. But by far the largest number came by train. Of the three major stations that served Manhattan, Grand Central was the largest, with forty-four platforms servicing sixty-seven tracks on two levels and covering more than forty-seven subterranean acres.

The police cruiser screeched to a halt at the security entrance on Vanderbilt Avenue. Jonathan opened the door and climbed out, Danni and the others following. Two transit policemen waited. "You the guys that just called?"

"Take us to the Roosevelt tunnel," said Jonathan. "As quickly as possible."

"The Roosevelt tunnel? You sure?"

"Yeah," said Jonathan. "Let's move it."

The calls had hit like a one-two punch during the drive in from the airport. The first had come from Benny's contact at the Secret Service fifteen minutes earlier. "Rashid is scheduled to speak at the United Nations tomorrow. His jet was due in to Teterboro in New Jersey at seven this morning, but it didn't show."

"Did they know where he was flying in from?" demanded Jonathan.

"Germany," said Benny. "He's booked into the Presidential Suite of the Waldorf Astoria."

"He's with Haq," said Danni. "No question."

Bob from DHS's phone rang five minutes later, and his pallor went from winter wan to half dead. "Traffic control at Grand Central got a call last night regarding a diplomatic request to use the Roosevelt platform."

"Where's that?" asked Jonathan.

"Back in the thirties, a special tunnel was built for Franklin Roosevelt so he could get in and out of the terminal without people seeing him struggling with his leg braces. The tunnel leads to a platform directly below the Waldorf Astoria. The idea was that FDR would get off the train and be able to access the hotel privately and get into his car in their garage."

"Below the Waldorf?" said Jonathan. "That's it, then."

"Who made the request?" asked Danni.

"The embassy of the United Arab Emirates, on behalf of Prince Rashid," replied Bob. "Homeland Security cleared it automatically."

The transit police led the way across the main concourse and down the east flight of stairs toward the lower level. The time was eight-fifteen, and the terminal was at its busiest. Trains arriving from Connecticut and Westchester County disgorged hundreds of passengers every five minutes. The floor teemed with commuters heading in every possible direction.

"Wait here," said one of the policemen. "I got my best team coming in."

"We don't have time," said Danni. "Let's move."

Bob from DHS was already out of breath. "You sure about this?" he asked.

Jonathan nodded.

"Take my piece." Bob handed Jonathan his gun. "I'm assuming you know how to use it. Now go. I'll make sure the CT guys find you."

The transit cops led the way down the stairs, making a sharp right and continuing to the end of the walkway, then passing through a set of doors and entering a restricted area, out of bounds to the tens of thousands of regular commuters. A lone unlit platform extended into the distance.

A four-car train sat parked at the siding. At that moment, muzzle flashes lit the windows, accompanied by muffled gunshots. Jonathan took off, Danni close behind and Benny following at a distance. A lone figure leaped from the back of the passenger car. A tall, formidable silhouette ran across the tracks, a hitch visible in his stride.

"It's Haq," said Jonathan, pointing.

A train pulled into the station on the closest track, blocking Haq from view. Jonathan jumped down from the platform and ran across the tracks, narrowly beating the locomotive. He turned to see Danni beside him. The area beyond them stretched into an endless gloom. "There!" he said, spotting the fleeing figure.

"He's got something on his shoulder," said Danni, running beside him, the raised tracks and uneven wooden ties turning their path into an obstacle course. Without the weight of the warhead to carry, Jonathan and Danni gained ground quickly.

Twice Haq turned to look over his shoulder to gauge their position. The second time, his eyes met Jonathan's and he slowed, recognizing him. The Afghan jumped onto a platform and headed toward the station. In seconds he was caught up in the crowd, one figure among dozens.

A policeman stood at the end of the platform. He had seen Haq running and raised his hands. "Stop!" he shouted. "You!"

A gunshot rang out and he fell. For a moment the crowds parted. Haq's back was a plain target. Jonathan heard an earsplitting blast by his ear and saw Danni squeezing off several rounds. But then Haq was gone again, heading toward the staircase that led to the main level.

"He's going into the main concourse," said Jonathan, breathing hard.

Danni kept at his side as they dashed up the marble staircase to the broad, cavernous space. He slowed at the top of the stairs, searching the crowd for Haq's dark head, the bag slung over his shoulder. He heard a shot and, directly beside him, a cry. He turned and saw Danni crumple to the floor, a hand to her neck, blood coursing through her fingers. "Go," she said, mouthing the words.

Jonathan hesitated, torn, then continued on. He glimpsed Haq heading to the center of the concourse. The sound of the gunfire was absorbed by the vast spaces. Only those directly near it responded, some cowering, others shouting. But their panic, like the gunfire, dissipated and was lost.

And then the crowds parted. Jonathan was offered a clear line of sight. He saw Haq unslinging the bag, drawing out the silver canister. An enormous American flag hung from the ceiling directly overhead. Jonathan raised the pistol, hesitating. There were too many people. An iron fear gripped him, and his arm steadied. Placing the sights on Haq's back, he fired three shots, slowly, accurately. Squeezing, never yanking.

Haq spun and fell to his knees, the warhead still in his clutches. With one hand he pried open the cover. Running, Jonathan fired again, and Haq slid to the ground. The canister rolled away. Jonathan snatched it up, opening it as he'd seen the physicists do inside the hangar at Islamabad airport. A pinlight glowed green. The LED showed the word "manual." He eyed the red button and yanked his hand away. Carefully he closed the cover and held the canister tightly under his arm.

Jonathan stood over Haq. "It's over."

The Afghan's black eyes stared back, straining to remain focused, still brimming with hatred and determination. "Never."

Haq's eyes opened wider and his head fell to the floor. He glared at Jonathan, his eyes lifting to the massive American flag hanging above him. And then he was gone.

Jonathan slipped the warhead into its leather bag. This was New York, and a crowd had formed around him. Someone asked Jonathan if the dead guy had stolen that thing from him. He heard police shouting to move out of the way. Turning, he looked directly into Emma's face. She was dressed in black slacks and a trench coat, her hair pulled back into a ponytail, looking no different from any other woman in the station. "You're okay," he said.

Emma nodded. "You stopped him."

"Yeah."

Emma stepped closer and put her arms around him. "Thank you, Jonathan," she whispered in his ear.

"I love you," he said, and a moment later something sharp jabbed his neck.

Instantly the world grew blurry and Jonathan felt himself fading away, darkness pressing in. He watched Emma take the leather bag from him, but he could do nothing to stop her. His body no longer obeyed his commands. His legs buckled, and Emma lowered him to the ground. She put her face to his and kissed him lightly. "I know," she said.

Jonathan blinked, and when he looked up again, she was gone.

EPILOGUE

"Hello, Jonathan. How are you feeling?"

"I've been better. You?"

"Docs tell me the shoulder'll heal in a couple of weeks. It's the heart they're worried about. Come on in. Make yourself at home."

Jonathan stepped inside Frank Connor's town house at 34th and Prospect Streets in Georgetown. A week had passed since Haq had been killed at Grand Central and Emma had disappeared with the bomb. Jonathan had spent a day in the hospital recovering from the dose of succinylcholine Emma had hit him with. Other than fatigue, there were no lasting effects.

With the aid of a cane, Connor led the way to the living room and sat down with a humph. "President wants to meet you," he said, smiling as proudly as any father.

Jonathan took a seat on the couch across from him. "No kidding. What'd you say?"

"No chance," said Connor. "I can't risk anyone taking a picture of you. He sends his thanks. If you're a good kid, I'll get you an autographed picture."

Jonathan smiled before growing serious. "Any word?"

Connor shook his head. "Disappeared without a trace. That's my girl."

"What are you going to do?"

"About what? Officially, we never even lost that cruise missile. No one wants to dredge up the past. Frankly, it's probably safer in Emma's hands than anywhere else. She called it her 'insurance policy.' You know something? She was right."

"And Rashid?"

"Claims that Haq hijacked him and his plane. We're letting it slide." Connor looked up from beneath his brows, his eyes narrowing. "For now."

Jonathan nodded. "Have you talked to Danni?"

"This morning. Lost a lot of blood, but she'll pull through. She's flying back to Israel tomorrow." Connor grimaced. "I bet she'll think twice before helping me out again."

"I don't blame her."

"She's a good kid."

"The best," said Jonathan.

Connor leaned to his side and labored to free a brown-tie folder from beneath a stack of magazines. "Did I tell you about Erskine's wife—Lina, Prince Rashid's niece? They caught her trying to hop a plane out of Dulles. Turns out her job at the Justice Department involved assisting the military in writing briefs for or against the inmates at Guantánamo. Apparently she had a big hand in getting Sultan Haq and his brother Massoud freed."

"What will she get?"

"Life without parole. They're putting Malloy's death on her, along with espionage. She'll have plenty of time to contemplate her soul at whatever supermax penitentiary she ends up in."

"What about Erskine?"

"Headed to Wall Street."

Connor spent a moment loosening the ribbon on the folder. "You know, I looked into the circumstances surrounding that B-52 that crashed in 1984. I found out that there was a second tragedy that occurred in that very same area."

Jonathan eyed Connor warily. "Oh?"

"Yeah, something right up your alley. An entire team of climbers was killed on Tirich Mir around the same time as that plane went down. In fact, it might even have been the same day. It was some UN-sponsored climb for peace to protest the Afghanistan war. I seem to recall that Tirich Mir meant something to you."

"My brother, Michael, was on that climb."

Connor nodded. "I'm sorry."

"It was a long time ago. I was just a kid."

Connor took a sheaf of papers from the folder and tossed them onto Jonathan's lap. The name S/Sgt. Michael R. Ransom was typed on a white label, and it was stamped "Department of the Army."

Jonathan opened it and leafed through the pages. Special Warfare School. Honor graduate. Green Beret. Commendations. Photographs. Shaken, he lifted his eyes from the papers. "He told me he washed out. Right after that, he went to work for a bank in Virginia."

"No," said Connor. "He didn't. He was put into a covert espionage program called Darklight. The bank was his cover. He spent four years there. At the time he was killed, your brother was working as a covert operative for the Defense Department. The expedition up Tirich Mir was his cover. He was supposed to install a long-range eavesdropping device to listen in on the Red Army's military communications."

Jonathan took this in, goose bumps prickling his skin.

"You ever wonder why we picked you for Emma all those years ago?" asked Connor.

"Only every day."

Connor freed a last file from the folder. "What did your father tell you he did for a living?"

"He worked as an accountant for the GAO."

"Really?"

Jonathan nodded, but his stomach had suddenly turned queasy.

Connor stood and handed him the file. "Read this. I think you'll find it . . . illuminating."

Jonathan stared at the folder, then stood and followed Connor to the door. "Thank you."

Connor fired off a lazy salute. "I'll be in touch."

Afterward, Frank Connor climbed the stairs to the third floor and entered his private sanctum. Though there was no one else in the house, he closed the door behind him and locked it. It took him a few minutes to get on his knees and open the safe, but he managed. The gun was there, as was his escape money. You never knew. But Connor wasn't interested in running away, at least not today. He didn't plan on leaving Division anytime soon.

Reaching inside the safe, he withdrew the heavy leather-bound volume that held pictures of all his agents, past and present. He needed another minute to get back to his feet and find a place to sit. By then his breath was coming hard and a light sweat beaded his forehead. Getting old sucked, but it sure beat the alternative.

Setting the volume on his lap, he opened it and flipped past all the photos to the first blank page. He spent a moment peeling back the transparent protective sheath. He had a new photograph ready, and carefully he affixed it to the firm paperboard.

The picture showed a tall, broad-shouldered man walking down a street in Oxford, England. His hair was black, already cut with gray. His eyes were dark as midnight. His expression was much too serious for someone so young, but then again, doctors tended to be rather on the intense side.

Connor pressed the protective sheath into place and passed his hand over the photograph.

"Welcome to Division, Jonathan."

Acknowledgments

It is my pleasure to thank the following individuals for their assistance in the writing of this book: Samuel Gordy, Dr. Douglas Fischer of the California Department of Justice, Dr. Jon Shafqat, Dr. John Alexander, Gary Schroen, Kyle Cornett, and lastly, my personal assistant, Susannah Szabo. I could not have written this book without their help, and that's all there is to it.

Also, I'd like to give a shout to my trainers at the Body Refinery in Encinitas, California, Michael Barbanti and Michael Luongo, who restore my sanity and health after too many hours sitting in a chair staring at a computer screen. *Res firma mitescere nescit* (have fun looking this one up!).

At Inkwell Management, I would like to thank Charlie Olsen, Lyndsey Blessing, Kim Witherspoon, Michael Carlisle, and, of course, my agent, Richard Pine.

At Doubleday, my thanks go to Bill Thomas, John Pitts, Todd Doughty, Alison Rich, Rob Bloom, John Fontana, and, last but not least, my editor, Jason Kaufman.